Upon a Mystic Tide

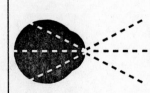

This Large Print Book carries the
Seal of Approval of N.A.V.H.

UPON A MYSTIC TIDE

VICKI HINZE

THORNDIKE PRESS
A part of Gale, Cengage Learning

GALE
CENGAGE Learning·

Detroit • New York • San Francisco • New Haven, Conn • Waterville, Maine • London

GALE
CENGAGE Learning®

LIBRARY OF CONGRESS CATALOGING-IN-PUBLICATION DATA

Hinze, Vicki.
    Upon a mystic tide : a Seascape Trilogy, book two / by Vicki Hinze. — Large print ed.
       p. cm. — (A seascape trilogy ; bk. 2) (Thorndike Press large print clean reads)
    ISBN-13: 978-1-4104-5276-4 (hardcover)
    ISBN-10: 1-4104-5276-X (hardcover)
    1. Marital conflict—Fiction. 2. Taverns (Inns)—Maine—Fiction. 3. Large type books. I. Title.
PS3558.I574U66 2012
813'.54—dc23   2012031048

Published in 2012 by arrangement with BelleBooks, Inc.

Printed in Mexico
2 3 4 5 6 7 16 15 14 13

Upon a Mystic Tide

CHAPTER 1

Body language rarely lies.

That Bess Cameron's boss, Sal Ragusa, stood about as stiff as a totem pole set her ragged nerves on an even sharper edge. While divorce never bares its pointed teeth without pain and suffering to everyone involved, in her case, it appeared those teeth would be mortally wounding far more than her marriage.

Resigned to yet another lecture, she held up a give-me-a-second finger, punched the tape labeled "Commercials" into the deck, pressed the play button, then rocked back in her squeaky chair. "All right, Sal. Go on."

"I'm really worried about you." He slumped against the recording booth's doorjamb, deliberately trying to look less concerned. Harsh light from the hall spilled across the WLUV 107.3 emblem on his T-shirt and swiped a slash across his clenched jaw. "This is the only way I know to protect you, and you refuse. When Millicent hears about your divorce . . ."

Bess would feel the bite of the teeth. She sighed. Why did formally ending a marriage that had died and been mourned long ago conjure intense hurt that felt so . . . fresh?

Seeing little productive coming from exploring that question and certain she'd miss nothing that hadn't been covered on countless other occasions, she let her attention drift from Sal's lengthy monologue.

The eerie green, red, and white light emitting from the booth's controls typically seemed familiar and comforting. Tonight, it made her uneasy, though she was enough of a pro to admit that the root of her discomfort really wasn't the light. It was her, inside — and for a good, logical reason.

It was late, nearly midnight, and she'd had so much on her mind lately that she hadn't been sleeping well. Big understatement there. And even though she considered self-analysis the fodder of fools for professional psychologists, Bess risked speculating on her unprofessional opinion of her current status. Diagnosis? She was physically tired, emotionally wrung out, spiritually drained, and about as sick as spit — a term she'd picked up from her friend, Maggie Mac-Gregor — of worrying. Prognosis? Grim.

From all indications, things were doomed to get worse before they got better. And exactly how much worse remained totally out of Bess's control.

The first commercial started playing. She tapped the mute button so it'd be transmitted but not heard in the booth, then checked her watch. They had three minutes to wrap up this conversation before she had to get back on the air.

Swiveling in her chair to face her boss, who unfortunately showed no signs of being winded or of winding down and ending his lecture, she again thought he'd be ahead of the game if he'd give in gracefully to his age instead of trying to keep up with the twenty-year-olds running around the station. To her own thirty-three, Bess figured Sal at fifty — maybe fifty-five — and fighting each year showing as if it were a thieving demon. He jogged to fight a tiny paunch, lifted weights three times a week at his posh French Quarter club to avoid unavoidable muscle sag, and tinted his hair an awful brown to hide persistent gray. His obsession with his appearance, like his tendency to talk first and think later, was at times saddening, at times maddening, but always tolerable because the man was fair, he had a good heart, and he was loyal.

With him, Bess never ranked second.

And now she had to oppose him. She suffered a flash of regret but, needing to wrap up this session of their "Great Debate," she interrupted. "I know you're trying to help, but I can't accept *this* kind of help. It's . . . wrong."

"And I knew you were going to say that. You always do." He propped a sneakered foot against the lime green wall. "But these are the only possibilities I see of saving your job. I've put out some feelers on this and, as soon as she catches wind of your divorce, Millicent *will* fire you, Bess."

A divorce *and* losing her job? Surely she couldn't be expected to endure both simultaneously — at least not with grace. And staring financial ruin in the face didn't do much to assist on the personal philosophy aspiration front. Bess chewed on her inner lower lip. Why had she made aspiring to grace part of her annual, personal motto this year anyway? Foolish. Especially with her knowing the divorce was coming — John certainly wouldn't lift a finger to stop it — and with patience still lingering on the list from last year, she'd finally given in and accepted that patience — or, more accurately, her lack of it — was destined to be a perpetual aspiration: a part of every year's motto. But she was still working on accepting the divorce and John's reaction to it. Now she had unwisely put herself in the position of having to strive to meet both *and* the threat of being fired and financially ruined too. All with grace. And all simultaneously.

Fat chance.

The fear of failure had the recording booth seeming small and stuffy and stifling hot. It smelled musty too, and the temptation to spout off at Sal to release some tension spread like a wildfire up her throat. She swallowed it back down, where it churned in her stomach.

Well, no one had promised life would be fair. Good thing, because these days her supporters cantered in few and far between. Sal was one of her most staunch. Alienating him would be just plain foolish, and Bess Cameron was not a foolish woman, at least not in most things — aside from in choosing her spouse and in saddling herself with overly ambitious annual mottoes she regretted January second and doggedly pursued until December thirty-first.

Having heard enough of this particular lecture, she squeezed the padded arms of her chair. Air swooshed out, hissing between her fingers. "I've been counseling callers at this radio station for more than six years, Sal. I'm a psychologist. I'm not superhuman or 'Wonder Woman,' and I certainly never claimed to be perfect. And I'm not committing felonious acts in my private life, I'm just getting a divorce."

"*Just* getting a divorce?" Sal lifted an arm. "A divorce is more than pertinent to your professional life, Bess."

Her temper again flared. And again, she tamped it, chilled her voice to cool. "Can you, or our esteemed owner, Millicent Fairgate, make a marriage work alone?"

Sal lowered his gaze to the tile floor. "No. No one can. But —"

"I see." Bess crossed her chest with her arms. "Why then am I expected to be able to do it?"

"Because *you* earn your living counseling people on marriage and relationships. *We* don't." He muttered a grunt. "You know Millicent is going to take the position that if you can't make your own marriage work, then —"

"I know how I earn my living." Bitterness burned in her stomach. Given half a chance, she *could* have made her marriage work. But John hadn't cooperated. She'd loved him enough to go the distance, to fight to keep their marriage strong. But he hadn't loved her enough to work at it with her. And he'd caused her more grief . . .

Bess put the skids on those thoughts. Counterproductive. A waste of time and of good energy. "I'm sorry, Sal, but neither of your options work for me. I can't live in this unmarried-married state of suspended animation anymore. Going ahead with the divorce is a positive step. It's an outward reflection of inner acceptance. A commitment to growth and, regardless of how uncomfortable or painful it is, personal growth is always positive." Let him take that rationale along as ammunition to fight Millicent Fairgate. Even she couldn't deny Bess deserved a life as much as anyone else. "And I can't lie — not even to save my job."

She forced a strength into her voice she just didn't feel. "If the truth isn't good enough for Millicent, then fine. Let her fire me. But I will *not* lie to these callers by pretending to be happily married when I'm divorced."

"You omit lots of personal details. You've avoided talking about your personal life for six years. Why does it have to be an issue now?"

He couldn't be serious. She studied his expression and held off a sigh. He was. "I haven't avoided talking about my personal life. Callers haven't been interested. They've wanted to discuss their troubles, not mine. But, as you so aptly put it, I'll soon be a divorcée counseling others on love and relationships. The press will be all over me, making my status an issue. And when they are and they do, I will not lie about it."

Sal slid her a look ripe with warning. "Think this through. If you're fired, you can't help anyone. You'll have no forum. If you omit publicly disclosing and discussing the divorce, you've got a shot at staying in a position to help others. What's the difference —"

As if the press wouldn't disclose it for her. As if she had a choice. Rationalizing, indulging in selective recall, talking without first thinking — as usual. *Get a grip, Sal.* Bess interrupted. "Even if the press gave me a choice — which they won't — the difference is that these callers trust me."

Sal's jaw fell slack.

Bess pushed her palms against the chair arms, then squeezed her eyes shut. Had she *really* just raised her voice to her boss? Good grief, she had!

She was losing it. After years of diligent effort at restraining herself and venting only when alone, she was losing it. So much for patience. And she could kiss off grace on

14

this discussion too. What had gotten into her? She just didn't do this sort of thing. *Elevating her voice.*

Worrying about the divorce; the disputed property settlement still hanging over her head and keeping her off-balance; her lawyer, Francine, throwing fits with monotonous regularity because Bess refused to take anything from John — as if she could and not die of humiliation — and now threats of being fired by WLUV 107.3's judgmental matriarch owner, Millicent Fairgate. *What else could go wrong?*

Nothing. Absolutely nothing. All bases stood covered.

Hardly a comforting thought but, on the upside, Bess was still sane. And when things *couldn't* get worse, then they *had* to get better.

The solace in that universal truth enabled her to level her voice. "I'm sorry, Sal."

"It's, um, no problem." He wasn't trying to hide his concern anymore and, if his grim expression proved a reliable indicator, that concern had doubled.

"Listen, I understand your logic, and your intent is good. But, to me, *that* omission would be lying, and I won't do it." She raked a thumbnail over her coffee mug handle. The grating friction felt good. "I can't."

His silence demanded an explanation. Though she'd rather not discuss her feelings further, she supposed he deserved to hear her reasons. He *would* oppose Millicent firing Bess, and Millicent wouldn't take his opposition kindly. If history proved telling, she'd retaliate. For his loyalty and heartburn in defending Bess, Sal would pay dearly, and be made darn miserable. Yes, she owed him an explanation.

Trembling, she set down her mug then grabbed a pen from the desk to have something less risky to do with her hands. "The people who call here believe in me. They feel comfortable talking with me because they know I'll be honest with them. If I lie to them, then what have I got left?"

He groaned. "Bess, you're taking this much too person—"

"I'd have nothing, Sal." That pitiful truth had the back of her nose tingling, her eyes stinging. Her heart aching. "Nothing."

Statue-still, his hands fisted in his jeans pockets, he stared at her a long minute, then blew out a sigh that reeked of frustration. "Okay." The lines etching his face shadowed in the dim control lights, tinting his skin with a ghoulish green glow. "Okay. There's a ninety-nine percent chance you'll end up canned and out on your keister, but I admire your principles. I always have." He sighed again, deeper. It lifted his chest and shoulders. "I'll do what I can to tame the shrew and to keep her hand off the ax."

"I appreciate it." Bess tried but couldn't muster a smile. Afraid her relief would show in her eyes, and she'd insult Sal by doubting his loyalty, she glanced down at her watch and checked the time. Less than a minute before she had to be back on the air.

He rolled away from the doorjamb. "How long until the divorce is final?"

"July tenth." Her heart slid up into her throat. Never would she have dreamed this really could happen to her and John. To anyone else, yes. But not to them. She dropped her gaze. Her wedding band winked in the control's lights, mocking her. She'd been so . . . sure.

"Three weeks." Sal rubbed his jaw. "More or less."

"More or less." She knew the exact number of weeks, of days, of hours. The minutes ticked away in her mind like a bomb set to explode. But admitting that to herself, much less to Sal, proved far too revealing for her comfort and, suffering plenty enough discomfort without heaping on more, she shoved those thoughts away.

He raked a hand through his close-cropped hair. The gray-root spikes with tinted brown tips sprang out from his head. "I have to be honest here."

Bracing herself, she hiked her chin. "Wouldn't have it any other way."

"A divorced shrink counseling callers on love and relationships isn't apt to sit any better with listeners than with Millicent. New Orleans is predominantly Catholic, and that's worth remembering."

A muscle spasmed, knotting in her neck. She kneaded at it. "I could lose some listeners, true. But if I lie, I lose a lot more."

"What *more?* We're a radio station. Listeners are everything."

"I lose them," she lowered her gaze to his chest, "and me."

Sal stared at the ceiling, mumbled something she couldn't make out, then glanced back at her. "I hate to say it, Bess, but one of us has to be less idealistic and more realistic here, and it doesn't appear it's going to be you."

Considering her position realistic and reasonable, she opened her mouth to object.

He held up a hand to stay her. "Look, I admire your principles — really, I do. And

18

far be it from me to say self-respect doesn't hold value. But it doesn't pay the rent. The public isn't exactly known for being forgiving. It won't let this divorce slide by unnoticed. You're right. You *will* take heat in the press — and worse."

Sympathy shone in his eyes. As if knowing she wouldn't appreciate it, he let his gaze slip away, back to the ceiling. "It kills me to have to say it, but now might be a good time for you to look into setting up a private practice."

Bess held off a frown. From the start, she'd resisted private practice, and the financial security it could bring, because the people who most needed her were those least likely to seek out counseling. She'd found her niche, her forum — the radio — and she intended to keep it. "You're firing me?"

"Not yet." His expression turned grim. "Just preparing you."

Underneath all the bluster, he was a good man. A really good man. "Thanks." She nodded to let him know she meant it. "Now it's only fair that I prepare you." She leaned forward, squared her shoulders, and looked him right in the eye. "We both know John Mystic and I have been separated six years. The piece of paper coming July tenth doesn't change anything. Not my job performance, my credentials, or even my name. Only my legal status changes." Risky, but she had to be totally frank. "I've lost all I intend to lose willingly, Sal. If Millicent wants me out of 107.3, then she's going to have to fire me, and she's going to have to make it stick." Bess dipped her chin and looked up at him, forced her voice and her gaze firm and steady. "I'll fight it every step of the way."

Sal rubbed his stomach, as if his ulcer were acting up again. "Maybe if you fought that hard for John —"

Bess spun on him. "Don't you dare!" Thoughtless comments were just Sal's way. He didn't mean them. But this time he'd hit too close to home, pegging some of her own unreasonable, irrational fears. Ones she couldn't afford to give any value to if she expected to come out of this divorce with a fair sense of self-worth.

Sal stopped midsentence, then slid her a repentant look. "Look, I'm sorry. That was out of line." He swallowed hard, bobbing his Adam's apple. "I just don't want to lose you. If you stayed married to the jerk, then I wouldn't."

Those kinds of remarks were expected to entice her? Bess swallowed a response so searing it set her temples to pounding. "I don't want to be lost either, but don't say things like that about John and me. You don't know how things were with us, and it's unfair of you to judge him or me."

"Yeah, you're right." Sal shrugged and his face turned red. "I guess I just want this whole sordid mess to . . . to go away."

So did she. "That isn't going to happen." Once she'd thought it might, that John would ask her to come home, but she'd accepted the truth a long time ago. He had no intention of trying to save their marriage. He didn't love her, and that was the sorry truth.

A painful ache shimmied through her chest. She clenched her muscles against it. Some dreams die so darn hard.

She checked her watch — ten seconds — grabbed the mike, then put a manicured fingertip on the tape player's eject button. "I'm out of time and I've got four lines lit up. If you'll excuse me, duty calls."

Looking pensive, dejected, and truly sorry, Sal lumbered out of the booth.

When he closed the door behind him, Bess started shaking, rattled from the bone out. Would she ever stop shaking again? Would her life ever be right again?

Never let 'em see you sweat, kid. Her

father's voice sounded in her head.

A hornets' nest of guilt stirred in her stomach. *I'm trying, Dad. I'm really trying. But it hurts and it's hard. I loved him so much.* She pulled in a deep breath, counted to three, then answered the first caller.

The next four calls were tame; normal problems she'd faced before, countless times. Taking a sip of coffee so strong and bitter it had to have been steeping since dusk, she grimaced, then answered the fifth. "*Love* 107.3. This is Bess."

"Dr. Mystic?"

Her married name? Bess frowned. She'd never used her married name on the air. "Dr. Cameron," she told the caller. "But I prefer Bess."

"My name is Tony."

Something in his voice unnerved her. Not the tone — nothing so mundane as that, though it was gravelly and odd. It was something . . . inexplicable. And it created the strangest sensations in her. As if he could see inside her, and he knew all her secrets . . . and more.

The little hairs on her neck stood on edge. She put her cup down on the desk. Shaking even harder, she laced her fingers, rested her hands in her lap, then chided herself for being ridiculous. No one could literally see

22

inside anyone else. They could perceive, interpret, intuit, but not see. "What can I do for you, Tony?"

"I've heard a rumor."

Warning flags flashed before her eyes. Warning flags gained by developing strong instincts that came with phone-counseling for over half a decade. Warnings she'd come to respect. Sight and physical observation, two very important tools to every psychologist, radio-counseling denied her. She'd had to compensate and her instincts, bless them, had done so for her, honing with experience to acutely perceptive. And, right now, those acutely perceptive instincts screamed that this wasn't a harmless, or a typical, call. That it carried serious repercussions and consequences — to Bess. And, worse, that no matter how depleted she felt right now, she couldn't retreat and regroup or run from them.

Her mouth drier than dust, she mustered her most professional voice. "Rumors are dangerous. Usually destructive." She paused to let that sink in. "Are you destructive, Tony, or does this rumor personally affect you?"

"No, I'm not destructive, and this affects me only in the broadest sense." He sounded uncomfortable. "But it is extremely important — enough to warrant this call."

"I see." Dread dragged at her belly. "Well, if the rumor is 'extremely important to you,' then you should attempt to verify it. Try to be open-minded. Strive equally hard to prove, and to disprove, the rumor. To come out of something like this with a clean conscience, it's imperative you be fair — and, if possible, you find out the truth without inflicting harm on anyone else." She automatically lifted her cup, but shook too badly to hold it. Hot coffee sloshed over the rim and scalded her hand. She bit her lip to keep from crying out, and ordered herself to get her nerves under control.

"I don't want anyone hurt. That's why I'm calling you."

This time, his tone was a dead giveaway. He wasn't being honest, and yet she innately knew he wasn't lying. The truth rested at some obscure place in between. "I see." She rubbed at her temple, not seeing at all. Maybe she was overreacting. Maybe he just needed a place to vent. She definitely needed to calm down. "I suppose then we'd better talk about this."

"Only if you're sure. This rumor affects you, Dr. Mystic."

A sense of doom blanketed the dread, and Bess dragged in a deep breath. How could a rumor about her be extremely important to him? She didn't even know him. Should she disconnect him?

Though sorely tempted, her instincts warned her against it. Warned her that this call was inevitable.

The pounding at her temples grew to a sickening throb. No, as much as she wanted to, she couldn't play ostrich and bury her head in the sand. Whatever was coming had to be faced. Hadn't she advised that very action to caller after caller? "If it's important, then go ahead, Tony."

"You're getting a divorce."

Bess swallowed a gasp, then a groan. Good grief. Not a question, a statement.

Sal shoved open the booth door. Wild-eyed, he swiped his hand back and forth across his neck, mouthing, "Don't answer! Cut him off! *Cut him off!*"

Blinking hard and fast, Bess broke into a cold sweat. It had been just a matter of time until word got out, but she should have had three more weeks and now, because of this Tony, she'd been cheated out of them. She resented that. Boy, did she resent it. Wasn't the divorce itself hard enough?

Sal grabbed her shoulder. "Cut him off!"

Bess reached over to the phone and touched a fingertip to the button. She tried, but she couldn't press it down. She just couldn't do it. Sliding Sal an apologetic look, she spoke into the mike. "This rumor is true, Tony. I am getting a divorce."

Sal muttered a curse, stomped out into the hallway, then slammed the door shut.

Oh no.

"I'm sensing your resentment and a little hostility, Dr. Mystic. There's no need for it, or for fear. I didn't call to give you a hard time."

He *sensed* it? Mystic. Not Cameron. Again. He hadn't forgotten, but deliberately had used John's name. Why? Bess frowned. Was John behind this? That would be atypical, true. She'd left him for neglect. It seemed highly unlikely he'd remember he had a wife now. And besides, this Tony seemed . . . sincere. Oddly pervasive, extremely perceptive, unwelcomely intrusive, but sincere.

Still, her instincts were good, not perfect. Was he sincere? Or was he setting her up for a fall? "If not to give me a hard time, why then are you calling?"

"To dispel the rumor."

A setup. "Well, now you have." Bess lifted a finger to disconnect the line.

"Wait! Don't hang up!"

Bess jerked back, stared at the phone as if

it were possessed. How had he known she'd been about to disconnect him? Could he sense *and* see her? She darted a glance around the booth, uneasy. No one around. Nothing amiss. So why didn't the impression subside? Why did she feel watched, observed — almost invaded? Absurd. If this hadn't happened so soon after the confrontation with Sal, if she'd had a few minutes to recoup and regain her balance, it wouldn't be happening.

"I called to tell you something too, Dr. Mystic."

Totally unraveled and fighting it, Bess chastised herself for letting her imagination run crazy. There was nothing unusual at work here, or about this call. There couldn't be. Tony likely worked at the courthouse and saw her divorce proceedings on the docket schedule, or something equally mundane and ordinary. There had to be a simple, logical reason prompting his call. Had to be. "I'm listening."

"My situation is hopeless. But yours isn't. Just don't lose hope, Doc. As long as there's life, there's hope."

As sincere as a summer sky. Concern. Empathy. Approval. All those feelings flooded through the phone from Tony to her. The back of her nose stung and tears

27

burned her eyes. She swallowed a knot of raw emotion. "I appreciate your concern, Tony, but my purpose here is to give help, not to rec—"

"You're hearing, but you're not listening. You've used your training and skills to help a lot of people. Now, you have to help you." He paused, then went on. "I know you sense what I'm telling you is more than just words, Doc, but sensing alone isn't enough. You've got to really feel it. To do something."

Bess *did* sense it, just as she sensed there was something unique about his voice, and that frightened her into denying she felt anything at all. Seeing Sal standing outside the booth's window in the hallway, she shrugged, feigning ignorance. His frown deepened.

She looked down at the mike, puzzled. What did Tony mean? *Really feel it. Do something?* About what? Exactly what was he up to — and why was he up to anything regarding her? *Who* was he? And what convinced her he wasn't a nut case? She'd had her fair share of them around here. Yet she'd bet her life Tony wasn't one of them.

As well as she knew she sat in the New Orleans booth, she knew he *could* feel all she felt, *could* hear all she heard. He *knew* all she knew — and *she* knew he still approved of her.

Bizarre. Intimidating. And violating. He had no right to invade her this way. Again she considered disconnecting him and ending the call.

Don't do it, Doc. Please. I want to help you.

Bess sat straight up. Tony's voice. Tony's "Doc." But not over the phone — *mentally!* What in the world was happening here?

Trust me.

She stared at the phone, stunned.

Please.

She darted a look back over her shoulder at Sal. His frown hadn't altered a bit; he clearly hadn't heard anything. Tony had conversed with Bess telepathically? But they were strangers. They couldn't be that closely linked mentally. Telepathy cases —

The sensation of something mystical happening sluiced through her. Bess's stomach flip-flopped. Pressing a hand against it, she denied the possibility, and fought the urge to protect herself by ducking into a dark corner. Her instincts had gone haywire. Besides, she couldn't run or hide. When something occurs inside your mind, where can you go?

She took a deep breath and then answered him. "Okay, Tony. I'm trying to really feel what you're telling me." She meant it and, if her voice lacked an ounce of courage, at least it carried the weight of her conviction.

Thank you.

You're welcome. She thought by rote, then gasped, surprised. They *were* communicating telepathically!

"Sometimes hope alone isn't enough." He dropped his voice to just above a whisper. "Sometimes you have to leap upon a mystic tide and have faith the sand will shift and an island will appear."

His words slammed into Bess. An odd tingle started at the base of her spine then slithered up her back. *A mystic tide. Shifting sands, an island . . .*

A metallic taste filled her mouth and a surge of anticipation she hadn't felt since before she and John had separated suffused her.

Mental communications, verbal puzzles. What was this man, some kind of psychic? "Tony?" Her voice cracked. She swallowed then tried again. "What do you mean?"

"Think about my message, Doc. Just think about it."

The line went dead.

Bess stared at the unlit button, wishing she could bring Tony back, wishing she could force him to explain. She tried silently asking him to return. But if he heard her, he chose not to respond. Instead, his message echoed through her mind, again and again, always ending with *think about it.*

For the remainder of her shift, Bess thought about it. During commercials, she studied on it, intrigued by Tony, and more by the message itself. But by the end of her program, Bess wasn't intrigued anymore. She couldn't *not* think about Tony's message. And it no longer intrigued. Now, it haunted.

And, for some reason that escaped her entirely, she had the strongest urge to — of all things — call John.

Ridiculous. Since she had filed for the legal separation two years ago, they'd only talked through their respective attorneys. John *would* believe her, but that was beside the point. The point was that Tony's call and message were driving her nuts. Fuel on the turmoil fire in what had become her complicated life.

How had this happened to her? She'd been so careful. So darn careful.

Too much was happening too quickly that couldn't be rationally or logically explained. And, as hard as it was for her to admit it, to get through it, she needed someone.

Oh, she could come up with her own solutions, but it sure would be nice to have a friendly sounding board. She obviously couldn't talk with John, or with her Yorkie, Silk. Her friend Miguel was out. He'd react to her telling him about the telepathy experience with Tony about as well if she'd announced aliens were invading the White House. Who could she trust? Who *wouldn't* think she'd lost her mind?

A friend.

Or friends.

Of course.

Knowing the perfect listeners, Bess snatched up her purse from the bottom desk drawer, then headed down 107.3's long hallway, toward the exit sign and outside door. She'd talk to T. J. and Maggie MacGregor.

"Shut up, darling."

Sassy, sparkling, very pregnant, dressed in forest green, and clutching a box of saltine crackers, Maggie MacGregor sidled up to her giant of a world-class artist husband, T. J., then pecked a chaste kiss to his chin.

"Maggie." His warning tone echoed through the cavernous riverfront art gallery they'd bought right after they'd married.

She wrinkled her nose at him, then turned toward Bess. "Ignore him. The man loves earning redemption points to stay in my good graces." Maggie shrugged, but her eyes danced with mischief, then went serious. "Okay, I agree. The job being threatened makes the divorce pill even more bitter to swallow."

"Darn right it does." Bess grunted and snatched a cracker. The cellophane wrapper crackled.

Maggie shifted the box of saltines then squeezed Bess's arm. "I know this doesn't make a bit of sense, but will you please just humor me and look at the painting?"

Standing toward the rear of the remodeled warehouse, Bess barely resisted an urge to roll her gaze up Lakeview Gallery's long, white columns to its equally white high ceiling. "Maggie, you know I adore you, but I've *just humored you twice* before today by staring at that seascape, and all I've gotten for my trouble is crossed eyes." Bess slid an apologetic glance toward T. J., who'd painted it. "Nothing personal."

He nodded, looking a little amused.

She scanned the sculptures, the paintings lining the walls, then looked back at Maggie. "I'm a little worried about all this stuff I've been telling you — seriously, you have to agree that my life's a cesspool right now — and, frankly, I'm not in much of a humoring mood."

"I'm sympathetic, Bess. Honest. But would you just trust me and do it?"

Bess lifted a hand toward the painting on the wall — T. J.'s masterpiece, according to Maggie — but held her gaze on her friend. "Frankly, I don't see why you're so enamored with it." Bess inwardly groaned at that less than diplomatic remark, then cast T. J. another apologetic look. "No offense, T. J., but in my opinion some of your other works are much more powerful."

"None taken." He looped a strong arm around Maggie's shoulders. "But you might as well give in, or my darling wife will resort to blackmail next."

"Maggie?" Bess guffawed. "She wouldn't."

"She would." Digging into the box, Maggie pulled out a cracker, lifted her chin, then crunched down on it. "I've already lost five dollars on this ordeal of yours. We heard Tony's call and I bet MacGregor here," she lifted her elbow to brush against T. J.'s ribs, "you'd come over to talk about this right away. He bet you'd fight it alone and come after work."

"So you lost a bet. That's not my fault." Bess smoothed her rumpled beige crepe skirt, then flicked at a cracker crumb on her lemon silk sleeve.

"The heck it isn't. If you were a tad less stubborn, friend, he'd owe me the five." Grunting, Maggie swiped her hands together, ridding them of cracker crumbs. "No options can be ignored in a bet with MacGregor — not even a little friendly blackmail." She pointed to the painting. "Now quit stalling — remember my delicate condition — and just look at it."

"All right, all right." Bess frowned. "But I have to say that you using this pregnancy as an excuse for being contrary is wearing thin."

"Amen to that." T. J. crossed his arms over his chest, rumpling his red plaid shirt.

Maggie slid him a killer glare, then grunted. "You adore me, MacGregor, and if you don't start helping me out here, I'm going to have to get drastic. Maybe even cry."

"Oh, man." He turned to Bess. "If our friendship ever meant anything to you, *please,* look at the painting. When Madam Prego gets wound up —"

"Would you two quit teasing here?" Bess propped her hands on her hips. "I'm telling you that this Tony guy was weird. What he said was weird. And what he knew went beyond weird and launched straight into spooky. It wasn't normal."

35

She squeezed her eyes shut, cursed the tremor in her voice, then looked back at her friends. "Ordinarily, I love your banter, but I'm dying here. Between the divorce, Millicent threatening to fire me, and this weird stuff with Tony haunting me every waking minute, I've maxed out." The words she'd been trained from the cradle never to utter, never to admit even to herself, poured out of her mouth. "I need . . . help."

The teasing light faded from Maggie's eyes, left them riddled with worry and with something else . . . hope? Yes. But hope for what? And, why was Bess's looking at the Seascape Inn painting so important to Maggie? It *was* important — Bess's intuition hummed it.

"Just look at it, Bess," Maggie said. "Please. Just do it."

Bess gave in and looked at the canvas. It was just a house. A huge gray Victorian with stark white shutters, sitting atop an ocean-side cliff. A common turret and widow's walk, a typical front porch that stretched end to end across the bottom floor. Pretty, but just a house.

"There." Bess looked back at Maggie. "I did it. Satisfied?"

"No," Maggie said sharply. "Really look at it."

Really feel it, Tony had said. Now, *really look at it* from a desperate-sounding Maggie. Apprehensive with the similarity, Bess wheeled her gaze to T. J. Stone-faced, he nodded and, no less apprehensive but certain now that something weird was occurring, Bess stifled a shudder and forced her focus back to the painting.

Sometimes hope alone isn't enough. Sometimes you have to leap upon a mystic tide and have faith the sand will shift and an island will appear.

Her heart hammered, thudding against her ribs, and she whispered on a brush of breath, "Tony?"

The painting seemed to come to life. The scent of its pines wafted over her and the cool sea spray crashing against its cliffs gathered on her heated skin. The gull flying through the fog in its misty sky cawed in sync with its ocean's rhythmic roar. Bess scanned the horizon. Her stomach rocking with the white-capped waves, she cruised with them to the shore, then up the steep and craggy granite cliffs. She let her gaze linger on the house itself, on its graceful turret, and on the narrow widow's walk that aroused such intense emotion in her, tears stung her eyes. She then looked on, to the attic room just under the eaves, and the cryptic sensation grew stronger.

The temperature plummeted.

An icy veil of a chill shivered up her spine.

And all the tension and pressure and strain she'd been feeling inside shattered.

Warm heat, energy as pure and tranquilizing as summer sun, seeped into her pores, and liquid, flowing sensations of peace and comfort and contentment spread through her, limb to limb, until she felt calm and at ease.

"How . . . odd," she mumbled. Absurd. Ridiculous. Impossible.

Wonderful.

Awed, Bess sucked in a wisp of a gasp. She'd never felt so empowered, so satisfied, such sheer joy in just being alive.

T. J. gave Maggie's arm a gentle squeeze. "That was it, honey. She had to admit she needed help."

Maggie pressed a fingertip over her lips. "Shh!"

He lowered his voice to a barely discernible whisper and eased toward the back room. "I'll call the airline and Miss Hattie."

Why did T. J. need to phone their friend from Maine and the airline now? How could he bear to miss experiencing this? Bess wanted to ask him, but the lure of the painting . . . She couldn't look away. Why hadn't she noted before its raw power, its soothing majesty? How could she ever have looked at this and felt it anything but magnificent?

Gingerly, as if being careful not to obstruct her view, Maggie stepped to Bess's side. "You don't want this divorce, do you, Bess?"

Captivated, she mumbled the truth. "It's inevitable."

"But is it what you want?"

"Does it matter? It's going to happen. Acceptance is positive growth." Bess's focus remained fixed on the canvas. "You know, Maggie, I look at this, and all my problems, even the divorce, seem insignificant. It's almost as if it's touched by . . . magic."

"You feel healed."

Bess smiled, spared Maggie a glance. "That's it exactly."

A look of empathy, of understanding, and — unless Bess mistook it — of relief flashed through Maggie's eyes. Relief seemed rather peculiar.

"You need a vacation," Maggie murmured. "Time away to just let go and to get things into perspective."

That sounded like heaven. And, looking at this house, possible. "Yes." The magnetism proved stronger than her will and Bess again mentally drifted into T. J.'s masterpiece. When her gaze lit on the turret room, certainty rippled through her heart. "More than anything else, I want to go there." It had been so long since she'd felt at peace. Six long years . . .

"Marvelous." Maggie sighed contentedly, stepped between Bess and the painting, then rested her arms on her distended belly.

Bess blinked, feeling almost as if she'd been under a spell and it'd been broken. That healed feeling disappeared, and she wanted it back. Desperately. "It is a real place, isn't it?" An anxious fear that it might not be gripped her.

"Oh, yes." Maggie nodded. "It's real. It's the bed-and-breakfast T. J. and I visit in Sea Haven Village, Maine. Seascape Inn."

"Your friend, Miss Hattie?"

Maggie nodded. "She's the innkeeper."

Bess's mouth felt stone dry. She licked at her lips. "I can't explain this, Maggie. I know it's going to sound crazy, but I have to go there. Now. Today."

"You don't have to explain — not to me." Maggie smiled. "T. J.'s making arrangements for you right now."

Bess vaguely remembered T. J. saying something about him calling Miss Hattie. How had he known?

Maggie cocked her head. A frown creased the smooth skin between her brows and she glanced off into space as if she were listening to something only she could hear. Seconds passed, and the strangest expression formed on her face. Worried, Bess clasped Maggie's arm. "Are you okay? Is it the baby?"

"No, no. We're fine." She patted her stomach, a fleeting smile touching her lips.

Despite her assurance, *something* concerned Maggie; it shone in her eyes. "I'm getting the strongest feeling that you're protecting me. I don't need that from you. Now, be honest. Are you two okay?"

"We're fine. I promise. It's, um, about Seascape Inn." Maggie brushed her gleaming red hair back from her face, clearly avoiding Bess's eyes. "When you get there, you might, um, see a man in an old Army uniform — one with a yellow carnation here in his lapel." She touched a fingertip to her dress, just above her left breast.

A shudder rippled up Bess's backbone. Why did this disclosure strike her as significant as Tony's message? "Okay."

"Trust him," Maggie said. "He's trying to help you."

"This has something to do with the painting." Certainty flooded Bess. "That's why you had me look at it before. You were hoping then —" Bess drew in a sharp breath.

41

"This man — he's the reason this strange stuff is happening now, isn't he?"

Maggie nodded.

Her wariness alerted Bess. "Is there something . . . different about him?"

Looking as guilty as sin, Maggie shrugged, stepped back to the tall column behind her, then sat down on the padded bench circling it. "To some. But I — I don't think I'm supposed to say anything more, Bess. Just trust him, okay?"

"You're sounding as weird as Tony."

"I know." Maggie grimaced, rubbed at her stomach, and rotated her swollen ankles. "Can you just trust me, too?"

For a long minute, Bess stared at her friend, not sure what to make of all this. But considering every aspect of her life lay in shambles already, what did she have to lose? "Why not? I always have."

Maggie swallowed and stilled, again as if listening. "Bess," she said, "I know this is stretching the bounds of friendship, but you might . . ." Her voice trailed.

"Might what?" Lord, but she hated to see Maggie distressed — especially in her condition. The baby was due in November, just five months away.

She turned away. "You might hear the man without actually seeing him."

A bolt of fear rocketed through Bess. Tingling head to heel, she stiffened her shoulders and stared hard at Maggie's narrow back. "Is he telepathic?" Tony was telepathic. Was there a connection?

"Sort of." Maggie looked back over her shoulder at Bess. "You've nothing to fear from him, though. Honest. If I thought for a second you did, I'd tell you."

Nervous. Evasive. Cryptic. So unlike Maggie MacGregor. "What aren't you telling me?"

She looked back in front of her, toward the white-carpeted floor. "It's . . . complicated."

Complicated. Well, that was comforting. "This man," Bess gave her instincts free rein. "He's not like us, is he?" Speaking her feelings aloud had her skin prickling.

Maggie twisted her lips and shifted on her feet, clearly uneasy. "If I say no, will you change your mind about going to Seascape?"

"No," Bess insisted with absolute certainty. The pull for those good feelings tugged more mightily than anything she could imagine. Nothing would keep her from going to Seascape Inn. "There's something special there, luring me. I have to see what it is." She couldn't explain her feelings fully; she didn't understand them herself. But the sense of mystery, of urgency, of irresistible allure was there, and so strong. It oddly promised that at Seascape Inn she could do what she hadn't been able to do here: sort through the remnants of her life and plan her future — a future without John.

"No, then," Maggie said softly. "He's not like us."

Bess had known it. But knowing and hearing it confirmed were two different things. Gooseflesh raised on her arms and she had the hardest time catching her breath. "Does this man have a name?"

"Yes, of course. But —"

T. J. breezed into the showroom. "You're all set, Bess. Miss Hattie's expecting you."

"Great." Bess glanced at Maggie and, seeing the lines of tension creasing her brow, backed off. Mystical events occurring or not, extra stress during pregnancy was bad for Maggie and the baby. If she said that this — whatever *this* proved to be — was all right, then certainly it would prove exactly that. "You can relax, Prego. No more questions. I said I'd trust you, and I will."

Maggie slumped against T. J. in obvious relief. "Thanks."

Bess smiled, kissed Maggie on the cheek,

then stretched up to place a peck on T. J.'s jaw. When she drew back, she stared at him, long and hard. "For you, I have one question. How did *you* know I'd be going to Seascape before *I* knew I'd be going to Seascape?"

His mouth dropped open, but no sound came out. He gave Maggie an inquisitive glance then, clearly not liking her nonverbal response, he returned a worried gaze to Bess. "Just a guess."

"Hmmm." Something told her not to push. And she decided to go with it. T. J. too had earned her respect and trust. "As it turned out, a darn good one."

"Appears so." Conspicuously happy to be off the hot seat, he grinned. "Your tickets are at the airport reception desk. American. Three o'clock flight."

"I'd better hurry, then." She moved toward the gallery's entrance door.

"Bess," Maggie raised her voice to be heard. "Don't forget to phone Francine. She said you've been ducking her calls, and she needs to talk with you. It's urgent."

"With Francine, it's always urgent." Bess paused at the glass front door. "Thanks," her gratitude stuck in her throat, "for everything."

"Be careful, okay?" Maggie had that worried gleam in her eye again.

It warned Bess what she didn't know *could* hurt her. Still, on looking at the painting, those good feelings had been so strong. Once she got to Seascape, things would settle out okay; she just knew it. She waved, then left Lakeview Gallery.

The bell on the door still tinkling in the back rooms, Maggie watched Bess disappear beyond the tinted-glass windows at the end of the riverfront walkway.

T. J. joined her. Looking out through the glass onto the busy street, he grimaced. "Think she'll call Francine?"

"Nope." Maggie looked up at her husband, her eyes shining. "But finally Tony's interceding."

T. J. rubbed their noses. "Did you tell her about him?"

Maggie ran her fingertips up and down the soft placket of his plaid shirt, between the second and third buttons. "Not exactly."

"Honey, you should have told her. Remember how you reacted to Tony? He scared the bejesus out of you."

He had. He'd gotten MacGregor's attention too. Cranky because he failed to mention that fact, she lifted her chin. "I hinted."

He looked at her with too-seeing eyes. "Okay, 'fess up. Why didn't you tell her?"

46

Maggie snuggled against him. "Worrying about Tony drew us together. I figured —"

"Matchmaking." T. J. grunted and clasped her shoulders. "I should have known. You're as bad as Miss Hattie."

"Miss Hattie's an angel, and you know it."

"Did I say she wasn't?"

"No, but you sure implied it. You sounded perfectly snotty, MacGregor, and you know I like snotty about as much as I like nagging."

"Facts are facts, honey. Have you forgotten those seventeen possibles she tried pairing me up with?"

"Not hardly. But she didn't know then you were there waiting for me."

"Point is, she still tried."

"Shut up, darling."

"Maggie." He leveled her with a warning look.

She snorted, not at all intimidated. "All right, MacGregor. So maybe I should have told Bess about Tony." She rubbed her nose against the side of his neck and whispered close to the shell of his ear. "But you've got to admit, we had some —"

"We had lots of," he agreed, then kissed her hard. When he lifted his head, he looked dreamy-eyed. "But you're forgetting a couple of minor details."

Maggie lowered her hands from his broad shoulders to his waist, then looped her arms around him and scooted closer, until they stood belly to thigh. "Like what?"

"For one, John and Bess are divorcing. As in, they don't want to be married to each other anymore. And, for another, they're not divorced yet. Bess isn't going to get involved with another man while she's still married to John."

"She's been involved with that yachter."

"Miguel Santos?" MacGregor grunted. "Come on, Maggie. Don't fall for gossip. They're just friends."

Maggie shrugged, then shot a worried look at the painting. "Bess *is* still crazy about John. She doesn't say it — she never has. But when I asked if she wanted the divorce, she said it was inevitable. Not that she wanted it. They belong together, MacGregor. I feel it down to my bones. Maybe that's what Tony's doing — stopping the divorce."

"Maybe. Or maybe it's not supposed to stop. Maybe Tony's helping them get through the divorce so they can move on with their lives."

It *could* be they were supposed to divorce. Not everyone who visited Seascape Inn discovered, or rediscovered, love. "Maybe," she agreed. "But I sure hope not."

"Bess has been under a lot of stress. I think you should have warned her about Tony."

"I couldn't." Maggie backed away then turned from the window.

"Why not?"

She sighed her impatience. "Geez, think about it, MacGregor. Bess hasn't made the connection between Tony and Seascape Inn yet. She believes Tony is telepathic, which doesn't scare her witless. But she *will* make the connection. And when she does — aside from trying to convince you I need a long vacation at a quiet sanatorium — how do you figure she'll react to me advising her to trust a ghost?"

CHAPTER 2

John Mystic had experienced only three gut-wrenching wants in his whole life: to marry Bess Cameron and build a home where they'd both be content and happy; to find Elise Dupree's missing daughter, Dixie; and to keep the truth about his parents a secret he would take with him to his grave.

He'd married Bess and built a home. Unfortunately, he'd never once thought it necessary to mention his wants, including keeping her and staying in it. He'd done everything humanly possible, but he hadn't found Dixie — yet. The painstaking search continued. And he'd kept the secret about his parents, though doing so had demanded he distance himself from his sister, Selena, who had a knack for making people talk. Otherwise, sooner or later, she'd have wheedled it out of him.

John also had learned a hard lesson. Sometimes, no matter what a man does, no matter how hard he tries, he just can't win. And too often when he loses, others also pay the price.

Knowing the secret had cost him his sister. The distance between them had hurt her. It'd hurt him and their uncle, Maximilian Piermont, too. Dixie's case had cost him his wife. And he, Bess, Elise, and Dixie, all had paid the price, in spades.

It shouldn't have happened that way, though John didn't know how he could have avoided it. He and Bess hadn't been married long when, with her blessing, he'd struck out on his own to open Mystic Investigations. Maybe if they'd been married longer, she'd have felt more secure. Maybe if he'd known what a closed society New Orleans was, he would have been better prepared for closed doors and not needed society matriarch Elise Dupree's case. But he hadn't known, and he had needed it. And so when tragedy struck Elise and she'd come to John with the story of her daughter Dixie's kidnapping — an elopement, according to the FBI — John saw solving the case as his big break. If he found the girl, kidnapped *or* eloped, his business would be set for success. Bess would be proud of him. And he'd have proven to her his worth.

He hadn't planned on getting emotionally involved with Elise. Bess didn't know it, but Elise had become the closest thing to a mother he'd had since he was three years old. He hadn't planned on Bess getting riled over the relationship, or on her forming the opinion that he was obsessing on the case, either. And he certainly never had planned on losing her over it. Events had snowballed and it all had just . . . happened.

By the time he'd realized their marriage was in trouble, it was too late for an easy fix. Things had gotten complex and, he admitted it, his pride stepped in. He couldn't find Dixie, couldn't stop looking for her. Couldn't tell Elise he'd failed her when she'd needed him most. And he couldn't, *wouldn't,* crawl back to his doubting-his-worth-already wife a failure.

Instead, determined to turn things around, he'd dug in his heels and formulated a plan. A simple plan. Find Dixie for Elise, paying her back for caring about him and trusting him with her daughter's life, for opening society's doors for him — and for her sound investment advice — and when all that had been settled, as a successful man Bess would be proud of, he'd reclaim his wife and his home.

It would've worked. Except Bess filed for

a divorce. And he still hadn't found Dixie. And, heaven help him, three days ago, Elise had died.

Elise's funeral this morning had been sheer torture. Bryce Richards, Maggie and T. J. MacGregor, Selena, and Uncle Max all attended to support John. Bess hadn't.

He thought he just might hate her for that.

Sometimes, no matter what a man does, no matter how hard he tries, he just can't win.

And so he'd come here. Back to where he always came when he needed support. Needed to feel close to her again. Needed to relive the good times and glimpse again elusive peace . . .

Through the car radio, Bess's familiar, silky-voiced sign-off snagged John's attention. "Rest easy, New Orleans. See you at twilight."

Innately alerted, he punched the knob, squelching the radio. Silence filled the car, and then subtle sounds of crickets and frogs carried in on the sultry night air. Parked in the driveway, his stomach tense and in knots, he again stared through the windshield into the dark windows of the empty house he and Bess once had shared. She was in trouble; he felt it.

During her radio program, not a hint of

anything being wrong had been heard in her voice. Bess was far too private, too cool and controlled, to let anyone know an imperfect ripple she couldn't smooth out by herself had trespassed into her world. They might have spent more of their seven-year marriage separated than together, but he knew her the way only a husband knows his wife, and something had Bess in a tailspin and doing some serious reeling. Question was, What?

Maybe she'd had a fight with her sorry Spaniard, Miguel Santos. Unlikely. She'd been seen all over the French Quarter with him lately, and seemingly everyone in New Orleans — eager to impart their backdoor censure of John's treatment of her, yet not bold enough to just do it — had made a point of telling him how happy she'd looked. No, not the Spaniard. Had to be something else. What, precisely, John hadn't a clue, but he certainly knew what *wasn't* the reason for her upset: their relationship and imminent divorce. Bess didn't give a darn about either, or about him.

An empty ache had him slumping, fighting a longing pang for the old days. They'd been happy once. Here. In this house. He squeezed the steering wheel. She'd loved this house. Why hadn't she stayed in it and demanded he leave? Too many memories? Too many shattered dreams haunting every room?

Those had been his reasons for moving out and leaving the house empty. As for her reasons, only she knew. He still couldn't believe she'd actually suggested they rent it. John grunted. He'd flatly refused, of course. The idea of another couple living in their home, sharing meals in their kitchen, making love in their bedroom . . . well, it got to him. Obviously, it hadn't bothered her. And that had gotten to him, too.

He let his gaze drift up the white brick to the second-floor veranda. How many nights had they come out of their bedroom door, tossed a blanket down on the veranda floor and, wrapped in each other's arms, dreamed into the stars?

Plenty.

But not enough.

And there never would be more.

Regret swam in his stomach. A future of silence engulfed him, dark and oppressive and yawning. He gripped the wheel tighter, making knobs of his knuckles, and frowned down at the front door. A spray of amber light from the streetlamp swept over the sleek landing and he imaged her standing there in it, greeting him as she had so often, open-armed and smiling. Oh, how he missed her. Sometimes he missed her so much.

Why had she done it? Why had she left him with no more than a phone call? Why had she waited years before filing for the legal separation, knowing it'd take over a year from then for the divorce to be final? Why had she left him at all? They'd been happy. She'd loved him, darn it. He *knew* she'd loved him.

The box-hedge outside the passenger door rustled. His neighbor, Peggy, spying on him again. He sighed. She'd report to Selena and, before sundown, he'd get another when-are-you-going-to-stop-going-over-there-and-get-on-with-your-life call. Didn't he wish he knew?

His gaze drifted back to the house. Maybe Bess had waited to file for the divorce because she'd feared losing her job. Millicent Fairgate was a real hard head who'd do anything to protect her legacy — the station. John never had liked her, and didn't know anyone who did besides Elise. A whiff of scandal and, in a finger snap, the social-minded airhead would fire Bess.

But, no, not the job. Slumping back in his seat, he rested his shoulder against the door, his hand on the gearshift. Bess could hold her own with Millicent and she wouldn't put up with that. Santos had to be the reason. Maybe Bess was ready to marry the guy.

Bess? Married to another man?

John's stomach soured, his muscles all clenched at once. Torn between denial, anger, and guilt — resenting all those feelings and more — he stiffened in his seat. Why had she done it? Why had she done anything that she'd done? And what difference did it make now? In three weeks, they'd be history. The divorce would be final, and their marriage would be over. It'd be too late.

It was already too late. Elise was dead.

The empty ache inside him deepened to a gaping hole. In finding Dixie, he'd taken too long.

The cell phone rang.

Ignoring it, he stared sightlessly at the house, feeling as lost and alone as he had in the early years, when he and Selena first had moved in with their Uncle Max. John had hated those feelings then. He still hated them — as much as he hated himself for coming here.

Yet he continued to do it. He looked down at the yellow carnation petal in his hand. Elise had died holding it. Where had it come from? He'd probably never know. Odd, but it comforted him. And after the funeral today, he needed comforting. He just hadn't been able to face that empty apartment alone.

The phone rang for the third time. He frowned at it, certain if he didn't answer it, the blasted thing would ring forever. When it rang a fourth time, resigned, he lifted the receiver. "Mystic."

"John, it's me, Bryce."

His lawyer calling him now? But they were friends, too, and considering the hour — a shade shy of dawn — this had to be personal. Since Bryce's wife Meriam's death, Bryce'd had his hands full with his three children, his practice, and his grief, but the predawn SOS calls had ceased months ago. Until now.

Couldn't anyone just be happy anymore? "The kids okay?"

"Suzie's still having nightmares. Her therapist says she needs more time to get used to losing her mom. Selena's talking with her, too, trying to help her get and keep both oars in the water."

"That sounds like Selena." She never had beaten around the bush.

"Yeah, I'd be nuts without her help on this." His indrawn breath crackled through the phone. "Hey, I didn't call to complain. You doing okay, buddy?"

He'd never been less okay. "I'm fine."

"I tried calling you at home . . ."

John looked up at the house. This was home. Not the apartment he lived in and avoided as much as possible. For six years home had stood empty. Now Elise was gone, too. Pain crushed him in a wrenching vise.

"I called on the cell a while ago but got no answer."

John sort of remembered the phone ringing earlier, when Bess had been talking to that guy, Tony. Weird message. Weird man. Maybe he and/or his message was what had Bess rattled. They'd surely given John the creeps. "Must have stepped out."

"Where are you?"

John sucked in a sharp breath. "Working on a case."

Bryce let out a ragged sigh, proving he knew exactly where John was at the moment, and it worried him. "I'm sorry, buddy. I know how close you and Elise were."

Close? She'd trusted him with her daughter's life. She'd called him dear heart. Close? *Close?* "She . . . mattered," he choked out. "Look, I've got to go. Thanks for the call."

"John, wait. As soon as you can, drop by the office. I know the timing is lousy, but we need to talk about this property settlement dispute. We're out of time."

The divorce was the *last* thing he wanted to talk about right now. "What dispute? I told you to give Bess whatever she wants."

"That's the dispute. She doesn't want anything."

Not anything? "What do you mean, she doesn't want *anything?*" John cranked the engine, turned on the headlights, then backed out of the driveway, swearing he'd come here for the last time. He'd listened to Bess on the radio for the last time too. If she knew he did either, she'd have a field day analyzing him.

Maybe she'd have better luck than he'd had. Why *did* he come here? Why *did* he listen to her program every night? Knowing she had become involved with another man, why *did* he still hunger for the sound of her voice?

Maybe he still loved her.

Impossible. He couldn't. He *wouldn't.* John Mystic was no woman's chump.

So why did he keep putting himself through this?

It didn't matter. He'd done both for the

last time. And how many times he had made and broken those promises to himself before didn't matter either. This time, he really meant them.

"I meant exactly what I said," Bryce told him. "Bess refuses to touch any of the assets you two acquired. Francine's having a virtual stroke, but Bess won't budge."

Bess's lawyer having a virtual stroke ranked as her problem, but Bess's refusal — that was another matter. An infuriating one. Was she sending John another of her infamous messages?

Probably. Probably her way of telling him she wanted nothing of his, of theirs, because it held no value to her. *He* held no value to her.

Yeah, Bess never had screamed her intent or opinions, or anything else, for that matter. Cashmere, eel-skin women like her opted for far more subtle means of torture. Always sending confusing signals and silent messages a man had to try to decode. Always analyzing their men too. But *his* cashmere, eel-skin woman wasn't going to get away with it anymore.

He should have stopped this a long time ago and hadn't. But, by gosh, he'd stop it now. She would *not* blow them off as if their marriage had meant nothing. He wouldn't let her do that to either of them. "She'll take half, and that's my bottom line."

"She's refused, John," Bryce said. "She'll accept nothing."

John frowned at the street. Between street-lamps and glaring neon signs, dark shadows muddied the pavement. "Why?"

"Francine doesn't have a clue."

"Do you?" They were friends too, and had been for years. Bryce, his now-deceased wife, Meriam; T. J. MacGregor and, more recently, T. J.'s wife, Maggie. John and Bess had been, or were, friends with them all.

"No," Bryce said. "She hasn't said a word about it to me. Whenever I try to bring up the case, she ducks the topic or gives me one of her this-conversation-is-unethical looks."

Oh, her settlement refusal was a message, all right. "Unacceptable." John hit the blinker and changed lanes to pass a battered green pickup with two German Shepherds loose in the truck bed. It seriously needed a new muffler, and the right-rear fender had rusted out.

"Francine says Bess isn't negotiable on this."

"She better be, because I'm not agreeing to her *nothing* business."

"Why not? Clearly, this is the way she

wants it."

"I said, unacceptable." He braked hard. Was he going to hit every red light in the city between Pontchartrain Drive and the apartment?

"John, as your lawyer, I have to point out how many divorcing spouses would love to be in your position on this. Especially those with your kind of assets."

"I'm not one of them, okay?"

"That's apparent. My question is, why?"

"I'm just not. Let's leave it at that." *Isn't this stupid light ever going to change?*

"Can't do it, buddy. Francine's going to want a reason. And if you expect Bess to go along with what you want, you'd better make it a good one."

John sped to the corner, then stopped at yet another red light. On the crossroad, cars whizzed through the beams of his headlights. Bryce was right. Bess wouldn't rant or rave, she'd just quietly refuse to budge an inch. "You want a reason? Okay, here it is. Bess is running on emotion, not logic. After that guy Tony's call, if Millicent Fairgate hasn't already, she's bound to fire Bess. She's going to need —"

"I'll be."

Puzzled, John frowned at the phone receiver, then put it back to his ear. "What?"

"You want her back." Bryce sounded incredulous.

John's stomach lurched. It was too late for that. He'd run out of time. Elise was dead, and Dixie was still missing. And only a chump would want back a woman who'd walked out on him.

The light turned green and he punched down on the accelerator. "I want to make sure she has the resources to take care of herself until she decides what to do with the rest of her life. You know how proud she is, Bryce. The woman's so stubborn she'd die before asking anyone for anything — especially me."

"I hear she's changing, though I can't say I know it for fact. But Santos did give her Silk, and she accepted it."

"Silk?" Three more blocks. Just three more blocks and he'd be there. "What does Bess need with fabric? She can't sew a stitch." When they'd gotten a little frisky and she'd caught the heel of her pump in her hem, he'd had to mend the slinky, hip-hugging slip she called a skirt. Man, her legs went on forever in that thing.

"Silk is a Yorkie."

A dog? A flash of anger raced through John's chest. Jealousy ran fast on its heels. "She accepts a dog from Santos, but won't touch a thing she acquired with her husband? That proves my point. It's not as if we didn't both work. She can't even use that excuse." Definitely sending him a message. Definitely. "I'm telling you, Bryce, she's not running on all cylinders."

Bryce softened his tone. "John, you and Bess are divorcing. Whether or not she's running on a single cylinder isn't any of your business. What I mean is, her job and future aren't your problems anymore."

Seething, John swiped at his blinker. "Until July tenth, she's my wife. That makes her problems my problems." He whipped into the parking lot, then cut the engine and the lights. "Now you call her shark of a lawyer and tell her Bess takes half, or no divorce."

"Be reasonable, John. If we go back into court without this being resolved, Judge Branson is going to throw a fit."

"We all have bad days, buddy. The judge can fend for himself. If Bess wants her divorce; she can have it — on my terms." He lifted the handle and opened the door. "I'm at home now. I'll drop by the office in the morning."

"John, wait!" Bryce sighed deeper. "I wish we could have delayed this until later. I really am sorry about Elise."

"Yeah, well, we do what we have to do." The ache in his chest doubled. "Give the kids a hug, and tell Suzie I said she can only have sweet dreams." He knew firsthand that losing a mother was rough on a kid. But it was especially rough on one so young.

He clicked his phone off, then got out of the car.

The air smelled of rain, heavy and sultry. He looked up, then stilled. Not the apartment but the hospital loomed in front of him, large and stark white against the cloudy sky. He'd automatically driven there, just as he had every day during the long weeks Elise had been a patient. She was dead now.

Dead.

His vision blurring, he looked up at the building. It seemed wrong. So clinical and cold, when Elise had been anything but. Why had she had to die? Why had he had to lose her, too?

Memories of three days ago, when he'd parked in this same spot, flooded back, and his knees went weak. Man, but he hadn't wanted to walk in there. He hadn't wanted to see her for the last time.

Knowing he'd failed her, he hadn't wanted to watch her die.

■ ■ ■ ■

At noon, John met with Bryce at his uptown office and heard the words that would forever alter his life: "Bess won't budge, and she's left town."

Bess had left New Orleans? John paced before Bryce's gleaming mahogany desk, cursing the sun for flooding in through the window when it should be storming. Sunshine seemed the ultimate insult to endure for someone confronted with ten tons of turmoil. "Where did she go?"

Fiddling with a button on his suit jacket, Bryce avoided John's eyes. "Sea Haven Village, Maine."

"Maine?" Pacing the plush carpet, John stopped beside a maroon leather wingback chair. Photographs Meriam had taken hung on the paneled walls. One of T. J. MacGregor's paintings held a place of honor, behind Bryce's desk, above a credenza. John glanced at the painting, but it was one of Meriam's photographs that captured his attention. A seaside ocean view from atop granite cliffs. A huge gray Victorian home. It was just a clapboard house. So why did it captivate him? "Does she know anyone in Maine?"

"I don't know. But she's at a bed-and-breakfast called Seascape Inn, the one T. J. and Maggie visit." Bryce laced his hands atop his desk. "Look, if you want this property dispute settled, then you're going to have to go to Bess and take care of it personally, one-on-one."

One-on-one with his wife was the *last* thing John wanted right now. He was still too shaky over Elise's death, and he had to get back to the case. Elise had known he'd lied to her on her deathbed about finding Dixie and, until he did find her daughter and see to it that she was all right, neither he nor Elise would know a minute's peace. "I'd rather not."

"I don't think your 'rathers' carry much weight on this." Bryce frowned. "The judge is threatening a hefty fine if this property dispute isn't settled pronto."

John shrugged. "Right now, I'd rather pay it."

"He's not fining you. He's fining Bess." Bryce lifted a hand. "She left town."

She didn't have the money to pay a hefty fine. Had she gone into private practice, then she'd have been set financially, but she'd wanted to help others more than assure her own financial security. John had understood that, had admired her for it. But that choice left her personally vulnerable now. And her vulnerability played a big part in him insisting she accept half of their assets. It was the only way he could be certain she'd have the freedom to follow her dreams.

He reached to his inside jacket pocket then pulled out his checkbook and pen. "How much?" She'd be ticked, but so what? She was already ticked. He'd outlasted her lawyer's lungs before; he could again.

"You can't cover it — Judge Branson's order."

John dropped a fist to the back of the chair. "Why is he doing this?"

"Because he ordered you two to settle this property dispute last go round and it still isn't done. He's taking your defiance kind of personal."

Figured. Only one in a hundred judges would get his bowels into an uproar over this, and theirs just had to be the one.

Bryce leaned back, propped his feet on his desk, then laced his fingers behind his head. "The way I see it, the ball's in your court, buddy."

"Looks that way." John plopped down in the wingback chair, exhausted from the mountain of things he'd had to do since Elise had passed away. Now this with Bess.

Nothing with that woman had ever come easily. Why should the divorce be any different?

"So what's it gonna be?" Bryce asked. "Are you heading up to Seascape to work this out with Bess, or are you going to watch your wife go to jail for contempt of court?"

CHAPTER 3

"Bess, dear, I'm so glad you're here. I was starting to worry. T. J. said to expect you just after noon."

Bess set down her bags in front of the Seascape Inn registration desk, then looked at the innkeeper, Miss Hattie. She *did* look like Norman Rockwell's grandma model, just as Maggie had said. Soft, round face, crinkled into a welcoming smile, imprints alongside her nose — obviously from reading glasses, which were absent from her face now — a peach floral dress and, in her left hand, the infamous white lacy hankie. A bubble of sheer pleasure trickled through Bess at finally meeting the much-adored woman. "I'm sorry. I should have called. I got lost coming out of Bangor."

"Happens all the time. Missed the sign for Sea Haven Highway, didn't you?"

"Yes, ma'am, I did." Bess glanced around the entryway and through the gallery. To her right, beyond a stately, brass-trimmed grandfather clock, she saw the parlor and the living room. A winding staircase partially blocked her view to the left, giving her but a glimpse of a dining room decorated with wainscoting and splashes of pink florals on navy blue. The gallery dead-ended in a cheerful looking kitchen done in white lace and washed oak. Charming. But it felt like a home. "I thought this was an inn, Miss Hattie?"

From the opposite side of the L-shaped registration desk, Miss Hattie smiled. "Actually, it's a bed-and-breakfast, dear."

"The name confused me."

Fingering through a little ceramic box with a lighthouse painted on its lid, Miss Hattie fretted, clearly distracted and looking for . . . something — ah, a key.

She passed it to Bess. "It's simple, really. Collin and Cecelia Freeport built Seascape as their private residence — remind me to tell you the legend. Lovely story. Just lovely."

Maggie had told Bess the story, but not wanting to rob Miss Hattie of the pleasure, Bess didn't say so, only nodded.

"Their son, the eldest child, was killed in the war, so their beloved daughter, Mary Elizabeth, inherited the place. When she became a widow, God rest her soul, she

72

converted the house into an inn. The Carriage House, too. It has a suite and extra rooms."

And a new roof. When driving around back to park her car, Bess had noted the Carriage House roof wasn't yet weathered like that on the inn itself. "Are all the Freeports gone now, then?"

"Oh my, no. Mary Elizabeth's son, Judge Nelson — he lives in Atlanta now — inherited the place. He opted for a bed-and-breakfast — no doubt due to my advancing years, treasure that he is — but neither of us saw any need to change the name. Seascape has been Seascape Inn for years and the locals would continue to call it that anyway."

A ceiling fan's spinning blades thumped overhead and smells of lemon oil and vanilla potpourri filled Bess's nose. The paneling gleamed as if freshly oiled and a little sachet of burgundy tulle and white lace lay on the desk near a green banker's lamp. She glanced over her right shoulder at the grandfather clock, oddly reassured by its steady ticks, and a sense of peace and calm similar to that she'd felt on looking at the painting of the inn at Lakeview Gallery washed through her. A smile curled her lips. "It's charming, Miss Hattie."

"It's home." Miss Hattie turned the registration book toward Bess, lifted then passed a pen from a wooden holder near the lamp. "I've lived here most of my life, dear. Can't imagine thinking of Seascape as anything more than home."

"You're as special as T. J. and Maggie claim." Angelic, through and through. Bess signed the register then returned the pen to its holder.

"Bah." Miss Hattie smiled. "But I've heard some wonderful things about you." She came around the desk and patted Bess's arm. "I don't care for feeling like a guest, so I never have them here. Think of Seascape as your home."

"Thank you." Bess cringed at what Miss Hattie would think at knowing how awful home had been.

She dabbed at her temple with the delicate white hankie. "Now, let's get you settled into the Great White Room. First light hits there, so lower the shades at night, and take advantage of the sitting room in the adjoining turret, mmm? T. J. says you're under a lot of pressure right now and we're to see to it you relax." She lifted a blue-veined hand and brushed back a lock of hair from Bess's face, her gentle green eyes concerned and comforting. "Gaze upon the ocean and dream a little, dear. Very soothing, dreaming. Brings peace to a troubled soul."

Peace to a troubled soul. All a home should do. Bess nearly cried. Home. Exactly what she needed to lick her wounds. How Miss Hattie had known that remained a mystery — and a blessing. Maggie often had said the innkeeper seemed aged and ageless, touched by magic. Maybe it was true. Bess gave Miss Hattie a watery smile. "I think T. J. and Maggie were right about you."

"Don't you worry, dear." Empathy and then certainty rang in Miss Hattie's tone. "Everything is going to be just fine. That's why you're here."

An odd feeling shimmied through Bess's chest. Miss Hattie knew the reason Bess had felt compelled to come here? "Why?"

The old woman smiled. "To heal."

Bess didn't want to dispute the woman, but she didn't think for a second Seascape could cure her troubles. True, she did feel . . . comforted. And oddly at peace. Miracles, truly, considering her circumstances. But for a full-fledged healing, she'd need a fistful of miracles. And that would be asking for too much, even for Seascape.

A heavy summer shower had the Blue

75

Moon Cafe bustling and its friendly owners, Fred and Lucy Baker, jumping to get everyone seated at the long wooden bar and at the red-checked, clothed tables fed and watered and comfortable.

Because Bess was *from away,* as Miss Hattie put it, the angelic old innkeeper filled Bess in on the identity of the rain-soaked people coming in to dry off: Horace Johnson, the baseball-capped mayor who owned The Store across the street from the cafe; Jimmy Goodson, the lanky, young, and shy mechanic who had been orphaned long ago, and who Bess already had met at Seascape. Miss Hattie clearly was very fond of Jimmy. The incredibly handsome Pastor Brown, whose single marital status Miss Hattie had pointed out twice, so far; and Sheriff Leroy Cobb, the bear of a man who sat at the bar and, along with his coffee, indulged in a slice of Lucy's blueberry pie that, in Bess's book, qualified as a slab. Sheriff Cobb, Miss Hattie explained, had grown up here and was now the county sheriff. But wherever his duties took him, he made it his business to drop by the Blue Moon Cafe every afternoon for pie, coffee, and lively conversation.

Trying to keep everyone's identity straight had Bess's head swimming. Finally, she gave up. Hearty and generous-natured, the villagers would tolerate any mistakes an outsider might make.

Even without Miss Hattie's insight, Bess would have recognized the postage stamp-size cafe as the village hub. It was small, but alive with conversation, laughter, and music. Garth Brooks, via the old jukebox on the far wall, belted out a song about thunder rolling. Its vibrations rocked together the seashells and starfish inside fishnets, hanging from the walls. A partition made of boat oars blocked the view of the kitchen, but someone in there — sounded like a teenage girl — sang along. Lucy Baker, a jean-clad, thirtyish redhead wearing a T-shirt with "I'm Not Old, I Just Need Repotting" emblazoned across the front, snapped her gum and buzzed table to table, refilling mugs of hot coffee from a carafe in one hand, and glasses of iced tea from a pitcher held in the other. The succulent smell of lobster drifted up from Bess's plate. It had been divine, as Lucy had assured her it would be. Must be true about the deeper, colder water making Maine's lobster the best.

"Isn't it wonderful, about Tyler and Maggie and the baby? I can hardly wait for November." Miss Hattie sipped from her

77

cup of steaming hot tea, her eyes shining her delight.

"Yes, it is." Secretly, Bess hoped she'd be asked to be the baby's godmother. With her and John divorcing, godmother likely would be as close as she'd ever come to having a child of her own. A little ripple of sadness slid through her chest. Well, at least T. J. and Maggie were happy. And Miss Hattie clearly took their well-being into her heart. That had Bess smiling at the dear soul. Since Bess's arrival, Miss Hattie, with her kind and gentle ways, her forever-mussed apron and floral dresses and her soft white, bunned hair, had hovered over, nurtured and pampered and spoiled Bess rotten, acting as if it were her personal responsibility to make Bess welcome and happy.

She'd half-succeeded. Never, including during her childhood, had Bess felt so welcome or comfortable anywhere as she did at Seascape Inn. The house itself seemed to open its arms and cradle her. Strange to imagine until she'd experienced it firsthand, but it felt as a home should feel, though none in Bess's experience ever had.

She let her gaze drift to the front door. A birdlike woman rushed in from the storm and tilted back her chin to look around. "Leroy Cobb," she said, her voice high-pitched and tinny, her eyes narrowing. "I knew I'd find you here."

Clad in a wet yellow slicker and floppy hat, she stomped from the door to the bar, dripping a trail of her path onto the wood-plank floor. Standing beside the sheriff's stool, she shook her finger at his reddened face. "You ought to have more respect for your elders than to make them run after you in this kind of weather, young man. I told your mama back when you were a boy that she needed to —"

"I'm sorry, Miss Favish," he interrupted, looking as if he wished he could crawl under the bar to get away from her.

Bess cocked her head. Amusing, considering he was thrice the size of the older woman.

"Pay her no mind, dear," Miss Hattie whispered over the table. "That's my next-door neighbor, Beaulah Favish. She's a good woman, but she's had some challenges that have troubled her more than a wee bit."

Ah, Batty Beaulah. Maggie had told Bess about her too. "I see." Challenges. Boy, could Bess empathize with that. If she didn't watch herself, when all her challenges settled out, people would be calling her Batty Bess.

"I'm telling you, Leroy Cobb," Beaulah

slapped at her slicker, spraying those seated at the bar, "I saw lights on up in that attic room at two in the morning. Now we both know darn well it wasn't Hattie up there. Something strange is going on at that inn and I expect you to handle it — better than you handled T. J. busting the cliffs with his hard head."

Most people would worry about the human head, not the granite cliffs. Bess lifted her brows, and whispered to Miss Hattie. "Our T. J.?"

"Mmm, I'm afraid so, dear." Miss Hattie's soft sigh coupled with her concerned look. "Beaulah is a dear woman, but she's a tad —"

"Eccentric?" Bess suggested, sensing Miss Hattie's unease, and that her generous spirit wouldn't permit her to say anything unkind about anyone.

The door opened and Miss Hattie's friend, Vic Sampson, the mailman Bess had met at the inn yesterday, came inside, hauling his leather bag. Worn and wet, it splotched dark, but he'd fastened the clasps to protect the mail. A moment later, he waved and grinned at her from the stool beside the poor sheriff. Understanding his silent message, Bess smiled back at the spry man who was in his seventies, like Miss

Hattie. He was clearly amused — and right. Beaulah certainly did have a strong set of lungs; she barely paused for breath.

Lucy stepped between Bess and her view of the conflict. "More tea, sugar?" She snapped her gum.

"Yes, please." Bess smiled and moved the red plastic glass closer, so Lucy wouldn't have to stretch. "You sound Mississippian."

"I was, but I converted. Now, I'm a hard-core Mainiac, and wouldn't have it any other way."

"Maggie didn't mention that, though she did tell me how all the villagers started calling Miss Hattie 'Miss Hattie' to keep you out of trouble with your mother."

"They sure did. Mama's a true southern belle and a stickler on manners. Back when I was growing up, I was a tad forgetful, which meant without everyone's help, Mama always would've been crawling my backside."

The villagers had adopted the traditional southern "Miss" to help Lucy remember. The caring in the gesture warmed Bess's heart, and convinced her Lucy Baker must be special or the villagers wouldn't have felt so protective of her. It also created a pang of envy. No one considered Bess that special. Not anymore.

Squelching thoughts of John, of the divorce, she watched Lucy pour the tea, then looked at Miss Hattie.

"I've been getting a lot of requests for your blueberry muffins lately." Lucy gave the edge of the table a swipe with a cloth. "I don't suppose you'd share the recipe."

Looking pleased, Miss Hattie dabbed at a droplet of tea on the table with her napkin. "I'll bring it by on my way to Millie's for the Historical Society meeting tomorrow — provided you don't draw Bess into your debate with Fred about angels being dead people or spiritual beings."

"Dang. With her being a shrink, we figured she'd have some lively opinions." Though disappointment flickered through Lucy's eyes, she nodded her agreement. "You drive a hard bargain, Miss Hattie, but folks would get into a snit if I didn't grab the chance to get that recipe. Appreciate it." She grinned and turned to Bess. "Miss Hattie's pie is a hit around here and everyone's sick of arranging church socials just to get a sample of her muffins."

"They don't." Flushing a pretty pink, Miss Hattie protested, her kind eyes twinkling.

"It's happened, and you know it," Lucy insisted, then whispered to Bess. "But don't mention it to Pastor Brown. He gets a mite

82

long-winded if provoked, and then the mayor snores and drowns out the sermon. Mortifies his poor wife, Lydia." Lucy sniffed and dropped her voice. "Even snooty folks don't deserve being mortified in the Lord's House."

"Mum's the word," Bess promised, crossing her heart with a swipe of her fingertip and grinning from the heart out. There were some aspects of small town life she adored. This bonding among the villagers was one of them. She cupped her glass.

Lucy's smile faded to a puzzled frown. "You're wearing a wedding band." She slid her gaze to Miss Hattie, who remained serene-looking, then back to Bess. "You're already married?"

"Yes, I am." Now why did Lucy look so disappointed? And why did Miss Hattie have that sparkle in her eye?

Looking resigned, Lucy stepped away, splashed tea into someone's glass at the next table, then called out to the man behind the bar. "Fred, darlin'."

When he looked at her, Lucy pointed to a cork bulletin board hanging on the wall just below a Budweiser beer clock, then used the same cut-off-at-the-neck hand signal Sal had used to nonverbally instruct Bess to disconnect Tony's call.

Bess sent Miss Hattie a questioning glance.

"Jimmy Goodson shops in neighboring towns for the villagers twice a week. Lucy keeps the list for him on the bulletin board."

"What's that got to do with me being married?"

"Nothing." She gave Bess an angelic smile.

"Miss Hattie, I do believe you're avoiding answering me."

The old woman's cheeks again went pink. "The villagers amuse themselves with friendly little wagers, dear. It's nothing important."

"I see." Bess said, not really seeing at all, and certain Miss Hattie preferred she didn't see.

"Not yet." Miss Hattie lifted her steaming white mug. "But soon."

Bess shivered and glanced at the rain-speckled window. Looked as if the storm was easing up. Had it been the storm — Lord, how she hated them — or Miss Hattie's innocent statement that had her on edge and uneasy? Had to be the storm. Why would such an innocent statement scare the socks off her?

"Have I told you about the village and how it came to be?"

Subject evasion. Clear and simple. "No,

you haven't."

Straightening the condiments on the table, Miss Hattie smiled. "It all started with a wedding. Lester and Dora Sanford's wedding, to be exact. They were relatives of my friend, Millie."

Getting a divorce, the last thing Bess wanted to hear about was a wedding. But Miss Hattie looked eager to impart the village history and Lucy Baker's pleading look cinched it. Bess had to ask. "Miss Millie who owns the antique shop down the street?"

"Yes, dear. That's her." Miss Hattie sipped from her cup of tea. "All this land was Lester's father's wedding gift to them. Financially blessed, the Sanfords. Anyway, Lester was a shipbuilder and he and Dora wanted to open a small yard to build fishing boats. He had contracts to build three lobster boats, so he and Dora opened the yard, right where Fisherman's Co-op is today."

"Ah, industry." Thinking the story over, Bess tabled her napkin then started to rise.

With a hand to her shoulder, Lucy Baker pushed Bess back into her seat. "This is just the beginning."

Lucy surely had heard this recounting a hundred times and still she looked twinkly eyed at hearing it again. Grinning, Bess looked back to Miss Hattie. "What happened?"

"Lester's family was very angry. They thought the shipyard was a foolish venture and Lester and Dora would end up bankrupt."

"A family rift over money." How many times did Bess encounter that in counseling? Far too many.

"Worse."

"And better, Miss Hattie." Lucy gave the next table over a good rubdown with the red cloth.

"I'm confused," Bess admitted. "How could what happened be both?"

Miss Hattie explained. "Lester told his family that, despite their opposition, he and Dora had decided to take a leap of faith and open the yard anyway. They sank all their money into the venture, not realizing they'd have a hard time getting people to come here to work."

"Why?" Bess couldn't bear the thought of Lester and Dora trying so hard only to fail.

"Roads weren't as good in eighteen ninety-two as they are now, Bess." Lucy plunked down a bottle of ketchup. "Commuting back then was work — in mud season, impossible. There wasn't anywhere close for the workers to live."

"Major obstacle," Bess mumbled. "How did they get past it?" Had they? She hadn't seen a shipyard here and Miss Hattie had said that it was where Fisherman's Co-op is now . . .

Miss Hattie tisked. "The poor dears were struggling something fierce to just keep their heads above water. And then Dora got an idea — enterprising woman, Dora — to sell off some of the land so that the workers could live here."

"No commuting." Bess smiled. "Works for me."

"It did for them, too."

Lucy let out a heavy sigh that worried Bess into looking at the woman. "Well, it worked for Lester and Dora until they made that train ride up to Lester's family's."

Frowning, Bess looked to Miss Hattie to clarify. "To heal the rift, dear."

"Oh." She glanced back at Lucy. "Well, what happened on the train?"

"It crashed and they died. Bad tracks."

"They *died?*" Bess stopped. "No, they couldn't have *died.*"

Miss Hattie patted Bess's hand atop the table. "I'm afraid they did, dear."

"But all those people moved here. What happened to the shipyard?"

"Lester's family shut it down."

Bess stifled another groan, but just barely. "Miss Hattie, no. He couldn't put all those people out of work."

"He sure did, sweetie." Lucy cracked her gum. "That's when folks turned to the sea."

"Ah, so that's how Sea Haven became a fishing village." Bess lifted her napkin to the table, again figuring the story had ended, and feeling better because the sea had provided for the villagers. They were still here, right? So it must have.

"But that's not the best part." Lucy pulled out the chair beside Bess, then sat down.

Bess lifted a brow. "Oh?"

Lucy looked at Miss Hattie, whose kind green eyes twinkled. "Go ahead, Lucy. I know how you love talking about the legend."

Maggie had told Bess about it, but Lucy looked as if she'd bust if she didn't get to relay the telling. Bess couldn't deny her the pleasure. "What legend?"

"The Seascape legend." Lucy tut-tutted. "It's wonderfully romantic."

"I enjoy legends." Clearly, Lucy enjoyed being romantic. Bess wasn't at all sure she believed in romance anymore. Once she had, with John. But that was over now.

"You'll love this one." Lucy bent her

elbows and leaned against the table. "It actually started before Seascape existed. Back when Lester's brother Charles inherited the land. See, Lester and Dora didn't have kids so when they died, the land went back to his dad. Charles eventually inherited it. He's how Miss Millie came to own it. Anyway, Collin and Cecelia Freeport were newlyweds, and Cecelia loved the hill where Seascape Inn is now. She'd sit there for hours and hours. Collin tried to buy it, but Charles was a land hog and —"

"Be gentle, dear." Miss Hattie pulled her white lace hankie from her pocket then dabbed at her temple.

"I wasn't being harsh, Miss Hattie. He was a land hog, truly." Lucy looked back at Bess. "But then Charles saw Cecelia and Collin on the hill. And he saw how much she loved it."

"So," Bess said. "He sold it to them."

"No, it was something Collin told Cecelia and Charles overheard that convinced him to sell the land to them."

Bess couldn't imagine. "What was it? Do you know?"

Lucy smiled. "That even though they couldn't afford it, if Charles would agree, Collin would take a leap of faith and buy the land."

"Just like Lester and Dora." A joyful warmth bubbled in Bess's stomach.

"Yep." Lucy whacked the table.

"So he sold them the land and they built Seascape."

"Eventually," Miss Hattie said. "They didn't have the money until nineteen eighteen."

Lucy cleared her throat, clearly ready to again be the storyteller. "They lived at Seascape all their married lives, Bess. Isn't that romantic? Collin was a wood-carver and Cecelia a healer. Have I mentioned that?"

"No," Bess said. "You haven't."

"Well, they were. And they were very happy, Bess. So much in love."

"Tell me about their children." Miss Hattie had said they'd had two. Bess hoped they'd been happy. Surely they had been, being raised in a home so full of love.

Miss Hattie's eyes clouded and Lucy answered. "They had two kids. A son who was killed in the war, and a daughter, Mary Elizabeth. She moved away and Collin and Cecelia stayed home and grew old together."

Envy slammed through Bess. She was supposed to have grown old with John. Now, she'd grow old alone. "Did they live a long time — happy together, I mean?" For some reason, it seemed important to know. Maybe to reassure Bess long, happy marriages were possible.

"They did," Lucy said. "And they were loved by all the villagers. Collin carved the cross that hangs above the altar in the church. He helped carve that bar too." She pointed to the bar where Fred stood. "Very community-minded. Both of them. And when Collin got cancer, everyone said it was Cecelia's love that kept him alive as long as he was."

"Defied medical science and that's the simple truth." Miss Hattie nodded to lend weight to her claim.

"Love can do that," Bess agreed. She'd seen it more than once in her practice. "So what exactly is the legend?" This wasn't the rendition Maggie had given Bess.

Lucy grinned. "It happened the night Cecelia passed on. All the villagers held a candlelight vigil out on the Seascape lawn. Mary Elizabeth was with her mother, of course. And when her mother departed, Mary Elizabeth swore that her father, Collin, came down out of nowhere and carried Cecelia's spirit away."

Ah, Maggie's version. Bess didn't know what to think about this. Having been at Seascape, feeling its comfort and warmth, she could almost believe it. Almost . . .

"It's true, Bess," Lucy said, as if sensing her skepticism. "You know what Mary Elizabeth really saw, don't you?"

Bess shook her head that she didn't. Why did her throat feel tight? Why did she feel so relieved that when Cecelia most needed her Collin he had come?

"Personified love."

Miss Hattie sighed. "Some don't believe the legend, of course."

"Many of us do, though," Lucy quickly added. "You know what I think, Bess?"

Again, she moved her head from side-to-side, indicating that she didn't.

"Fred and I disagree. He thinks Cecelia's healing magic lingers in the house. But I think it's Seascape itself that has magic because all that was really important to Cecelia took place there."

"I don't understand." Bess frowned.

"She loved her husband, her children, healed the sick — everyone at Seascape. She was the only medical help around. When a place holds that much magic, it doesn't just disappear." Lucy smiled softly. "No, Seascape held magic then, and it holds magic now. The kind of magic that lives on forever."

"Love." The word came out before Bess

realized she'd spoken it.

"Love." Lucy slid back her chair and stood up. "Isn't it romantic?"

"Yes. Very." Wishing she'd known that magical love with John, Bess looked at Miss Hattie. "It makes sense, doesn't it?"

Dabbing at the corner of her eye with her hankie, Miss Hattie nodded.

"Collin risked everything in the world he had for Cecelia." Bess couldn't fathom it.

Miss Hattie's gentle green eyes grew piercing. "True love is always like that. Don't you think?"

A sweeping chill settled over Bess's skin. Something important had just been revealed to her; the sensation crept through her, and she couldn't shake it. "I suppose so." Like Tony's message, she didn't understand this one, or how it applied to her, but she had no doubt that it did apply.

"That's as love should be, anyway. When both people are truly committed."

A little ache rippled through Bess. "I can't imagine a love like that." Realizing she'd spoken aloud, heat surged up her neck and she let out a nervous giggle. "Don't we all wish we could?"

"Someday you will."

"Maybe." Not for a second did she believe it. But Miss Hattie clearly did, and Bess didn't want to be the one to shatter the woman's illusions.

Lucy gathered their dishes.

Miss Hattie's fork slipped off her plate, hit the table, then clanged. She passed it to Lucy. "Bess, may I ask you a question, dear?"

She really didn't want to answer personal questions, but Miss Hattie smiled so sweetly, and she looked so charming, with her bun a little worse for the wear from the wind on the walk over from the inn to the village. "Sure."

"I understood you to say you and John have been separated for a long time."

"Yes."

"Why do you still wear his ring?"

Lucy paused her gum-snapping and rag-wiping of the next table, avidly listening and trying hard to pretend she wasn't. Bess shifted on the wooden chair, then moved the silver-knobbed salt shaker next to the pepper at the end of the table, nestled to the wall. A ketchup bottle there was half-full.

"I didn't mean to intrude, or to make you uncomfortable." Miss Hattie gave Bess's hand a pat atop the table. "If you'd rather not answer, dear, then, please, don't."

"No." Bess had wondered the same thing

herself. It was time she knew the answer, and she half-considered thanking Miss Hattie for nudging her into searching for it. She looked up from the metal napkin holder stuffed with white paper napkins and shrugged. "I guess at first I kept wearing it because it felt comfortable. I was used to it, you know? And," this proved harder to admit, "I think I never really believed it was over for John and me. By the time I realized it was, I — I don't know. I just didn't want to take it off."

The tiny gold band winked at her, and she vividly recalled their wedding ceremony and John putting the ring onto her finger. "I suppose it sounds kind of foolish now, but I promised him on our wedding day that I'd never take it off." She let out a nervous, little laugh. "So I haven't."

"Doesn't sound at all foolish," Miss Hattie said. "Promises are made to be kept."

Yes. Yes, promises are made to be kept. Yet, John had made promises too and he'd broken them. He'd vowed to always love her, but he hadn't. He certainly hadn't loved her anything like Collin had loved his Cecelia. In fact, John couldn't have loved Bess at all. A lump of sadness swelled in her chest and she cursed herself as forty kinds of fool because that truth still had the power to hurt her so much. It shouldn't hurt even a little. Not anymore. "After the divorce is final, then I'll take it off."

"A few more weeks, hmmm?"

Bess nodded. A flurry of motion caught her eye. Lucy rushed over to Fred, then whispered something into his ear that had him smiling and letting out a muffled "Hot dang!"

Lucy popped him on the thigh with her red rag. Fred flushed purple and grunted out a hasty apology for cursing — not that it did him any good. Lucy's glare warned that he had not yet been forgiven and reminded Bess of the killer looks Maggie leveled on T. J. Fred looked about as worried as T. J. usually did, too: not at all. Bess cocked her head. Maybe she should have laid a glare or two on John. At times, she'd wanted to, but her rigid upbringing had kicked in, and she just hadn't been able to lose her composure and feel comfortable about it. Now what was Fred scribbling on that bulletin board?

The phone rang.

Lucy answered it, then yelled out: "Bess, it's for you."

"Me?" She frowned at Miss Hattie. "Here?"

"I forwarded the calls from the inn, dear.

Tuesday is my errand day and Lucy takes calls for me."

"Ah." Bess slid back her chair, walked over to the end of the bar, then took the receiver from Lucy's outstretched hand. The sheriff, Bess noted, was actually backing out of the cafe with tiny Beaulah Favish right on the toes of his boots, still bending his ear and demanding respect.

"Hello," Bess said into the receiver.

"Bess, come home. I miss you."

Miguel. Bess internally groaned. This week's redhead evidently had dumped him. "You miss Silk." If he'd choose his women on something more than hair color . . .

"Her, too." He confessed. "Is she liking Maine?"

"Loving it. So am I, in case you're wondering." He often used Silk as a go-between, for some reason feeling more at ease asking about her reactions to things than Bess's. "Coming here was the best idea I've had in a long time."

"Wonderful, even if it does cramp my nefarious plans to seduce you."

Bess laughed aloud. Miguel seducing her was about as likely as her seducing John Mystic. "And I thought you loved challenges."

"Only in regattas, Angel. I prefer eager

women."

"Ah, the redhead escapes. What happened this time?"

"A true friend wouldn't ask such indelicate questions, Angel." He cleared his throat. "Tell me, what must I do to make this woman . . . eager?"

"I'm standing in the middle of a crowded cafe at the moment." And receiving far too many interested looks for her liking. "Could I put on my shrink hat and see what's gotten your synapses misfiring later?"

He laughed. "You're supposed to console me. I'm nursing a broken heart."

"Sorry. Condolences, of course." With a broken heart once a week, sympathy waned.

"A true friend would stop this unnecessary exodus, come home, and sail the world with me on *Daybreak* until I'd recovered."

She twisted the phone cord. "Friends don't sail around the world together when one of those friends has a job to get back to in a few weeks — namely me." Provided Sal fast-talked Millicent into not dropping the ax. "And if I left here now, I'm wagering that before I could get home, you'd have a new redhead in tow."

He laughed, then turned serious. "It'd make me feel better if you'd be reasonable and let me buy the station. Then you'd be free to do exactly as you pleased."

"No." Bess wiped at a nag of an ache in her forehead. This, she did not need. "It isn't that I don't appreciate your offer, it's that —"

"You don't want the support of a friend," he finished for her.

"I don't want your money." How many times had they been through this?

"But —"

"Don't push on this, okay, Miguel? Please." She paused to bury the tremor in her voice. "I'm a little shaky right now."

"I don't wish to make you shakier but, when I tell you the news, you might change your mind."

That the news wasn't good came as no surprise. Was good news possible anymore?

"I saw Millicent Fairgate at a charity ball at the Clarion last night. She'd only just heard about you divorcing your John. Need I say she was less than pleased?"

"No." Bess's stomach coiled into a nest of knots. "I can imagine well enough, I think." Raging, most likely.

"Hmmm, I suggest you double your worst expectations. Then you'll be close."

Bess grimaced. At least the wait for the ax to rise before it fell on her head was over. Millicent would fire her; it wasn't a question of *if* but of *when*. "I'm expecting her to can me. She can't do any worse."

"I wouldn't bet on that."

"What do you mean?" What else could she do to Bess? Nothing came to mind.

"You're forgetting the woman is a powerful influence in New Orleans. Nearly as strong as Elise Dupree. She can close a lot of doors that until now have been open to you."

Elise Dupree. The older woman who had hired John to investigate the kidnaping/ elopement of her only daughter, Dixie. The case that had obsessed John. The other woman — the one who had come first with him. "Not much I can do about it."

"You can let me buy the station."

"No." That, Bess couldn't do. She'd look like a laughingstock. Worse, she'd feel like one — and she'd feel bought and paid for by Miguel Santos.

Miss Hattie touched Bess's arm. "Just a minute, Miguel."

"I'm sorry to interrupt, dear, but I have to get to Millie's Antique Shoppe. She's gotten in a curio she's anxious for me to see."

Bess smiled. "Thanks for joining me for lunch. I enjoyed your company."

"Me, too." Miss Hattie squeezed Bess's forearm, then snapped closed her rain slicker. "I'll see you at home later on."

Bess nodded and Miss Hattie moved on down the bar to speak briefly with Vic and Horace Johnson, who immediately removed his cap as a show of respect to Miss Hattie. A light rain still tapped at the cafe windows, speckling the glass and running down the pane in rivulets. Soon, it would stop. "I'm back," Bess said to Miguel.

"As your friend, I'm asking you to reconsider. I've spoken with Sal and he would stay on. It's not a solely altruistic thing I'd be doing. I'd make a great deal of money."

"No. Please, no." Even she would view Miguel buying the station as him having to buy it to keep her employed. Everyone in town already thought they were lovers.

A buzz sounded in the background. "I've got another call," he said. "Maybe my redhead apologizing, eh? Hug that rag of a dog and think kindly of me."

"Silk is hardly a rag, Miguel, and she takes serious exception to being called one. As does her owner."

"Ah, I've gone too far, haven't I?"

"Indeed." He hadn't. "We'll expect a box of treats delivered by two P.M. tomorrow."

He laughed. "Very well. A box of biscuits —"

"We call them cookies."

"Cookies, then, for your Silk, and a surprise for you."

"Only the cookies, if you please. I'm not ready to be bribed."

"Okay, Angel."

Bess hung up the phone. Back at her table, she again started shaking. Three days at Seascape Inn, and she'd been calm and content. But one phone call from New Orleans and here she sat again rattling worse than the old Chevy she had driven — and John had sworn was held together with spit, rubber bands, and baling wire — on their first date.

Understandable, but pitiful. She and Miguel were just friends. What difference did it make if he thought she couldn't carry herself without him buying the station and taking care of her? A friend *should* show more support and faith in a friend's abilities, true, but that notion likely hadn't occurred to Miguel. Anyway, she'd refused his bailout offer. And Millicent learning of the divorce had been inevitable — and a worry hanging over Bess's head. At least now it was done and Bess knew to expect the you're-fired call anytime.

She sipped from her glass of lemon-tart tea. There was a silver lining here, though she had to stretch to find it. Positively, absolutely nothing else in her world could go wrong.

"Hello, Bess." A man's voice sounded from right behind her.

Recognizing it as John Mystic's proved her mistaken.

Rain dripping off his tan trench coat, John watched Bess's slim shoulders go starch stiff. She didn't turn to look back at him. She'd recognized his voice, all right, and she was *not* happy.

People in the crowded cafe hovered at the bar, whispering dollar amounts and dates to a man wearing a gold nugget ring on his pinkie finger, who wrote furiously on a bulletin board. What was that all about?

A minute passed. Then another. And still Bess didn't turn around.

Out of patience, and figuring she'd surely recovered from the shock of him being there by now, John circled to the other side of her table. "May I sit down?"

She stared up at him, as beautiful as ever. Her hair was still the color of light beer — a comparison that once had surprised her into laughing — but she wore it longer now. How long exactly, he couldn't tell, though it kissed her shoulder. She had it pulled back from her face and caught at her nape in an aqua and white dotted bow that matched her white blouse and sandals and aqua slacks. That color combination did wonderful things to her blue eyes. Right now, they were stretched huge and clouded, evidencing her upset and giving her a vulnerable look that jerked hard at protective cords he'd thought he'd severed. If she knew he saw either emotion, she'd die, so he kept his expression bland. The last thing either of them needed was more emotion packed into this tense moment.

Her still perfect complexion and high cheekbones brought back too many memories of how tender and soft her skin had felt against his roughened palms, and those memories kicked his heart straight into overdrive just like the night he'd first seen her at T. J.'s art showing and had fallen in love with her. John had vowed to himself on the spot she'd one day be his wife. She had. And, remembering that now, proved time hadn't much changed him, either. At least not inside. But it was too late for them, and that he had no choice but to remember.

Promise me, John. You swear? On your mother's grave? Elise's deathbed plea that he make things right with Bess replayed in his mind. Every muscle in his body clenched.

"Hello, John." Bess gazed up at him.

John not *Jonathan.* Passive. Totally in control. The same old story. Vintage Bess. A little bolt of disappointment set off an ache inside him that nagged as persistently as a gnat, a vengeance-seeking desire to see her lose control — just once. Just . . . once. "May I sit down?" he repeated.

"I was just leaving." She stood up. The napkin that had been in her lap tumbled to the floor. "But you're certainly welcome to my table."

As greetings went, he'd stupidly hoped for better, and expected worse. At least she hadn't walked off without acknowledging him. He lifted the napkin and set it onto the table. "We have some unfinished business to attend to, and since you don't seem to be answering your attorney's calls . . ."

"Francine phoned *you?*"

"No, she called Bryce."

Bess looked less than pleased, but kept her opinion to herself. That hadn't changed, either. "Is there some place a little more private we can go to and talk?"

"Sorry, I'm on my way back to Seascape Inn."

"We can —"

"No, we can't," she interrupted, her chin quivering. "I don't want you there." She

105

walked over to the cash register at the bar.

He followed, stopping beside her, near a burn on the floor. Why was everyone so interested in them talking? "I'm a guest at the inn, too, Bess. Sorry if that offends you, but it's the only place in the village that accepts guests and, like it or not, we do have to settle some things."

She frowned at him. "Very well, then. Let's settle these *things* on the way. Then, as soon as we get back to the inn, you can leave."

John shifted aside. She wasn't making this easy on him. He didn't like it, but could he blame her? "Fine. The sooner, the better."

That rattled her — her lip twitched — but, Bess being Bess, she recovered quickly and masked her expression. Few would have noticed the telling sign. But she was his wife, and John wasn't one of the many. Would Santos have noticed?

She dropped her bill and money onto the bar. A pretty redhead stood behind the register, looking pleased about something. She let her gaze rove over John — not in a man-to-woman kind of way, but in an assessing one that had him shifting on his feet and Bess snickering behind a faked cough at him being on the hot seat.

"Your change," the redhead told Bess,

then swung her gaze to John. "So you're new in the village, Mr. —"

"John Mystic," he said. "I'm Bess's husband."

The woman's grin grew to a beaming smile. "Ah, I see."

"We're divorcing, Lucy," Bess chimed in, sliding him a did-you-have-to-say-that look. "July tenth."

Lucy hiked a speculative brow and nodded. "Sorry to hear that, but I hope you'll both be very happy."

"We will."

"Definitely."

That Bess answered at the same time as he had raised John's hackles. But Lucy's smugness didn't strike him as unfriendly. Actually, it seemed more endearing in a way that reminded him of Elise when she had the inside scoop on something he didn't and, before passing the information over to him, was teasing him with it.

His heart suffered a deep, lonely pang. Elise. It seemed impossible, but she really was gone. How long would it take for the raw pain to ease to an ache?

"Hope you enjoy your visit to Sea Haven." Lucy wiped at the bar with her red cloth. "Pretty up here in the summer, and lots cooler than New Orleans."

It was. And less humid. He glanced at the window and noted the rain had finally stopped. "Thank you."

Bess mumbled an "I'll see you next visit" then headed toward the door. John nodded to Lucy, then followed Bess.

Just outside, she stepped past a large, rusty anchor leaning up against the building, and then off of the porch.

"Watch out for the —"

She promptly stumbled.

Just before her knees kissed the wet dirt, John grabbed her arm. "Cat."

The cockeyed critter let out a screech loud enough to wake the dead in the cemetery across the street. Bess groaned.

"It's not hurt," John assured her, his voice as gravelly as a rock pit. She stood so close. Smelled so good. She'd always worn *Ritz* cologne. And it never had smelled quite so alluring on any other woman's skin. After all this time, was he really standing in an overcast, rain-soaked parking lot in Maine holding Bess in his arms?

Her eyes darkened to deep, ocean blue. "Thank you. I'm fine." She pointedly looked down to where his hands clasped her arms.

One of them — he couldn't tell for certain which one — shook. When he loosened his grip, she backed away.

"If you have something to discuss with me, you should have just phoned. You shouldn't have come here." Looking almost stricken, she turned on her heel and took off down Main Street, toward the inn. "I don't want you here."

The sun shifted behind a dark cloud and the wind picked up, tugging at his coat. Watching her storm down the slick asphalt, he seriously considered sitting back and watching her go to jail. But her stricken look preyed on his mind. He was angry at her for blatantly not wanting him here, but he understood it. Bess was worried *and* rattled. Not that she'd care, but she made him as uncomfortable, too. And he was in enough trouble without this. Until he found Dixie, he'd know nothing but trouble, and he had no choice but to accept it.

First things first.

He caught up to Bess near a little bench overlooking the jagged cliffs, then fell into step beside her. She didn't acknowledge him. Inwardly sighing in tandem with the sounds of the sea, he figured if ever they were to make any progress, he'd again have to make the first move. "Look, Bess, neither of us like it, and we don't have to like it, but we do have to get this property settlement dispute hashed out." Amazing. He'd gotten that out sounding calm, despite his deathbed promise to Elise weighing heavily on his conscience.

"It's already settled." Bess hastened her steps. "I don't want anything."

He stepped around a mud puddle that Bess tromped right through: yet another sign of her upset that didn't show on her face or sound in her voice. "Obviously," he drolled in a tone he forced dry, "you haven't yet talked with Francine."

Her blush proved him right. "Before I left, I told her to just handle it."

Bess couldn't even be bothered with something as important as ending their marriage? He could shake her. And he would — if he weren't opposed to physical violence, and if he didn't feel so guilty because he'd made her feel as she did. He inhaled the tangy smell of sea spray and listened to the waves crashing against the granite cliffs. She'd splashed up her slacks from the knees down. On a scale of one to ten, the mud puddle stomp rated a firm seven. "Francine can't handle it."

Fisherman's Co-op was ahead on the right. Just off the edge of its slate slab porch, two little boys were playing in a mud puddle, having the time of their lives. The youngest sat down and splashed muddy water all over his cocoa-colored skin. His laughter warmed John's heart. Wow, to be that carefree and in love with life again.

At a mailbox across the road, Bess turned left onto the fir-lined gravel drive that led up the slope to the inn. Though the rain had stopped and the sun, for the moment anyway, had broken through the heavy clouds moving away, the huge Victorian was still wet: a deep slate gray that perfectly matched John's mood. A turret stretched up above the roof toward the sleet-colored clouds and, on looking at it, the oddest feeling swam through John. An eerie feeling. Not bad, just eerie. A harbinger of some kind. Strange . . .

He glanced at Bess. The wind whipped at her hair and tiny tendrils pulled free from the bow, kissed her cheeks, and clung. He envied them, which only made his mood darker. "Did you hear me, Bess?"

"Yes." She squinted up at him, against the sun. "Why can't Francine handle it? I left explicit instructions. No settlement. That should make things easy." Stepping past a small limb that had fallen during the storm, she continued on up the sun-dappled drive, gravel crunching under her sandals. "I know you don't like complications that keep you from your work."

The case. Dixie's case. Bess might as well have said it specifically. So, her resentment against Elise and his job as a private investigator still needled Bess. A gust of wind sent rain collected on the leaves pattering to the ground. And even after all their time apart, her resentment still stung. Especially now that Elise was . . . gone. The tight fist of loss gripped his chest. "True, I don't like complications," he told Bess. "So why are you causing me trouble?"

Bent over, inhaling the faint, sweet scent of a blossoming delphinium, she looked back at him as if genuinely surprised. "Me?" She straightened, letting her fingertips linger on the soft-looking petals. "How much easier can I make this for you?"

Good question. He wished he had a good answer, but he didn't. If anything existed that would make their divorce easy for him to swallow, he sure hadn't found it. "A lot. You can be reasonable and accept your half of our assets."

Without a word, she turned and walked up the steps onto the columned front porch that stretched end to end across the front of the house.

Littered with hanging baskets of alyssum and pink geraniums, and a special planter of blossoming zinnias; with white wicker furniture and a comfortable-looking swing; the porch invited tranquility — definitely at odds with Bess's mannerisms and his feelings. She was still in control, though, by gosh. Vintage Bess. Always in control, no matter what. "Well, are you going to be reasonable?"

A crooked sign hung to the left of the front door. "Seascape. Established 1918." Bess straightened it. "Look, I don't want anything, okay?"

"No, it's not okay."

She shot him a glare that he'd be feeling in his grave. "It's my choice, Jonathan, and I've made it." She reached for the doorknob.

He leaned against the door, shoulder to wood, and stared at her. *Jonathan.* Only Bess had ever called him that. He'd missed it. And he hated that he'd missed it. Hated that he'd missed her. She was stubborn, strong, and so beautiful it hurt him to look at her. His stomach curled and he fisted a hand in his coat pocket. "Your choice affects me, too, yet you've locked me out of the decision-making process. That's hardly fair."

"So who said life was fair?" Her eyes widened, and her pupils dilated. "Life is *not* fair, John. I hate to be the bearer of bad news, but this is the real world, and one day you're going to have to live in it just like the rest of us. In the meantime, could you please move aside so I can open the door?"

A barrel of anger bounced around in his gut. He should let her have it, but he couldn't. He'd done this to her. How, he wasn't sure. But Bess had never been this way before and, Lord knew, before her death, Meriam Richards sure never missed a chance to tell him he was to blame. Bess and Meriam had been close. Bess hadn't told him why she'd left him, but she'd evidently told Meriam. "So you'd rather go to jail than to touch anything of mine — or of ours?"

"Jail?" Bess's jaw fell slack.

He nodded.

"Why in the world would I go to jail?" She snorted. "I hate to break it to you, darling, but me not taking your money isn't a crime to anyone but you."

Darling. Once the endearment had struck him nearly as powerfully as her Jonathan. It didn't anymore. Now it rang as empty as an echo. As solid as a reflection. But his hunch had been right. She didn't know about the judge's order. "I hate to break it to you, *darling,* but it *is* a crime — at least according to Judge Branson."

"Don't call me that." She clamped her jaw

shut and shuttered the anger from her eyes. "Judge Branson? What have you done to me?"

"Me?" How typical that even this was John's fault.

"Well, who else?" She jerked at his coat sleeve to tug him away from the door.

"Don't get physical, Bess, unless you're serious about it." He lifted his brows.

She jerked back as if he'd burned her. "Would you just move?"

"Not until you apologize. I haven't done anything to you, and I don't appreciate your saying I have — and I don't appreciate your *darling,* either. You walked out on me." He started to object to her calling him Jonathan as well — his name was John and what once had been her pet name for him and had made him feel so special now grated at his ears — but he couldn't bring himself to actually do it.

"Here we go again." She let out a sigh that could power a substation for a week.

"If you'd talk to me just once about this, it'd be done. But, no, not you. You walk out and consider yourself above even giving me an explanation."

"If you don't mind, can we get back to this jail business?" She swept her hair back from her face. The wind tore more of it loose from the bow at her nape and she held it back with a cupped hand. "Why is Judge Branson jailing me?"

"Call your lawyer, *darling.*" John slid away from the door.

She frowned at him, deliberately holding it so he wouldn't miss it. "You know exactly why and you're just being contrary by not telling me. I never liked that about you — your being contrary. In fact, I hated it."

She'd hated it. She'd hated him. And maybe it was time she regretted both. Yeah, maybe it was *past* time. "You loved it." He gave her his best killer smile. "And me."

"I hated it, I said." Pain flashed through her eyes. Anger chased it and burned. "And at times, heaven forgive me, I've hated you, too."

She meant it. He nearly staggered from the blow. Both blows. That she'd felt these things *and* that she'd admitted feeling them. Bryce had said she'd changed, but . . . Double-checking, John baited her. "Liar."

"Don't you wish?" She grumbled then shoved past him and strode into the house.

John watched her back. Well, for the first encounter on a reunion meet, it could be going a lot worse. Could be better, too. She had let him peek inside her. That was a plus. But she had no right to still be beautiful to

116

him. No right to still make him ache. And no right to make him remember how good the good times had been between them. Why did just looking at her still turn his gut inside out?

A champagne-colored mop of a dog, sporting a jiggling pink bow atop her head, ran across the entrance floor, nails clicking, tail wagging, and tongue hanging out. It passed the registration desk, where Bess stood flipping through mail, and came straight to John. Smiling he scooped up the tiny ragamuffin. It couldn't weigh more than three pounds.

"That's Silk." Bess tossed an envelope back onto the counter between a green banker's lamp and a wooden pen holder, then reached for the dog. "She's mine."

Silk whined at Bess and licked at her wrist, sending her a pleading message: *Look but please don't touch. I'm comfortable right where I am.* John rewarded the pup with a good ear scratch.

"Stop being rude, you ungrateful vagabond." Looking miffed, Bess grabbed the dog.

Poor Silk would pay for her loyalty lapse. Did Bess send her subtle messages, too? "Judge Branson is ticked because you left town without having the property settlement finalized. He's holding you in contempt."

Bess looked up at him, clearly surprised John had told her. She couldn't be any more surprised than he was. Why *had* he told her?

The dog, he figured. Being met at the door by someone — well, something — glad to see him. He shrugged and took back the dog. "Save you a call to Francine."

"Contempt is absurd. The dispute *is* settled." She frowned at Silk, who was licking at John's hand, then snatched her out of his arms, tucking her into her own. "The dog is mine, Jonathan."

"Half-right." He leaned against the wooden registration desk. "The dog is yours, but the dispute isn't settled — and it won't be until you agree to take half of our assets."

She stared at him. The house grew oddly silent, almost as if it were waiting. The stately grandfather clock opposite the desk ticked, and a soft whir of the ceiling fan's spinning blades overhead pulsed out a humming *thump, thump, thump.*

"I can't do that." Bess looked over at the ceramic boxes atop the desk.

"Well, I guess we won't be getting a divorce, then." He met her puzzled stare with a rock-hard, steady one. He wasn't going to bend on this, and the woman had best realize it right up front.

"Fine." She turned, hooked a left, and then started up the stairs. "It's just a piece of paper and doesn't change a thing."

What did *that* mean? Ending their marriage was no more than a formality to her? His ego took another stab. Hadn't she bludgeoned it to death already?

He frowned up at her, her slim hips swaying step to step. His groin tightened, and his deathbed promise to Elise flitted through his mind. "You can't just walk out this time, Bess. You're going to have to face me sometime and tell me why."

She stopped on the landing, below the two portraits of Seascape's original owners, Collin and Cecelia Freeport. According to Miss Hattie, their love was a legend. And, simply put, John envied them. Even after one of them died, they'd known more of love than he'd ever known in his life and, from all indications, more than he ever would know of it.

Silk squirmed in Bess's arms. She absently patted the dog, and glared down at John. "I'm not walking out. I am, however, leaving."

Figured. Cut-and-run. Vintage Bess. "Bad idea, but no surprise." John grabbed the banister. She was upset, all right. All cashmere and eel-skin and cool elegance on the outside, but mad as heck inside. About an eight on the scale, he figured. "When you're packed, yell. I'll carry your bags down."

She lifted her chin. "I can take care of myself, thank you."

"Fine." He started up the steps. When she reached the top and he the landing, he stopped beneath the portraits. The temperature dropped ten degrees and a cool breeze that seemed to come from nowhere chilled his skin. He shivered and walked on, prickly and feeling . . . watched.

Seeing no source for that either, he pushed the feeling aside. Imagination, no more than that. Only he and Bess were in the house. Miss Hattie was still having tea with Miss Millie at the Antique Shoppe. "In case you're interested," he topped the stairs and turned the corner, "the fine is ten thousand dollars."

At the end of the hall, Bess stumbled against a hand-carved bookshelf, then collapsed onto a plump window seat cushion. *Tall Ships* tumbled to the floor. The mullioned windows above her head let in soft gray light that swept over a white Berber rug and on down the shadowy hallway of closed doors.

"Ten *thousand* dollars?" She sounded breathless.

Oh, boy. A ten response if ever he'd seen one. Definitely a ten. He returned the book to the shelf, straightened its spine to match the others, then sat down beside her on the bench. Now that he had her attention — she was as pale as a ghost — what did he do with it? "Or jail."

"Good grief." Silk scooted off her lap and crossed the cushion to John.

"Only you would do this to me." Anger flashed in Bess's eyes. "Only you."

"Hey, Doc," he used his pet name for her without thinking, "I haven't done a thing here, except to try to pay your fine."

"You didn't." She dragged her lip between her teeth but still failed to hide her frown.

"I did. Ask Bryce." John gave Silk's back a stroke. "Branson refused to let me cover it — even though it was *our* money."

"You set me up, didn't you? You paid off Branson to make this divorce even tougher on me." She stood up, stiff-spined and hands fisted, but her voice remained oh-so-cool. "I knew you were a jerk, John Mystic. I didn't know you were vicious or crooked."

She knew better. It was anger talking. Bess's rendition of pulling out the heavy guns. "Now why would I do that?"

"To punish me."

"What for?" As if he ever had punished her for anything.

"For divorcing you and wounding your overinflated ego by refusing to touch your fortune." She blew out a breath reeking of frustration. "That really galls you, doesn't it? That you can't buy me off to soothe your conscience just eats you up inside."

Buy *her* off? Soothe *his* conscience? *She'd* walked out on *him*. Man, but this infuriated him. How could she stand there looking so beautiful, sling arrows that cut right through his heart, and look so unaffected and calm? She more than infuriated him. And her accusation made him sick. What kind of man did she think he'd become? "I never tried to buy you, Bess. Never."

"Admit it. That *is* what this is all about. You. Mr. Hotshot Private Investigator who's got it all. Looks, money, the whole nine yards. You've always had everything your way — until now. Well, consider this reveille. I will *not* bend and take your money, Jonathan. Why in the world your mother —"

He snapped his head up. "Don't!"

"Oh, right." Bess slapped at a crease in her slacks. "I forgot that your mother is a forbidden topic. Excuse me, Mr. Mystic, for breaching yet another of those areas of your life where you shut out everyone — including your wife."

His chest went tight. This wasn't getting them anywhere. Her standing there huffing with righteous indignation, him sitting here feeling like a put-upon slug. "Let's stop this, okay?" What in the world had come over her? In all their time together he'd never seen her act like this. So . . . emotional. And again the secret about his parents weighed heavily on his soul. If not for knowing what the truth would do to Selena, he could risk telling Bess. But he couldn't afford the risk because Selena would have to pay the price.

"Gladly." She visibly grabbed control and slid back behind her sleek mask of porcelain-skinned indifference. "You can lie to me, but you can't lie to yourself. This is about ego — yours. And about money."

"Listen to you." He shook his head and stood up. "You're an intelligent woman, but do you realize how stupid you sound right now?"

"Jonathan, do not insult me." Her chin quivered.

Whether near tears or near committing murder, he couldn't decide. "Okay. Yeah. Yeah, you're right, Bess. You're exactly right. I've busted my buns to turn a modest inheritance into a fortune and, thanks to

Elise's investment advice, I succeeded. Now, I just can't stand the thought of not giving half of it to you to spend on that sorry Spaniard." He shrugged. "Makes perfect sense to me." Silk yapped. "Makes sense to her, too."

"You leave Miguel out of this." Bess narrowed her eyes. "And knock off the sarcasm. It's counterproductive."

"And not telling me why you're ending our marriage isn't?"

"Would you stop already? What's the difference anymore?"

Their relationship really was over. There wasn't a shred of hope. A sick feeling settled in his stomach. Anger, denial, rose to fight it. He'd promised Elise. "No difference at all. In fact, you should check with Francine. Maybe there's some obscure legal precedent set where a man wanting his wife to be financially secure qualified as abuse. You could sue the socks off me. Humiliate me some more — though with you being seen all over town hanging onto Santos, you'd have to work hard at it. What are the odds of pulling it off, do you think?"

She rolled her gaze ceilingward. "I do not *hang* all over anyone, and I refuse to listen to this. Miguel is my friend and he has nothing to do with this. You're making a mockery of — of this entire situation."

John stepped closer. Her back to the wall, they stood chest to chest, and he dropped his voice. "This situation is our marriage, *darling*. And if anyone is making a mockery of it, it's you."

She shoved against his shoulder, passed him, then entered her room — the Great White. Just inside the door, she spun around to face him. *"You* are making a mockery of this, John. You've told me I'm going to jail." Hopping on one foot, she tugged at her sandal strap, then slung the shoe to the floor.

It hit the planks with a firm *thunk* that sent Silk scurrying under the bed, diving for cover. John half-considered joining her.

Bess reached for her other shoe. "You've had your fun. Now would you please just . . . go away?"

"Fun?" Taking five to cool down, he glanced around the large room decorated in blues and soft greens. The adjoining turret room windows were open. The shades were up and the sheer curtains billowed in a sea-scented breeze. "Right. I always thought the idea of you behind bars was a real hoot, Bess. Hey, if Francine pulls off the abuse bit, maybe we can get adjoining cells."

"That's one of the most ridiculous things

I've ever heard come out of your mouth and there have been some real winners."

He stepped closer and looked down his nose at her. "Another thing we have in common."

She glared up at him. The fire died in her eyes. They went soft, vulnerable, and she was trying so hard not to let him see either. The anger drained right out of him and the urge to kiss some sense into her, to kiss her until she understood he only wanted reassurance she'd be independent and cared for, slammed into him with the force of a sledgehammer. "Why do we still have the ability to hurt each other so much? *Why?*" He didn't want to hurt Bess. He'd never wanted to hurt her.

"Jonathan, don't," she whispered breathlessly, her chest lifting with rapid breaths and brushing against his, the pulse at her throat pounding against her creamy skin.

Sliding his hand up her arm to her bare shoulder, he gave her a puzzled frown.

"Don't kiss me." She swallowed hard and her lips parted. *"Please."*

She feared him kissing her. Feared it. . Heaven help him, the magic was still there. He'd hoped it wouldn't be — prayed it wouldn't be. But it was. And he'd never expected it'd be so . . . strong. "Bess, I —"

"Please."

There is hope. See it in her eyes. Give it time.

John let her go then stepped back, condemning his conscience and himself for wanting that kiss. The look of relief on her face stung. "When you're ready, I'll, um, carry down your things." He nodded toward the neat row of tapestry luggage just behind her.

She turned to look, then went rigid.

Silk parked on her haunches at the foot of the bed, alert, ears perked. She, too, sensed Bess's sudden tension. John frowned. "What's wrong?"

No answer.

"Bess?" A creepy feeling slithered up his back. "Answer me."

"My bags." She stared at them. "They're packed."

"You did say you were leaving."

She looked up at him, her eyes wide. "I didn't pack them. When I left here, my luggage was empty and in the closet."

This rattled her. Why exactly, John didn't know. But he didn't like it. "Maybe Miss Hattie packed for you."

"Why would she?" Bess frowned at him then looked back at the bags as if they were betrayers. "I'm booked here for another two weeks."

"I arrived." Seeing her upset got to him. Okay, they'd once loved each other, so upset was natural, he supposed. But it sure shouldn't produce an almost irresistible urge to take her into his arms and kiss her until her fear gave out. That it did irritated him. She'd walked out on him. What more proof did he need that she couldn't care less about him? And knowing that, why couldn't *he* care less about *her*?

You promised.

He frowned at his conscience. It'd become a real nuisance lately.

For Elise, you swore you'd set matters right with you and Bess. Have you sunk so low that you're comfortable lying to Elise and breaking your word? A man's word is his bond, Jonathan.

Jonathan? John's skin prickled. His conscience never before had niggled at him using Bess's name for him. And it never had used anyone else's voice either. This time, it had done both.

It wasn't his conscience.

John looked down the long shadowy hallway. Empty. Who owned this man's voice? *Where* was he? Had Bess heard — ? Wait a minute. John paused to remember

128

and analyze, mentally sifting back to the last time he'd had this odd feeling and heard this stranger's voice. It had been at the hospital. When Elise was dying. This man, whoever he was, however he was doing this, had helped John then. Had told him to give Elise peace. To let her go, and to tell her he'd be okay without her. A shiver raced up John's spine and set the roof of his mouth to tingling. How was the man getting into John's head?

"Miss Hattie was with me at the cafe."

Reeling, John blinked and looked at Bess. It took him a moment to mentally shift back to the luggage problem. "Miss Hattie was here when I arrived."

"You're right." Bess looked relieved. "She joined me there. She stayed behind because she was expecting a guest. Obviously, you."

Something strange was going on here. A man talking to John inside his head. Bess's luggage being packed. He didn't think for a second Miss Hattie had packed it. She hadn't even come upstairs to show him the Cove Room. That friend of hers, Jimmy, had given John the nickel tour. But John darn well intended to ask her — just as he intended to find out the identity of this man talking to him. Evidently, whoever he was, the man was trying to help. Someone bent on harm sure doesn't help a guy get through the death of a loved one as the man had with Elise. But why would he want to help John? "Apparently, Miss Hattie figured you'd run."

Bess grimaced at him, clearly at ease again now that, in her mind, the mystery had been solved. Should he tell her it hadn't been? No. She was stressed already. Her lip was twitching double-time. He'd solve it first and then tell her.

"I'm not running, John." She grabbed the handle of her case, then slung the shoulder strap of the garment bag over her shoulder. "I'm leaving. There's a difference."

"Not where we're concerned." Silk barked near his ankle, wanting attention. He picked up the dog and scratched her ears.

Bess held out her hands for Silk. When John passed her, Bess flashed him a pleading look. "I don't want your money."

"You have no choice, darling." No way was she going to toss yet another guilt trip on him. She'd be self-sufficient or married to him, and that was where the buck stopped.

"I'd rather spend a month in jail."

The barb hit home. Hard. "Fine. And when you get out and this still isn't settled, then you can spend another month in jail. I wonder if Sal Ragusa will do remote tapings of your program. Be a shame to lose your job, too. Oh, but I guess WLUV wouldn't have much use for a jailbird counselor, would it?"

"Sometimes you are a total and complete idiot as well as a jerk, John Mystic. Sometimes you're a vicious jerk. And sometimes —"

"I'm adorable. I know." He smiled, doing his best to melt the meanness right out of her. "But try to control yourself, hmmm?"

"Not a problem."

"Are you going to look me in the eye and tell me you're unaffected at seeing me again? Come on, Bess, you might pull that stunt on your sorry Spaniard, but I know you. It's always been there between us, and it probably always will be." Better to acknowledge it and watch its power fizzle than to hold it in and let it gnaw at him.

"It — *what?* The only thing between us is a divorce."

"The magic."

She screwed up her mouth to say something — scathing, he felt sure — then changed her mind. That hated mask of indifference slipped solidly back into place.

"Stop calling Miguel that. Stop needling me. Just stop everything." She raked her hands through her hair, squeezed her eyes shut, and hissed in air between her teeth. Quickly, she dropped her hands and sent him a cool, droll look. "The truth is, for me, the magic is gone. I don't want you, John. I just don't. Okay?"

"Uh-huh." He let his gaze drift down to her pulse throbbing at her throat, then down to her fisted hands. The lady hadn't come unglued, true, but she was a far cry from unaffected. Though he knew he risked one wicked backfire, he wanted more. He wanted unglued, snapped, and out of control. Just once. Just . . . once. "Right."

"That *is* right."

"Sorry, synapse misfire. I forgot you said you hated me."

"Not you. Your actions." She headed toward the door. "If you're going to throw my words back into my face, at least get them right."

He had gotten them right, but her surly expression proved she wouldn't appreciate the reminder and, while he wanted her unglued, he didn't want her unraveled. Contrary to popular belief, he wasn't the heartless jerk Meriam Richards and half of New Orleans had accused him of being. "No problem. Though I don't typically repeat lies. Or rumors."

Bess's jaw dropped open — no doubt to blister his ears — but, without uttering a sound, she snapped it shut, snatched Silk, then shrugged. "I guess that brings this conversation to a close."

"I guess it does." He let his gaze slide down her length. "You'll look great in stripes, darling."

"Shut up, John. Would you just shut up?"

Bryce had been right. She *had* changed. But John hadn't expected this. He kind of liked it. Sassy, saucy. Not a loss of control, but certainly not indifference. A surefooted step in the right direction. Yeah, he liked it a lot. Except . . .

He grimaced. Except it evidenced how much pressure she was under. Bess endured. She survived; took whatever life tossed her on the chin, then went on to pursue her goals. And no matter what happened, she never, *never,* showed her emotions like this. Definitely riding the edge. And knowing it stirred those husbandly instincts to nurture, to surround, and to protect her. She'd hate that. More likely than not, she'd throw one whale of a fit. And that prospect stirred his blood. She'd never let him, or anyone else, see her riled, but he'd imagined it a million times. And when he did, few things could rival Bess. She was magnificent.

She left the room then headed down the stairs, struggling with her heavy luggage.

He followed her. The second time she mis-stepped and nearly tumbled, he couldn't bite his tongue anymore. "I'd be happy to help with that."

"No, thank you." Giving Miss Hattie's banister spindles a real workout, Bess bumped and grunted her way down the stairs.

Stubborn. To the bone, stubborn. "Your party." Even fuming inside, he noted that the farther from the Great White Room they walked, the cooler the house felt. All the warm feelings he'd had on entering it had gone. Now, it was downright chilly and he was edgy as a straight razor — and more certain by the minute Miss Hattie hadn't packed Bess's bags. But they were the only three people in the house now. If not him or Bess, and not Miss Hattie, then *who?*

Good question. One he wanted answered.

By the time John reached the back door leading out to the mud room, he felt like a moving chunk of ice. Bess was walking out on him again. This time, in person. And this time, it hurt every bit as much as it had before.

Outside, they cut across the lawn, rounded the side of the greenhouse, then went on to the little lean-to where guests parked their cars. The sun was shining brightly on her sleek black BMW, but it looked dull, as if the sheen had been stripped from its paint. Curious. When he'd parked beside it earlier, it had gleamed. "Your car could use a good waxing."

She unlocked the door then tapped a button to pop the lid on the trunk. When it sprang open, she tossed her luggage inside. John frowned. "It'll rattle like crazy in there like that."

He moved over to the trunk and re-arranged the cases, snuggling them tightly to the sides of the car and to each other. "That'll work."

"Thank you." The words were stiff enough to walk over to him without benefit of sound waves.

"You're welcome." Why did it have to be like this? Why couldn't they just talk? This whole encounter wasn't going as planned. And a lot of the responsibility for that was his. He'd stunned her, showing up here without warning, then knocked her for a further loop by throwing the news about jail onto her shoulders.

He slammed the trunk shut, then leaned back against it. "I'm sorry, Bess. We got off on the wrong foot here. Can we start over and discuss this settlement like two rational adults?" That should do it. The doc loved rational discussion.

"There's nothing to discuss." She got into her car. "I'm not being testy, Jonathan. I just can't be flexible on this issue. It's . . . personal."

He walked around to her window then leaned down, propping his forearms on the window frame. Silk watched him intently from the passenger's seat. Bess had strapped the mop into a safety belt. Cute. "Too personal to discuss with your husband?"

Her eyes darkened to sapphire blue, that same shade they'd deepened to whenever they'd made love. A rivulet of desire trickled down his center to his core. She was the only woman who ever had affected him so intensely. And he was losing her all over again.

No. No, that's how it felt, but it wasn't true. A man couldn't lose what he didn't have. And he didn't have Bess. Not anymore.

She looked straight ahead, through the windshield and off into the pines. "There was a time when I'd have given anything to talk to you. But you were too busy then, and now it's too late."

That she was right tormented him nearly

as much as the husky sadness in her voice. He'd never meant to hurt her. He'd loved her. And he should tell her that. But she looked a breath away from tears, and Bess's tears would cut him to shreds. "I'm sorry, Doc." Inadequate, but all he had that he could give.

"Me, too." She put her key in the ignition. "Me, too."

There was nothing left to say.

His insides ripping apart, he backed away from the car and again heard her condemning words: *It's just a piece of paper and doesn't mean a thing.* But the divorce did mean something. It meant a lot. To him.

Giving him a look laced with regret and hurt, she cranked the engine.

It ground, then died.

She tried again. Then a third time. And then a fourth. When the grind wound down to an intermittent whimper, she accepted the truth and looked at John. "It won't start."

The ice encasing John's heart melted and a bubble of anticipation burst in his chest. A second chance?

A second chance. Don't blow it.

That man's voice again. John looked around, but saw no one — not that by now he expected he would. This voice came from inside his head. Strange as it sounded, or would sound to anyone else, if he had any intention of telling anyone else, which he certainly didn't. Who the man was didn't matter — not right now. Right now John had a second chance with Bess. A chance he wanted down to his toenails. Whether because of his deathbed promise to Elise, or for himself, John didn't know. Cowardly, but he didn't *want* to know. Not yet. Not until he knew how this chance would pan out.

Not until he knew if it would prove a miracle, or a curse.

CHAPTER 4

Leap upon a mystic tide . . .

"Bess?" John opened her car door. The hinges creaked. "What's wrong?"

Did she dare to get out? Could she stand on her own? Her knees felt like cream cheese. "Um, I'm fine." Tony? Here? Conversing with her in Seascape Inn's backyard as if he were standing right there between the Carriage House and the lean-to?

"You don't look fine." Worry shimmered through John's voice.

"I said, I'm fine." Grace. Think grace. And patience. Lord, but she needed to think a lot about both. Her lip twitching, she'd snapped at John like a world-class shrew. Her parents would have been mortified or worse.

It was all John Mystic's fault. So much on her mind, being this close to him, thinking at all, much less straight, constituted a major undertaking. Why couldn't he just have called so she'd only have had to deal with his voice? That would have been challenging enough, but, no, she had to deal with *all* of him.

Outrage kindled a fuse of anger and she glared at him. If he'd had to come, then at least he should've gotten slouchy or something — *anything* to tone down his megawatt appeal. But he hadn't. And so every time she glimpsed him, she saw him being loving. If that were all she saw, she could probably fight it. But there was also a deep sadness in him that shone in his eyes. She didn't understand it, and that made it, and unfortunately him, all the more attractive. It jerked hard at her heartstrings and created nearly an irresistible urge to hold him.

Irritated at herself, she slid over the sun-warmed seat, brushed aside his offered hand, then stepped out of the car. "I don't understand this." Big understatement there. A lot was happening she didn't understand. "The car ran great two days ago, and now it won't start."

"Pop the hood and I'll take a look."

Recovering from the shock of hearing Tony's message again, from the effect of being near John again, she pulled herself together. "No, but thank you." She couldn't owe John Mystic one thing more. Not one thing more — especially not for kindness. He'd stunned her, showing up out-of-the-blue, but she'd recouped now. And she knew what she needed to get through this divorce: Anger.

Okay, so she was tossing grace and patience right out the window, and she was rationalizing. But right now she didn't give a fig. She'd do what she had to do to get through this and then later, when she didn't see him, didn't smell him, or hear his deep-timbre voice, then she'd sort it all out.

I take exception to being ignored, Bess.

Good grief. She *couldn't* be expected to deal with both of them at once. *Go away, Tony — unless you're going to tell me the meaning of your mystic tide message. That's the only thing I'm interested in hearing from you right now.*

Would if I could, Doc. But there are things you have to discover for yourself.

"Typical male," she groused.

John frowned at her from the front of the car. "Well, excuse me for trying to be nice."

Good grief. She'd spoken aloud. *See what you're getting me into, Tony? More trouble. Would you just go telepath with some other tortured soul? I'm kind of busy losing what's left of my sanity here and I really don't need any outside help to see the job done.*

He laughed.

"Jerk." She must have an invisible sign on her forehead only men could see. One that said "Nag Me."

"What?" John stiffened his spine.

Terrific. A telepathic intruder *and* a soon-to-be-ex-husband ready to nip at her backside. Just terrific. "Not you, John," she said. "Tony." Now why had she admitted that? John would think she'd lost her mind. Well, shoot. Maybe she had. Talking telepathy. Lusting after the man she was divorcing for breaking her heart. Odds looked darn good she was in deep mental kimchee here.

You could give him the benefit of doubt.

Hah! Easy for you to say. Not me. No way. Been there, done that, didn't work, don't intend to do it again. And I thought I asked you to go nag somebody else.

I like nagging you. You're naggable — and stubborn. Crimney, cut the guy a little slack.

Fat chance.

But he's going through a rough time.

Aren't we all? Her marriage on the skids, her parents peeved to the gills because she was getting a divorce when divorces are so unseemly, her job in mortal jeopardy and, the ultimate insult, her hormones in warp-speed mate-mode, lusting after John Mystic. Oh, yes. Aren't we all?

142

This is different.

He broke my heart, and if I let him, he'll do it again. She slammed her car door shut. *Now would you just go away!*

John walked around the car then leaned against the back fender. "Who's Tony?"

"Tony?" Bess feigned ignorance and the out and out lie had her flushing heat. Boy, she could just see herself trying to explain Tony. "Did I say Tony?" Her emotions were churning too close to the surface; John would see her, inside. She turned away. "I meant Jimmy Goodson. I'd better go call him."

"Okay, then. Who's Jimmy Goodson?" John's voice carried to her.

He was following her back to the house. If there were justice, so much as a speck of it, he'd have gotten slouchy, the arrogant pig. Bess couldn't stand slouchy men — and he knew it. He'd stayed perfect to deliberately torture her. And he *knew* blue was her favorite color for him to wear. Why couldn't he have worn neon orange or lime green? She hated both those colors. And why, in the name of everything good, after all that had passed between them, did she still need a barrier for protection against him? "Jimmy showed you around here, remember?"

"Ah, I'd forgotten his name."

"He's also Miss Hattie's mechanic and can fix whatever broke on the car."

"Okay." John sounded hurt.

She glanced back at him and nearly cringed. So much pain in those eyes. What had hurt him so deeply it'd put those haunted shadows there? "I really do appreciate your offer to help, but I have to take care of these things myself now."

"You always have taken care of everything."

And that bothered him? No, surely she'd misread his remark. John Mystic would never admire a helpless, shrinking violet who couldn't handle her challenges without running to him to fix everything all the time. He'd be fed up in a week.

He opened the back door, walked inside, shrugged out of his trench coat, then snagged it on a wall peg. Wearing a pale blue shirt and hip-hugging jeans that did wonderful things for his body, and wicked things to her libido, he crossed the mud room, then stepped into the cheerful kitchen.

Ah, I see you still have a thing for him in jeans, too.

I do not. What did Tony mean — *too?* Good grief, he couldn't see what she saw in her mind's eye. Not with the images of John that had been floating through there. Tony

144

couldn't!

Calm down, Bess, and quit lying to me. Tony laughed. *I'm tapped into your thoughts and you're trying to deceive me? I expected better from you.*

Stuff it. Go away. Would you please just go away? She'd never again be able to meet her eyes in the mirror. Never.

Honesty is the very least I'd think your conscience would accept. The man is your husband. Why can't you admit you find his body attractive and you'd like to —

"Tony!" Good grief, was the man trying to give her a heart attack by embarrassing her to death? *Quit intruding. Lord, isn't anything sacred around you?*

"Tony?" John stilled.

"Slip of tongue." Bess shrugged, feeling like a fool.

Oh-oh, he remembers me.

You know John? How do you know John? Is he behind this? She pulled in a sharp breath. *Did that slug-lover con you into nagging me to death?*

Nagging you to death? Tony sounded surprised, then sad. *No, Bess. I'm trying to nag you into life. So far, you're flunking at living it on a grand scale. Why are you hiding from yourself and from John?*

Tony's surprise she could tolerate. But this grief and disappointment in his voice pricked at her pride. *Who asked for your opinion?*

"Wait!" John frowned at Bess. "Are you talking about that weird caller Tony who let the cat out of the bag about our divorce?"

Oh boy. So he'd heard the call, too. *See what you've gotten me into now?* "Yes, John. That Tony."

Isn't it interesting?

What? Bess grunted. *Would you go away? I'm getting dizzy, trying to keep up with both of you.*

That he listened to your program. Isn't that interesting?

It was. Bess's heart flipped over in her chest. Why had John listened to her program? *Maybe he didn't listen to it. Maybe Bryce told him because of the divorce being mentioned.*

Bryce has three small children. I seriously doubt he was awake.

Bess scrambled for an explanation. The idea of John listening to her show unnerved her. *Maggie. Maggie might have told him. Or T. J. They were listening.*

Did you hear that? Your husband just called me weird. Can you believe it? I take serious

146

exception to being called weird, Bess.

From his disgruntled tone, Tony did indeed take serious exception to the slight. Though not feeling particularly kindly toward John, her sense of fair play insisted she disclose her honest opinion on the matter. *Talking to someone without benefit of speech in two different states does bend a little low to the weird side, Tony. And for the record, I'm living my life just fine. Though I thank you for your interest, I don't need you meddling.*

Bess reached for the wall phone, hoping to forestall any more discomforting remarks from or about Tony. "I really need to call Jimmy before he closes," she said to John to fill the silence and tapped in the number for the garage from Miss Hattie's list. "He's shutting down early to drive Vic to the Grange dance tonight."

Chicken. You can't run from him or avoid him, Bess. You're going to have to talk this out sooner or later — before the divorce can go through. You might as well do it and get it over with now.

Go away!

All right. I think I will. I'm sure not much appreciated around here. But before I do, I want to ask you one question. Have you been thinking? I asked you to think about my message.

You really need to do that.

Good grief. A pouting telepath and a ticked-off ex. And she'd thought she'd hit bottom before. Ha! *I've thought about it. Too much. And it still doesn't make a bit of sense.*

Think some more, and lighten up on Jonathan. He's grieving.

Grieving? Haunted eyes. Air of sadness. He *was* grieving. *What's he lost?*

Tony didn't answer.

Bess called him, asking again, but had no luck. *Now you go. Typical male. Drop a bomb, then depart. You guys are really aces at that.*

"Who's Vic?" John reached into the cabinet for a glass and then filled it with ice at the refrigerator door. Cubes plopped into his glass. One fell onto the floor. Silk scarfed it up and crunched down on it.

"Vic Sampson. The postman." Bess frowned at the dog. Ice wouldn't hurt her, but why was she following John's every step? *Little traitor.*

Silk sniffed and yapped for another cube of ice.

John fished one from his glass and gave it to her, then filled the glass with tea from a ceramic pitcher on the white-tile countertop. "You sure learned a lot about everyone here quickly."

Bess shrugged and listened to the phone

ring for the third time. Had Jimmy already gone? "Village life is like that." Silk yapped, this time wanting lemon. If John gave her a wedge, Bess swore she'd sock him in the nose.

John scooped Silk up, tucked her into the bend of his arm, then reached for the white petal bowl holding the lemon.

"She's a dog." Bess jerked the bowl out of reach. "She can't eat lemon rind."

"I wasn't going to let her eat it."

Bess propped her hand on her hip. "Are you going to tell me you weren't reaching for a lemon wedge, Jonathan?"

"No. But I wasn't going to let her eat it. Just lick it."

Bess held off a frown by the skin of her teeth. He'd sure never responded so quickly when she'd wanted attention. A flash of jealousy zipped through her and, behind the phone receiver, she grimaced. Wouldn't he just love it? Knowing he'd reduced her to being jealous of a dog. Lord, but this was ridiculous. Absurd nonsense she had to nip in the bud.

"Blue Moon Cafe."

"Lucy?" What was Lucy doing answering the phone at Jimmy's garage?

"Yeah. Who is this? It sounds like Bess Mystic."

"It is Bess Mystic." *Mystic?* Had she said that? Her face went hot. And, darn him, John noticed. His eyes gleamed and the corner of his mouth curved up in an I-knew-it smile. Well, she wasn't going to give him the satisfaction of stammering, or of correcting herself. "I meant to call Jimmy's shop."

Silk licked at the moisture on the underside of John's chilled glass. He put her down and showed her where Miss Hattie, the thoughtful sweetheart, had put matching blue water and food dishes for Silk in a niche by the fireplace beside the big, antique radio.

"You did call Jimmy's," Lucy said. "He's already headed over to the dance, so I'm taking his calls."

"I see." Bess toed the floor where it met the wall. Well, great. Now what did she do? "Would you ask him to come to Seascape as soon as he can? My car won't start."

"Sure will. But it'll be morning before he checks in."

Someone talked to Lucy in the background. The man's voice came through the phone garbled and Bess couldn't make out his words.

"Wait a second and I'll ask," Lucy said. "Bess?"

150

"Yes?" John was just standing there, lean hip against the cabinet near the sink, staring at her. Lord, but the man still looked too gorgeous for his own good and for her peace of mind. She had to get out of here. Fast.

"Fred wants to know if you're really going to divorce John. I tried to tell him you were, but he wants to hear it from the horse's mouth, so to speak. Not that Fred thinks you're a horse, or anything. Dang, you know what I mean."

Bess should be peeved, but who could be peeved at Lucy Baker? "It's all right, Lucy."

"Oh, good. See, Fred, I told you she'd understand. Fred says thanks."

"He's welcome."

"So are you going to divorce John?"

Bess's heart slid up into her throat. "Yes, Lucy, I am."

"She is, Fred."

"Too bad." This time, Fred's voice came through loud and clear. "Some woman'll snatch him up in a heartbeat."

Bess wished it had been muffled. "Probably will." Maybe she'd have better luck than Bess at keeping him snatched up. "Thanks for passing my message on to Jimmy, Lucy. Bye."

"Sure thing, sugar. And I'm sorry about Fred's, er, indiscretion."

Certain Lucy was leveling Fred with another killer glare and maybe even with another swat with the table-wiping rag, Bess cradled the receiver. "Too late," she told John. "It'll be tomorrow."

He sat down at the round, light-oak table, then fingered a yellow daffodil in the porcelain bisque centerpiece. "So you're stuck here."

"It appears so." Why did he look pleased about that? Lacy white curtains fluttered at the window behind him. The light breeze carried the scent of honeysuckle and the sea. More importantly, why was she pleased about the delay?

"I'll be right back." John stood up, then headed for the mud room door.

Furious with herself, Bess watched him go. Okay, so he was every bit as gorgeous as ever. He'd gained muscle at thirty-two he'd lacked at twenty-seven. But did just looking at him have to stir memories of them making love? Mentally, only once since he'd joined her at the Blue Moon had she actually seen the man in his clothes. Where it concerned John, imagination was a terrible thing. Memory was worse.

And the real thing was most awful of all. His black hair was longer now on his nape and at his ears. Gleaming and sexy. How she'd loved the feel of it between her fingers and against her shoulder. And his eyes. Cobalt blue and every bit as mesmerizing as T. J.'s painting of the inn. Maybe more. That new sadness in their depths only made him more appealing. What had put it there, she didn't know, but it burned soul-deep. And, far too much for her liking, it had her aching to just hold him until the sadness disappeared. He was grieving, Tony had said. But what had John lost?

Likely not solving Dixie's case yet for Elise. So far as Bess knew, the case was the only thing capable of arousing that kind of emotion in the man.

And, if she had a lick of sense, that sorry truth would convince her to stop wanting to heal him. She couldn't hold him *that* long. She'd tried. And she'd failed.

Watching the curtains blow in the breeze, Bess pulled herself stiff. What was wrong with her? All this notice of him physically. Emotionally. And calling herself Bess Mystic. Absurd. Ridiculous. Before today, she'd *never once* called herself Bess Mystic. And wasn't it just her luck to have this atypical slip of tongue when the man stood within earshot?

Maybe it's your conscience trying to tell you something.

Tony. Good grief. Bess closed her eyes, counted to ten, then spoke aloud. "You again?"

Afraid so.

"Did you make me do that — call myself Mystic?"

Now how could I make you do anything, Doc?

He had a point. "What's John grieving?"

The back door snapped open.

Startled by the sound, Bess jumped, then saw John coming in, hauling her luggage. "You didn't have to do that."

"I know." He walked through the kitchen to the gallery, then started up the stairs.

"John?" The grandfather clock ticked loudly, certain and steady.

The third step creaked. He paused and looked back down at her.

If he'd asked, she'd have refused his help. So he hadn't asked — or so she suspected. Yet suddenly it seemed very important not to suspect, but to know. "Why?"

"I wanted to." He started to say something more, but instead turned, then continued on up the stairs.

When he reached the landing, she leaned against the railing and looked up at Cecelia's picture. A flash of warmth sizzled along Bess's skin.

An unselfish act — for you, Bess. Just for you. To feel needed. You wouldn't let him feel needed with the car. Don't you know everyone needs to be needed?

Bess frowned. Tony, answering the question John wouldn't. But he was way off base on this being needed thing. "Thanks, Jonathan."

"You're welcome, Bess." He looked surprised and sounded wounded. And then he looked wounded, too.

What had she done to offend him?

Maybe you didn't offend him.

What do you mean, Tony?

Maybe the sincerity in your simple thank you touched the man.

Absurd. This is Jonathan, Tony. He doesn't get touched — at least, not by me. And he doesn't need to be needed by me, either. John appreciates independence.

Are you sure about all this?

Was she? Why did she want to think she had touched John? Tony was definitely wrong on the needed front, but could she have touched John? Why was she fighting the urge to run up the stairs and to apologize to him? And why was her silly heart chugging like a steam engine pushed to the max?

She swung her gaze to Cecelia's portrait.

155

She'd been a healer. And the villagers had loved her so much that they'd held a candlelight vigil on the front lawn the night she'd died. When told the legend of Collin and Cecelia's love, Bess had gotten chills. If she died, would there be even one person willing to stand on her lawn?

John had talked about magic between them, but what Cecelia and Collin had, *that* was magic. At one time, though, Bess had thought she and John'd had love. She sighed. But they hadn't.

Or maybe they had . . . and they lost it.

Squinting against the light from the chandelier high overhead, feeling its heat radiate and blanket her skin, she looked up at Cecelia's portrait. "How did you hold on to it? I tried and couldn't do it. I wanted to — Lord, how I wanted to — but I just . . . couldn't do it."

Warm feelings of comfort and love filled Bess. The sense of peace she'd first felt at Lakeview Gallery and on first entering Seascape shimmered through her again now. In the entryway behind her, the grandfather clock ticked softly, luring her attention. The ticking sound grew louder and louder until it filled her ears, until her blood picked up its rhythm and tapped it at her temples. An odd tingling started in her toes, spread up her legs, through her torso, then up her neck, and into her head. Woozy, adrift, she heard only the clock, ticking in sync with the beats of her heart.

The temperature plummeted.

An ice-cold chill swept across her skin.

And a phrase echoed through her mind in an unearthly, pulsing whisper:

The . . . magic . . . lives . . . The . . . magic . . . lives . . . The . . . magic . . . lives . . .

"Tony, is that you?" It *could* be him. It *had* to be him; he was the only telepath around. But it didn't sound like him. Well, it did sound odd and gravelly like him, but this voice sounded different too. Softer. More elusive. Less . . . solid.

It's me, Bess. Inside. Sorry, I got a little overemotional.

Thank goodness. You scared me. I was beginning to think the place was haunted.

He laughed out loud, deeply and from the heart. *Now wouldn't that be absurd?*

Yes, it would. That he could so easily admit to becoming overemotional surprised her. She'd never be able to do that.

Never say never, Bess.

Excuse me?

You'll eat your words every time.

Are you going to intrude on my every thought? I don't like that, Tony.

157

Physician, heal thyself.

Because I don't like your intrusions, I need healing?

You need healing because you hide your feelings. Think about it, Doc.

Don't you start that think-about-it business again.

Middle age weight gain.

What? You're making me crazy, trying to keep up with what you're talking about.

That's what comes from saying never — middle age weight gain.

Tony, you're not making a lick of sense.

I'm making perfect sense.

Not to me.

Really, Bess. Middle age weight gain is a direct result of eating your words — all those I'll-never-do-this-or-that vows you make during your youth that you end up breaking as an adult. He sighed. *Words really put the pounds on a body, Doc.*

She laughed out loud. *You're ridiculous.*

So what's wrong with being a little ridiculous once in a while?

Another important message. Bess stilled and went solemn. *Enough to earn you the silent treatment for a month or longer.*

You're not a child anymore, Bess.

No, but some lessons learned are ones that stick with you.

Especially lessons frequently reinforced.

I don't want to talk about this anymore.

Okay. But let me ask you one question. Just because something happens often, does that mean it's right? Or that the lesson holds value?

Bess blinked, then blinked again. *No, it doesn't.*

Ah, you're finally getting it.

He sounded smug. For some reason, that didn't bother her a bit. Funny, but knowing heart to heart that someone approves of you makes a lot of their irksome little traits endearing. And he really did have her best interests at heart. *Tony? Why were you so emotional?*

I'd rather not say.

Please.

He sighed. *Because I see things you can't yet see or ones you choose not to see.*

What kind of things? She ran a fingertip along the smooth banister. It was so slick and smelled faintly of lemon oil. Miss Hattie pampered everything in the inn. Did the Atlanta judge owner realize what a treasure he had in her?

I'm not free to tell you specifics — professional ethics. For now, be content to know that the magic lives.

Content? He had to be kidding. This was

the most awful news she could have received
— ten times worse than Millicent Fairgate
firing her. Bess tried to look away from Cecelia's portrait and couldn't. Too pre-
occupied to remember speaking wasn't
necessary, she spoke aloud. "No, Tony. The
magic can't be there for me and John. I
won't let it."

I don't think you have a choice. He gentled
his voice.

"But loving and losing him the first time
nearly killed me. I can't go through that
again." Fear crawled up her back. "I won't!"

Shivering, she jerked her gaze away from
Cecelia's sweet face and locked it on the
hardwood steps. Bathed in mellow light
from the chandelier overhead, the stairs
gleamed, as glossy and well-tended as the
rest of the sprawling home. This couldn't be
true. She wouldn't let it be true. There
would be *no* magic — not between her and
John Mystic.

The magic lives.

Bess groaned and turned, rushed down
the stairs, then raced back to the kitchen.
She had to get away from here. The sooner,
the better. She couldn't trust herself around
John. And certainly not here with him.
Strange things happened here.

Something Maggie MacGregor had told

her niggled at Bess's memory, but stayed just out of reach. "No matter," Bess told herself. "No matter."

She had to get away. John already had hurt her more than any man should be able to hurt a woman. Yet here she stood, wanting to heal the sadness from him, having to fight to keep from opening herself up to all that agony and pain again. Hadn't she learned *anything* from the last time with him?

Leap —

He'd followed her. "Shut up, Tony." Bess stuffed a glass under the running faucet and filled it with cold water. Her hand shook so hard that water splashed all over the counter and floor. "I mean it. I've got all I can handle right now and then some. I don't need you or your messages driving me up the wall, too."

Touchy.

"Darn right."

Crimney, Doc. You can't deny the truth. Accept it.

"I can't. I won't! It . . . hurts."

But pain is an affirmation of life. Be grateful you can feel it. Be grateful your situation isn't hopeless. Be grateful you have a second chance to love.

"But it *is* hopeless, Tony. Don't you see? John doesn't love me. He never loved me."

The magic lives, Bess. Whether you stay or go, that isn't going to change because it lives in you.

The full weight of his words hit her. She slid bonelessly down the cabinet to the floor and sat there in the puddle of water. Tears, stinging her eyes, spilled over, then trickled down her cheeks to drip onto her blouse. "Oh, Tony. What am I going to do? You're right. It does live. After all this time, I still feel it. I love what he does to a pair of jeans. I love what the way he looks at me makes me feel. I don't love him — I'd have to be crazy to love him. Worse than crazy. But I want him. I want him so much I ache in places I didn't know I had." She bent over and buried her face in her hands. "What am I going to do?"

Jimmy Goodson raised up from under the hood of Bess's BMW and let his gaze slide from Bess to John Mystic, then back to Bess. They looked scared of each other, and kind of like Jimmy felt every time he saw Nolene Baker over at the Blue Moon Cafe. Jelly-bellied, Miss Hattie called it. When Nolene outgrew being jailbait, he'd be twenty-six. Then he'd ask her out on a date — if she wasn't still sweet on Andrew Carnegie Johnson. The mayor's son, whose mama insisted he study to be a lawyer, had a lot more to offer a girl than the grease monkey orphan of a drunk, even if Miss Hattie did say it only matters what a man is inside. 'Course, Nolene's parents having to get married so Nolene wouldn't be illegitimate wouldn't set well with Lydia, Andrew's mama. She wanted more than for Andrew to be a lawyer. Yeah, that social-climbing snob definitely had her eye on politics for Andy. A wife with parents who'd had to get married might just keep Andrew from snatching up Nolene. But if it did, then did Jimmy still want Nolene? He was crazy about her, no doubt about it. Maybe him hoping she'd be crazy about him was asking for too much, considering his own parents and all. Maybe her just settling for him was the best he could hope for. Might be foolish, him wishing that just once someone besides Miss Hattie thought he was special.

Deflated, Jimmy looked at Bess. "I'm gonna have to take 'er to the shop."

Bess nodded and shoved her hair back from her face. It was loose and she looked kind of pretty for an older lady.

"Any idea what's wrong?"

"Not yet, Mrs. Mystic." Jimmy scratched his head. "Isn't any of the usual. Starter,

163

plugs, points, distributor — all check out fine."

"She prefers Bess Cameron, Jimmy."

His face went hot. "Yes, sir." He turned to Bess. "Sorry, Ms. Cameron."

"It's no problem," she said, her gaze sliding to the dirt telling him it *was* a problem but she didn't want to embarrass him.

John stepped to the front of the car, between it and the tow truck. "I'll help you hook it up."

In minutes, they had the BMW chained up and the safety-catches in place. Good to go, Jimmy headed down the gravel drive, back toward Main Street. He looked in his rearview mirror and glimpsed Batty Beaulah Favish hiding in Miss Hattie's orange tiger lilies, decked out for bird-watching with her binoculars.

Jimmy guffawed. Crazy old bat. Only birds she ever watched were Seascape guests. Right now, she had her peepers locked on Bess and John Mystic. They were heading toward the cliffs. Tourists did that a lot. Though Jimmy couldn't recollect any of 'em watching the ocean more than T. J. Mac-Gregor had, before Maggie had come to the village.

Bill Butler's oldest boy, Aaron, stepped out from behind Beaulah. He had his dad's antique spyglass in his hand, mimicking her in her ghost-hunting again. Jimmy grunted. "Crazy old bat."

At the end of the drive, Jimmy toed the brakes and waited for the sheriff to drive past. He was heading down Main Street, toward the village. Too early for his afternoon visit to the Blue Moon. Likely he was keeping an eye on that group of motorcyclists down at the cafe. They were kind of dusty from their ride, but they were good people. Up here from Arizona and on their way to the hill country to do a benefit for charity. Just goes to prove Miss Hattie's right: When you look at folks, you see what you expect to see instead of what's true about 'em.

Jimmy debated. Left to Fisherman's Co-op? Or right to the garage? He probably should swing by and tell Aaron's folks he had that spyglass again. Leslie would be gone to the auction most likely, but Bill would be there, running the store and keeping an eye on their other two boys. They were having themselves a time in that mud puddle. Yeah, Jimmy should drop in on Bill and give him the word, but then Bill would be ticked to the gills at Aaron . . .

"Naw." Jimmy turned right. Best let the kid have fun while he could. Though if he broke that glass, his dad would fillet his backside. Batty Beaulah really ought not be filling Aaron's head with nonsensical stuff such as ghosts, though. Sure, odd things kind of happened at Seascape. But they happened because Miss Hattie was so good. Hadn't she always said that good things come to those who try to live right? Shoot, everyone in the village knows she lives as right as a body's able — and she never lies. 'Course good stuff happens at the inn. She lives there.

At the shop, Jimmy parked then unhooked Bess's car from the tow. Horace Johnson watched from his old gas pumps next door at The Store, his *Local Yokel*–emblemed baseball cap pulled low over his eyes. Lydia griped about those old-fashioned pumps all the time. Said they made the place look like something out of the Stone Age. But Jimmy kind of liked 'em, just as he did the old glass postal boxes down at the post office. It was comforting, knowing a man could count on some things staying the same.

He looked back at Bess's BMW. Strange. Out at the inn, its finish had looked stumbled, as dull as dirty brass, but here it shined as if freshly waxed. He scratched at his neck. Strange that the car wouldn't kick over too. Nothing wrong he could see that ought to keep it from starting . . .

The betting over at the Blue Moon had started, and Bess and John had looked at each other all jelly-bellied. Jimmy stared at the car. Why not? It was worth a shot.

His stomach knurled. He got in, hit the seat lever to get his knees out of his gut, then keyed the ignition. If his hunch paid off, he might just win enough to buy Miss Hattie one of those yellow tea rose bushes she'd been wanting on his run over to Boothbay Harbor. He sure would like making her happy. "Come on, baby," he whispered from between his teeth, gripped the BMW's steering wheel, then turned the key. "Come . . . on."

The car cranked right up. The engine purred sweeter than Candy, the cockeyed cat, when she'd gotten a bowl full of Lucy's cornbread scraps at the Blue Moon.

A slow smile tugged at Jimmy's lips then spread over his face. He unfolded his lanky body, eased out of the car then into the shop, heading straight for the phone.

He dialed and then waited.

On the third ring, Lucy answered. "Blue Moon Cafe."

"Lucy?" Elbows bent, he leaned against the counter. Was Nolene over at the cafe, or had she and some of her friends hauled it over to the shopping mall? He didn't much care for her venturing that far from the village with just a bunch of girls. Things happened in the city and, for all her bluster and boasts of being grown-up now, Nolene had been protected her whole life. Lucy Baker was a fine mama. "It's me, Jimmy."

"Hey, sugar."

"Listen, how's the betting going on Bess Cameron and John Mystic?" Jimmy wiped a grease spot off his knuckle with a red shop rag, then tossed it onto the scuffed counter. In the breeze, the fan belts hanging on nails slapped against the far wall and ruffled the pages on the girlie swimsuit calendar that gave Pastor Brown hissy fits. The smell of the salty sea mixed with that of oil. No matter what Lydia Johnson said, it was a pleasing scent.

"Betting's been brisk."

Jimmy had expected that. "What's Lydia Johnson down for?" Horace's uppity wife was as snooty a woman as they come — nothing like Miss Hattie. 'Course, Miss Hattie was the finest woman to ever set foot on this earth, and measuring up to her was impossible. But, for all her faults, Lydia did have a nose for smelling romance; Jimmy had to give her that.

"Twelve dollars and twenty-one cents."

Hefty bet for Lydia. "For or against them getting back together?"

"Against." Lucy sighed. "A shame, but I'm inclined to agree with her, Jimmy. They've been separated a long time, and when he showed up here this afternoon, Bess went as stiff as a plank and as white as one of Bill Butler's sails. Miss Millie's betting for 'em, though, bless her heart. I think she's missing Lance. It's close to what would have been their anniversary, and she's waxing a little on the sentimental side."

"Don't you worry about Miss Millie. Hatch will perk her up," Jimmy said confidently. About the only time Hatch ventured from the lighthouse over to Miss Millie's Antique Shoppe was when she was feeling down. Vic said Hatch had a built in radar that went off whenever Miss Millie was out of sorts. After seeing it prove true time and again, Jimmy believed it.

"Saw Hatch headed that way not more than an hour ago. He stopped by Landry's Landing and got some of Miss Millie's favorite tea."

"That should do it, then." Miss Millie loved her tea. Jimmy looked out through the left, big bay door. It was open. The right one remained closed. The BMW gleamed in the weak sun. He rubbed at his chin. The light stubble of his beard grated against his hand. Maybe Lydia was right this time. Bess had been dying to leave Seascape and, if her car had started, she *would've* left. But, out at Seascape, nothing Jimmy had worked on had gotten the BMW fixed, and yet he comes back to the shop with it and, without him so much as putting a wrench to it, the car cranks right up and runs sweeter than honey.

That was proof enough for him. "Put me down for twenty, Lucy — *for* them getting back together." If this worked out, Miss Hattie would be tickled with her yellow tea rose bush. He smiled at that. Even when his own mother had been alive, she hadn't been half the mother to him Miss Hattie had been. He'd never figured out why Miss Hattie had taken to him, but because she had, he loved her more than anybody else on earth.

"That's pretty steep. You sure, sugar?" Lucy sounded worried.

"Yeah, I'm sure." The glimmer on the car grew to a gleam that darn near blinded him. When he'd brought John's bags upstairs and given him the tour, and he'd seen that Miss Hattie had put John in the Cove Room, just across the hall from Bess in the Great White Room, Jimmy had been suspicious. That, the car not starting up with its dull paint all glossy again now, and those jelly-bellied looks between them . . .

Inspiration struck. He'd keep the car out of commission for a spell, just to help things along. A little insurance never hurts, Miss Hattie says. So long as he didn't lie to Bess, things should work out fine. "In fact, make it twenty-five."

Jimmy grinned. Shoot, with her stuck here, how could he lose?

CHAPTER 5

John sat at the kitchen table. Hatch, a bent and little, crusty salt of a man with leathery skin, a stubbly chin, and eyes as wise as the ages sat in the opposite chair, finishing the last of a cup of coffee that still steamed. A yellow bandana tied at his throat, he tucked its ends under the collar of his white shirt.

"I think Miss Millie's all right. We had a little tea and a long chat." Hatch looked over to Miss Hattie, near the fireplace. Her old rocking chair squeaked and, on her forward rocks, a string from the worn red-and-white-check cushion dragged low, touching the floor.

"I'm so glad you dropped by to see her." Miss Hattie looked at John. "Millie gets a little sad this time of year. She's a widow now and it's close to what would have been her wedding anniversary."

"That can be rough." John let his gaze drift from her to the empty fireplace grate.

He'd learned that first through Elise and then, after Bess had left him, firsthand. He'd suffered through anniversaries, birthdays, and Christmas celebrations alone for six years. But Elise had been a widow for a long time. She'd withstood all he had a lot longer — and because John had failed to find Dixie — without her daughter there to offer her comfort. A wave of regret grew to a gale in his stomach and wrenched his heart. Did Miss Millie have children?

He refrained from asking. If she didn't, then she still had suffered as had Elise and, if Miss Millie did, he didn't want to know it right this second. He was depressed enough.

Hatch set down his cup. "Dropping the mail off for Vic today gave me a good excuse to stop by."

"Danced too much at the Grange last night again, didn't he?" Miss Hattie's emerald eyes sparkled. "My, but that man is hard on his feet."

John smiled. She was a special woman; an innate sense of goodness and caring emanated from her.

"Yep, he sure did." Hatch grinned. "We took Millie over, to get her out of the house. And he dipped her one time too many. Ain't his feet hurting him this time. He threw his back out of whack. Probably be down a couple days."

"Oh, dear. I'll have to take over some —"

"Now don't start your fretting, Miss Hattie. Since you have guests, Lucy's seeing to him." Hatch stood up, hiked his pants, then tossed Vic's worn mailbag onto his shoulder. "I'd best be getting on over to Beaulah's before she makes her afternoon run down to the Blue Moon to test the sheriff's good nature."

"Hatch, don't be unkind. Beaulah is just a little . . . persistent."

"She's nuttier than Lydia Johnson's fruitcake and that's the truth, Miss Hattie."

She didn't dispute him, but she didn't agree with him either. John thought her the soul of diplomacy — and that Hatch must be right.

He headed toward the back door. "John, bring your wife over to the lighthouse and I'll give you the tour. I can't be lighting the lamp. The Coast Guard would pitch a fit. I'm summercating, but I'll tell you the history of it — if you bring me a couple of Miss Hattie's blueberry muffins." He grinned from under the brim of his hat. "I'm partial to 'em."

"Thanks." John smiled. "I'll see what I can do." The muffins would be far easier to bribe than Bess's agreement to go anywhere with him.

Hatch gave them a gap-tooth grin, then left through the mud room. Whistling a jaunty tune, he limped past the kitchen window, a youthful spring in his step.

John watched him round the edge of the house. "He's a good man."

"Yes, he is. Very wise, too. People are often deceived by his rustic looks. Some foolish souls even have called him 'Popeye.' "

With his weathered, wrinkled skin and virtuous ways, John could see that, though Miss Hattie's lip curling told him that neither reason had solicited the nickname. "Why 'Popeye'?"

"He loves the sea and smokes a corncob pipe." She paused, tilted her head, then grunted. "I have to say, though, it's been a good ten years since I've seen it lit."

"My great-grandmother used to smoke one of those. Mortified my Uncle Max. She died when I was really young, and I haven't thought of that in years." He couldn't honestly say he'd thought of her much either. It'd just been too long. And too much pain had clocked in between losing her and losing Elise.

"May I say something, Jonathan?"

Jonathan. His senses went on alert. Now where had she heard him called Jonathan?

"Yes, ma'am."

"One of the challenges in aging is that we watch the numbers of those we love — and of those who love us — dwindle. That's a hard thing about life, and going on."

"Yes, ma'am, it is." His grandparents, his parents, Elise. All he had left now was Selena and his Uncle Max and, busy with their own lives, they had little time for him. Honestly, because of the secret, he had to admit, he hadn't made much time for them either. Or for Bess . . . and getting him to see that had been Miss Hattie's intent.

Subtle, but effective. A special woman. Noble. Her chin dipped to her sewing, he stared at her white-bunned crown. "May I ask you a question, Miss Hattie?"

"Certainly, dear." She smiled up at him.

"Why didn't you ever marry?"

She stopped rocking. Her eyes glazed over and, in her mind, she'd left her Seascape Inn kitchen for a journey into her past; John knew it as well as he knew he sat in her kitchen.

Her eyes went sad and her voice took on a faraway tone. "I was engaged to a wonderful man." She brought her gaze to John, and he sensed her reluctance to leave the memories of her fiancé behind her. "He was a soldier."

And a good man. Her cadence reeked of pride. "Why didn't you marry him?" She obviously loved him.

"He died saving the life of another man."

"All those years ago, and yet you still love him." What did a man have to do, what could he do, to make any woman love him that much?

Bess's words again haunted him. *It's just a piece of paper and doesn't change a thing.*

The skin beneath Miss Hattie's eyes crinkled. "I love him with all my heart." Her conviction burned strongly in her voice, in the gentle upthrust of her chin.

War was hard on the men and women who fought it, and on those left behind. Because of that war, Miss Hattie had been cheated out of a lifetime of loving, of marrying, and having a family. She'd have made a wonderful wife and mother. Saddened by her loss and touched by her devotion to her soldier, John softened his voice. "I'm sorry he didn't make it home."

She raised her brows. "But he did, Jonathan. A part of him never left home. With my every breath, he lives on in me."

Cecelia and Collin's rare kind of love. Elise and Clayton's kind of love. An empty ache gnawed at John's stomach. He and Bess never had known that kind of love. At least he hadn't, and he didn't think Bess had, either. And he feared he'd die without ever knowing it.

Miss Hattie turned on the big, antique radio behind her. Big band era music drifted through the kitchen, and she softly hummed along with it. Her head bowed, she studied the embroidery in her lap. She was sewing the Seascape Inn logo onto a new batch of crisp, white napkins. Yellow thread.

She had a fondness for yellow; nearly every flower in the house was some shade of it. Some soft buttercup, some bright and sunny. Those on the kitchen table, upstairs in his bedroom. There'd been yellow flowers in a crystal vase in Bess's room, too.

And in Elise's hand.

A cold chill raced up his spine. When she'd died, Elise had held a single flower petal. According to the florist John had consulted for accuracy, one from a yellow carnation. And yet, of all the flowers in her hospital room, there hadn't been a single carnation . . . or a single yellow flower.

Was the color significant to women of that age? Miss Hattie and Elise had been relatively close to the same age. Well, not really. But there had to be an explanation to that flower petal and an answer to the mystery of how Elise had gotten it. During her entire

178

hospital stay, he had been the only visitor permitted to see her.

"Miss Hattie, why are all the flowers around here yellow?" Maybe she could at least shed some insight.

"They hold a special place in my heart, dear. My soldier adored yellow flowers."

Personal, not a custom of the time or any reason he could apply to Elise. "I see." And all these years later — several decades — Miss Hattie still held them dear.

What did Bess hold dear and special in her heart?

John pushed aside an empty plate, and pressed his finger to a crumb of pie crust that had fallen onto the table. At one time, he'd thought he could answer that. Now, he knew he didn't have an inkling. He'd never asked her. Not easy to admit, but true. Maybe on this second chance, he could try a little harder. And maybe the information he'd learned from his phone call with Bryce earlier would help him to do just that.

"Jonathan." Miss Hattie looked up at him again and stopped rocking. "I wouldn't presume to intrude, dear, but I think you should know something about Bess."

He frowned. "Oh?"

"She's . . . concerned about you."

Bess? Concerned about him? Right. If it

wasn't so sad, the idea would be funny. If she were concerned, which she wasn't, she certainly wouldn't be concerned after their next round of discussions on the settlement. She'd be furious. Maybe even let him see a little more of that sass. Inwardly, he smiled. He could hardly wait. "Oh?"

Miss Hattie nodded, her bun jiggling. The lights set her soft white hair to sheening. "She senses your grief and doesn't understand it. Haven't you told her about losing Elise, dear?"

"No, I haven't." He couldn't hold Miss Hattie's worried gaze, and let his fall to the needlework in her lap. "She and Elise . . ." He frowned. "They didn't get along."

"I understand." Miss Hattie lowered her tone just enough to prove she really did understand. "Far be it from me to suggest I know your wife better than you do, but she is worried, Jonathan. It would ease her mind to know the reason you're grieving."

He sighed. "I can't tell her. I thought about it, but I can't. Elise was . . . special."

"I know, dear, and you aren't certain Bess's reaction will be kind or compassionate." Miss Hattie stuffed her sewing into a little black bag with yellow flowers on it, then set the bag onto the floor beside her rocker. "But Bess *is* kind and compassionate. She's special too, and she feels your discord with her is what has you sad. She feels responsible."

Some part of John took satisfaction in that. It wasn't a part of himself he took pride in or one he wanted to emulate, but it was real and there. "She's only concerned because of the settlement. It's the last obstacle between us and her freedom."

"It is?"

He nodded. "Bess is in love with another man, Miss Hattie." Man, but those words hurt coming out of his throat. They left his tongue bitter, and his heart hollow. He grimaced. *Chump.*

"She is?"

Again he nodded. "I think she filed for the divorce because she's decided she wants to marry the man — though that's just speculation."

"Is this true?" Wide-eyed, Miss Hattie looked puzzled.

"I think so." The divorce would cost Bess her job. If not to remarry, then why do it? She loves her job.

"Well, haven't you asked her, dear?"

He shrugged. "Only a thousand times — about why she's divorcing me, that is. Not about the other." There was no way he could say that twice about her marrying another man without being sick all over Miss Hattie's kitchen. "She won't discuss the matter with me."

"Hmmm, I can't say I'm surprised. If she's truly in love with another man —"

"No, Miss Hattie," he corrected her. "I mean Bess won't discuss with me why she wants the divorce. It's very frustrating."

"Oh." The old woman nodded, her expression pensive. "Well, I'm sure as certain it *is* frustrating." She started rocking and, after a long moment of clearly mulling over the matter, she cocked her head. "Jonathan, dear."

"Yes, ma'am."

"Far be it from me to tell you your own mind, or Bess's, for that matter . . ."

Realizing she wanted permission to offer her advice, he encouraged her. "Go on, Miss Hattie."

"Perhaps you should use a little . . . gentle persuasion to get Bess in a more talkative mood, and then ask her again."

John nearly fell off his chair. "Miss Hattie, are you suggesting that I seduce Bess?"

"Well," the dear woman shrugged, her face as pink as the geraniums on the front porch, "there are worse ways to find out the truth, dear, you must agree, and you are married to Bess, so I can't see how this could actually be seduction. It's more like . . . encouraging. Yes, encouraging. That suits, doesn't it?"

"Encouraging suits." Loving her logic, John laughed out loud. "You're a treasure."

She smiled. "Why, thank you, Jonathan."

"But even if I wanted to, I don't think I *could* seduce Bess. Remember Santos?"

"Ah, her sorry Spaniard."

John laughed again. "He is that."

"I'm afraid voices carry in the house." She lowered her gaze. "I truly wasn't eavesdropping."

"I know that, Miss Hattie," he assured her to rid her of the wrinkle of worry creasing her brow.

"Well, I'd be remiss if I didn't say that I think you're mistake —" Miss Hattie stopped midsentence, stared up at the ceiling as if listening, then changed tactics and smiled. "I'm sure you know best, dear."

John sipped from a tall glass of iced tea. Extra lemon. Tart. It slid down his throat, cool and refreshing, and buried the chump. Bess didn't care about him and he wouldn't be suckered into thinking she did or that he could seduce her. She wouldn't like his new spin on the settlement, that was a given. But if she'd been reasonable and accepted her half, then he wouldn't have been forced to revert to drastic measures to make sure she didn't have to rely on anyone else for her needs. She'd be ticked. Furious. But would the drastic measure work?

That remained to be seen. If it did, the heck she was sure to put him through for his trouble would be worth it.

The phone rang.

"It's for you, dear," Miss Hattie said, not missing a stitch of her sewing.

How could she identify the caller *before* answering the phone? On the second ring, John went to the wall beside her, then lifted the receiver. "Seascape Inn."

"John Mystic, have you lost your mind?"

He stared at Miss Hattie, disconcerted. It was for him. "Selena," he said into the receiver, "calm down." Silently, he cursed Bryce. The man hadn't wasted any time calling her.

"Bryce called at the crack of dawn. I'd have called as soon as the sun was up, but Miguel Santos phoned me, too. So has Francine. In fact, I've spent an entire day listening to people gripe and swear you've lost your mind, brother dear. I defended you, of course, but if half of what they're telling me is true, I'm inclined to agree with them."

"Why?" John leaned against the door casing and stared out the window at the lush lawns. A butterfly was having a field day in Miss Hattie's peonies.

"Why? You *have* lost your mind!" Selena drew in a hissed breath that crackled through the phone wires. "You're suing Bess for —"

Bess walked into the kitchen. Terrific timing. "I asked you to calm down, Selena. Now, I'm telling you to do it. This is my affair and I'll handle it as I see fit."

Bess sat down at the table and sipped from his glass of tea. Just like the old days. Every muscle in his chest clenched. And angry because it had, he semi-shouted at Selena. "Don't you and your partners have enough to do to keep you busy?"

"Enough, John. Leave this alone, okay?" Selena's voice went soft, pleading. "Bess has made her feelings quite clear. Can't you just accept that it's over and let go?"

He'd promised Elise. Failed her when she'd needed him most. He'd never wanted this stupid divorce or to lose Bess. Now he had a second chance. No, he couldn't "just let go." The magic was still there. True, that hadn't been enough to make a successful marriage before, but maybe — "You're stepping over the line, Sis."

"Somebody's got to keep you from self-destructing. I know you're still going to the house and parking in the drive. I know you're still listening to her radio shows, too. You've got to move on, John. For you. And you've got to let her move on, too."

Bess dragged a fingertip down his glass. He envied it. She had shadows under her eyes. Beautiful, and worried. But Miss Hattie was wrong. Bess's worry had nothing to do with him. He was just a piece of paper. She worried about all the trouble and turmoil in her own life. Bess resented turmoil. She probably missed Santos, too. That, John resented. "Take care of your seniors and kids and stuffed bears, Selena, and leave my business to me. And tell Peggy to give the box-hedge snooping a rest."

Darn. Bess heard him. He thought he'd been talking low enough so that she wouldn't, but he hadn't. Her cheeks flushed a dusty rose, nearly the same shade as her silk robe. Wrapped and belted at her waist, it clung to her curves. She had no right to be so alluring. Sitting there covered neck to heels and still looking sexier than in any teddy she'd ever let caress those lush curves.

"But, John. I'm worried about you. It hasn't been that long since Elise died, and I know you're hurting. You're vulnerable, you know? I don't want to see you hurt more."

Selena was worried. He softened his voice. "Look, honey, I'm fine. Really. And I know what I'm doing."

"Sure as heck doesn't look like it from here. Suing Bess for —"

"I've got to go, Selena. And tell Bryce there's a thing called attorney/client confidentiality that he'd best start adhering to or I'm going to start losing my sweet disposition."

Bess sent him a look flatly stating she didn't think he had a sweet disposition to lose. He frowned at her, and held it so she wouldn't miss it. She let her gaze roll to the ceiling, and he nearly smiled. He didn't, of course, but he could have. As soon as he got off the phone and hit Bess with "Settlement Proposal Number Two," she'd lose that superior smug look.

He could hardly wait.

"Bryce was worried about you, too," Selena said. "You have to see that this is one crazy stunt you're pulling, John. If Bryce wasn't concerned, he wouldn't be a very good lawyer."

"Okay, you're all on record as being officially worried. I'll talk with you later."

"John, don't do this. Do you hear me? Don't do —"

He hung up the phone. Miss Hattie and

Bess were talking softly. The tune on the radio switched from horns to piano, soft and smooth and mellow.

"I'd rather have one of your blueberry muffins. Lucy's pretty excited about them," Bess told Miss Hattie. "Is that okay?"

"Of course, dear. Whatever you like." She nodded toward the counter at the plate of muffins next to the ceramic canisters. "I've been a wee bit concerned about your lack of appetite lately, though you don't look the slightest bit peaked. Do you think she looks peaked, John?"

She looked red as a beet with embarrassment. Bess didn't like being the focus of attention. Feeling a little contrary because of that "sweet disposition" look she'd laid on him, he studied her slowly, intently, weighing every nuance of her every feature. His body went hard and that reaction he hadn't anticipated. If the woman wasn't just so blasted beautiful to him.

"No, she doesn't look peaked." John slid back into his chair and saw himself taking back his glass of tea, rubbing its rim where Bess's lips had touched. Hard to tell for sure with her robe — he couldn't see beyond temptation — but maybe she had lost a couple pounds. Her eyes were shadowed. Her cheeks were a little more hollow, too.

Worry spiked through him, but if he asked, she'd know she still mattered. Couldn't have that. He'd *chump* himself and she'd sweet-disposition and mind-your-own-business look him into the next century. Instead, he poured himself a shot of steaming black coffee then returned to his seat and frowned down into a flowered cup far too delicate for his huge hands. Maybe it would cool him off. He must have been crazy, thinking he could assess her without getting hot and bothered. He never had been able to do it. Still, that she might be ill concerned him and, heck to pay for it or not, he had to ask. "Why aren't you eating? Are you sick, Bess?"

She stilled at the counter, squared her shoulders, then turned to look back at him. "No, I'm fine. Just a lot on my mind."

Like Santos, the divorce, the settlement, her job. Yeah, John could see it. And as soon as conversation allowed, he'd be adding to her list of worries. That had guilt knocking at his conscience's door. He ignored it. The only reason he'd sunk so low as to pull this stunt was because she'd left him no choice. He'd see to it that she never had to depend on anyone for her financial needs. That reassurance would compensate for the additional guilt he'd have to lug around. When

189

you had a heap already, what was one more shovel's worth? He compromised as best he could to soften the blow. "I don't like adding to the list, but we need to talk about something."

She filled a cup with coffee from the pot. Her hand started shaking; coffee sloshed in the carafe. "Fine."

Giving him a smile as false as her worrying about him, she returned to the table, then sat down. Weak sunlight filtered in through the windows and Bess's hair looked like spun gold, far too tempting to not want to touch.

The chair legs scraping against the floor sounded gritty and good and reminded him he shouldn't be thinking these kinds of things about her. At least not until she accepted his proposal.

Would she accept it?

Yeah, she would. He'd box her in if he had to, but she would accept it.

Miss Hattie stuffed her sewing into her bag. "Would you two prefer privacy?"

"No!"

"No!"

Simultaneous reactions. Miss Hattie jerked, then eased back down into her rocker and shifted her gaze uneasily to the ceiling.

John glanced to Bess then back to Miss Hattie. They'd made her uncomfortable and he hated that. "I'm sorry."

"Me, too." Bess shifted in her chair. "I guess it's pretty obvious we'd rather not be alone together."

"Understandable." Miss Hattie gave them a warm smile that had John feeling even more guilty for startling her. "Divorce is seldom easy. I admire you both for treating each other kindly." She pulled out her sewing again then counted her stitches. "So often couples want only to hurt each other. It's such a sad thing, isn't it? To hurt so much that you want to hurt back?" Her round cheeks tinged pink. "Not that either of you would do that, thank goodness."

John frowned at the yellow porcelain daffodils in the table's centerpiece. He'd been looking forward to dropping his bombshell on Bess for a good hour. Now, he couldn't do it. Not without feeling like a jerk. And Bess was staring at her muffin as if she expected it to burst open and suck her down. Looking as guilty as he felt because in their earlier encounter they both *had* wanted to hurt each other.

"Kindness is more my style, Miss Hattie." Bess lifted her gaze to John's, across the table. "I don't want to hurt or to cause hurt.

191

I just want peace."

He didn't want to hurt her either. Couldn't she see that? "So do I, Bess."

Miss Hattie cleared her throat. "Perhaps I should go water my flowers."

"No!"

"No!"

"Very well." Miss Hattie again lowered herself back to her rocker pad. And again she sent a concerned, questioning look ceilingward.

Everyone fell quiet. John fidgeted. What did he say to an angelic-looking woman who thought he was one of the good guys or to the woman divorcing him who still put knots in his stomach? He didn't have a clue.

Rocking back and forth, Miss Hattie looked to the end of the fireplace mantel. "Oh, my. I almost forgot." She stretched and grasped the brown box then passed it to Bess. "While you two were busy with Jimmy and the car, a package from Miguel Santos arrived. I'm sorry, dear. I'd forgotten it."

"It's no problem." Bess took it. "Actually, it's for Silk. Cookies." She looked to where Silk lay curled into a ball on the rug at Miss Hattie's feet. "She certainly doesn't mind."

John suffered a twinge of sheer jealousy. Silk didn't mind. Snoozing there before the fireplace, she didn't seem to mind at all. At least all was well in somebody's world.

Bess opened the box. It crackled then split. Smiling, she pulled out a dog biscuit. "Silk. Wanna cookie?"

Another gift Bess would accept from that sorry Spaniard. And still, she'd touch nothing of her husband's. Man, but that rankled, and it made him even more determined. She *would* relent. He would *not* bend on this. Not now, not ever.

The puppy perked up and padded over to Bess, tail wagging and eyes alight.

"Sit and say please," Bess instructed.

The mop dutifully obeyed, sitting and lifting her right paw. John couldn't repress a grin. Silk took the cookie into her mouth, then promptly ran to John. When he lifted her up, she dumped the cookie into John's jean-clad lap.

"What am I supposed to do with it?"

Bess smiled. "She wants you to hold it for her."

His insides quivered. Bess's smile lit up the room, lit up a life that'd held nothing but dark shadows since Elise's death. The back of his nose tingled and misty-eyed, he looked down at the pup. "Saving it for later, huh, squirt?"

Silk barked once, wiggled until John put

her down, then returned to the rug. Miss Hattie had left; her rocker still moved but she was no longer in it, nor in the kitchen. He hadn't seen her go.

"Here, I'll take it." Bess held out a hand for Silk's cookie.

Santos's cookie she'd take. But nothing from John. Fury coiled tight in his stomach then exploded. He slipped the cookie into his shirt pocket, taking far more pleasure than he should in Bess's what-are-you-doing expression.

"I'll be needing some of these." He laced his hands atop the table. "That's what I wanted to talk with you about."

Her brow crinkled. "Do you have a dog?"

"Not yet." He glanced pointedly at Silk. "But I will soon."

Bess stood up. "Jonathan Mystic, you can't mean to try to take my dog!"

Genuine emotion? From Bess? Without seduction or deliberate provocation? Good grief, he couldn't believe it. "Of course not, Bess. You know I'd never *take* her." He leaned back and folded his arms across his chest. "I'm only asking for visitation rights — maybe joint custody."

"What?" Bess bumped the table. Coffee from her cup sloshed over the rim and splattered onto her robe. She grabbed a dish cloth from the counter and swiped at the spill. "Are you crazy?"

Definitely genuine emotion. Irksome that Santos's dog aroused it, but at least it was there. If Santos had tapped into it, then there had to be a way for John to tap into it, too. "You're the doc, darling. You tell me."

She walked around the table and stared down at him, her eyes glittering. "You are *not* getting visitation rights or joint custody of my dog, Jonathan. I got Silk *after* we separated. She's mine."

He smiled up at her. She was close to letting that facade crack. So close a good thread jerk would snap it. "I think you'd best check with Francine, darling. You got Silk after you walked out on me, true. But *before* you filed for legal separation. In the eyes of the law, Silk is *ours.*"

Bess drew in a sharp breath that had her chest heaving. "We'll see about that."

"I already have. But," he waved toward the phone, "call Francine. You'll feel better getting the facts straight from her."

Bess fumed. Her face flushed, her eyes seared, then went stone cold. "You are one sorry son of a —"

"Bess!" Miss Hattie gasped. White-faced, she leaned against the mud room door, the bunch of yellow daisies in her arms crushed to her chest.

Bess swallowed the rest of her words, then muttered a tight-lipped, "I'm sorry, Miss Hattie. If you'll please excuse me." She stomped out of the kitchen, past the gallery's grandfather clock, then on toward the stairs.

John stared at her back. If her spine got any stiffer it'd snap in at least three places. Flustered himself, he wasn't exactly sure what to do. Should he go after her? Let her get used to the idea before hitting her with his proposed settlement? Either way held distinct risks.

"John, dear," Miss Hattie walked over to the counter and set down her flowers. "I don't like to intrude, but I can't stand seeing you two so upset. If I might offer you a bit of advice, please, tell Bess about your loss."

"I can't, Miss Hattie. I thought I could, but Bess is just as bitter toward Elise now as she was six years ago. Losing her is bad enough. Bess wouldn't understand that I feel as if I've just buried my mother. She's never understood."

A frown creased Miss Hattie's soft brow. She folded a pleat into the skirt of her flowered dress, fidgeting with her fingers, and mulling over the matter. Then she sighed. "I see."

"Don't say that. Bess *always* says that and she doesn't see a thing." He stood up, looked at her, and let her see his regret in his eyes. "I'm sorry. I don't mean to take this out on you. I just —"

"You hurt, dear. I know. No apology is needed."

"Thank you." He turned and stopped, then looked over the slope of his shoulder back at her. "Miss Hattie, did you pack Bess's bags?"

Her face went pink and she averted her gaze.

"Miss Hattie?" Now what about that question induced discomfort?

"No, Jonathan, I didn't."

"Any idea who did?"

"I don't like to speculate, dear. So often guesses are inaccurate."

She knew. And he should push her. But Bess and he already had given the elderly woman more than enough shocks and startles and grief for one day, so he let it go. Another time would come, one when she wasn't looking so vulnerable. "True," he agreed, then strode out of the kitchen.

Miss Hattie watched him turn onto the stairs, then blew out a shuddery sigh and stared up at the ceiling. "I hope you know what you're doing here, Tony, because I've certainly got my doubts about these two."

The lights flickered once, then again.

Miss Hattie frowned. "All right. You don't have to get persnickety. I wasn't questioning your judgment, darling, only theirs. It seems to me that too much hurt has passed between them for things to ever again be right. If the man won't turn to her even in grief and she won't turn to him even when facing serious challenges, when *will* they turn to each other? My guess is that they won't. Not at all."

The lights snuffed out and stayed out.

Miss Hattie calmly reached into the kitchen drawer near her left hip, pulled out a candle and matches, then lit the wick. When the flame lit up the kitchen, she grunted. "Maggie MacGregor was right about you, Tony Freeport. You *do* have an attitude."

The temperature dropped and a cool breeze fanned past her shoulder. The candle's flame went out.

Resigned, Miss Hattie began arranging the flowers in the dark, hoping John and Bess wouldn't prove to be one of the intended couples here who failed to meet their destinies.

Though she hated to admit it, that did

happen at times. Those two clearly loved each other, but a lot of obstacles stood in their way. Maybe too many obstacles.

The candle flamed to life.

Then again, Miss Hattie smiled, maybe not.

The sound of raised voices carried down from overhead.

"Oh, dear." Cringing, Miss Hattie bit down on her lower lip then hummed to drown out their actual words and busied herself arranging her yellow daisies. "Well, a little darkness does create a safe haven for a little spirited discussion." It *could* help.

Or it could complicate matters and make them worse.

She was *not* sick. She *was* eating. And she had *not* lost weight.

Did John think she should lose a few pounds?

"Idiot! What difference does what he thinks make?" Because it did matter and she didn't want it to, Bess tossed her coffee-splattered robe onto the bed and stared at her stunned reflection in the dresser mirror. The scraps of lace she called bra and panties looked stark against her pale skin and the soft-hue blues and greens in the room.

She gave the antique white and brass

phone on the desk a longing look. It worked only when it wanted, but she willed it to ring, willed Francine to call her again and tell Bess the legal opinion given earlier had been a mistake.

But the phone didn't ring.

Francine didn't call again.

And there'd been no mistake.

John Mystic, determined to have his way, really had demanded legal visitation rights with Silk.

Bess had to accept it. Acceptance was always positive growth. But wouldn't the press just have a field day with this lawsuit? Bess could just see the headlines: RADIO HOST TO THE LOVELORN SUES FOR DIVORCE. HUSBAND GLADLY DITCHES WIFE BUT FIGHTS FOR CUSTODY OF DOG.

She could pitch a fit. A foot stomping, yelling at the top of her voice, raging fit. And Millicent Fairgate, whose call Bess had expected and had dreaded the entire day, surely would come no later than nine A.M. tomorrow. She'd likely as not fire Sal, too, because he hadn't fired Bess over Tony's call. Muttering, Bess paced a furious path between the braided rug beside the four-poster bed and the adjoining turret room window.

The curtain was open. A chilly breeze blew in, smelling of the sea and — heaven help her — of rain. Shivering straight down to her bones, she plodded back toward the bed. "Perfect. Just perfect."

Never let them see you sweat, kid.

Her father's teaching replayed in her mind and suddenly she was angry. So very angry at him. "I've listened to you my whole life, Dad. Maybe if I'd stomped my feet a few times and yelled once or twice, I wouldn't be in this fix. Tony was right. What's wrong with being ridiculous now and then? And what's wrong with being angry and showing it? Oh, I know the drill by rote. A *lack of self-discipline is so unseemly.* Well, I've tried being seemly and it sucks dead canaries. Burying my emotions, never letting anyone see me sweat — I'm a psychologist, for goodness sake. I know what you demanded from me was unhealthy, and yet I did it anyway — to please you and Mother. But neither of you were pleased. You never will be and you'll never approve of me. So okay, I accept it. Positive growth. Now I want *my* approval. Listening to you two cost me everything. Starting now, I listen to me."

Feeling better at having come to a decision on *this* worry, Bess stopped pacing at the turret room windows. The strong wind now had the filmy curtains billowing nearly straight out. Not just rain coming. A storm.

Figured. Positively, absolutely figured.

She stomped her foot. It felt pretty good, so she stomped it again. Then she returned to pacing, putting her heart into it. When it failed to rid her of steam, she added deep-breathing exercises. The moon clung on the horizon, beneath the swirl of angry, gray clouds and their eerie, misty tentacles. A brilliant flash of lightning split the night sky. A horrendous clash of thunder followed. The windows rattled and the lights flickered, then flickered again.

Bess stopped dead in her tracks. Not just a storm. A wicked thunderstorm. The lights dimmed, then went out.

A thin, silvery streak of moonlight slanted across the floorboards and the braided rug. Odd. With the storm there should be no moonlight, and yet there was. How could that be?

Please, not this, too. Not a storm, too. Not now. A blink from tears, she moved toward the bed, determined to plop herself into it, jerk the covers up over her head, and not come out until the world again got civilized. She'd had all she could stand of her starring role in "The Perils of Pauline."

Her foot tangled in the edge of the rug.

202

She stumbled, fell face first down to the hardwood floor, breaking her fall with her elbows. Pain shafted up her arms and she bit back a wail.

Well, if this just wasn't the last straw. Stinging tears flooded her eyes then spilled down her cheeks. She should stop them, now, before she lost complete control. But a good cry could be therapeutic, could clear some of the frustration from her system. Hadn't she often prescribed a marathon crying jag on occasion for just that purpose?

Someone touched her arm.

She gasped.

"It's me." John sat down on the floor beside her. "Are you hurt? I heard you fall."

"Only my dignity." Her voice caught, ragged. He hadn't heard her fall. The rug had muffled it. He'd remembered how much she hated the dark and storms. And now he knew she was crying. Lord, was there no end to the humiliation?

"Come here." He pulled her into his arms.

Yet another act of unselfish kindness. Cecelia would like that. Bess shouldn't like it but she needed holding, and she was so tired of fighting everything — including him — alone. Swearing she wouldn't, she snuggled closer. When he closed his arms around her, she shivered. Feeling safe and secure, and unafraid. She should be terrified. If she had half an ounce of sense, she'd be scared witless.

He pulled her into the wedge between his bent knees, his feet flat on the floor, his shirt soft against her skin, his jeans rough against her side.

"Aren't you going to ask me a bunch of stupid questions?" She curled her hands to her chest to keep from winding them around him. He smelled so good, like John, and he still wore the same cologne. *Obsession.* How he'd laugh at her if he knew she'd bought a bottle and sprayed her spare pillow to help her get through stormy and lonely nights.

"No. No questions." His heart raced, thudding hard against the side of her face. He brushed at her wet cheek with a gentle stroke of his thumb. "These tell me plenty. You've talked with Francine."

"Why are you doing this?" She looked up but the darkness shadowed his face and she couldn't see his expression. Grateful for that, for knowing he couldn't see hers either, she dropped her voice to a whisper. "Do you hate me that much?"

He lifted her chin with an upward nudge then smoothed her hair back from her face. "I don't hate you, Bess."

The moonlight slanted over his face and,

though the look in his eyes contrasted with his words and an unspeakable sadness tainted his tone, relief fluttered through her. She was rationalizing but weak right now, she needed the crutch. Being held in the warmth of his arms couldn't be good for either of them. They were both vulnerable. And with them, vulnerability equated to danger. The magnetism between them always had been too strong. Yet she didn't move away. "Why, then? Why Silk? Jonathan, I'll look like a fool and so will you."

"Let's talk about it later. Right now, just let me hold you. You're shivering."

And she would be as long as she was in his arms. She hated it that he could still do this to her — but not enough to want him to stop. The storm was nearing; she smelled the rain, and wished she'd closed the window. "I think we've got a classic case of —"

"Please don't start spouting jargon, Bess."

He pleaded for far more than that; though for what exactly, she didn't know. "A classic case of all or nothing," she amended, using laymen's terms. "You don't want me, but you don't want to let me go for fear someone else will want me. You want to just hold on to me." His arms gripped her tighter. "Am I right about this?"

"At the moment, Doc, I am holding you."

He clearly meant to sound flip, and he would have, to anyone but Bess. She heard that telltale tremor in his voice, the husky one that betrayed him. John was not calm, but highly emotional — and hungry.

John? Hungry for her? Hot desire rippled through her body. Memories of other times, of other storms, flooded her, swamping her with vivid recollections of times of tenderness and lovers' secrets shared: situations and feelings best forgotten.

She tried to pull away.

He held her tighter. Let his hand drop to her bare back, graze her cool skin. "You used to sleep naked." His voice went huskier, sexier.

"I've changed." She had, but not in that respect. "Are you going to tell me why you're doing this with Silk? You don't really want visitation rights with her, John."

He skimmed Bess's side. "Maybe I resent you leaving me by phone. Maybe I think I deserved for you to tell me you were leaving me face to face."

She looked up at him, into the underside of his chin. The sliver of moonlight splayed over it and it looked as hard as the granite cliffs beyond the turret room window. She drew back then rested her hands on his rock-hard thighs. "Maybe I resent you staying gone three days without a word. You didn't call — not once, not even on Christmas." Chilled, missing his warm, sure hold and, stupidly, the comfort of it, too, she snuggled back to him. "When you finally did call, all you said was, 'Sorry, darling. I forgot.' " She slapped at his thigh. "That was a rotten thing to do to me."

He rested his chin on her crown. "You knew I was following a lead."

"Kidnapers," she snuggled closer still and curled her knees until they rested against the underside of his firm thighs. "You were following kidnapers who might have murdered Dixie and I thought, maybe you." After putting Bess through that, holding her seemed the least he could do. Oh, but she'd been terrified.

He guffawed. "You never believed she'd been kidnaped, Bess. You sided with the FBI, remember? Convinced she'd eloped."

"I'm not sure I believe she was kidnaped now. But I didn't know it for a fact, Jonathan. And when you don't know for fact, you worry your beliefs are wrong. I worried myself sick over you. Do you know how long three days can be when you're worried someone you — ?" Nearly saying *someone you love,* she stopped cold. A slip of the tongue. A momentary lapse of memory that things were different now. "I was worried sick."

He cupped her face in his big hands. They were strong, good hands, and not quite steady. "I believed she'd been kidnaped. Why couldn't you believe me?"

"Because the evidence was shaky at best. It wasn't anything personal, John."

"Nothing personal? For a wife to not have faith in her husband?"

Genuinely surprised, she grunted. "This didn't have anything to do with faith in you. That's absurd."

"It did from where I stood."

She'd hurt him? She didn't want to answer him. Didn't know how to answer him. "It doesn't matter now."

"It matters to me." His fingertips stroked her jaw, the sides of her nose, her lips. "Why, Bess?"

"I was afraid you were dead." Her voice cracked and a tear slid down her cheek and onto his fingertip. "I was afraid I'd lost you forever, and —." A sob swelled in her throat. She couldn't go on.

"So you left me." He tilted her face into the silvery moonlight.

Praying it wasn't a mistake, she let him see the anguish he'd put in her eyes. "I loved you then, Jonathan."

He swallowed hard. "I loved you then too, Doc."

He was shaking. So was she. Their gazes locked and he leaned toward her. The truth, sadness, and regret tortured his eyes, and that urge to nurture, to heal, struck her hard. It would be so easy. So easy to move those scant inches, to lean to him and to kiss him. To let her body tell and show him all the turmoil she was feeling inside. But she couldn't do it. They were divorcing. They weren't the same people now they'd been then.

And they couldn't go back.

"But that was then, wasn't it?" she asked. "It isn't now. We don't love each other now."

He let his hands slide down her neck, then down her ribs to her waist. "Come here, Bess." The gentle pressure of his urging hands, the smell of the sea and him, so familiar and so long missed, conspired and proved far stronger than her will. "I want to kiss you."

Her heart skipped a pounding beat then nearly careened out of her chest. "That's not a good idea. In fact, it's a lousy idea."

"I know. But I'm going to do it anyway."

Knowing the magic was still there between them physically, she'd be a fool to do it. She'd be forty kinds of fool. All that pain.

That emptiness. That desolation of losing what they'd had. The disillusionment on again realizing they'd had nothing more than a mirage. "Please, don't."

"Tell me you don't want to know what it'd be like, Bess. Tell me that after all this time, you haven't once thought of it or wondered, or dreamed about us being together again."

She couldn't. Her body remembered too well exactly how it'd been between them. But that was physical. It wasn't love or any basis for a strong, enduring marriage. It was lust with a kick. No less, but no more. "No."

He bent low and whispered close to the shell of her ear. "Liar."

"Okay, I've wondered, I've dreamed, I've even fantasized," she confessed. "But I don't want to know enough to find out." The costs were too high.

He laughed, low and husky, his broad chest rumbling. "You never could lie."

She couldn't, not to him. And it only made her look more foolish to try now. Though in the shadowy darkness he likely wouldn't see it, she gave him a solid frown. "You should have gotten slouchy, Jonathan. If you had a single compassionate bone in your body, you'd have become a real pig."

He slid her a wicked smile and dipped his

chin, descending closer to her mouth. "Sorry, darling. My wife has a strong aversion to sloppy men."

"Sorry, indeed." The man was too charming for his own good — and definitely for hers. But the temptation, hearing him again refer to her as his wife; she couldn't resist him any more now than when they'd first met. Even less now because she *knew* what she was missing: the magic.

He touched their lips, his voice a throaty whisper that had her quivering. "I have to feel you again, Bess. Just . . . once."

He looked so good; felt and smelled and sounded so good. "Just once," she swore, unsure if it was a promise to him or to herself. Not caring at the moment which it proved to be, only wanting to again feel all she'd once felt when in his embrace. Safe. Secure. Loved . . .

He rubbed his lips to hers, gently, teasingly, with little pressure, and yet the impact was potent, powerful, stunning. She stiffened, certain she had trodden too far into a place that could bring her pleasure but even more pain. Once his mouth left hers, once his arms no longer cradled her and she could no longer feel his warmth, she'd ache for him. She didn't want to acutely remember those early months of their separation, to have those memories sharpened by rediscovery. She didn't want . . .

Oh, heaven help her, he tasted good too. A little groan of submission vibrated in her throat and she glided her hands up his thighs to his narrow waist, then finally circled them around his back. "Darn you, Jonathan." She tunneled her hands through his thick hair — longer, more luxurious, more tempting — then settled into the kiss.

Heady at her feminine prowess, at the frantic drummer's beats of his heart, she swore that if he let her go, she might just float. They were divorcing, but the magic was definitely still there.

Heaven help them both.

He left her lips, blazed a trail of hot kisses to her jaw, to the soft underside of her chin, to the shell of her ear. "Bess," he whispered, raking her lobe with his teeth.

Awash in a sea of remembered sensations, she couldn't think, just let her head loll back, and let the tide of reawakened passion take her. "Hmmm?"

"It's storming." He kissed his way down the column of her throat to the soft hollow. He buried his nose at her neck, inhaled her scent and nipped at her skin, supping. "The Shell Room has a deck. That's nearly a veranda."

Yes. Oh, yes. She opened her mouth to agree.

Lightning flashed. An angry clap of thunder boomed, shaking the house and, Bess swore, her teeth.

The electricity came back on as abruptly as it had gone out. Light flooded the room. *Every* light turned on — the overhead, the lamps on either side of the bed, the banker's light on the desk — even those that hadn't been on when the power had been interrupted — and the alarm clock's red LCD flashed 12:00 and its alarm shrieked a steady, deafening blast.

What was she doing?

She pulled out of John's embrace, scrambled to her feet, then grabbed her robe. When she'd shoved it on and tightened its belt so hard she could barely breathe — a firm reminder to keep the blooming thing on — she looked at him, sitting there on the floor, one knee on the rug, one bent and on the bare floor, smiling up at her. "Wicked, Jonathan."

The devil danced in his eyes, right alongside desire. "Who?"

"You!" Even hazed with those emotions, the sadness remained. Grieving, Tony had said. She didn't feel brave enough to ask John what he grieved. Whatever it was hurt

213

him so badly that even in her arms he couldn't forget the grief for a moment's time. That was a forceful blow to her ego and a solid reminder that she had caught him but had failed to hold him.

Digging deep, she schooled her emotions, then turned off the alarm. When the room went silent, she let her teeth sink into her lower lip, determined not to stew on this kissing business or to make too much of it. They'd both been curious. No more than that. "This was a bad idea." She looked back over her shoulder at him. "People who are divorcing don't kiss as we did and they certainly don't make love."

His hair mussed from her fingertips, he cocked his head, looking darling, danger-ous . . . and very tempting. "Do they have sex?"

Wicked *and* cute, the rotten grub. Her palms itched to touch him. She stuffed her fists into the pockets of her robe. "Definitely not."

"Oh." He hauled himself to his feet, then stared at her, caressing every curve, every plane of her body, from head to heel. When his gaze returned to hers, desire burned in his eyes, yet the sadness remained. "A shame. We might have been lousy together at times, Bess, but in bed wasn't one of them."

Boy, was he right about that. "I don't suppose that much matters anymore, either." She forced herself to hold his gaze, locked her knees to stay upright, and ordered her feet to stay still. Every acutely honed instinct in her body shouted at her to cross the floor and take him to bed.

"No, I don't guess it does matter anymore." He walked over to the dresser, then dragged a blunt fingertip down the spine of a silver-edged comb on a little oval tray. "Unless . . ."

What was he thinking? She frowned at his broad back. Sinful what the man did to a pair of jeans. And to her blood pressure. "Unless?"

He turned to face her, leaning a hip against the dresser, stretching out his long legs and crossing one foot over the other, his arms over his chest. "Unless you want to compromise."

She walked around the side of the bed to the little bench at its foot then plopped down. Her robe spilled open, exposing a healthy expanse of bare legs. She grabbed the fabric edges and clamped them together. "I know I'm going to regret this, but tell me what's working in that twisted mind of yours."

"I'm not going through with this divorce unless you accept your half of our assets."

She frowned, holding no illusions. He was dead serious. "And, according to Francine, not without half of my dog."

"That's the part that's negotiable."

"Uh-huh." Bess eyed him warily. He looked a little too cocky for her comfort, and she recognized only too well that half-smirk of his for the signal it was. He was about to drop a bomb. Right on her head. "Negotiable. As in . . . ?"

"I'll forget the visitation rights and joint custody of Silk," he said.

"If I do what?"

"Give me two weeks with all of you. No mention of the divorce whatsoever. Just you and me and —"

"Sex."

He shrugged. "I prefer making love, but if you can't bring yourself to it, then, yes, sex will do."

"Good grief. Are you serious?" She stood up. "You're propositioning me?"

"No, I'm not."

She propped her hands on her hips and stared him down.

"Okay, I am, I suppose — if you choose

216

to look at it that way." He thumped a fingertip to his chest. "I didn't choose to, by the way."

"Just how *did* you look at it, Jonathan?" Her teeth ached from holding her jaw so tight.

His eyes gleamed, the look in them heated. "Differently."

"Why do you want to do this?" He couldn't be serious. He couldn't *really* expect her to be a wife to him again for two weeks over a dog. Not that she didn't love Silk, but this was absurd. Ridiculous.

"Why not?"

Evasion. Clear and simple. "I can think of a dozen good reasons right off the bat. The best is that I don't sell myself — not even for Silk."

He narrowed his eyes. "And if you did, you wouldn't sell yourself to me."

"No, I wouldn't." She'd be an idiot to do that knowing he could hurt her. And how unchivalrous of him for pointing that out and adding insult to injury. In less than a minute, he'd taken her from proposition to prostitute. What was left?

He stepped closer. "Nothing of mine. No part of me. Right?"

He was angry. The white slash of his jaw tightened. Didn't he see that any part of him would only have her doing anything for a glimpse of the rest of him? All or nothing. That's how it *had* to be between them. It couldn't be all. They'd tried that and Bess had ranked a sorry second. That left only one option: nothing. "No, John," she said softly, a sad tremor shaking her voice. "No part of you."

An ice-hard look clouded his eyes. "Regrettable." He walked to the door. "I'll take odd weekends with Silk. You and Santos can have even ones." Out in the hallway, John softly closed the door.

Santos? Now why would John think Miguel —

Okay, Bess. Give over.

Bess nearly jumped out of her skin. *Tony, would you stop that? You scared the heck out of me.*

Why did you turn him down?

"Good grief." Avoiding the braided rug culprit that had started all this, she walked to the turret window, propped her knee on the window seat's soft cushion, and stared out into the night. The rain had started. Strong winds gusted through the trees, whistling. It was going to be a bad one. "I thought you'd gone, Tony."

You're avoiding my question. Why did you refuse his offer? I know you want those two weeks as badly as he does.

"I don't."

Tony sighed. *You're doing it again, Doc.*

Lying. Inwardly she sighed. Having a man inside her thoughts was getting to be a royal pain in the posterior. She leaned farther out the window, searched the gloomy sky. "The only thing I'm doing is seeing if there's a full moon tonight."

What?

"There's got to be some reason you men are all talking crazy."

Nice try, but it won't work. I recognize avoidance as well as you do, and I'm not going to let you lie to yourself, or to me.

"I've already admitted the magic's still there." She dragged a hand through her hair. "What more do you want?"

The truth.

Shutting the window, she frowned. She sank down onto the cushion, folded her arms and rested them on the window ledge, then dropped her chin atop her knuckles. Her breath fogged the glass panes. "The truth is I'm going to lose him. And my job. And likely full custody of my dog. I can't risk losing any more." Like she'd told Sal, she'd lost all she intended to lose willingly.

And two weeks with Jonathan will put more at risk?

She grunted. "Two minutes with him puts more at risk." Lord, how she resented that. "I'll just get hurt again. I don't need a refresher course on what he can do to me, Tony. I remember too well."

He needs you. He can't admit it, but he needs you more right now than he ever has needed anyone in his life.

"Lord, you've got an imagination. That man has never needed me. He's wanted me, and, yes, I know he wants me again — for two weeks — but need?" She shook her head. "No, Tony. I needed John, but he's never needed me."

He does, Doc. Why else would he make such an outrageous proposition now? Why not five years ago? Three years ago? Why now?

"You tell me."

I have. I've said it before, but it's worth repeating. You're hearing, but not listening.

She gulped in a big breath of air. The rain pattered on the roof of the porch below her window and the answer came to her. "He's grieving."

Yes! Grieving.

"Do you know why?"

Elise died, Bess.

Her chest went tight. She bit down on her lip. Elise died, and he hadn't told his wife.

"I'm sorry."

Tell him. Don't you understand, Doc? Because he didn't find her daughter for her —

"He feels he failed her." Bess stared at a limb on the nearest fir, her heart aching. "Miss Hattie knows, doesn't she? That's what was behind her treat-each-other-kindly lecture earlier."

Hattie knows, but that isn't what's important.

So John had told Miss Hattie, but not his wife. Second . . . again. But, in an odd way, it made sense. Miss Hattie invited confidences and exuded motherly nurturing. And she wasn't divorcing him. "What is your point, Tony?"

My point is that John needs you. Elise meant a lot to him. He's hurting, Bess.

No one had to tell her how much Elise meant to John. Bess had lived with it. "Of course, he's hurting." And Elise's death, and not their divorce, had put the sadness in his eyes. "She came first with him." Bitterness crept into Bess's voice.

Have you ever asked him why?

"That would be absurd. I'd look like an idiot."

Well, maybe you should risk it, Doc.

Tony, sarcastic? Yet she suffered the shudder that had become all too familiar lately. A significant message had just passed be-

221

tween them. "Maybe I will."

Now would be a good time.

"Man but you're pushy."

If that's what it takes.

She frowned. "Until I do, you're going to nag at me, aren't you?"

I have to say that I resent your nag word, Doc. I don't nag. I merely . . . encourage.

He nagged. "Well, if you're going to *encourage* me until I ask him, I might as well do it now and get it over with. Then will you go away?"

For a time.

She stood then lifted a potpourri-filled seashell from the desk. For some reason, the feel and scent of it soothed her. "I'm really not all that comfortable with this telepathy stuff." She hoped he wouldn't take offense, but likely he would. Seems everyone did these days.

Trust me. You prefer it.

"Prefer it to what?"

No answer.

"Tony?"

Still, no answer.

No sense pushing. He'd just drop his bomb and depart and, before he did, she wanted to know something else. Bess let her teeth sink into her lower lip. "Did Elise suffer?"

Yes, she did. Sadness tinged his tone. *Intensely. John stayed with her, and that helped her a lot but it was . . . difficult for both of them. She died in his arms, Bess.*

And he had been devastated because she had.

Yes. Devastated. Nearly destroyed. And swamped with guilt that wasn't just. His failure haunts him, Doc. He needs comforting and compassion or he might never heal.

"And you want me to give it to him."

You are his wife.

"Until July tenth, yes, I am." Back at the window, the little shell cupped in her hand, she stared at a raccoon traipsing across the lawn. It didn't have enough sense to get out of the storm either. "If I give him those two weeks, when they're over, who's going to heal me?"

When it costs you nothing, it's easy to reach out to someone else and give, but it's when you pay the steepest price, you reap the most precious rewards.

"My reward will be a broken heart." A lump of emotion squared in her throat. She swallowed it down, already envisioning the pain that would come at the end of those two weeks — if she were foolish enough to give them to John.

Or perhaps a healed heart. Who knows?

*Maybe in giving to each other, both of you
can forgive. Think about it, Doc.*

She groaned. "I still haven't solved your
last think-about-it puzzle and you're already
laying another one on me. Just hearing you
say that awful phrase sends cold chills up
and down my spine."

Leap, Doc. Leap.

"No way." My feet are staying firmly on
the ground.

Regrettable.

The temperature in the room dropped a
solid twenty degrees. An icy chill feathered
across her arms and an unusual pressure at
the soft spot under her collarbone had her
feeling light-headed and winded. "Tony,
something's wrong with me."

*I'm sorry, Bess. I'm trying to make a point
without having to just come right out and say
it.*

"You're scaring me."

The pressure ceased. The room warmed.
She blinked and blinked again. One by one,
the lights started going out. First the lamp
on the desk. Then the one to the left of the
bed. And then the little tulip lamp on the
right. "Tony?" Her voice was shaking.
"What's happening here? Do you know?"

Yes, I do.

"Would you explain it to me?" Her heart

rate sped to a canter. Only the overhead light kept the room from being plunged into darkness. And Tony sounded so strange. Sad, but resigned. Why? "It's . . . spooky."

You'll understand soon enough.

Bess sighed. "I'm about sick of people telling me how I'm supposed to feel and react, Tony. In fact, I'm more than sick of it. I've just determined to listen to myself, to do what I think I should do, and here you come along telling me I'll get what you mean soon enough. True, you helped me see the light where my parents were concerned, but stop protecting me. And stop confusing the heck out of me with cryptic messages. If something you have to say is important —"

Oh, it's important, Doc. Vital.

"Then drop the puzzles and spit it out. All this cryptic stuff does is confuse me and make me crazy. If you know that and you persist, then why should I listen to you?"

I'd rather not explain my reasons, but I can solve the mystery.

"Then do it!"

All right. But remember you asked for this.

The overhead light clicked off.

Boo.

CHAPTER 6

The Cove Room was dark.

It didn't matter; John could see its forest green and brown decor, the cherry wood furniture placement, the antique washstand in the far right corner near the three south windows — even the little terracotta trinket box with blueberries and vines on its top that Miss Hattie had put up atop the armoire today. A thank-you gift from Bess, Miss Hattie had told him. One she'd thought John might like in his room.

He hated that darn box.

Bess had bought it. She'd chosen it. And every time he saw it, or even thought of it, he imagined her long, slender fingertips smoothing the berries and touching the leaves, outlining its oval shape then lifting it into her hands, her looking at it, and smiling. And every time he imagined those images, he was sorely reminded that, in the terracotta box, she'd found value. In it, she'd acknowledged worth.

Two gifts she never had awarded him.

And he was sorely reminded that the fault for that was his.

Leaning against the window casing, gazing out through the rain and onto the cove, he glimpsed the village, then let his focus drift to the pond and the gazebo. There were still lights burning over at Beaulah Favish's house. He guessed she was having a restless night, too. Releasing the green drapes, the white sheers behind them, he turned then forked an impatient hand through his hair. Bess. He'd failed her.

The room temperature dropped from chilly to cold. He went back to bed, pulled up the quilts, then stared at the shadows on the cathedral ceiling. He'd failed Bess and Elise. The two most important people in his life. When growing up, Selena and Max had been a team; John the outsider. It'd had to be that way. With parental ties to a cult, what kid could hold on to innocence? He'd no choice but to back away from Selena, to keep the secret. At least in him doing so, she could hold on to innocence. Then had come Bess, and then Elise. Elise was gone now and, no matter what his heart wanted him to do, he couldn't crawl back to Bess a failure.

It wasn't a question of his pride, but a matter of hers. When he'd wanted to risk going solo and open Mystic Investigations, she'd been supportive. When the crème de la crème of New Orleans wouldn't let him into their ranks, she had steadfastly insisted that he'd find his way. He had. Thanks to Elise. And it was then that Bess's support had ceased. She'd accused him of becoming obsessed with finding Dixie. In truth, he probably had been. With Elise's social standing — none ranked higher, and only Millicent Fairgate came in at a close second — solving the case would have set him up for life. It hadn't been the money. It'd never been the money. It had been, and was, a sense of worth. Bess never had understood that. And the more doubts she'd expressed in his judgment, the more determined he'd become to proving her wrong.

The oak outside his bedroom window cast shadows on the sloped ceiling. He stared at them. No, he couldn't go back to her, or ask her to come back to him permanently. Not now. Though his inquiries in Portland, where he'd originally lost Dixie's trail, looked more promising now than ever before, he still hadn't found Dixie. And he couldn't stand to have Bess look at him and for the pride she'd once felt in being his wife to be absent from her eyes.

He rolled over and jerked at the quilt, stared forlornly at the boxes of case files stacked near the desk and along the wall. Even if he found Dixie now, it would still be too late for him and Bess. She'd had no faith in him. He'd have to be a chump to want a woman who'd had no faith in him.

His blasted pillow had lumps. He gave it a punch with the heel of his hand. Man, he hated lumps. In his pillow, and in his pride.

He didn't want just sex with Bess, though honesty forced him to admit that he did want sex with her. What man in his right mind wouldn't?

Grunting, he smiled up at the dancing ceiling shadows. That wasn't likely to happen soon, however. She'd really been ticked about Silk — a solid eight on the scale — and even more so about his proposition. Definitely a ten, that. He'd talk her around, though — eventually. She wouldn't do it for him, of course, and he wasn't going to fall into that chump game of pretending she was. She'd do it for her dog — or so she'd tell him. Bess held tightly to her pride. And knowing that, he'd given her what she'd needed to accept him back into her life: a valid reason that wouldn't wound her feminine spirit.

Pretty clever that it would also give him the ammunition to encourage her into a property settlement palatable to him. Her depending on another man financially was out of the question. They couldn't have forever, but they could have two weeks. He'd use them wisely. He'd forget anything and everything but Bess. And he'd store enough memories of them together during those weeks to last him the rest of his life.

Unless she stuck to her raised-hackles position and kept turning him and his proposal down flat. Proposal. What a laugh.

And if she did that — continued to refuse — what would he do? What could he do to further entice her?

His nose pressed to the clean pillowslip that smelled of sunshine and the sea, he mulled the matter over. He'd have no choice but to get more creative and, if necessary to save her from herself, downright nasty. He wouldn't like it, but he'd do it. And he'd stop his conscience's traitorous thoughts about wanting her to really want him. If she did — and her kiss earlier tonight indicated that she did — then, great. But if not, then he'd be content without her wanting him. To get through a life without her, he needed those two weeks.

Desolate, he turned over and stared at the

little crystal clock beside the bed. Served him right for falling in love with a woman content to be self-contained. Well, she might not need him, but she sure wanted him. Though it warred hard on his male ego, he found solace in that.

The little clock's ticks grew loud, then louder, drowning out the patter of the rain against the window and the creaking floorboards from across the hall, where Bess paced in the Great White Room, agitated as all get out. She hated storms.

Some men rushed home when the icemaker broke. When the car got a flat. When a sock got stuck in the washer's drain hose, and the laundry room flooded. Not John. Bess had handled all those things alone. He'd rushed home when it'd stormed.

"What I'd give for a sign that she doesn't hate me." Passion and desire were important, but not all-important.

She wears your ring.

John sat straight up, searched the shadows for the speaker. As a courtesy to his logic, which insisted this wasn't happening, that he wasn't hearing another man's voice again inside his own head, he clicked on the lamp. The room was empty.

Logic accepted the inevitable and John frowned, then turned the light back off, not much caring for the feeling of his flesh crawling. "Who are you?"

A friend.

He wasn't an enemy; he'd tried to help John.

Either you're very clever or I'm slipping.

"Excuse me?"

It usually takes a lot longer for men to realize I'm not their consciences talking to them. It's more challenging with women, of course. In the early days, I'd try to disguise my voice, but that was hideous, not to mention ineffective.

The man — whatever he was — was rambling. Ah, John figured out the reason. To give John time to adjust. "I already knew you weren't my conscience. But I also knew you were trying to help me."

Terrific. It's amazing how many people flip out on recognizing the truth.

The man wasn't going to tell John his name so he saved his breath and asked another question. "Are you an angel?"

He laughed. Deep and lusty.

"I take it that's a 'no.' "

It is.

"Then how are you doing this?"

Getting into your head, you mean?

John shuddered at that description. "Yeah."

It doesn't matter. What does matter is that you asked for a sign that Bess doesn't hate you and you've been given one.

"I have?" John frowned at the darkness. When? What had he missed?

Didn't you hear me tell you that she still wears your ring?

"That didn't sound like you."

I was a little, er, emotional. It was me.

"Bess still wears her wedding band?" Surprise raised John's voice an octave. Why hadn't he noticed that?

You were a little busy noticing . . . other things . . . about her.

John frowned. "Watch it."

The man chuckled. *Still jealous, I see.*

"Protective. Until July tenth, she's my wife."

You've nothing to fear from me.

"Why is she still wearing her wedding band?"

The lingering traces of teasing and laughter left the man's voice. Reverence replaced it. *She made you a promise. On your wedding day. Remember?*

John did. She'd promised never to take her wedding band off.

A goofy grin tugged at the corner of his mouth. Odds of him getting his two weeks without a lot of grief were looking pretty good.

He'd been given a sign.

And you're missing the point of it.

"What is your name?" He recognized the man's voice. Who it belonged to, exactly, still eluded John, but he'd figure it out sooner or later. The tone sounded distinctive. He'd heard it before — somewhere.

Does it matter?

"Yeah, it does." Did it? He wasn't sure, but he wasn't in the mood to be accommodating. "I'd like to know who I'm telling to get out of my head."

The man laughed. *You don't lack for courage, I have to give you that. It'll come in handy in dealing with the doc. The woman does have her moods.*

Courage? No, it wasn't courage, but simple deduction. If the man meant to do any kind of harm or was capable of harm, he'd had more than ample opportunity already. He was trying to help. Weird as this was, it wasn't frightening; only frustrating because John knew the man's identity. He'd just forgotten from where. But his remarks about Bess rankled, and he meant to let the man know it. John cooled his voice. "Of course, Bess has her moods. Don't we all?"

Sure we do. Relax, Jonathan. I wasn't find-

ing fault with your wife. I meant it as a compliment.

"Didn't sound like one from here."

Everyone knows moody women love most passionately. Everything they feel — good, bad, or indifferent — they take into their hearts. They're lusty on life.

John laughed. "Bryce sure could have used you on that PMS case he tried a couple months ago."

Bryce?

"My divorce lawyer."

Ah, yes. Bryce Richards, Meriam's husband.

"Used to be. Meriam is dead now."

I know. The man sighed. *How are their children?*

"Suzie, the oldest, is having wicked nightmares." John couldn't believe this. He was sitting in bed, stark naked, having a conversation with a man he couldn't see, could only hear in his thoughts, who knew not only his every desire and dark thought, but knew Bryce and Meriam, and that they had kids. Who knew —

A shiver raced through his back and hopscotched up his spine. "You're Tony."

I am?

"Yes. The Tony who called Bess. That's where I heard your voice — on the radio."

I gave you the creeps.

235

"You did." John lay back on his pillow. "How are you doing this? Are you talking with Bess like this, too?"

It's a gift. And, yes, Bess and I have chatted quite a bit lately.

From his tone, he wasn't pleased with the results. "Are you psychic?"

Not exactly.

Hedging. Big-time hedging. "What exactly are you?"

Bess says I'm telepathic. I say, at the moment, I'm late for an appointment. I'll see you again soon.

Bess says. But was Bess right, or wrong? That, Tony hadn't said. "Question is, will I see you?"

Maybe one day.

"Wait! You packed Bess's bags, didn't you?"

Yes, I did. She'd made her mind up to leave and had to learn for herself that she really didn't want to go.

He'd done something to her car, too. Otherwise the finish wouldn't have gone from shiny to dull and it would have cranked. Bess had to keep that car in excellent running condition. She kept everything in her life tidy and neat and orderly. But there was no way a telepath could mess with a car's finish. Was there?

We'll address the car another time.

That suited John. His gut instinct warned him that small doses of this strange and weird business would be easier to digest. "Tony, do you think she'll come around?"

On the settlement? Or on you loving her enough in two weeks to make her want two more?

Until Tony had said it, John hadn't fully realized his motives himself. But he couldn't deny that maybe a small part of him — the chump part — wanted two more weeks, and another two and, after that, still another two. But it was too late. "There can't be two more. Not until I solve this case for Elise, for sure, and it's doubtful then."

I'm sorry for your loss, Jonathan. Elise was a good woman.

"Did you know her, too?" John tried and failed to keep his surprise from his voice.

I know you loved her. That alone tells me she was special.

John had loved her. And he'd never, not once, told her. But Tony really hadn't answered his question. And he wouldn't — even if asked directly. "Yes, she was special," John said, feeling the blinding pain of loss, the empty ache that hurt so deeply he couldn't identify where in his body it started or stopped.

Biological or not, mothers are special.

"Yeah." John frowned. "Yeah, mothers are special."

So are wives.

He didn't want to talk about Bess. Talking about Elise had reopened the wound of losing her, and he was losing Bess too. "How did you know about my mother?" And how did Miss Hattie know about Elise? Wait . . . of course, Tony had known Elise. He'd been with John in the hospital. Told him to let Elise go, to give her peace.

Yes, I was there.

"I thought you were my conscience then."

I know.

"You helped me a lot. Thanks."

My pleasure.

"Are you talking with Miss Hattie too?"

Don't I wish? Tony's voice shook with longing. *But, no, I don't exactly talk to Hattie. I . . . can't.*

"Tony?" Very confused by the emotion trembling in Tony's voice, John prodded for a more specific answer.

I know many people, Jonathan. Most, from the heart out. I can arrange a lot of things. Even a three-way conversation where no one has to speak aloud. All manner of things. But I have to weigh the total effects of any action I take. I have to consider the emotional impact along with everything else. Sometimes, I confess, that's a crapshoot.

"Big responsibility."

It is. But the learning involved is worth it. And unless I miss my guess, you're going to be learning a lot of new things about your wife. Things you never dreamed you'd learn. Things she's only discovering for herself.

"What kind of things?"

I can't say.

Elise and her flower came to mind. "Do you know anything about the flower petal I found in Elise's hand?"

She needed a little guidance to find her way . . . home.

Home? What did that mean? "I don't under—"

Nor do you need to. I would like to say something, though I'm not sure you're ready to hear it. Sometimes the costs of keeping secrets — regardless of how noble the intentions are behind it — are just too steep, Jonathan.

A streak of sheer fear shot up John's spine. "You know about my parents?"

Yes, I do. I understand your reasons for keeping silent, and I'll never betray your confidence. You've my word on that. But I wish you'd think about all you've lost because of this secret already. Maybe it's time to reconsider the value of keeping it to yourself.

His bedroom door swung open. "Jonathan?"

Bess. In a panic. He stretched and clicked on the bedside lamp. "What's wrong?"

Her robe hanging low on her shoulder, her eyes wild, she hurried across the room. Banging her hip against the tall stack of boxes near the desk didn't even slow her down. She grabbed her side and rushed on, stopping beside the bed.

"I know this is going to sound crazy, but I'm telling you it's the truth."

Nails tapping on the floor, Silk came in and settled down on the rug. She seemed calm, but his wife certainly wasn't. Bess was highly agitated, shifting her weight from foot to foot, wringing her hands. In all their married life, she'd never, not once, wrung her hands. "What's the truth?"

She started to say something, but changed her mind and turned pleading eyes on him. "I can't talk about it yet." She stepped closer, bumping her knees against the mattress. "Can I sleep with you tonight?"

Surprise streaked up his spine. *It's just a piece of paper and doesn't change a thing.* Six years. Six years, and she simply says, *Can I sleep with you tonight?* Did she mean sleep or *sleep?* Her *Ritz* perfume settled over him, and again he remembered that moment in her room where her robe had fallen open and he'd gazed upon those long, lovely legs of hers that went on forever. His throat went tight, his body hard. "Sure." He lifted the quilts.

She crawled onto the bed, over him with a none-too-gentle knee to his stomach, and then finally settled her head onto the pillow beside him. His heart chugged. Was she scared? Ticked? What? Tangled up inside, he couldn't sort out his own emotions much less hers. He'd get her calmed down first, and then at least he'd stand a chance of finding out what was going on here. "The pillows have more lumps than my mashed potatoes."

"This one certainly does." She squashed and fluffed it then lay back down. "You were a lousy cook."

"Hey, at least I didn't set off every smoke alarm in a two-mile radius." *Ritz.* She'd come to him robed in slinky silk and *Ritz.*

"Beat starving, too." She scrunched down, buried herself to her chin under the quilt.

"Your culinary skills weren't the greatest, either. Though you did burn a mean piece of toast."

"I'm a great cook." She slid him a wicked grin. "I burned everything on purpose."

He guffawed. "You burned everything because you can't cook."

"Nonsense. I said, I'm an excellent cook."

"Ha. Remember, darling, this is me you're talking to, not your sorry Spaniard. I shared your bed *and* your kitchen for over a year. You can't cook."

Seeing that she'd calmed down immensely, he turned off the light. As it went out, John saw her sinful smile — and the truth. "You tricked me, didn't you? You burned everything so you wouldn't have to cook."

"I never tricked you or lied."

"You definitely did." He'd been had.

"Jonathan, each and every meal I burned, I swore I was a good cook."

She had told him that — every time. And he'd fallen for it — every time. "You're good, Bess. Really good."

"I hate cooking."

He couldn't see her face in the darkness but whatever had sent her running in here still had her as tense as strung wire. She wasn't ready to talk about it yet and, if he knew nothing else about Doc, he knew she wouldn't utter a word until she was good and ready. "Why didn't you just tell me you didn't like to cook?"

"What if I had and then you'd said you

didn't like it either?"

He frowned at her. "Well, I guess we'd have done something drastic like toss a coin, rotate nights, or maybe even hire a cook. Pretty grim scenarios." He sighed. "Yeah, with stakes like those, I can see why you chose to deceive me."

"I didn't deceive you. I told you straight out I could cook."

She had a point.

She wears your ring . . . chump.

Watch it, Tony — and take a hike. This is private.

I happen to agree — on both counts.

Both?

This is private and, right now, she is one moody woman.

She's upset, not moody. Do you know why?

Yes.

Well, aren't you going to tell me?

I am. I'm going to tell you good night. He made a production of clearing his throat. *Good night, Jonathan.*

Tony had gone; John could feel it. And, for some reason — likely the fault of the woman beside him — the room had suddenly grown a lot warmer. "Bess?"

She wasn't touching him, but he felt her body heat all along his side. Maybe she wanted to make love. Her needing him physically beat her not needing him at all. "Is this your way of telling me you've accepted my proposal?"

"Fat chance."

He'd figured, but he'd still had to ask. "Are you wanting to make love, then?"

"Frankly, yes . . . but I'm not going to."

That she'd admit it, even as she denied them both, surprised him. He'd been right, thinking protection and not desire had brought her to him. But protection from what? She sounded cool and controlled, but she wasn't. He admired her discipline, but just once — just once — he wanted her to abandon it. With him.

"John," she whispered. "I wouldn't mind just a hug, though. I'm chilled to the bone."

Just a hug? *Just a hug?* Could he give her *just a hug* and stop there?

Six years, he'd ached for her. Contemplated a million reasons why she'd left him. Hurt for her, and hungered like a starving man for her to need him for anything. And now, inside of three weeks of divorcing him, she admits she needs him — if only to hold her for a minute. Naturally, she waits until he's vulnerable. Naturally, she waits until she's in his bed and nothing but that filmy excuse of a silk robe separates her skin from his. And, naturally, she levels him with that soft and husky I-trust-you-Jonathan voice that set him on fire. How could she trust him to demand no more than a hug when he couldn't trust himself? He'd try — he really would — but with all these memories crashing through his mind . . . Them together, Bess whispering lovers' secrets in his ears. Could he do it? He was only human.

But she trusted him.

Trust.

And for the first time ever, she'd admitted that she needed him. She . . . *needed* him.

His throat tight, he prayed he wouldn't let her down.

From the creaking floorboards, she'd paced a hundred miles in her room before coming to him, claiming herself cold. It was warm in here, quickly growing hot. She wasn't frigid, she was frightened, but he'd give her the lie — and the hug. And no more. Not even if it killed him.

Never would she regret needing him and telling him she did. He reached for her.

Grunting, she shifted farther onto her side of the bed, away from him. She'd clearly changed her mind. Disappointment so sharp he swore it cut through his soul stabbed him.

It's only a piece of paper . . .

Chump.

His chest went tight and, though he was furious with her for taunting him, he still ached to hold her. He lay on his hand, trapping it under his hip, to keep from pulling her into his embrace. It'd been such a long, long time. And he might never again have the chance to hold her. Might never again feel the sweet agony of her needing him.

"What are those boxes? I'll have a bruise on my hip the size of Maine."

"Case files." The moment had passed. He hadn't responded quickly enough. She'd pulled out her armor and hidden back behind it.

"Dixie Dupree's files?"

"Yes." Here it came. More censure. The desire swelling in his heart fell like a rock off a cliff. Resentment replaced it.

"So you're up here following a lead."

"I'm here to settle the property dispute."

"But there's a chance of a lead too."

Was she pleased or upset? "Possibly. Hopefully. A man in Portland might have some information. He's checking it out."

"I see."

"Don't say that, Bess." He tunneled his fingers through his hair. Maybe he should just tell her he needed the hug. What would she say? Do? "I hate it when you say that."

"Why?"

Likely she'd laugh at him, or sear his ears with some scathing remark. She certainly wouldn't respect his honesty. Needs were weaknesses to Bess. In herself, and in her husband. "Because too often you don't see and it really sets me off that you say you do."

"Oh." She sighed. "I hope your lead pans out."

She didn't. But saying she did was proper and right. Vintage Bess. Push all the right buttons. Even if nothing's hooked up to them. He played her game. "Thank you."

She rolled over onto her side, facing him, and lowered her voice. "I have to tell you something. I should have told you before, but the time just hasn't seemed quite right. No, that's not true. I didn't want to talk about it, but now I do."

He waited. She'd get around to it, as she did everything else: in her own sweet time. His heart rate sped up a notch. Was she finally going to tell him why she'd left him?

"I'm sorry about Elise." Bess's voice went ragged. "I can imagine what you think of me, not showing up at her funeral, but I didn't know she'd died until . . . recently. Long after the funeral." Bess swallowed hard, saying things in the dark she'd never have said to him in the light of day. "If I'd known, I'd have been there, Jonathan. You know I would have."

"Would you?" He hated the hope in his voice as much as he'd hated her for not coming to the funeral. That she'd brought up Elise stunned him. And it made him wary.

"Of course."

The woman was lying through her teeth. "You hated Elise."

"I didn't. I envied her."

That took a moment to digest. A lot of people probably did envy Elise, especially those who only saw the image of her: wealthy, powerful, answerable only to herself. But he'd seen the real woman. The widow who continued year after year to grieve the loss of her husband, Clayton. The mother who didn't know if her daughter was dead or alive and feared with every breath *that* moment was *the* moment Dixie was being tortured, raped, or murdered. The woman who'd taken him under her wing and had called him *dear heart:* rich words to his motherless ears that had helped soothe the pain of empty years of longing to be considered dear to anyone.

"I really am sorry. I know you loved Elise and she loved you."

"She didn't," he said. "She never said she did."

"She loved you, John. Trust me on this. Elise Dupree loved you with all her heart."

A tear slid down his cheek and his voice went gruff. "I felt as if she did. But just once . . ."

"You wanted to hear the words."

He squeezed his eyes shut. "Yes."

Bess patted his upper arm, then lay back down on her pillow. "Did you ever tell her you loved her?"

"No." And, man, but did he regret that now. "I thought she'd — It doesn't matter anymore. She's gone."

They fell quiet, then a long moment later, Bess turned back toward him, onto her side. "John?"

Her perfume settled over him like a soothing blanket. *Ritz.* Nothing else in this world ever smelled so good. "Hmmm?"

"You can still tell her."

Face to face with Bess in the darkness, he saw only her shadowy outline. "She's dead, honey. How can I —"

"By pretending that I'm her."

"It's not the same."

"No, but it will give you a sense of closure. You need that." Bess cupped his chin. "Please, do it. Say to me whatever you wish you had said to her."

Foolish, but this seemed really important to Bess. Maybe the idea of helping him appealed to her — though, after his stunt with Silk, he couldn't imagine why she'd want to do anything but wring his neck. And yet the night Tony had called the station, he'd mentioned her using her skills to help others, and her needing to now use them to help herself. Maybe in doing this for John, she would be helping herself. Maybe she too needed to feel needed. And maybe before, John had failed to let her know she had been.

A *second chance. Don't blow it.*

A memory. Not Tony. John swallowed hard. "All right."

He closed his eyes, thought back to the night Elise had died. Remembering it now just as it had happened then, with him walking into the hospital weak-kneed, knowing he'd failed her, and not wanting to watch her die . . .

"I knew you'd come, John Mystic."

He stood beside Elise's hospital bed. It was dark outside, but the dim glow of the fluorescent light above her bed glared on the window pane and her ruby amulet flickered in it. Swaddled in white linen, she looked so pale and wan, so little. He had a hard time reconciling the vibrant woman of a few months ago and this small, frail-looking woman with sunken, frightened eyes. "Where else would I be?"

She managed a semblance of a smile. "Sit down, dear heart. I need to say some things and there isn't much time."

A nurse he hadn't seen before came into the room and checked Elise's blood pressure. When she was done, she frowned down at Elise. "Oh, my. Someone missed this." She reached for the clasp on Elise's amulet.

"No." Fumbling, Elise reached up and palmed the necklace.

John sat up straighter. "Leave it alone."

The startled nurse looked at him. "But a patient wearing jewelry here is not advisable."

Because he knew the importance of the amulet to Elise and the nurse didn't, he softened his voice. "Leave it." On the day Elise's only child, Dixie, had been born, Elise's beloved husband, Clayton, had given mother and daughter matching amulets. He'd died a long time ago, and Dixie had been missing for nearly seven long years. "She's more comfortable with it on."

"All right, Mr. Mystic. But the hospital can't accept responsibility."

Responsibility. Didn't anyone care about

comfort and meaning and compassion anymore? Did everything have to be judged, ruled, and settled based on finances? "No problem," he said more sharply than he intended.

The nurse's expression sobered. Wordlessly, she tucked the blood-pressure cuff under her arm, then left the private room. Her shoes squeaked down the hallway, then faded into silence.

"John?"

He scooted nearer to the bed, then clasped Elise's hand in his. "I'm right here."

"It's getting close," she whispered, her lips dry and cracked, her eyelids drooping. "I feel my body shutting down."

His heart wrenched and a wall of regret and guilt and grief slammed through his chest. He dammed it deep inside. "Shh, save your strength."

"I have to tell you —"

"It can wait until you're stronger." She couldn't die on him, too. Not now. *Please, not now. Not yet!*

"You have to face it, dear heart. I'm not going to get stronger."

"Don't say that." She had to get stronger. *Had* to.

"John, I'm dying. We both know it. Please, let me say what I have to say."

He dipped his chin and stared at the white sheet draping over her thin chest. His eyes burned like fire. It was wrong, but he had to do it. Had to give her what peace he could. "You've got to get stronger." He forced his gaze to meet hers. It was one of the hardest things he'd ever done in his life. "I reached that lead at Dockside — the bar in Portland."

"Keith?"

Heat gushed up John's neck, flooded his face. "Yes." He blinked, unable to hold her gaze. "We've found Dixie and . . . and she's coming home." Heaven forgive him, what was he doing? Lying to her? Lying to Elise?

"Wonderful. I never doubted you'd find her. From the moment I hired you, I knew you'd never give up." She winced and dragged in a deep breath. "That's why I made you executor of my will. Everything is in trust for Dixie under your care. When you find — When she gets here, you tell her I love her. Tell her I never gave up hope, and neither did you."

A knot of tears clogged his throat. Elise knew he'd lied. Even in this token attempt at offering her comfort and peace, he'd failed.

"Promise me." Her eyes misted.

"You know I'll take care of Dixie." He

gently squeezed Elise's cool fingers. "You know I will."

"I do know, dear heart." Her breathing grew more shallow, as ragged as if she had to fight for each puff of air. "I want another promise from you."

Her grip was weakening. He was losing her. His throat went tight. "Anything."

"Go on with your life."

"Elise, don't." Oh, this hurt so bad. Why did losing someone have to hurt so bad?

"Promise me." She brought her free hand to her amulet and breathed deeply. "Your devotion to me cost you your marriage. I know it did. You needed a mother's love and, not knowing what happened to Dixie . . ." Elise swallowed a sob then looked at him, regret shining in her damp eyes. "I needed a child's love just as badly, John. But I was selfish. I thought after you found Dixie, then you could go back . . ." Regret, self-directed anger, flooded her voice. "I was a foolish old woman, insisting you neglect your wife to find my daughter. I'm sorry. I want your promise that you'll set matters right with Bess."

"*I* chose. *I* wanted to find Dixie. You didn't break up my marriage, Elise. I did that all by myself. Not intentionally, but I did it."

"Bless you for trying to spare me, but I

know the truth." Pain twisted her expression and her voice cracked. "I just — I can't bear to die knowing you love her and it's my fault you're apart. Once I'm gone, you'll be alone."

Tears in the old woman's eyes fell to her soft, wrinkled cheeks. "I can't bear —"

His heart ached as if it were ripping right out of his chest. Unable to hold her gaze, he lowered his to her amulet. "I promise," he whispered the words she needed to hear, knowing full well he wouldn't live up to them. "I'll do whatever it takes to make things right with Bess." At that moment, to give Elise peace, he'd have told her anything, agreed to do anything.

"You swear?"

He blinked, then blinked again, his heart boulder-heavy at telling another lie. "Yeah, I swear."

Her voice weakened to a reflection of sound. "On your mother's grave?"

Oh no. *Oh no.* Pain seared through him. He couldn't lie. He couldn't — and Elise knew it. He'd have to follow through on this. There was so much he wanted to say. So much, and yet the words wouldn't come. If the dam broke, and he let the emotions walled behind it out, he'd never recover. She'd be comforting him instead of him comforting her. He couldn't do it. But he could try with Bess. For Elise. He *could* try. "I swear."

"Good. Good." She swallowed hard, and groaned. "It hurts, John. Dying with dignity is so hard. I've lain here and regretted things I haven't thought of in years." She rubbed a fingertip over his thumb. "Remember the day I hired you to find Dixie?"

He nodded. "I remember." He'd been elated. Finally, his break had come. His chance to prove himself. "I'm so sorry she isn't here with you now."

Elise stiffened. "You won't give up. I knew it then, and I know it now. You'll find my —" She gasped, reached up to touch his face, her blue-veined hand trembling.

A knot of raw terror slid up his throat, slammed against his ribs. "Elise?"

He palmed her fragile fingers against his jaw, his heart thumping like a jackhammer, threatening to burst through the wall of his chest. "Elise?"

"It . . . hurts."

She's lingering for you. A man's voice sounded inside John's mind. *Tell her it's all right to go. Tell her you'll be okay.*

I won't be okay. I'll be alone!

Tell her, John. Give her peace.

Peace. Oh God, peace. His conscience was

256

right. She deserved peace — and so much more. Tears slid down his face, wetting their entwined fingertips on his jaw. *Please! Give me the strength to let her go. Help me!*

He dug deep, pulled up courage and gentled his voice, praying it'd be steady. "It's okay, Elise." Nothing should bring a person this kind of pain. Nothing! "I'll be all right."

He'd never be all right again. Never. He had no one left to lose. "You can . . ." *Could he do this?*

You can, John. Help her. You can.

He let his gaze lovingly embrace her, taking each line, each impression of her face into his heart and memory, knowing that too soon his memories would be all he had left of her. He'd miss her so much.

For heaven's sake, John. She's suffering. Help her!

Crumbling inside, cursing the cancer killing her, he swallowed a hard lump from his throat. "Let go now, Elise. It's . . . all right." He blinked hard and fast. "I — I don't want you to hurt anymore."

Relief shone in her eyes. "I . . . lo . . ." Her hand fell slack.

And in her open palm lay a single flower petal from a yellow carnation.

He clasped their hands, palm to palm, crushing the flower between them. The dam inside him burst and the things he wanted to say spilled out on a rush of breath. "Oh, Elise. I'm so sorry I failed you. I'm so sorry I never told you that I love you. I'm so sorry —"

She stared at him through sightless eyes. She couldn't hear him anymore. Hadn't heard him tell her he loved her.

She was gone.

Internally, his guttural moan of mourning grew to a tortured keening. Raw and wounded, he clenched her frail fingers tightly, leaned his forehead against her still breast, and cried.

The funeral had been held on Wednesday.

Not that it would have mattered to Elise, but all the New Orleans elite attended. It was the first time John saw some of the self-indulgent of the bunch sober, much less solemn. Their reverence, like their affection for her, pleased him. He'd been adamant that only those wishing to pay sincere last respects to Elise Dupree would be welcome in St. John's Church or at the cemetery for the graveside service. Everyone cooperated, with the exception of Millicent Fairgate, who mourned a little too enthusiastically to be genuine. John had expected she would. The woman was a vulture and, now that

Elise was gone, Millicent would reign as society's new matriarch. But she would never, never, hold a candle to Elise.

Elise had assumed the crème de la crème embraced her because of her powerful connections, but the truth was the woman had been respected and loved. Knowing it would have stunned her, and that gentle, unassuming quality had been but one of many which had drawn him and others to her. Everyone had come to support John — except Bess. He'd hated her for not coming, never dreaming she hadn't known about the funeral. But she was here now. Giving him now the support he'd needed then — and more.

She didn't prod him. Instinctively, she seemed to know he had to relive this to collect his thoughts. To make sure that this time he said all he wished he'd have said then. He thought he might just love her for that.

Ready, John raised up onto a bent elbow and looked down at her face. "I loved you, Elise. I don't know why I was afraid to tell you that. Maybe I thought you'd stop caring about me. I never told you a lot of things I meant to tell you."

"What things?"

"How much I admired you, for one. No

matter how many times the FBI insisted Dixie had left, you had faith in your daughter, and you stuck with the search. You never stopped believing in her. You were a good mother, Elise. The best."

"What else?"

Bess didn't sound like Bess. Her voice had deepened to a rough rasp. Was she crying? "I should have thanked you for not giving up on me. You never did. Not even when you were facing death without your daughter. I'm so sorry I didn't find her in time to be there with you then. I'll always regret that."

"Anything else?"

Not a trace of bitterness lingered in Bess's voice. What had changed? "I'll miss you." He pressed a kiss to Bess's forehead, his voice as gritty as sandpaper, his heart doubly raw. "I'll never forget you, and I'll miss you until the day I die."

Bess pulled herself up and wrapped her arms around him. "I'll miss you, too."

Whether she was speaking for herself or for Elise, John didn't know. He didn't want to know; the words were precious to him either way, and would be for a long time to come.

He held her for a long moment, letting the hurtful hold on his heart ease. When

Bess drew back, he forced himself to let her go: a hard, hard thing to do.

She lay back against her pillow and adjusted the covers. "Do you feel better?"

"Yeah." She'd said it for Elise. To comfort him. And Bess *had* comforted him. Yet a tiny part of him suffered a sharp stab of disappointment that she wouldn't be the one missing him.

He lay back down. Playing this role game had to have been hard for her. She'd openly admitted she'd envied Elise. And yet Bess had done it. For him. Just for him. "Thanks, Bess."

She didn't answer; he guessed she'd fallen asleep. The minutes stretched out and his lids grew droopy, though with her in his bed, smelling of *Ritz* and wearing only that flimsy robe that taunted him with all he was missing, how in the world he was supposed to sleep, he hadn't a clue.

A good half-hour later, she whispered, "Jonathan?"

An adrenaline rush surged through his veins. "Hmmm?"

"Are you all right?"

She meant about Elise. "I'm fine, Bess." Fine? He was losing his mind. Awash in memories of kissing her, holding her, being held by her.

"Good." She turned from her back onto her side.

Three minutes ticked by, then ten. He tried to be patient, knowing she'd get to the heart of whatever was preying on her mind in her own time. Working through it at their current rate of progress, she'd spill it out along about dawn.

"Jonathan?" Her whisper sounded even softer, as if maybe she hoped he'd be asleep and didn't want to risk waking him.

Another adrenaline kick. "Hmmm?"

"Since you're okay now, can I have my hug?" She drew in a sharp breath. "I'm — I'm not . . . okay."

Too emotional to speak, he opened his arms, but, he swore, not his heart.

CHAPTER 7

Bess breathed against John's neck. "I don't love you anymore."

"Of course not."

She quirked a brow at him. "Are you mocking me?"

"No. I'm a logical man, Bess." He curled his arm around her shoulder and drew her closer to his chest. The sheet bunched between them. "I know your feelings have changed. We've changed. How could our feelings be the same?"

They had changed. Though she was scared stiff, being in John's bed and feeling his strong arms around her, well, it helped to keep the demons away. Right now, with it storming outside, she couldn't think about Tony or his *boo*. She didn't dare to think about it or she'd fall apart.

John let out a little sigh.

Irked that she lay in his arms nearly tattered and he could sound so content, she didn't fight feeling grumpy. Let him hear it, by gum. "I don't want you, either."

"Of course not."

She couldn't tell for sure but she had a sneaking suspicion the foul man smiled. He clearly knew she wanted him every bit as much as he wanted her. And because he was under the misconception that she was in love with Miguel, she didn't know whether to be insulted or comforted by that. A flighty female in love with one man, lusting after another, or a fool in lust with the man she was divorcing. Pretty sorry choices. And darn tragic. At least John wasn't calling her a liar to her face.

But he knew she'd lied.

And he knew that she knew he knew she'd lied.

Well, shoot. Either way, she looked like a fool. She frowned down at his chest. Her heart raced like a rabbit's, but his rose and fell in smooth and even rhythms. That unfairness irritated her, and she deepened her frown. "I don't love you, I don't want you, I'm not backing down on the settlement or accepting your proposition, and I'm leaving here just as soon as Jimmy gets my car fixed."

"I know, I know, you'll back down or stay married to me, and I expected you would leave." He sighed. "And it's a proposal, not a proposition."

What the heck was the difference? The end result was the same. And why didn't he sound bothered by her refusal? If he was sure-bent on this proposal — proposition is what it was, and at least one of them should call a spade a spade — why did he sound so calm about her leaving him? Actually, the man sounded bored, which didn't do her disposition a bit of good. "Well, you were right. I will leave. Just as soon —"

"As Jimmy fixes your car." John inhaled deeply and rubbed her arm, shoulder to elbow. "I heard you, Bess."

Bored and indifferent; the manners of a pig. "Right."

He turned, pinning her to the bed. Hovering over her, he whispered against her mouth. "Liar."

"I'm not lying, Jonathan," she insisted, knowing darn well she was lying through her teeth. If she went home now, she'd next see John across a courtroom, be tossed in jail for nonpayment of the fine. She had to stay out of Louisiana until she figured out a way around Judge Branson's order. Francine wasn't going to be a bit of help. And John's kind of help was worse than offensive. What kind of man propositioned his wife, for goodness sake? And what was she going to do to get out of this first-rate fix?

"Either tell me the truth or I'll kiss it out of you, Bess. That's a promise."

Cursing her fluttering heart, she let out an indelicate snort. "Sounds like a threat."

"Whatever." He rubbed the end of her nose with his chin. "It's a fact."

Arrogant jerk. He knew the effect he had on her and he was taunting her with it. Again. Bess sighed. Why did he take such pleasure in humiliating her? "All right, I'm lying. I do want you. But I don't want to want you, and that's the truth. In fact, I resent wanting you. It makes me angry with me, and with you — which is only fair since you don't want me and yet you're doing everything humanly possible to entice me to want you. I really don't understand why you're doing that when —"

"I never said I didn't want you," he interrupted her lengthy monologue. "How did you twist around my proposal and draw that conclusion?"

"For two weeks, you want me." She sounded disgruntled, and she was disgruntled — and just fed up enough to not give a flying fig who knew it anymore. The man would probably go to his grave laughing at her because she'd been so easy to humiliate and rattle and yet she still wanted him. He'd surely be telling jokes about her long after he hit heaven.

He cupped her face in his hands. "If the two weeks bit bothers you, we can eliminate it as an obstacle."

Her heart slowed to a deliberate thump. Did he mean he wanted her back forever, then? She studied him to make sure he wasn't baiting her, but there wasn't a trace of sarcasm in his voice. Its absence confused her. He *was* angry with her, she'd have to be an idiot not to see that, but he did want her. She'd felt it in his kiss, seen it in his eyes far too often during their good times to deny seeing it now. Yet he was holding back from her; that she didn't see but sensed, and it had her wary of him and of his motives. "The time stipulation doesn't sit well with me and, if I didn't admit it, I wouldn't be honest."

"No problem." A devilish lilt in his voice left her breathless. "If it makes my settlement offer easier to swallow, we can cut the time back to one week."

She shoved him away from her. "You are one sorry jerk, John Mystic."

He laughed, the demented man. Couldn't he tell she was furious with him? "I came to you for comfort. Not for you to seduce me, or to threaten me — or to humiliate me. I've had quite enough of that lately without you adding more, thank you very much."

John stilled, his cobalt blue eyes no longer twinkled in the lamp light. Now they glittered with an anger so intense it had her wincing. "Who's humiliated you?"

"Who hasn't?" she spat. "And anyone who missed will certainly get another chance when the media gets a hold of this dog-custody lawsuit of yours."

His voice dropped a notch. "You can avoid it. You have a choice, Bess."

She snorted. "Some choice."

"Jail and bad press, or me. Those are your options."

"Yes, they are." With a sigh that ruffled the linens, she jerked at the quilt, leaving him as bare as the day he was born. "I should be furious with you for pulling this stunt."

He stacked his hands behind his head. "You are furious with me."

"I mean even more furious than I am, and I darn well shouldn't be coming to you, especially not to you in your bed, for comfort." Determination lit in her eyes and she tossed back the quilt then rolled toward the edge of the mattress.

"Comfort?" John pulled her back. "From

the storm?"

"Yes," Bess licked at her lips and scooted farther away from him, "but not the one raging outside." This storm raged within, and attacked her on all fronts. She had so many worries and fears she didn't know which to fight first. And that had her feeling overwhelmed, and too weary to fight any of them. "I really just want you to hold me." Oh, but that was hard to admit. And she'd done it in a whimper, no less. Again, she could kiss off grace. Yet, she didn't regret it. He'd understand now that she really was asking him for that which her parents had trained her never to ask from anyone. That awful, weakness-provoking "H" word. And John would be decent about it. He wouldn't force her to say the word *help*. He'd give her what she needed without making her ask; he always had.

"Just to hold you?" He laughed in her face. "Now what would your sorry Spaniard think about that?"

Miguel wouldn't be in the least surprised, Bess supposed, but, grumpy and embarrassed, she didn't disclose that tidbit to Jonathan. Couldn't he react as she expected him to — as he would have before — just once?

"Never mind. You don't have to speculate." John let out a sigh and took her into his arms. "If my wife wants comfort then, by gosh, I'll give it to her."

"Grudgingly," she muttered against the crook in his neck.

"Don't push, Bess."

"I'm sorry." She truly was. He didn't sound very controlled, though he clearly tried to, and he didn't sound very compassionate either. But at least he was holding her and that, shameful as it was, did bring the comfort she sought and make all her troubles a little easier to bear. Maybe, if he held her long enough, she could sort through them and figure out what she was going to do. Right now, her biggest worry was Tony. She shivered hard.

"Are you cold?"

"Freezing," she lied. Not being honest with John rankled but it disturbed her far less than the truth about this particular worry — and it would be far easier to discuss in the dark. She turned off the lamp.

John pulled her back into his arms, tight against his chest, then he slung a leg over her thighs. The heat was wonderful — and nearly as disturbing as her fear. That lust with a kick had her hormones rocketing to warp-speed mate-mode, and raging. "I could explain, but . . ."

Could she really? *Boo* from a man thought to be a telepath was pretty darn hard to believe, much less to explain. Especially to John. He would believe her, all right. He'd believe she'd gotten too tied up inside some patient's head and had slipped beyond twilight herself. "I guess I can't explain, after all." Feeling forlorn, she plucked at the edge of the quilt. "Even to me, the whole thing sounds just too bizarre."

John felt her despair. Tension had her neck muscles knotted. Her head against his chest, he rubbed at the lumps until they melted. Finally, he had a clue; in addition to all her other troubles, which even he admitted numbered many and no small part of them were due to him, she had come to some realization. About them? About herself? About Santos?

Tony had told John to expect . . . Ah, shoot. Tony.

She rubbed at John's foot with the arch of hers. Glad that some things hadn't changed, he pecked a kiss to her forehead then gave her an opening he half-hoped she wouldn't take. This Tony situation *was* pretty bizarre. But it wasn't threatening. "Bess, does this internal storm have something to do with your weird caller?"

271

"Tony?" she asked, sounding as weak as a beggar.

"Yeah." Tony *had* been talking to her, too. He'd admitted that.

"Yes, it does."

The anguish in her voice hit John hard. He rubbed tiny circles on her back. Should he admit that Tony also had been talking to him? With Tony's cryptic messages, John felt as if he'd been plunked down in the middle of a play and no one had bothered giving him a copy of the script. He didn't like it. Evidently, Bess didn't like it either.

At least she wouldn't think he was crazy. Small solace, and one he wasn't convinced should be a solace. She'd been genuinely surprised that he'd felt offended at her siding with the FBI about Dixie and lacking faith in John's judgment. Maybe Bess had learned something here. Maybe he should take the risk and see if now she would hold onto the faith.

The truth slammed into him like a hurricane's storm surge hits the shore. Mystic tide. Leap. Island.

No, it couldn't be that simple. Tony's message couldn't be that simple.

"Bess," John made his decision. "Has he been talking to you . . . without a phone?"

Bess sat up and clicked on the bedside

lamp. Its pear-shaped shade had suffused light pooling on the nightstand and on the bed. She sat up, folded her long legs Indian-style, and faced John. "I do need to talk about this, but I don't want you think I'm . . . unstable."

He was dying to know. Why couldn't he make himself look to see? *Was* she wearing his ring? What if she'd taken it off? Wouldn't that mean that he'd blown this second chance already? If he had, the sooner he found out, the better — right?

Wrong. Watching hope die hammered the soul hard. And his soul had suffered about all the hammering it could take for one night.

She mumbled something he couldn't make out, talking to her hands. Not wringing them, though she was giving the edge of the quilt fits. "I know you're stable, Bess."

"Tony *is* talking to me without a phone," she confessed, then glanced up at John, letting him glimpse her appreciation of his support. "I thought he was telepathic." She stared right back down at her hands. "But now I know he's . . . not."

And that scared her senseless. John sat up, too, nude as a newborn, and knee to knee, confronted Bess in the roundabout way she definitely needed to draw the same conclusion John had drawn. "Maybe he's something similar. Psychic?"

She lifted her gaze to his, sucked in a little gasp, then pulled the quilt up to cover him from the waist down. Her hands trembled, but her cheeks flushed pink and her eyes warmed. "He, um, said he wasn't."

That admission brought with it a grimace. And now her chin trembled, too. Tony, not him, had been the reason for the grimace and, while John was relieved by that, he didn't like seeing her distressed. She wore some kind of ring. But he'd only glimpsed a view of it from her palm. Why wouldn't she turn over her hand? He wanted her to, wanted to know. Really. "If he isn't a telepath or a psychic, how is he communicating with you?"

"I don't know." She shuddered and rubbed a chill from her arms.

Lying to him, again. Well, maybe not lying, but not being totally honest. If she didn't know, she certainly had her suspicions, yet, he softened toward her, it wasn't obstinacy that had kept her from sharing them with him. It was her fear of how he'd react. John draped the quilt around her shoulders. "How long have you been hearing him?"

"Since that night he called into the station

with the rumor of our divorce."

"And he gave you that message."

Bess nodded, remembering then that she'd been so certain they were experiencing telepathy. So certain. Didn't she wish she could be certain of that now? His one word message, however, pointed distinctly and irrevocably in a different direction. One she wasn't ready to admit to herself, much less to John. It was absurd, of course. Ridiculous. So much so, she couldn't bring herself to even think that awful "G" word.

But what other explanation was there?

The storm outside hit with a vengeance. Rain pelted against the window and the side of the house. Lightning flashed so frequently the Cove Room seemed illuminated by a strobe light. And the clashes of clapping thunder pierced Bess's ears, set them to ringing.

"I've been thinking about his message that night," John said. "What do you remember him telling you exactly?"

"You mean about leaping upon a mystic tide?"

John shook his head. "No, before then."

Surprised, she raised her brows and twisted the covers. Their bare knees rubbed and she shifted away. "Have you figured out what he meant about the tide?"

"Not yet." Sounding gruff, he grabbed the quilt then pulled it back up over his thighs.

His gaze went hot; his gruff voice, husky. "I am human, honey." He wagged a finger toward her robe.

She noted the gap and gave its lapels a solid tug, then held the quilt draping her shoulders closed at her chin. "Sorry."

He nodded and cupped a hand over her foot. "What did Tony say right before the tide message?"

Bess thought back, though concentrating was darn difficult. Between the almost constant thunder and lightning and John staring at her and rubbing delicious circles into her arches, it was a wonder she could think at all. He remembered how much she hated storms, how much she loved having her feet massaged. "Not to give up hope. That so long as there's life, there's hope."

"That's it!" Realization shone in John's eyes.

And Bess didn't get it. *"What's* it?"

John shoved aside the quilt, took her other foot in his hand, then rotated her ankle. "Just before Tony told you that, he said, 'My situation is hopeless, but yours isn't.' "

"Yes." So what did that mean? What was John seeing that she was missing? Unrequited love certainly wasn't uncommon enough to warrant John's eureka reaction.

"Think about it, Bess."

"You sound just like him. I hate that awful phrase." She cringed then frowned at John. "Every time I hear it, another bomb drops on my head."

"Like the words or not, would you stop and just think about this?" John squeezed her instep. "He said his situation was hopeless. Then right afterward, he said —"

"That so long as there's life, there's hope."

A shiver of pure terror shot up her spine. She'd known it but, Lord, she hadn't wanted to know it. She'd denied it and prayed she'd be permitted to go on denying it. "He has no hope, Jonathan."

"He has no life, Bess."

Determined not to faint, not to hyperventilate, or to give in to sweet oblivion, she sat statue still for a long moment, then let her gaze drop to John's chest. That it was still rising and falling in smooth even motions when she felt frazzled to the core both comforted and infuriated her. "He warned me from the start," she finally said.

"And tonight something happened with him that frightened you."

"Scared the fool out of me, and that's the truth."

"What happened?"

If John had demanded she tell him, she wouldn't have. But he hadn't. He'd asked in a soft, sweet voice that said he knew she was reeling. She couldn't *not* tell him. This was bizarre — beyond bizarre, and scary as heck — but it *was* happening.

"He, um, gave me a message," she said, resolving to look him in the eye even if it killed her. But she couldn't do it. The sheet and quilt lay rumpled near his waist. She lifted her gaze but, at the mat of hair on his chest, stopped cold.

"Honey, what did he say?"

John sounded so calm. Lord, how she envied him that. And how she resented him for it. She looked up into his eyes. They were solemn, serious, and questioning. Maybe she shouldn't tell him. Maybe she should protect him from the truth for so long as she was able. It would be the humane thing to do. Not the easiest for her, but the most humane.

No. No, she couldn't. She'd tried protecting him before and it'd backfired. She'd fallen under the misconception that his relationship with Elise had been entirely different from what it had been. She'd misjudged him, and she had to live with that. It had been a difficult lesson, but she'd learned from it. Tonight, when they'd been doing the role-playing and she was Elise, he'd kissed her forehead. At that moment, for the first time, Bess had known the truth. John had never had an affair with Elise Dupree. She'd come first with him, true, but for some other reason. Not because they'd engaged in an affair.

This time, Bess would share her fears with him. What more did she have to lose? "Tony just said one word, John."

"It must have been some word. I've never seen you so rattled."

She was shaking, and very close to tears. "Don't start giving me fits about getting emotional. Frankly, I'm doing well to not already have soaked your sheets."

That worried him. He dug his fingers into her hip. "What was the word?"

"It was a question." Why didn't she just say it and have it done? The delay wouldn't lessen the shock, only his response to it. And if that wasn't a good reason for a delay she didn't know what was.

"All right, then," he said from between his teeth. "What was the question?"

"Well, it wasn't actually a question." She went back to wringing her hands. Good grief, she couldn't keep her thoughts straight. With the contents of them, she couldn't really blame herself, though. Who would want to keep *these* thoughts straight? "I asked if he was a telepath. He said he wasn't. I asked how then was he talking to me without speaking. He told me we could solve the mystery, and then I stupidly asked how. I never should have asked that. Never."

She paused for breath, uncertain if she could say the rest without falling into a dead faint. That she hadn't fainted before in her life made no difference. She'd never before encountered this type challenge either. And, in the way she dealt with it, patience and grace could just fend for themselves.

"Well," John muttered in a whispered shout, *his* patience clearly deserting him. "What did he say?"

Taking exception to his tone, Bess glared at John. "Boo."

Hattie climbed the stairs up to the attic room just after dawn. The temperature change midway didn't surprise her; she'd become accustomed to it years ago. She paused in Tony's room — the one, when he'd reached his early teens, he'd asked his parents, Collin and Cecelia, to let him move into. He'd been growing up, making the change from boy to man, and had wanted to exert his independence, and to feel confident of their acknowledgment of his rites of passage. Being compassionate angels, and wise and loving parents, they'd given it to him.

To the right of the stairs sat his bed and desk and the chest that, now and then, held his clothing. All the dustcovers lay puddled on the floor like puffy, white clouds. Again, not uncommon, though, for years, on finding them off of the furnishings, Hattie religiously had replaced them. But for the last decade or so, she'd replaced them or not depending on the temperature of the room. If it felt cool enough to raise goose bumps, she'd left them where they'd lain. If not, then she'd replaced them. Today, the room felt cool, but not chilly. Tony wasn't here. And that left her feeling a little bereft, and a little sad that she'd come up here.

The wall nearest the stairs was covered solid with shelves full of his treasures. His baseball cap, his favorite fishing lure, his own photo of her in her yellow, floral dress. She'd worn that dress the night he'd proposed and, when she'd accepted, he'd sworn that yellow flowers would forever be his favorite. Remembering that vow had him stealing her heart all over again.

She let her gaze drift to a little silver frame, a photo of him and Hatch. She'd snapped it the day they'd gone fishing and had found that silly doubloon. They'd been as excited as if they'd recovered a trunk full of gold. Anthony Freeport. Her beloved Tony. Tony . . . She lovingly caressed his familiar face with her gaze. His hair was a mess. He'd been embarrassed about that but, my, how she'd loved it. Tony was touchable. Loveable. And, oh, how she'd loved him! How she still loved him . . .

Her heart wrenched. She sucked in a steadying breath and, wistful, looked around. It'd been a long time since she'd been up in this room; since Maggie and T. J. MacGregor's visit, when she'd wanted so desperately to help them heal and had been at a loss as to how to do it. And she wouldn't have come here again now — the material reminders of Tony being in the house were a comfort, but seeing them, touching them, smelling them, when she couldn't see, touch, or smell him . . . well, that still hurt.

Yet she couldn't be spiney about this. Jonathan would call it spiney, wimpy. Bess, no doubt, would have a mile-long clinical name for it. But spiney was good enough for Hattie. And, to get to the widow's walk, she'd had to not be spiney and to come to the attic. When John Mystic had left the house in the middle of a violent storm, she'd had to see where he was going.

She walked to the little door leading out onto the narrow widow's walk. Rain beat hard against it, so she only cracked it ajar enough to glimpse the cliffs. He hadn't yet moved. Continued to sit there on the jagged cliffs as still as a shadow, staring out onto the ocean.

He wasn't used to Maine's climate. Jacketless and rain-soaked to the skin. Even in summer, especially during a storm, he should have on something to protect him from getting a chill. Miss Hattie tisked, fretting. "And no boots either." The granite cliffs were treacherously slick when dry, much less wet. She wanted him to come back inside and get warm — the dear man had to be as cold as ice — but, if he tried, with one misstep, he could tumble to his death. And, being from away, he likely didn't even realize his danger.

Panic surged through her. She had to do something besides worry. But what? *Oh, Tony, where are you when I need you?*

Back in his room, something fell. She frowned, shut the little door, then searched to see what it had been. The silver-framed photo of him and Hatch lay face down on his dresser.

Understanding the Message, she smiled. "Yes, dear. I'll phone him straightaway."

She left the attic in a rush for the stairs.

Tony watched her go. Leaning against the doorjamb at the top of the stairs, he craned his neck until she turned at the landing near his parents' portraits. In truth, he was more than a little miffed at his beloved. *Where are you when I need you?*

That stung. Hadn't he promised her when he'd left to go to war he'd return to her? Hadn't he vowed his undying love and steadfast support? In all the decades since his death, hadn't he proven to her time and again that he'd meant the vow he'd made when mortally wounded on the battlefield?

He'd sworn that, though they couldn't be together, they'd never be apart.

All these long years, he'd kept his word. He hadn't let her see him because to see each other and to not be able to hold, to touch, would be far too painful for them both. But he had given her signs of him being there with her. She frequently talked to him and he found ways to answer her. And yet she lacked faith in him keeping his word.

He resented that as much as he resented giving John Mystic the creeps. As much as he resented Bess's fear on realizing he wasn't the telepath she believed him to be. He'd steer clear of them for a while now, and give them time to accept the truth about him — and from Hattie to let her know he didn't much appreciate her slight.

John and Bess had reacted normally, of course. In fear. Tony sighed, hating that. When Bess had believed him a telepath, she'd been frisky. He'd thoroughly enjoyed her barbs and demands. Once people learned the truth about what he was, they rarely acted so open. She'd been a breath of fresh air — and far too clever. John had, too. A shame they'd suspected and picked up on the truth so quickly. Tony could have used more preparation time.

Getting these two together had become the biggest challenge he'd faced in a decade. They loved each other; he knew they did. But they were so caught up in what they *thought was real* about each other that what *was real* got lost in the shuffle.

Whether or not they stood a chance together was entirely up to them. For now, he'd done all he could think of to do to steer them in the right direction. If they didn't settle their differences soon, though, he'd have no choice but to get . . . creative.

Dangerous, that. And drastic. But what other choice did he have?

He stared out the widow's walk window. Hatch hiked over the cliffs in his yellow slicker and black boots. A shame that his wise friend knew the answers to all John's questions about Dixie Dupree and John didn't know enough to ask the right questions. Maybe this meeting on the cliffs would provide an opportunity. Then again, John was so confused and centered on his feelings for Bess, it probably wouldn't. The man loved her, but as long as he felt he was a failure, he'd never make a move toward a reunion.

A real shame he had this to contend with as well as the secret about his parents. Tony turned away from the window. In a pinch, Hattie had expressed a lack of faith in him, too. And, justified or not, a part of him understood exactly what John Mystic felt.

Betrayed.

And angry.

Rain pelted him, as cold as ice. John should be shivering, but the truth was, he was too numb to feel a thing.

Tony. A ghost. A *ghost?*

Bess had denied the "G" word, of course. But John couldn't deny it. He rolled the yellow carnation petal that had been in Elise's hand when she'd died between his forefinger and thumb. It made sense.

Well, it didn't make sense. But Tony being

a ghost had the puzzle pieces fitting into place.

"Fine storm we're having, ain't it?"

John looked over the rocky cliffs toward the lighthouse. Trudging gingerly through the patches of chickweed sprouting from the sand-filled crevices, Hatch limped closer, then finally sat down beside John on the craggy rocks. "Yeah, it's a great storm."

Hatch reached under his slicker, pulled out his corncob pipe, then perched it in the corner of his mouth. "Ain't but one thing can drive a man into a fine storm without so much as a slicker. A woman. Actually, trouble with a woman." He stared down, out past a lone oak's low-slung branch to the angry waves beating against the narrow strip of a strand below. The wind roared, blowing up the face of the rocks then over them, bending the tall grass and weeds and shivering through the trees. "Yep, women. Ya gotta love 'em."

John sighed. "I think men must be half-nuts, Hatch."

He grunted, then leaned back onto his elbows and lifted his weathered face to the rain as if it were warm sunshine. "The ratio's closer to two-thirds, in my estimation."

Was the man ridiculing him? John slid him

an accessing glare. But, seeing not a hint of scorn or guile in Hatch's expression or manner, John dropped the glare and sighed again. "Truth is truth, and Bess has me hovering at a hundred percent."

"She's a moody woman." Hatch didn't open his eyes.

Tony had said the same thing. This time, John wouldn't assume it an insult. "Takes everything into her heart?"

"Yep, and pretends she don't feel, when her heart's cracking from being too full and holding inside all she does feel." Hatch nodded. "Pull up a blade, son. Ain't as good as a pipe stem, but gnawing on a tender blade helps a man with his worrying."

What could it hurt? He'd tried and tried and never had gotten a good look at her hand. It'd seemed almost as if she'd known he'd been attempting to see her ring and she hadn't wanted him to do it. John pulled up a blade of grass then stuck the end of it between his lips. "You call it moody. I call it her cashmere, eel-skin control." Just off the shore, a gull dove for a fish. It must be starved to hunt during a storm. Starved, John grunted, or a male with a moody mate. "She's a lot less reserved than she used to be, but I want to break through all of it."

"I expect you do. It's hard on a man's

pride to know his wife's taken another man."

"It is!" John nodded enthusiastically. "She's made me a eunuch and doesn't even think about it, much less see it."

"Bet when people start riding her about Silk's custody suit, she'll be doing some thinking then."

"How did you know about that?" Rain dripped down from his forehead into his eyes. John swiped a finger across his brow.

"Word travels fast in the village."

Bess too had said that. "But who told you?"

"When it's stormy, the phone lines go a little crazy. Anyone can listen in on any conversation. If asked, they'd likely deny doing it, but I figure, what the heck? If it's my phone and I pick it up and hear somebody else talking, then I can listen to what they're saying without so much as a twinge of guilt. If they don't want me to hear what they're saying, then they ought not be talking on my phone."

John grinned, betting Bess didn't know word traveled so fast around here with the help of Ma Bell.

And maybe Tony.

White caps littered the ocean and pounded the shore, lifting an angry sea spray. Rain trickled down John's cheeks to his chin and stung. "Hatch, have you ever heard Seascape Inn is haunted?"

"Sure. Dozens of times."

"Really?" John turned from the sea to the old man. There had to be a connection. Tony and Seascape. Had to be more than coincidence.

" 'Course. Usually about 3:30 in the afternoon."

Totally confused, John frowned. "What?"

"Batty Beaulah — er, don't mention to Miss Hattie I called Beaulah that."

John bent his knee then wiped his face on his sleeve. "I won't."

"Batty Beaulah swears the inn's haunted. Drives Sheriff Cobb crazy with her *sightings* — usually down at the Blue Moon Cafe. He drops by there every day about 3:30 for coffee and some of Lucy's pie."

Batty Beaulah wasn't quite as batty as everyone thought. Did Tony talk to her, too?

Hatch flicked at a brown weed that clung to his slicker. "Have you heard about the second time the sheriff tried to dodge Batty Beaulah at the Blue Moon?"

"No, I haven't." Nor had he heard about the first.

"Got his ample hide wedged under the bar. The sheriff always has been a slow learner — and as stubborn as the pastor is persistent at nagging Jimmy about taking his girlie calendar off his shop wall." Hatch grunted. "For a while, it looked as if they'd have to bust the wood to get the sheriff unstuck. That had Fred Baker hostile, and Lucy fretting something fierce."

Lucy. The redhead at the Blue Moon Cafe the day John had met Bess there. The one who'd reminded him of Elise.

"Collin Freeport had helped Fred's daddy build that bar, and Fred always admired Collin's wood carvings and was right fond of the bar because he'd helped build it. Fred would rather have cut the sheriff than the wood, seeing's how the sheriff had been fool enough to get himself stuck in the first place."

By the skin of his teeth, John repressed a grin. "I'll bet that opinion stirred up a heated debate."

"Better than some of the Village Council meetings. And they get pretty spirited."

"Did they bust the bar?"

"Naw. Jimmy Goodson saved the day. Fine boy, that Jimmy."

The car mechanic. "How?"

"He greased up the sheriff like a pig set for auction with a couple cans of 10W30 motor oil, non-detergent — Pennzoil, if I recollect proper — then slid the sheriff right on out of there." Hatch scratched at the gray stubble on his chin. "Seems sacrilege that when he finally got free, Batty Beaulah stood there waiting for him. In my estimation, the man had suffered enough, but evidently God felt a mite different on the matter."

Envisioning the big, burly sheriff diving under the bar to avoid the tiny, birdlike Beaulah had John smiling. "Women, eh?"

"Yep, women." Hatch clicked his tongue and winked. "Ya gotta love 'em."

John shook his head, a grin tugging at his lips. "Hatch, do you know Tony?"

"Sure. We were good friends. The best. Me and him and Vic were the Three Musketeers of Sea Haven Village. Why we —" Hatch paused then squinted and sent John a withering look. "Don't you be playing games with this old man. I know Hattie Stillman, and ain't a day goes by she don't talk about her soldier."

Tony was Miss Hattie's fiancé? Her soldier?

Of course. Another piece of the puzzle slid into place. "She does talk about him. I just wondered if you knew him."

"Everyone around here did — except the Butlers." Hatch nodded toward Fisherman's

Co-op. "They weren't living here then, though Bill's Uncle Mike was. He knew Tony. Used to take us fishing back in the old days before he retired and Tony got himself killed."

Tony *was* dead.

A ghost.

And Batty Beaulah was as sane as John and Bess, which could, or could not, be saying a lot.

Hatch sat up and fiddled with his pipe. Rain rolled down his neck then disappeared under his slicker's collar. "I'm thinking maybe Bess is as confused as you."

A seal waddled off a rock just offshore and flopped into the water. "Yeah, most likely." At least he'd confirmed that Tony was a ghost. When John had started to say the "G" word, Bess nearly had fainted. Worse, she'd started wringing her hands again. So he'd hushed and let the word hang in the air between them like an echo. Unspoken, but there. "She's facing some rough situations."

"Yep, times are hard — especially for a moody woman."

John put Elise's flower petal back into his wallet, then shifted his weight onto his hip and shoved the wallet back into his pocket. "I'm doing my best to help her. Not that she considers me anything more than a hellhound bent on torturing her heels."

"You ain't. You love her."

Surprised, he slid Hatch a how-did-you-know-that look.

The crusty old salt of a man shrugged. "You're sitting out on the cliffs in the middle of a storm, boy. I ain't a rocket scientist, but I got the picture clear enough."

"Yeah." John sighed. "I love her. I don't want to, but I do."

"What you want don't matter, does it?"

"Doesn't seem to." Why didn't he resent that more? Even two days ago he would have resented it immensely. He *had* resented it immensely. Why not now?

"I'm thinking sometimes confusion is a good thing. 'Specially in women."

Gooseflesh prickled at John's skin. He looked at Hatch. "Why?"

He took his pipe out of his mouth and squinted against the rain pelting at his face, deepening his wrinkles to grooves. "Because when a woman's confused, she don't stop to think. She just acts on what she feels." He shrugged. "Comes in handy."

With his tongue, John rolled the tender blade from the left corner of his mouth over to the right. "Yeah." Anticipation filled his stomach and a smile crept to his lips. "Yeah."

"I'm thinking, if while a woman's all confused, a man was to go after what he wants most, then he might just get it."

"Maybe." John weighed the possibilities. "But he might also reach out a hand and draw back a nub."

"There is that." Hatch nodded his agreement, then snorted. "But, shucks, boy, what's life without a few risks?"

"Risks are one thing. Failure's another." John looked back out onto the water, not wanting to see censure against him in Hatch's eyes. "I was one lousy husband, Hatch."

"I'm told it's a job a man's gotta grow into. Shame it don't come with a training guide, ain't it?" Hatch spit onto the rocks. "Definitely an oversight, in my estimation."

"Yeah." On-the-job training without a Policy and Procedures Manual. John never before had looked at marriage quite like that. It made sense. "You know, you're onto something here. Bess is always sedate — even when she's fired up. I want to see what she's really like, underneath the mask." Heat crawling up his neck, he lifted a little stone and rubbed it between his forefinger and thumb. The gritty sand clinging to it sprinkled onto his jeans. "I guess that makes me a sorry man."

"Maybe. We all got our demons, you know." Hatch shrugged. "But, more likely, I'd say it makes you human."

John supposed it did. Hoped it did. Miss Hattie had been right about Hatch. He *was* a wise man.

Hatch drew on his unlit pipe. "Why does she hide her feelings?"

Opening his mouth to answer, John realized he didn't have the foggiest notion. Hadn't he asked her that either? They'd been busy buying dishes, climbing career ladders, making love. But surely they'd talked about some of this stuff. They *had* to have talked about it. He thought back, but couldn't recall a single discussion. Shame filled his stomach, turned his tongue bitter. And another shovelful of guilt dumped onto the heap. "I don't know," he confessed.

"You *were* married to her."

"I still am." Bristling, John grimaced. "I told you I was a lousy husband."

"Lousy or not," Hatch hauled himself to his feet, "it's looking like you might get that chance you're wanting — provided you move your rear and get to her before she breaks her neck trying to get to you."

John wheeled around. Bess was slipping and sliding her way across the cliffs. "She's going to kill herself." He scrambled to his feet.

Hatch shoved his pipe stem back into his mouth and squinted. "Possible."

"Darn." John looked for footholds in the craggy cliffs and, using them and patches of weeds as he'd seen Hatch do, he started making his way toward her. "Bess," he paused to shout, "don't move. Just stay where you are until I get there."

"Women." Hatch turned back toward the lighthouse. "Yep, ya gotta love 'em."

John skidded and nearly did a split. His groin muscle pulled tighter than an arrow-nocked bow. "Or kill 'em."

"There is that, too." Hatch waved without looking back.

The strong wind and rain had the rocks slicker than if they'd been doused in oil like the sheriff. Bess, thank goodness, had decided for once to listen and stood still, shivering down to her toes. No jacket, of course. She had no more sense than John. And her jeans were as soaked as his, too. So was her blouse, and it was thinner. Red silk. Drenched red silk that lay plastered to her skin.

He finally reached her. Standing toe to toe in the pouring rain, he glared down at her. "What are you doing out here?"

"I was worried." She looked up at him, defiance burning in her eyes. "I woke up and you were gone. Miss Hattie said she thought you'd come down here."

Mascara streaked down her cheeks, and still she looked beautiful to him. "Didn't she tell you the cliffs were dangerous?"

"Of course. Why else would I risk coming out here?" She shoved her drenched hair back, spraying him with rain. "I was afraid you'd fallen."

Right. Bess worried about him? Did she think he was stupid *and* gullible? She'd *hoped* he'd fallen, more likely. No, Bess didn't care; she just wanted him out of her way. And that angered him. With her, and with himself. Why did it matter? Why did she matter? Selena had been wrong about a lot of things, but she'd been right too. Bess *had* made her feelings for him clear. "Sorry to disappoint you, darling, but we're still going to have to go for the divorce. I'm not going to fall off the cliffs and kill myself to spare you the trouble — or the embarrassment — of ending our marriage. And I'm not going to let you fall either."

She flinched. His words clearly stung her. He probably should apologize, but he wasn't going to do it. He'd called this as he'd seen it.

She looked up at him, blinking fast. "I don't want you dead, John."

"Don't you?" Crazy woman, coming out here, sliding all over on the rocks. She'd already nearly given him heart failure. Definitely scared ten years off him. And she expected him to believe she didn't want him dead? He grabbed her arm and started leading her back toward the house. "Is that why you're telling me these lies about you caring and worrying about me when you don't and you aren't, Bess? Because you're wishing me well? How dare you take chances like this with your life."

"What's wrong with you?" She jerked loose from him and stumbled, tearing her jeans and skinning her knee.

The bright red blood had John's stomach churning. "Be still and let me see."

"It's just a scrape." On her feet again, she stepped more carefully, onto the path then down the stone steps to Main Street.

"I'm sorry." From the flush in her cheeks he could forget worrying about her being cold. In fact, he should be more worried about seeing her steam. "Did you hear me?"

"Everyone in the village heard you, Jonathan." Clench-jawed, she looked toward the lighthouse, then toward the village. Seeing the road was clear, she crossed then started up the sloped drive back to the inn. "Bellows carry over the stones and through the trees."

Bellow? Had he — ? Well, he guessed he had been a little excited and raised his voice. "I'm sorry. I didn't mean to shout."

She gave him a curt nod that would have been cute if he'd not been ticked at her for scaring him. And she was limping. Yet another shovelful of guilt dumped onto his personal heap. At this rate, he'd soon be buried. "Does it hurt?" He nodded toward her knee.

"Immensely."

On the gravel drive, John finally caught sight of the back of her hand. His heart nearly stopped. Tony had been right. She *did* still wear John's ring.

His emotions snapped like live wires — surprise, disbelief, confusion, pleasure, and pride — coupled and tumbled with each other, bombarding him. His heart full, he scooped her up into his arms.

"What do you think you're doing?" She rocked against his chest and glared at him. "Put me —"

He kissed her quiet. And he decided that, if when he was done she refused to stay quiet, then he'd just kiss her again — however many times it took for her to get the message. She wasn't slow, she'd figure it out. Seeing her sliding on the cliffs had rattled him and he needed time to let the fear settle. Seeing his ring still on her finger gave him something he'd never thought to have again with her: hope. This second chance was real. Real.

She looped her arms around his neck. "I take exception to your high-handedness, Jonathan." Her words were as stiff as her jostling body.

"Noted." Maybe giving her an excuse to come unglued would help with the stress. She had been under a lot of pressure lately. Yeah, he'd let her vent . . . for a while. Maybe she'd even spout a little sass. "But you earned it, woman."

She bent his ear all the way back to the inn.

Inside the house, between the kitchen and the gallery, she grabbed hold of the doorjamb and repeated to Miss Hattie all the slurs slung at him during the hike, pausing intermittently only long enough to insist he put her down.

He endured and ignored, then turned to Miss Hattie, who had the most angelic smile on her face he thought he'd ever seen, and sighed. "I'm taking Bess up to doctor her knee and to see what I can do about her disposition, Miss Hattie. Honestly, I think the odds favor the knee healing long before the attitude improves, but I'll do what I can. Would you keep an eye on Silk?"

"Certainly. She's quite comfortable on the rug."

"Don't talk about me as if I'm not here, Jonathan." Bess sent Miss Hattie a he's-hopeless look. "Ignore him. He's going through one of his macho phases. I'll have him over it soon enough, though."

Her emerald eyes twinkling, Miss Hattie nodded and turned her attention back to her chicken and cheese casserole. "I'm sure you will, dear."

John guffawed and headed toward the stairs. "Women, ya gotta love 'em."

"Jonathan, I don't appreciate your cave man attitude —"

He kissed her lips.

Miss Hattie chuckled under her breath and popped her casserole into the oven. "Men." She set the temperature knob to three-hundred-fifty degrees then clicked the oven on. "You can't live with 'em or without 'em."

The lights went out.

She frowned ceilingward. "If you ruin my casserole, Anthony Freeport, I'm sure to be in a sour mood for a week. Vic's particularly fond of this dish and he's down in the back — as you well know."

She waited, but the lights didn't come back on. Above stairs, John and Bess had gone quiet. Well, that was a good sign, wasn't it?

Unless they weren't speaking to each other again.

The lights flickered on, then went right back out.

Tony was miffed.

Sighing, Hattie reached into the drawer and pulled out a candle and matches. Now what in the world was she going to do with a raw chicken and cheese casserole?

John plunked Bess down on the marbled countertop beside the bathroom sink. Her bottom stung nearly as much as her knee. They were both soaked to the skin, though they'd stopped dripping somewhere between the mud room and the upstairs bath. Now, she was cold. Freezing in fact, and her blouse clinging to her skin had her nipples peaked, and the rest of her covered with goose bumps. She looked down at the ripped knee of her jeans and at the bright-red blood covering her knee cap. It wasn't deep, just a scrape, but John acted as if she'd been shot.

"Don't move." Sliding her an I-mean-it look, he then started rifling through the cabinets. He tossed a box of cotton balls onto the counter near her hip then grabbed a brown bottle of peroxide from the shelf.

"Why are you acting as if this is such a big deal, Jonathan? It's a scrape, for goodness sake." She tossed her rain-soaked hair back from her face, sure she looked like something that crawled out from under a rock while he looked gorgeous. His hair, still dripping wet, splashed droplets of rain onto the soaked shirt molding to his chest like a second and third skin. It wasn't right. Or fair. Even peeved at him, the sight of him left her breathless.

He wet a washcloth at the sink, then grimaced at her. "Lose the jeans."

"Excuse me?" She had to have heard him wrong.

He leaned a hip against the counter, his stomach brushing her thigh. "Don't give me a hard time, okay, Doc? I'm tired, grouchy as a bear with a thorn in its paw, and trying hard to absorb all this about Tony. I am *not* in a good mood. And I am *not* interested in a debate. Now lose the pants."

"I haven't exactly been in paradise myself lately, you know? And I'm quite capable of cleaning my own scrape." Fluttering her fingertips, she shooed him toward the door. "Why don't you just go on and get some sleep and maybe you won't be so —"

He kissed her quiet. His hand at her nape, under her hair, he pulled her closer, her shoulder pressing against his chest. Stunned, it took her a moment to recoup, then, clipping his shoulder, she pushed away. "Stop that, Jonathan. You can't keep kissing me every time I say something you don't want to hear. It's absurd. Rid—"

He kissed her again. This time, planting himself against the counter between her thighs. One hand holding her head, his lips slanting over hers. His body heat radiated through their clothes and stole her chills. A delicious shiver coursed through her, heating her blood, setting it to pounding through her veins. And long before she was ready to end this kiss, he lifted his head.

Her face burning, she stared at him and twisted her mouth to verbally let him have it right between the eyes.

He quirked a brow at her.

Knowing the penalty for uttering so much as a single syllable, she fumed with a gaping jaw . . . and said nothing. Her time would come. And when it did, then he'd regret this macho manure.

"Are you ready to play nice now and ditch the jeans?"

Arrogant pig. The time was now. She steeled herself for the onslaught. "I'll handle this myself. I thought I already told you that. In fact, I'm sure I did. Between the first and second kisses you stole, I think. Or was it the second and third?" She gave him a saccharine-sweet smile. "Hmmm, I can't seem to —"

He kissed her yet again. And this time she was ready for him. When he slipped between her thighs, she curled her legs around him, wound her arms around his neck, too, and threaded her fingers through his hair. He'd always loved that. Especially right . . . there at his nape, just beneath the soft hollow behind his ear. Yes, oh, yes. He was going to leave this kiss far differently than he had left the others.

She pressed a fingertip to his chin. Yet, far from satisfied herself, she lingered, kissing him a little longer, a little deeper, stealing a little more of the magic.

His response was immediate and enthusiastic. Dazed, mesmerized, she gave herself to the kiss, vowing never again would she set out to teach her husband a lesson that didn't involve touching him. Learning never had been so pleasant for teacher or student.

"Bess?"

"Hmmm."

"We'd better stop this."

She nipped at his earlobe. Lord, he tasted sweet and smelled heavenly. *Obsession* and rain and warm man. "Uh-huh." Sounds were infinitely easier to manage than words.

He laved the hollow of her throat with his tender kisses. "I need to see to your knee."

Her knee? Oh, yes. Yes, her knee. She tried to clear her thoughts, but it was useless. In his arms, she staggered, lost in a sensual fog so thick and deep and dense she couldn't gather a thought to clear. "I need . . ."

"Me." John plunked her back down onto the counter.

Bess swayed. Her bottom was cold. She looked down. Her legs were bare. Where were — ? She looked down. Her jeans lay in a puddle on the floor. "Good grief. You did that without me even knowing it."

He grinned like the precocious, arrogant pig, slug-lover he was. "You were busy." A cotton ball in hand, he tipped the opening of the peroxide bottle against it, then slapped the bottle down, and the cotton ball to her knee.

It stung like fire. "Ouch!" She stared at the little *Occupied* sign on the counter next to the toothbrush holder and seriously

307

considered whacking him in the head with it.

"Be still, honey." He gentled his touch. "It'll be over before you know it."

Honey. Good grief. She couldn't very well whack a man calling her *honey.* "Hurry."

He glanced up, the devil dancing in his eyes. "Impatient to kill me, eh?"

She grunted. "Something like that."

Not looking at all worried, he tossed the cotton ball into the trash. "Do you want to shower with me first?"

"First?" A jolt of anticipation sneaked past her outrage and streaked to her core. She stared at the antique-brass soap dish and willed desire away. "I don't think so, Jonathan. I think first I'd like to sock you in the nose."

"Not exactly romantic, Doc, but if it'll get me another kiss like the last one . . ."

"Forget it." She scooted off the counter. Her knee locked up and she stumbled against him.

He lifted her into his arms and headed for the door. "I agree. We'll wait on the shower until . . . later."

"Jonathan!" she shrieked. She hadn't meant to shriek, of course, but, darn the man, he confused the heck out of her. First he wanted her, then he didn't, then he did again — though not for as long. And when she tried teaching him a lesson about kissing her quiet, she ended up tricked right out of her pants. How in the world he'd done that, she'd no idea. But he had done it and . . . well, whatever. She was just too weary of worries to worry about anything anymore. What harm was there in one little shriek, anyway? At this point, she'd *welcome* a month of silence.

Letting her head rest against John's shoulder, she focused on the books in the hand-carved shelves at the end of the hall. He was taking her back to her room. That was fine. She'd change her clothes, crawl into bed — without him; *definitely,* without him — then pull the covers up over her head. She'd said she was going to do that before and not come out until the world was civilized again. Well, she hadn't done it then. If she had, she wouldn't be in this mess. Another lesson learned: *Follow your instincts.*

John set her down beside the bed, then caressed her with his gaze. His wet jeans clung to his hips and muscular thighs. Memories of them together stirred and churned in her, sent heat swarming to her belly. She tightened her muscles against it. "I'm not going to bed with you."

"I know." He stared at her mouth.

"I mean it, Jonathan."

"I know you do."

His easy agreement had her even more jittery. "People who are divorcing don't sleep together."

He looked into her eyes. "We have."

"We have not." Lord, what an imagination.

John rubbed at his neck, then at his jaw. "I could have sworn I woke up this morning with a woman I thought was you on top of me." He pointed to the curve of his neck. "Her mouth was right here."

Bess wished the floor would open up and suck her down. But, like everything else, it wasn't cooperating. Now why didn't that surprise her? "I meant, we're not having sex."

"Good." He grabbed her by the waist. "I always preferred making love with you, Bess. And I have to say that, when I brought up the settlement proposal, I was a little ticked at your wanting to just have sex." His eyes twinkled knowingly. "Not nearly as . . . fulfilling as making love."

Flustered, she slapped at his hands and backed up a step. "I meant that we wouldn't be doing either, Jonathan, and you know it." A saint didn't have the patience needed to deal with this man.

"Oh." He stilled, nodded, and then turned for the door. "Well, I guess we can talk about Tony, then."

From one mine field to another. Lord, spare her — and heal her mind. It had to be sick or she wouldn't be feeling so disappointed that John's grand desire had stopped as quickly as a hot-air valve snapped shut. "I'd rather not."

"I'd rather not either, Bess, but the fact is we're caught up in some kind of mystical situation here. We have to accept it."

"Please, don't say it. Tony's just . . . Tony. He's a telepath with psychic insights. That's all." She hated the begging plea in her voice, the rationalization in her thinking, but she just couldn't take any more mental assaults right now. She just couldn't.

"Bess —"

"*Please*, Jonathan. *Please*, don't say that awful 'G' word. *Please*."

"He's a ghost, darling."

She covered her ears, turned, then crawled onto the bed, setting her sore knee to aching. "I'm not listening. I won't listen to this."

"You're not acting very doctorly." John stepped toward her.

Bess held up a hand to keep him away. "No, I'm not. But I'm not feeling very doctorly either. I'm feeling a lot of things — I have ever since Tony's first call — but I haven't once felt doctorly." She licked at her lips, her mouth as dry as sawdust. Admitting that hadn't been nearly as hard as she'd expected it would be, but what she really wanted — needed — was a few minutes alone to collect her composure. And, if her husband had an ounce of compassion in his huge body, he'd give her the time. "Why don't you go dry off and then we'll talk?"

He studied her, as if running a sincerity check. Well, she was sincere, so let him assess to his heart's content. She *would* talk to him — later. But first she had to have a good talk with herself. Her emotions were rioting, and rioting emotions and John Mystic made for an explosive situation. A few minutes alone and she'd regain control.

"All right, Bess." He moved to the door then stopped, one hand on the knob. "But as far as I'm concerned, this thing with Tony is settled. He is what he is, just as we are what we are. If he meant to hurt us, we'd be hurt. Remember that, okay? And you might also remember that you have a lot more to fear in refusing my proposal than you do in talking to a ghost."

"Do you realize how ridiculous that sounds?"

"Doesn't matter. Truth is truth, ridiculous sounding or not."

Essentially the same thing Tony had said. They both had a point, but she didn't have to like it. "You're right. Go dry off and we'll talk." She'd lock her door and not open it until Jimmy had her car back in running condition and parked outside in the driveway. And he'd be quick about getting it there or she'd nag him more than Beaulah Favish nagged Sheriff Cobb.

"Liar." John went stiff-shouldered. "You know, Bess, sometimes you're the most annoying woman I've ever met. You supposedly loved me once. Enough to marry me. But even with that between us, you'd rather lie to me than to tell me the truth. I just don't understand you."

"I don't understand you, either. I never have."

"I loved you, woman. What more did you need to understand?"

"You never loved me. You said you did and for a while, I believed you did. But you didn't."

"I'm not going to argue the point with you. I said I did, I did, and that's that. The subject is closed."

She lifted herself to her knees on the bed. Putting weight on her scrape, she grimaced and fell back onto the pillows. "You're very good at that."

He let go of the doorknob and put his hands on his hips. "At what?"

"Closing subjects." She waved an arm in frustration. "Do you realize we've been married for seven years and I've seen your sister Selena exactly twelve times, your Uncle Max half that many, and not once have I ever seen either of your parents? *Not once*. What kind of man won't introduce his wife to his parents? Won't even discuss them with her? I don't even know your mother's name, Jonathan."

Bess's self-esteem took a nosedive. What kind of man? One clearly ashamed of his wife. What other reason could there be for distancing her from his family?

"You married me, not them. And you walked out on me six years ago. So what's the difference?"

"Here we go again." No. No, they were not going to rehash old news. "Did your parents disapprove of you marrying someone beneath you financially? Was that it?" Darn it, now she was going to cry again. She just didn't understand it. She'd never been a weeper. Her father would have been disgusted, her mother mortified. And neither of them would have spoken a word to her for a month. Maybe two.

"You're right," John's eyes glittered, dark and angry. "The subject is closed." He grabbed the knob and tried to jerk the door open.

It wouldn't budge.

John tried again. The knob was turning, and the clicking sound proved the slide-bolt was freeing from the jamb. So why wouldn't the door open?

"What's wrong?"

"It's stuck." Clamping his jaw, he looked at the thing. Didn't appear swollen and he failed to see any reason it shouldn't open. But it wouldn't. His gaze lit on the brass hinges. No problem. If the knob wouldn't work, the hinges would.

He looked around for something to work with, rifled through the desk drawer and, in the long center one, he found a letter opener. It wasn't a screwdriver, but it would do.

"What are you doing?" Bess scrambled off the bed and stood beside him.

Crouched down at the door, he removed the lower pin from the hinge, then stretched up to remove the top one. "The door won't open, so I'm taking it off the hinges." He couldn't talk about his parents. He'd never had the luxury of doing that with anyone.

And if Bess ever had loved him, she'd have respected that.

"It won't do any good."

The top hinge pin popped out. He braced to catch the door. It didn't shift so much as a fraction of an inch.

"John." She touched his arm, her hand trembling. "Jonathan, it's not the door."

"What?" John darted his gaze to her.

"It's Tony." Bess lowered her voice to soften the blow. "I feel him here, and I think he means for us to stay put."

You're exactly right, Bess, I do.

John and Bess locked gazes.

Tony?

Yes, Jonathan?

Would you open the blasted door, please?

Of course.

Now?

No, Bess. Not just yet.

When?

That depends on the two of you.

Oh gosh.

Bess, you can stop shaking like a leaf I'm not going to hurt you. Jonathan was right about that. I mean you no harm.

What are you going to do to us, then?

Nothing.

Then why keep us locked in here?

You need a little time together, Jonathan.

Terrific. He's encouraging again.

What?

Encouraging. I call it nagging, but he takes offense to the word. He "merely encourages," he says.

That's right, I do.

So we're staying here until we're encouraged. Well, I'm so glad you two cleared that up for me.

How long you're here, Jonathan, depends entirely on the two of you.

What do you mean?

I'm encouraging you, as Bess suggested.

To do what?

Jonathan, don't shout at him. He's a ghost, for pity's sake. Do you really want to tangle tempers with a ghost?

To do what?

Ah, that's much better. Bess is right. I do strongly oppose shouting. Hattie's father was a shouter and it upset her immensely.

You know Miss Hattie?

They were engaged, Bess. Tony died during the war.

Bess gasped.

Are you going to faint?

No. No, it's not that.

Well, what is it?

It's that real love — like the legend of Collin and Cecelia.

317

A little different. They got to spend their lives together. For Hattie and me . . . it's been different.

But you're here. You're still here.

I love her.

Yes. And you made her promises that you've kept. Bess slid John a reprimanding look. *Even dead, he kept his promises.*

Bess, don't be hard on Jonathan. Sometimes promises perceived as broken aren't.

What?

Sometimes the person who promised is doing his best to keep his word. It doesn't look like it, and maybe you don't feel as if that's the case, but it is. Sometimes there are extenuating circumstances. Wouldn't you agree, Jonathan?

John looked away, his jaw carved of granite. *Maybe. Maybe not. Look, we'll try to keep that in mind — your opposition to shouting. So what's the plan?*

The plan?

What do we have to do to get out of this room?

It's really simple. You and Bess should have no difficulty whatsoever. All you have to do is to talk to each other.

We've been talking.

As Jonathan said earlier, Bess, truth is truth, and what you've been doing is shouting and

318

evading the truth.

I get it.

You do? What does he mean, Jonathan?

We'll be stuck in here 'til hell freezes over.

That's absurd. Ridiculous. Tell him it isn't so, Tony.

I can't.

What?

Quit shouting. He's a ghost, remember?

Sorry.

I have every intention of letting you out.

When?

When?

Just as soon as you both get civilized.

Good grief.

Like, I said. 'Til hell freezes over.

Jonathan, I don't appreciate the innuendo that I'm —

Innuendo? I said it straight out, Bess.

I insist you apologize for it, too.

Civilized! Tony shouted to gain their attention. *Both of you!*

Now you've done it, Jonathan Mystic. He's furious.

Me?

Yes, you.

I suggest you stop slinging blame and think about my message. I told you it was significant, Bess.

What message?

His "leap upon a mystic tide" one.

I heard it on the radio, remember? Do you know what it means?

No.

Do you, Jonathan? Tony asked.

No.

Then you'll both stay here until you do.

"You can't be serious!" Bess spoke aloud. "Tony? Tony, don't you leave us here."

John waited for it to occur to her that Tony had gone. John had recognized it instantly, the second he could no longer hear Bess's voice inside his head. Tony had told John he could arrange three-way conversations, but John hadn't realized that during them he and Bess would be able to communicate with each other telepathically.

"I don't believe this!" Bess groused, began pacing and verbally blasting all men.

A minute passed, then two, and then two more. And still she showed no signs of winding down. Surprised, John lay down on her bed and watched her pace the floor, shout curses on Tony's head — and more than a few on John's own. Her eyes glittered a blue that put the ocean to shame. Her face flushed a ravishing pink that captivated him. Riled and unmasked, she was just as he'd always imagined she would be: magnificent.

And still so beautiful that looking at her hurt.

Bryce had said she had changed. And, man, had she. Never once in their marriage had he seen her so loose with her emotions. In bed, she'd been warm and passionate, clearly loving and, at times, lusty, but even then she'd held a part of herself back. Out of bed, she'd been all cool and sleek, cashmere and eel-skin. But now, now, she was feisty, fiery; totally adorable — and even more desirable.

And just once before she divorced him and married that sorry Spaniard, John had to see if she'd changed in bed as well as out of it. Just once, he had to see her in his arms, them loving, and her not holding back.

Just once, he had to know that, to her, he held value.

CHAPTER 8

"Well, how long is it going to be before you can get to it, Jimmy?" The tulip-shaped phone receiver at her ear, Bess glided her thumb along the edge of the little vanilla-scented shell on the desk and looked out of the turret room window at the flower gardens, at the forest and hills beyond them.

"It's kind of hard to say."

Covertly, she glanced over at John Mystic. Planted squarely in the middle of her four-poster bed, his head on her plump blue pillows, he lay stretched out, his hands stacked behind his head, his legs crossed at his ankles, and his to-die-for body wrapped in her silk robe. It was the only thing she owned large enough to cover the essential parts of him until his own clothes dried — or until Tony got over his snit and let them out of this room. Jonathan *should* look ridiculous. But he didn't.

Lust with a kick. Inwardly, Bess sighed. If

the man had an ounce of decency or compassion, he'd have gotten slouchy. "Do you have *any* idea?"

"I ain't exactly sure how long it'll be, Mrs. Myst— I mean, Ms. Cameron. The rain has me pretty backed up and, with the wind blowing like it is, I can't be putting your car or anyone else's up on the rack."

"But the rack is inside, isn't it?" The Great White Room was spacious, charming. But with John in it, it seemed small and close and crowded, as if its heavy furniture suddenly had grown too large and its spackled ceiling and paneled walls were closing in on her.

"Yes, ma'am. The rack's inside the shop, but I have to have the bay door open — Village Ordinance — and it creates a kind of wind tunnel. Could knock your car clean off."

"All right." Bess suffered a shaft of disappointment. To get past it, she focused on the sweet-smelling, yellow daffodils in a slender cut-crystal vase atop the chest of drawers, at the two heavy-stemmed water glasses beside it. "But please, as soon as you can, okay?"

"Yes, ma'am. As soon as it's time. You can count on it."

"Thanks." She cradled the receiver,

grabbed her hairbrush from the dresser, then walked over to the turret room. Dragging the bristles through her hair, liking the grating friction against her scalp, she looked outside. Wind whipped through the pines, blowing blustery sheets of rain that had leaves dancing and the window panes spotting. Miss Hattie's impatiens were taking a beating. Feeling a little bruised herself, Bess lifted her gaze to the gloomy, swirling clouds. Turbulent. But not a bit more so than she felt. This entire situation rattled her. It was just too bizarre.

Panic welled in her stomach. Hoping the sound of her own voice, the feel of her own senses, would reassure her she was all right and would keep panic at bay, she pressed her cheek to the cold glass. "Still raining like crazy out there, John."

No answer.

She glanced over at him. "Are you napping?" His eyes closed, his expression relaxed, the arrogant jerk reeked of peace. "We've been stuck in here for hours. How can you nap?"

He let out a heartfelt sigh that really irritated her and pulled himself up on an elbow. "It's not easy with you spewing fire and brimstone. Why don't you give it a rest?"

"Because I'm angry. And I'm hungry and thirsty. And I'd *really* like to see the inside of a bathroom again, preferably in the near future." Because she'd lost control of her emotions in front of him, because she'd banished patience and grace to obscurity forever with her outrageous tirade, she'd also embarrassed herself half to death. But she refrained from mentioning it. No sense being redundant and, if the fire burning her face fairly gauged, only a blind man would miss knowing it without being told. Jonathan Mystic, smirk intact, obviously was not a blind man.

She slapped her brush onto the desk. It landed with a *thunk* and, catching a whiff of the potpourri, she lifted the shell. Why the little thing had a soothing effect on her, she didn't know. But considering her agitation, she'd take any soothing she could get from wherever she could get it. Lord, but she was tired. Fear of Tony zapping her and John to Pluto, or doing something equally horrid and unprecedented, had her anxiety hovering at skyscraper level. Never in her life had she undergone such a potent adrenaline surge. It'd thoroughly depleted her energy reserves. Her lids were drooping and her limbs felt like lead. To recharge her batteries, she needed sleep in a bad way. Right now, she couldn't tell if her own behavior ranked passive, aggressive, or repressive. Forget trying to analyze Jonathan's. Tony's, however, was easy. Definitely aggressive. And manipulative.

She stifled a sigh. Sad, but that embraced all the emotion she could muster. "Aren't you at all concerned about being held prisoner, Jonathan?"

"Of course I'm concerned." He didn't so much as crank open an eyelid.

"Well, would you just spare a minute to look like it?"

"Quit snipping at me, Bess. I didn't lock us in here."

He was right. "I'm sorry." Skirting the rug that earlier had tripped and landed her in her husband's arms, she walked over to him. "Can we please just get civilized so we can get the heck out of here?"

"I've been civilized. You're the one who's called Tony everything under the sun and paced grooves in Miss Hattie's floor. I'll bet she won't appreciate what you did to the sill, trying to open the window either."

"It's just a little gouge." Good grief, could her face get any hotter? "I'll have it repaired — if we ever get out of here." If Tony had meant that they had to solve his puzzle before leaving this room, they'd die of old age staring at these walls — or of starvation. Surely he hadn't been serious. He *couldn't* have been serious. Could he?

"You need sleep." John folded a hand over his chest. "When you're tired, you're always cranky."

"I am tired." She was cranky, too. And getting crankier. Rubbing the instep of her left foot with the arch of her right one, she debated asking Jonathan for a foot massage then decided against it. He sounded prickly and more rejection from him she didn't need. "I told you I didn't sleep well."

"You slept like a rock, darling." He grunted, punched his pillow, then returned his arm to his chest. "You were in bed with me, remember?"

"I didn't say I didn't sleep, Jonathan." Lord, did the man have to notice everything? And why wasn't he uncomfortable, lying there swathed in pink silk? He should be disturbed, his male ego wounded. Instead he had the audacity to look totally at ease and . . . cute.

Her stomach furled and she cast a pleading look at his clothes. Still and lifeless, they hung on hangers snagged to the turret room drapery rod. She stared at his shorts, silently ordering them to get dry now so he could get his sexy self back into them and stop lounging in her bed, on her pillow, nude beneath her robe, with her silk caressing his skin . . .

Her heartbeat sprinted from a crawl to a canter. The flutters in her belly grew stronger and a groan eased up her throat. She swallowed it back down. *He* was making her crazy. Violating her territory, her senses. Making her remember things better forgotten. She fisted her hands and clamped her jaw. "I said I didn't sleep well, not that I didn't sleep. There's a difference."

"Oh." Clearly ignoring her stiff tone, he patted the mattress beside him. "Well, come take a nap with me, then we'll get civil."

Why bother? The man was too slow or too stubborn to know he'd been verbally swatted. Stubborn. He might be many things, but slow didn't rank among them. And she *was* tired; beyond tired, actually. Thanks to the non-slouch in her bed, she'd gotten little sleep last night and, between worrying about him on the cliffs, the storm, and Tony's surreal antics, she'd spent the entire morning in trauma. It might only be late afternoon, but it felt like the back side of midnight. Maybe if she slept a few minutes she would feel better.

Fighting a yawn, she crawled over John, brushing his stomach with her knee, then settled off his side, dead certain she'd never nod off for so much as a wink. Not with him so close, radiating heat and looking more tempting than a quart of Double Chocolate Fudge ice cream. Not a wink, not a chance.

He turned off the lamp. Though only late afternoon, the storm had the room filled with dusky shadows. "You know, you always do that."

She scrunched the pillow and tugged at the hem of her sweatshirt. July in Maine didn't resemble it in New Orleans. The room was downright chilly. Tempted to slide under the comforter, she opted to freeze. When he looked scrumptious and smelled so sweet — Lord, but she loved that *Obsession* cologne of his — and when she *wasn't* scared witless, creating a warm cocoon with John Mystic definitely wasn't a smart move. "What do I always do?"

He forked his fingers along his scalp, ruffling his hair. "Crawl over me rather than walk around."

She hadn't thought about it, but she always had done that. "Does it bother you?"

"No. But it used to be a lot more fun." He grinned mischievously and cracked open his left eye. "You used to take your time up top and visit a little."

She had. Yet more heat spiked up her neck to her cheeks. She quickly turned away, stared at the vanity in the corner. Her hip smarted, where she'd banged it on the boxes in his room: a firm reminder to keep her mind on the business at hand — which certainly did *not* include complicating matters further by again getting physically involved with John. It was disconcerting, not being terrified and being in bed again with a husband she hadn't made love with in six years. But it wouldn't be making love. It . . . wouldn't.

Her head was convinced. Abstinence and avoidance definitely rated wise on its choice list. However, her body rebelled. Before it would agree, it needed a deep and serious dose of convincing. The magic kept challenging her logic, and her senses rioted, plaguing her with an acute awareness of his every nuance. And that knocked her further off-kilter, upsetting her even more. Only John could portray a woman's fantasy of masculinity while wearing a dusty pink woman's robe. Only he could smell like the earth and man and the sea and something so uniquely him that a woman craved burying her face at the cove of his neck and inhaling deeply. Only his sounds and sights and scents could make a woman yearn to touch him so desperately that the thought alone had her fingertips tingling and her blood heating and rushing through her veins.

It wasn't fair. Or just. But what in life was either? She flopped onto her back with the grace of a beached fish. "We've got to find a way out of here."

"We've got a way out. All we have to do is to talk, remember?"

She couldn't get situated. No matter what position she tried, she ended up fidgeting.

"Come here, Bess." John stretched out an arm and curled her to him.

She shouldn't do it, but she was exhausted. What harm could a little snuggle do anyway? She scooted closer on the plump comforter and cuddled to him.

"Better?" His warm breath fanned her neck.

Heaven. "Better." She sighed and closed her eyes, wishing that were anything but the truth. What should she do with her hands? Before, she'd have draped her left one over his chest, let it meander over the hard ridge of muscles and bones and warm skin that reminded her of steel sheathed in velvet. But she couldn't do that now. "May I ask you something?"

"Sure."

She tilted her neck. His eyes were closed and he still looked relaxed. Considering their circumstances with Tony, how could John be comfortable? And didn't being in bed with her and holding her in his arms have *any* effect on the man?

Best steer away from those kinds of thoughts. "Tony asked me a question I couldn't answer. It got me to wondering, and I thought maybe I'd ask you — not that the answer makes any difference now." She sounded like a rationalizing idiot in denial.

John rubbed little circles on her shoulder. "If it doesn't make any difference, then why wonder about it?"

She half-shrugged. "I'm curious." Her right hand captured beneath her pillow, she figured the only way she could *not* touch him with the left one would be to stuff it under her side. That didn't work. Felt as if her arm was ripping from its socket. She frowned into the dim light. Now what? She couldn't hold her arm midair for however long they lay here.

Good grief. What difference did it make? It was just a touch — and there certainly didn't have to be anything sexual in it. His chest was just a comfortable place to rest her hand; no less, but certainly no more. And he didn't appear to hold qualm one about touching her. Those little circles on her shoulder felt delicious. So why should she feel uncomfortable at touching him?

Giving in, she lowered her hand to his hair-roughened chest, over his heart. Bare skin? Lord help her, the robe gaped. Her stomach surged to her throat and her heart knocked against her ribs. Why, oh why, couldn't his clothes be dry and he be in them?

"If I answer your question, then will you let me have my nap?"

"Yes." His grumpy tone hadn't fooled her. He just didn't want to be asked questions he might not want to answer. "Back when we were together, why did you put Elise's needs before mine?"

"I didn't." He sounded genuinely surprised.

"You did." She forced the bitterness from her voice and rubbed a tiny square on his chest to apologize. "You left me alone over Christmas, Jonathan."

He tilted up her face with a thumb under her chin. If it hadn't been too dark, they'd have seen eye to eye. "I never put Elise's needs before yours. *Never.* Your desires, maybe, but never your needs. And that Christmas was about Dixie as much as it was about Elise. And about me."

What did that mean?

He paused a long moment, then dropped his voice. "You don't understand, do you?"

Bess grunted, "Uh-uh." She didn't dare to risk words for fear he'd stop explaining.

"You're strong and capable, Bess. One of the most independent women I've ever known. If you want something done, you do it or you have it done. I wasn't worried about you being able to take care of yourself. You were safe and at home. Fine. And whatever might come up, I trusted you to handle it. You always had. But Elise was in a panic. All in the world she had was Dixie. Can't you imagine a mother's fear at not knowing if her daughter is dead or alive? Elise was falling apart at the seams, Doc. And then there was Dixie." He let his hand sweep down the length of Bess's hair. "She was just a kid. A scared kid who *wasn't* safe at home but held captive. A kid in the hands of kidnapers who could have been doing only heaven knew what to her."

Bess started to remind him that Dixie might well have been in the arms of her fiancé but knowing now that before he'd taken those comments as a lack of faith in his judgment, she held her tongue. "In other words, Elise and Dixie needed you, and I didn't. Is that what you thought?"

"Well, yes." He cocked his head. The satiny pillowslip rustled. "I got a lead, Bess. I *had* to check it out. Not knowing what was happening to Dixie, I couldn't ignore it until after the holiday. What kind of investigator would do that? What kind of man would do that? If your husband put something that important on hold, would you respect him?"

"I don't know." That honesty wasn't very flattering. But she'd looked at this from a different perspective for years and weighing these new views would take a little time. She'd thought she'd analyzed to death the dynamics at work in their relationship, but now she had doubts. Had she looked at the big picture and not just her own version of it?

"Be honest with me. And with you."

"I don't think I would respect him much," she finally decided.

John stopped his hand at her nape then worked his fingers up under her hair, against her skin. "What if the lead had panned out? What if I'd stayed home, pretending everything had been fine, ignoring Elise's feelings and her fear for her daughter and, after Christmas, I'd gotten up to Portland and had found Dixie dead? I'd have to live with wondering if I'd done what I should have done. Wondering if I'd given just a little more, tried just a little harder, been just a little less selfish, I might have been able to save her."

Steep, steep repercussions. Ones Bess, though ashamed to admit it, never had considered. Close to tears, she kept her eyes squeezed shut. "I understand." She'd thought he hadn't cared. Not true. He'd cared a great deal. For the child incapable of caring for herself, and for Bess. He'd trusted her to be capable of caring for herself *and* of understanding his what-if fears. She hadn't. And only now did she see how unfair she'd been to him.

His words echoed through her mind: *I loved you, woman. What more did you need to understand?*

He had loved her. In his way, he really had. But he'd been unfair to her, too. Three days of worry. Three long, fear-ridden days that had seemed to stretch on forever. He thought her strong. Capable. But she wasn't. So many times, she'd wanted to lean on him. To reach out, to ask his opinion, his advice. But she'd been afraid to do it. What if he'd reacted the way her father had reacted? What if any display of weakness or dependence had repulsed Jonathan?

The truth struck her with the force of a

sharp right hook. She'd been unfair, too. Jonathan was Jonathan. He wasn't, nor would he ever be, like her father or anyone else. All men were not alike — how well she knew it. And how tragic that for all her training and experience she'd failed to see that simple truth in her own situation.

Her grandmother's words about not being able to see the forest for the trees came to mind. Rubbing her fingertips, Bess mulled on the wrong she'd done. It was too late for it to matter, of course, but still, she'd like to know the truth. Standing outside the forest, no, she'd never see the trees. But if she ventured inside . . .

A few minutes slipped past. Maybe it *was* time she found out how he'd react.

Finally, she worked up her courage. Her stomach churned and, though chilled, she broke out in a sweat. This was a monumental moment in her life, and she didn't much care for monumental moments. By far, she preferred smooth personal sailing. "Jonathan?"

"Hmmm?"

Her throat went dry. "I needed you, too."

His hand, sweeping her hair, stilled.

A long tense moment crept by. Then another. Her nerves stretched taut. Why didn't he say something — *anything* to put her out of this misery? "I — I understand why you did what you did now. I should have seen that then, but I didn't." She stared at him in the semidarkness, grateful for its shielding cloak. Looking into his beautiful eyes, she'd never have the courage to say what she wanted to say. What rested deep in her heart. "I just wanted you to . . . know."

"Thank you, Bess." His voice sounded husky soft, a tremor from cracking.

She had to admit to the rest, too. It was time. Lord, could she do it? She had to try. To at least try. "I'm not always . . . strong, or capable, or self-sufficient. I try, but I don't always succeed." *Hard. So hard, this.* "Sometimes I really needed you too, and I had to struggle to not burden you with my . . . challenges. *Troubles. Worries. Concerns. Problems. Fears. I needed you!* "I know you admire women who take care of themselves."

He turned and his minty breath fanned her face. "I admire you. I always have. You needing me wouldn't have been a burden, Doc. It'd have been a blessing."

Cotton-mouthed, she swallowed, afraid to believe. "That's what Tony said."

"I agree with him — on that." John paused, as if collecting his thoughts, then went on. "I never wanted you to feel you couldn't talk to me about anything. I felt shut out. Unessential." He cupped his hand over hers on his chest. "I wanted us to share everything."

"No, you didn't. We have to be brutally honest here, Jonathan. You might think you wanted to share everything but you truly only wanted to share some things. The comfortable ones. Otherwise your parents wouldn't have been — or continue to be — a taboo subject."

Against her forehead, his jaw went chisel hard. "Sorry, but I can't talk about them."

"Can't or won't?"

"Can't." He swallowed hard. "I — I want to. I just . . . can't."

Disappointment ricocheted through her, rib to rib, heart to soul, and hope of them finally understanding each other, finally making genuine progress and settling their differences, died. Before, she'd shut him out. And he'd shut her out. Now, she was trying — Lord, but was she trying — to be open and honest, and still he shut her out. Just like before. She couldn't make their relationship — might as well call a spade a spade, their marriage — work alone. He had to do his part, too. "Fine."

"Fine."

She turned over onto her side, her back to him, rested her head on his upper arm, then closed her eyes. Burying the anger, disappointment, and bitterness, as she'd buried everything else for most of her life, she stilled.

Nearly asleep, she missed his warmth. They'd come so close to harmony. She hated this emotional distance between them. Hated it. Maybe she could try again. Nothing ventured, nothing gained, right?

She licked at her lips, hoping she didn't get her head bitten off for her trouble. "I hope your lead calls, Jonathan, and I hope you find Dixie. I really, really do."

The covers rustled beneath them. He scooted closer, fitting himself to her spoon-fashion and pulling the end of the coverlet up over them. "Bess," he whispered softly, then placed a kiss to the cove of her neck.

"Hmm?" Lord, but it felt good to be cradled in his arms. Cocoons might not be smart, but they sure were cozy.

"I have a confession to make."

Had he thought it over and been repulsed by her confessing her weaknesses, after all? She snapped open her eyes and stared at the dim outline of the dresser, her heart nearly careening out of her chest. "Okay."

"I hate that terracotta berry box you

bought for Miss Hattie."

"What?" Bess tried to rear but was thwarted. Tossing a leg over her thighs and an arm over her midriff, he held her firmly in place. She lay back down, her cheek pressed to his hair-roughened arm. It felt . . . soothing. "Why?" The box? Why would he hate the box? She'd never expected this.

He hesitated a long moment, then answered. "Because you chose it."

Her heart felt squeezed. "I chose you, too, Jonathan."

"But that was then." Sadness rippled through his voice and shimmied into her heart.

"Yes, that was then." She shifted back, closer, trying to get off her sore hip, and to steal more of his heat.

He let out a little groan. "I'd, um, really appreciate it if you'd be still a minute."

"Sorry." Statue-still, she stared sightlessly into the shadows, telling herself nine-hundred logical reasons why she shouldn't turn over and make love with her husband. And she accepted each one of them as valuable and valid, as logical and wise. But one reason refused to balance out on logic's pros and cons scales. The magic.

It was still there.

And, Lord help them both, it was *so* strong.

Tired of fighting it, she shifted, preparing to turn.

John clasped a firm hand on her hip. "Unless you've thought this through and you're sure, don't turn over." His voice low and gravelly, laced with warning. "I mean it, Doc."

Her head ordered her to be still and not to move a muscle. Making love with him would be foolish. It'd negate their legal separation. They'd have to go through the entire divorce process all over again. This wasn't a reunion. It was lust with a kick. That hadn't been enough to hold him before, and she'd just end up losing him all over again. More mourning. More pain. More emptiness and struggling to build a life without him. Did she need that? Want that? No. Only a fool would, and she was no fool.

Or was she?

Maybe she was the greatest kind of fool. Her heart still urged her to turn, to grab this chance with both hands and to hold on tight. Love or lust, one night or forever, she wanted him. What difference did the divorce make? The timing of it? It wasn't as if she intended to remarry. She didn't want any other man. She wanted this man. With her whole heart.

"And don't forget Santos." John's voice dropped a decibel and went hard. "I can't hold you in my arms and make love with you, knowing you're thinking of him. I . . . won't."

Jonathan jealous? Of Miguel? And sounding equally bent on convincing himself as on convincing her? Her heart gave a little lurch, and her logic popped in with a discomforting thought her heart agreed she should accept. Whether or not they physically made love didn't really matter. Not being physical wouldn't protect her emotions. When John Mystic again exited her life, she again would mourn him. "There's only you and me here, Jonathan," she whispered.

He sucked in a deep breath, and his hand on her ribs trembled. "Then come here and let me love you."

She turned over.

He pulled her to him, aligning their bodies "It's powerful stuff, Doc, telling a man you once needed him."

How she must have hurt him with that. He'd felt as much an outsider in her life as she'd felt in his. To know, yes. Yes. To know you're not only wanted, but needed. To feel

vital and important to another human being. To matter. Powerful feeling. Powerful . . . and humbling.

She slipped her hand under his arm,
around his waist to his broad back. "I know
we should talk and settle our differences
first. We should know what this means to
us. Will we be together again just this once,
or does this mean more?"

"I don't know." He kissed a trail along her
jaw. "I only know I want you."

He wanted her. Wanted *her.* A trickle of
sheer pleasure streaked from the underside
of her chin straight down her middle to her
core. How many times had she lain in bed
and cried because she'd never heard those
words? How many times had she imagined
him giving her what he now offered? And if
she refused now, how many times in the
years ahead would she regret it?

Still, one of them had to remain grounded.
Consequences would follow. They'd both
pay them. "It'll cause problems with the
divorce, Jonathan."

"Right now, that doesn't seem important."
He kissed the lobe of her ear, the soft spot
behind it, the pulse point throbbing at her
throat. "Did you mean it, Doc?"

Would it be important later? She arched
her neck, let her fingertips drift over his

back. "Did I mean what?"

"That you needed me."

The fierce hope that she did shimmered in his voice and arrowed straight into her heart. A lump of regret that she hadn't told him, hadn't let him see just how much she'd needed him, settled squarely in her throat and she promised herself that, regardless of what tomorrow brought them, tonight John Mystic wouldn't doubt anything she felt for him. "I needed you then," she confessed, "and I need you now."

A groan rumbled down deep in his throat. He rolled her onto her back, then hovered above her. His arms suffered a tremor and his heart pounded against her chest like a frantic drum. "I needed you then too, Doc."

Oh, how she wished she could see his eyes! She was a fool to ask, but she had to know. Her heart just had to know. "And . . . now?"

Cupping her face in his hands, he vowed, "I need you now. I . . . need."

He covered her lips with his in a searing kiss. Breathless, Bess dragged her hand over his shoulder, along its blade, and shoved her silky robe away from his warm skin. She needed, too. To touch him, to love him. To feel the magic.

The phone rang.

Bess snapped her eyes open, but either he hadn't heard it, or he'd chosen to ignore it. On the third ring, she broke their kiss. "Jonathan, the phone."

"Forget it," he murmured against her lips, sliding his hand along her thigh. "They'll call back."

He touched a particularly sensitive spot, and she shuddered. "It could be important."

"Not more important than this. Not to me."

Her woman's heart filled and, joyful, she kissed his clavicle to let him know it. "What if it's the man from Portland?"

John went stiff in her arms. What if it was Keith? "I'd better get it."

John crawled out of bed. Of all the times for anyone to call. Why not when they'd been fighting? When she'd been ranting? Why *now?* He grabbed the receiver then growled into it. "Mystic."

Bess turned on the little tulip lamp, then propped on an elbow and called out to him from the bed. "Don't bite off anyone's head, Jonathan."

Rumpled and flushed and hungry-eyed, she looked good enough to devour. Whoever was calling had twenty seconds. John was a reasonable man — and a realistic one. He couldn't wait any longer than that to get back to her.

"This is Keith, down at Dockside."

The Portland man. The bar where John had lost Dixie's trail six years ago. How had Bess known? Tony? John's heart started a low, hard beat. "You have news?"

"Yeah. The man you want is back in Portland. His name's Gregor Samuels and he'll be here tomorrow at two."

"I'll be there." John swallowed hard. "Thanks."

"No problem."

The line went dead.

John hung up the phone, his hand shaking, and turned to Bess.

Sitting Indian-style in the middle of the bed, her eyes blazed. "I heard. You're leaving, aren't you?"

"Provided Tony will let me out, yes. It's a lead on Dixie, Bess. I have to check it."

Bess's heart shattered. After six years, Dixie couldn't have been kidnaped. Elise never had been contacted with a ransom demand. And after her death, if Dixie had eloped, then wouldn't she have come home? If for no other reason, wouldn't she have come to claim her inheritance?

That left only one explanation, and Bess couldn't bring herself to think it, much less to say it out loud. But knowing it; knowing

John had to realize Dixie's status too; knowing that, in their own way, she and John were trying to settle their differences and, maybe — just maybe — trying to put their marriage back together, it hurt for him to again leave her to follow up on a lead. It devastated her that even now, even after all they'd been through together, she still ranked a poor second.

Isn't it interesting?

"Tony! Good grief, would you please knock or something? You scared me out of my socks."

"Tony, I'm glad you're here. I need to go to Portland. It's important. Could you please, please, let me out of here?"

Isn't anyone going to ask me what's interesting?

"Okay, Tony. What's interesting?"

Thank you, Jonathan. Isn't it interesting that you two are so very opposed to being stuck here together and yet for hours neither of you has tried to open the door?

"Jonathan, don't do it! He's a ghost, for goodness sake."

Primed for a strong shout, John shut his mouth, held his tongue, and strode to the door. Though he hadn't replaced the hinge pins, they were back in their slots. He grabbed the knob then twisted it.

The door swung open.

"You were bluffing. Darn it, Tony, why did —"

"Jonathan, darling, don't rile him." Bess crawled out of bed, came to John's side, then put a restraining hand on his arm. "What will we gain?"

For the record, I wasn't bluffing. I was proving a point.

"Lord help us, another puzzle."

Yes, Bess. But one you'll surely understand — if you dare.

Knowing exactly what Tony meant, she looked up at Jonathan, her chest tight with fear. Yet another monumental moment. She dredged up her courage, swallowed her pride, and then confessed the truth. "I didn't try the door because I didn't want to leave."

"You didn't?"

She'd been about to make love with him and he asks her that? Shocked herself, though, she couldn't hold his surprise against him. She gave him a slow, negative nod.

John looked down at her, his eyes bright and tender. "Me either, Doc."

Ah, sweet progress. I suggest you both think about that.

■ ■ ■ ■

She sat in the gazebo, staring out onto the moonlit pond. The gentle wind nipped at her hair, ruffled her white blouse and slacks. If she'd worn any other color, John might not have seen her; she sat so still. Deep in thought, he suspected, dragging a hand through his hair. Since Tony's last stunt and Bess's confession, John had thought plenty.

He loved her. He always had, and he always would. But could he stay married to her without destroying them both? That, he didn't know. Nor did he know how she felt about him. Needing him — dear heaven, nothing in his life ever had made him feel that good — was a far cry from still loving him. And how did Santos fit in? It didn't seem possible Bess loved the man. It wasn't her style to love one man and make love with another. John frowned. And they *would* have made love — had Keith not called from Portland.

That certainty had John's heart racing, his stomach knotting, and all of him regretting the interruption. It beat at him like a series of potent punches. The bottom line was that, yes, they were resolving their differences. But they hadn't resolved them yet.

And exactly what that resolution entailed, they'd neither determined nor stipulated. But from John's side of the fence, only one point of agreement couldn't be waived. He had to settle this case. He had to find Dixie and put the case, and the guilt, behind him. After all it'd cost him, he couldn't crawl back to Bess and their marriage a failure. He just couldn't do it. And, by her own admission, she wouldn't respect him if he did.

He walked on, across the rocky leaf-strewn ground, into the gazebo, then stopped beside the slatted bench. She didn't turn around; kept staring out onto the pond. Sprinkled with moonlight, it shimmered as if star-studded with diamonds. "Bess?"

"Hmmm?"

No surprise. She'd known it was him approaching. Still acutely perceptive. So why then couldn't she perceive all his feelings for her? Was it a blessing that she couldn't, or a curse? "Don't you think you should come inside? It's late and it's getting cold out." She didn't have on a sweater. She had to be chilled.

"I've been thinking."

"Me, too." He stepped over and put a hand on her shoulder. "You okay?"

She looked up at him, her eyes sad, her

tone resigned. "You're leaving."

How he wished he could say no. But nothing had changed and, until he settled this case, peace for him, for Elise, would remain as elusive as any hope of a reconciliation with Bess. "In the morning." Would she miss him? Be glad to see him go? Pray he didn't return? "But I'll be back tomorrow night."

"Maybe." She shrugged. "That depends on what happens at Dockside, doesn't it?"

"Yeah." She knew him better than he knew himself. He lowered his hand from her shoulder, then fisted his hand and stuffed it into his slacks pocket. "I guess it does."

Bess stood up and tilted her chin, then leaned back against the lattice-work railing. "I hadn't planned on spending my time here the way I have."

Because she didn't sound as if she regretted the way she had spent it, he smiled. "Me either."

"I wanted to go out to Little Island and cook clams in the rocks. When you bake clams that way, the seaweed is very important."

"As soon as I get back, we can go."

She stared up at him. "Are you coming back?"

"Yes."

"Why?"

Good question. "We haven't settled anything." A strand of her hair blew over her cheek. He thumbed it away from her eyes. "In fact, a lot less between us is settled now than before we came to Seascape."

"I've been thinking about your proposition —"

"Proposal." Frogs from down at the pond croaked throatily, and something scurried in an evergreen bush off to the left. Ah, the raccoon.

"Whatever. I've thought about it and I've decided, okay. You can have your week."

His heart nearly rocked through his ribs. "What changed your mind?"

She lifted her hands to his chest, let her right one drift up over his clavicle and circle his neck, then tugged, pulling him down to where she could reach his mouth. "You, darling. Only you," she whispered, then kissed him.

Man, the things this woman made him feel. And so gentle, this kiss. So gentle and loving it filled him with a longing that burned soul-deep. He kissed her back, giving her the tenderness he'd too often denied her, letting her know that, while he wanted her, his feelings for her ran deeper than lust and desire and passion. Those feelings were there, but others were too. Ones that were stronger. So much stronger . . . and freer. Untethered and boundless, those feelings were founded in love.

She lifted her head, then pressed her cheek against his chest. Her arms looping his waist, she snuggled to him, then gave his sides a firm squeeze. He held her tighter, his heart so full he feared it'd burst, her *You, darling. Only you* echoing through the chambers of his mind. "Bess, what exactly does that mean?"

Rearing back, she looked at him. "I don't know. Maybe I'm sick of the world and all its problems and I want to just forget they exist for a while. Maybe I just need . . ."

"Me?" he asked around a lump in his throat.

She laughed. "Arrogant pig."

He nearly dropped his teeth. "What?"

"Arrogant pig." She rubbed his nose with the tip of hers and held her smile.

He grunted. An endearment if ever he'd heard one. "And how does it feel to know that you once loved this arrogant pig?"

She pretended to think about it. "I'll let you know in a week."

"Fair enough." He pecked a kiss to her lips, light and teasing. "Just so we understand the terms here. No mention of the divorce, no mudslinging from the past, and no games. We're a married couple, very much in love, enjoying a summer vacation in a sleepy Maine fishing village." Why had he added that about love? Why delude himself? The answer came far too easily. *I . . . need.*

"Okay, provided you agree to my terms too."

"Which are?"

"No saying things we really don't mean, no taboo topics, and, at the end of the week, no custody suit over Silk."

He let his arms slide down her shoulders then locked them at her back. "That leaves only one issue to be solved."

"The money settlement." She swallowed hard. "Jonathan, I know you don't understand this, and you clearly think I'm being unreasonable about it, but I'm not. I can't take your money. I just . . . can't."

"Even though it's your money, too?" Why was she so adamant about this?

"Yes." She looked down at his chest. "Even though it's my money, too."

There was some deeper reason than the value alone he'd suspected at work here. Was it tied to her thinking he opposed any dependency? Surely she realized he was every bit as dependent as she was. And theirs were joint assets. He wanted to ask, but she looked fragile, as if she'd wrestled with all she could stand to for a while. He'd find out her reasons soon enough. She'd set the terms — no secrets. So he'd give her a few days, and then he'd just ask. Surely she'd tell him. She'd named the condition, after all, so she hardly could renege on fulfilling it now. "We'll work it out, Doc." He pressed a tender kiss to her forehead. "Can we change the terms to seven days together rather than a week?"

"Ah, Portland." That he wanted his full seven days with her made her smile. "I suppose — provided you'll be reasonable on any request I might have."

"The sound of that makes me a little nervous."

"A week of marriage to you again makes me nervous, too."

"All right. I agree." She couldn't think he *wasn't* nervous about this. He wouldn't be human.

"Good." She ran her fingers over the front of his royal blue shirt, waist to collar. "While I was thinking, something else occurred to me."

"Oh?" Now *that* really made him nervous.

She nodded. "I was thinking that I'm miserable with you and without you. So I might as well be miserable with you."

"Geez, Bess. I'm not sure my ego can take a week with you."

"Seven days," she corrected.

"Seven days." And he'd fill each of them with enough memories to last him a lifetime. "But I'll risk it."

"I'm glad."

"We're agreed then?"

"We're agreed."

"Okay." He started breathing again. "From here on out, not a word about the divorce or us not being together."

"Fantasy time."

"Right."

"Okay." She raised her chin offering him her mouth. "Then let's start this fantasy out right."

He growled from deep in his throat and tugged her closer. "Woman, I do like the way you think."

Her kiss was lusty, carnal, meant to incite and enrage his every sense. And it did that . . . and more. Their lips meshed and their hands explored, growing familiar again with a renewed awareness that this gift was one neither of them had expected, couldn't have anticipated, and yet relished.

When she broke the kiss, her breathing erupted as ragged as his. He grunted in total male satisfaction.

"Jonathan?" She nuzzled his neck.

"Yes?" His knees were shaking.

"We're not having sex together tonight."

Disappointment stabbed him. "Oh?"

"No." She drew in a breath that had her chest brushing against his ribs. "We're going to go over Dixie's files. Together."

"Honey, you don't have to do that. I know how upset —"

Bess pressed a fingertip to his lips. "Shh. I want to, Jonathan. Maybe if we'd taken more interest in each other's work before, we wouldn't have stumbled around hurting each other. Maybe we would've understood the significance of some things we didn't grasp. Our professional lives were a large part of who we were. We needed each other, and yet we kept our professional lives separate. It was a mistake I don't want to make again."

She made sense. But was her reasoning for not making love because she'd had second thoughts about Miguel, because it would complicate the divorce, or because she just didn't want John? Her kiss told him she wanted him, but could that be his wishful thinking? Did he dare to trust his instincts?

New agreement and new terms. No secrets. "When will we be together again?"

She looked up at him, solemn-eyed and serious. "When it's right."

He didn't understand. But she hadn't denied they would be together, only clarified the timing, more or less. "Right? Could you be a little more specific, darling?"

She lifted a gentle hand to his face then let her fingertips slide along the curve of his jaw. "When it's making love, Jonathan. You were right. I've never had sex with you. Never. And I don't want to start now. When it's right, we'll know it. Then we'll make love."

The back of his eyes burned. His body rebelled against the wait, but his heart took flight in it. Tony once had said to give her time. That there was hope. John hadn't believed him then but, if this lead panned out, if John solved the case, then maybe there *was* hope for him and Bess — long-term. Maybe during their seven days together he *could* love her enough to make her forget how lousy a husband he had been. Maybe he *could* love her enough that she'd forgive him. And then maybe he could forgive himself.

Never in his entire professional life had so much ridden on a single lead. What if it went sour? Fell flat? What if it proved to be just another false shot in the dark? What more could he do?

Fighting panic, he darted his gaze back to Seascape Inn. *Tony. Tony, I can't lose her again. I can't!*

A phantom wind whipped up. Swirling leaves and sand, it carried an ominous message:

Have faith that an island will appear.

Part of Tony's leap message to Bess. Leap. Leap? Did John dare? After all the pain and suffering and loneliness — the gut-wrenching loneliness — did he dare to have faith and leap? Faith in what? In himself? In Bess?

John had no idea.

CHAPTER 9

John leaned against his car and looked down at Bess, who stared at the ground. Why did he feel he was deserting her rather than simply checking out a lead on the case? Why did he feel guilty? "Honey, I have to do this."

"I know." She sighed up at him. "It's okay."

Dark smudges shadowed the skin beneath her eyes. She hadn't slept well. Neither had he, though he suspected their reasons different. She'd worried about Tony, dreaded Millicent Fairgate's you're-fired call which, according to Miss Hattie, Bess expected today. John had thought of nothing but her, across the hall and one room away. "You're not resting."

"No."

"Me either. When I get back, we're sleeping in the same bed. We don't have to make love, but we will sleep together." That seemed the only way either of them would get any rest.

"Sounds good to me." She gave him a smile that told him she'd known exactly what he'd meant.

He smiled back at her, immensely relieved and more than a little surprised. He'd been primed with a half-dozen logical reasons — the doc loved logic — to convince her, and missing out on the debate left him feeling a little cheated, and a lot happy. She'd known that his desire for her was there, but this went deeper than desire of the flesh. It went to the core: contentment of the soul.

He clasped her hand then rubbed the length of her forefinger with his thumb. Soft and smooth. Creamy skin. "Would it upset you if I said I'd miss you?"

She shrugged. "Will you?"

No lies. They'd promised. "Yes, I will."

"Then, no. It wouldn't upset me." She stepped closer, leaning against him, wrapping her arms around his waist. "In fact, I kind of like knowing it."

She'd changed so much. What had happened to her cool facade? To that slick cashmere, eel-skin control? He didn't miss it. He liked this open and honest Bess. Even if he didn't know what to expect from her. She was real. Touchable. "Do I dare to ask if you'll miss me?"

"I won't."

No lies, they'd said. But he had to work at it to keep disappointment out of his voice. Why had he asked? Set himself up? *Chump.* The breeze caught a leaf and it floated on the wind toward the gazebo and pond. "Oh."

"Oh?"

"Yeah, oh."

"Were you hoping I would?"

No secrets. He forced himself to meet her eyes. "Yeah, I was."

She smiled. "I would miss you, but I'm going to be too busy."

"Doing what?" He smoothed back a strand of hair from her face. Light flickered in a clump of firs, near the gazebo. He squinted to focus. Someone was . . . watching them. Who would — ? Ah, the binoculars again caught the sunlight. Batty Beaulah Favish. Doing her spying patrol. Though harmless, Miss Hattie must get tired of this "bird-watching" business.

Bess claimed his attention. "I'll be catching up on the case by reading the files."

He smiled and kissed the tip of her nose. "Honey, when I get back, we're going to have to have a long and serious talk about priorities. Missing me should come first."

"Fat chance."

She hadn't mentioned the divorce, but she didn't need to. His day seemed a little less bright for the reminder. He kissed her quickly, afraid of showing her too much, then opened the door and slid inside the car.

Bess tapped on the window.

John cranked the engine then pressed the button to lower the glass.

"Be careful, Jonathan." Her eyes went soft. "And just so you know, even though I intend to be very busy, I'll probably miss you . . . just a little."

His heart beating a wild tattoo, he cupped her chin with his hand and kissed her hard. "I'll take just a little."

"You'll take everything . . . for a week."

"Seven days," he corrected her. Was she complaining, or holding him to a promise? He couldn't tell from her tone but either way, the threat sounded darn good. "Bess, why did you agree to this proposal? Was it because of the bad press?" He'd wondered half of the night, and he didn't want to spend all day today again wondering. Hard to admit it, even to himself, but he prayed it wasn't her pride or her fear of humiliation.

She looked down at the rocky dirt, dragged the toe of her sneaker across a smooth rock, then met his gaze. "I need peace, Jonathan. I don't have it without you. And I'm not content. With the way things have been between us, I don't have peace or contentment with you either. But I feel closer to having both with you than without you."

He nodded. "I see."

"Do you?"

Who could miss that plea for understanding in her eyes? A stone would have to understand. "Yeah, I do. You're miserable either way, but misery loves company."

"Yeah, that's it."

He stroked her knuckles with the pad of his thumb. Were it her left hand, the one bearing his ring, he'd have kissed it. "We're a sorry pair, aren't we?"

"We are." She took in a breath that stretched the beige fabric of her blouse. "Hurry back, okay? Sorry singles don't hack it on our seven-day stint, and I've told Bill Butler over at Fisherman's Co-op we need some clams."

"I'll do my best." John put his hand on the gearshift and thrust the car into drive. "Take care of you, Doc."

"You, too." Bess stepped back from the car and again watched him leave her. But this time, she had a better grip on what ranking second meant. True, he no longer loved her. But if he did, she now understood that he would be ranking her second only in his urgent priorities. Not in his heart.

So why did seeing him go now still hurt as much as seeing him leave then? Why didn't she trust him to come back?

And why did she wish that, if only for one shining moment, he loved her again?

The afternoon came and went.

Miss Hattie had gone to visit with Vic, whose back was still giving him fits, and Bess had eaten a sandwich for dinner at the old desk in John's room. She'd gotten through an amazing number of files.

The back of her neck cramped and a dull ache throbbed between her shoulders. Time for a break. She straightened up and looked at the file folders littering the room. Though neatly stacked, hardly a floorboard or a snippet of the rug was uncovered. John certainly had worked hard; Bess had to give him that.

She stood up, stretched a kink from between her shoulder blades, then walked down the hall toward her own room. The house was quiet. The storm had run its course and a cool breeze filled the hall. The hair on her neck lifted. She stopped in her tracks. The breeze blew chilly, almost cold, and steady. Where was it coming from?

The inn wasn't air-conditioned — no need for it — and had no visible vents. Wary, she looked back over her shoulder, down the long hallway at the line of closed doors to the dead-end at the Shell Room. No doors open. And no open windows . . .

A draft? The inn *had* been built a long time ago, and older buildings always have drafts. Yes. Of course. A draft. That's all there was to this seemingly sourceless breeze. Besides, Tony was here. If anything strange went on, he'd nip it. He'd definitely protect the inn and everyone in it.

A ghost being in residence was bringing her a sense of security, not inciting fear? That stunned her into smiling. But Tony could hardly be a typical ghost. He certainly ranked atypical to any she'd ever heard of, and it didn't seem likely other ghosts could be as wonderful as him. If there were other ghosts. An uneasy shiver traipsed up her backbone. Could there be others?

She wrapped her arms over her chest. No. Not here. Tony wouldn't tolerate other ghosts being here. Not around Miss Hattie. Dear Miss Hattie . . .

With her nurturing ways and golden heart, how had she borne it? Loving and losing Tony, still loving him all these long years after he'd died? Amazing. A miracle, really. Denied a lifetime with her Tony, she hadn't become bitter at what she didn't have, but seemed genuinely heartened by what she did. There was a lesson there; Bess knew it. Probably several.

In so many ways, Tony, Miss Hattie, Seascape Inn itself — with its rich heritage of love and healing dating all the way back to Collin and Cecelia — taught such unassuming, earthy, and gentle lessons about life and love. Wonderful, powerful lessons. Healing lessons.

Healing. What was happening between Bess and Jonathan proved that, and so much more. And even if things didn't work out with them being together long-term, Bess would never forget the things she'd discovered about him, or about herself, here.

Yes, Millicent Fairgate would still fire Bess. No, she still couldn't accept John's money. Yes, she still loved the man to distraction and didn't have a clue if he loved her back, though he obviously wasn't indifferent toward her. But she felt a great deal more comfortable with herself now, with her feelings. And that was nothing short of a miracle. One she owed to Seascape and Tony and Miss Hattie — and, Bess strongly suspected — to Jimmy Goodson for all but highjacking her car.

Centered inside the small vaulted alcove at the end of the hall, beside the bank of mullioned windows, she reached to the left of the hand-carved bookshelves that flanked the thickly cushioned window seat, then let her fingertips drift over the spines of the orderly books. And she owed Maggie and T. J. MacGregor, too. Without them, Bess wouldn't be here. She'd be at home in New Orleans, falling apart at the seams.

She turned from the hall into her bedroom, then grabbed her robe. Remembering how adorable her huge husband had looked wearing it had her smiling. Lord, but he was gorgeous.

The robe in hand, she left her room, heading down the white Berber rug, then into the hall bath. Automatically, she reached past the antique brass soap dish for the little *Occupied* sign on the tan marble counter near the sink. Though alone at the inn — well, except for Tony — she slipped it onto the nail on the outer door, and wondered. Could Tony leave Seascape?

Having no idea, and not wanting to upset Miss Hattie by mentioning him and reminding her of her loss, Bess took the step up at the inner door into the bath, then debated between a long soak in the scrumptious-looking garden tub and a hot shower. The tub would relax her, but she had a good deal more work to do tonight, so instead she opted for the shower.

She stripped, tossing her jeans, blouse, and underwear into a heap just off the edge of the white, half-moon rug. After adjusting the water, she opened the glass door, stepped inside, then let the massager showerhead pound hot water on the cramped muscles between her shoulder blades. Her thoughts again drifted to John. In his search for Dixie, he certainly had turned over every rock. Amazing determination. A sliver of wistfulness laced with envy slipped through her heart. If only either of them had been that determined to save their marriage . . .

Minutes later, dried, robed, refreshed, and rejuvenated, she headed back to John's room to work further on the files.

She'd been back at the desk for only a few minutes when Miss Hattie called out from the Cove Room's door.

"My goodness!" Her eyes stretched wide, Miss Hattie scanned the stacks of unboxed files that were piled, wedged, and stuffed into every corner and crevice created by the king-size bed and cherry wood furniture. "Bess, dear, you're up to your ears in paperwork!"

"Literally." Bess smiled. "How is Vic feeling this evening?"

"Better, now that he's had some of my chicken and cheese casserole. It's his favorite." She frowned. "I'm afraid, though, that I'm in for a challenge at trying to keep him down until he's healed enough not to do himself further damage." She wrinkled her nose. "A Mainiac through and through, you know." She let out a little sigh. "I do so wish he had married. Vic is such a loving soul. He'd have made some lucky woman a fine husband."

Didn't Miss Hattie realize that the man was in love with her? Bess had seen signs of it the first day she'd met him. Hat in hand at the mud room door, he'd seemed flustered. And when Miss Hattie had invited him in for coffee, he'd looked as pleased as if he'd been the blue ribbon winner at the county fair.

"I brought you a cup of warm milk." Miss Hattie raised a burgundy marble mug. "Thought maybe it'd help you sleep better, since Jonathan hasn't yet returned from Portland."

Stepping gingerly, she wound through the maze of files and passed Bess the mug, a smile creasing her gentle, round face. "I hope you won't feel I'm intruding, dear,

371

but I have to say how very pleased I am that you and John have reconciled."

Heat rushed up her neck to her face. Bess focused on the stubby brass vase near her mug that held a single yellow daisy. "It's only temporary, Miss. Hattie."

"Oh, my. I'm afraid I misunderstood." She let her gaze slide to the floor.

"I know we've spent a lot of time behind closed doors lately. We've been discussing the terms of the divorce."

"I see."

"Would you believe the demented man propositioned me?"

"Propositioned?" Miss Hattie sat down on the foot of the bed. "Propositioned? Jonathan? My goodness."

Bess nodded and sipped from her mug of milk. "I was just irked enough to accept — though I made him sweat for a while, just to keep him honest."

"Ah, you said proposition but you're meaning his Happy Marriage Proposal."

Miss Hattie looked immensely relieved, though Bess couldn't imagine why. "Proposal, proposition — whatever you want to call it, it boils down to the same thing."

"Hmmm, he mentioned it to me."

"He did?"

She nodded. "I daresay, by the end of the

week — or was it two weeks?"

"It was two but we negotiated it down to one."

"Whatever for?" Pushing a pin back into her snowy hair, the dear woman frowned. "Oh my, I do apologize, Bess. I shouldn't be asking such personal questions."

"I don't mind." Bess licked at the milk mustache above her lip. "Actually, it feels good to talk about it."

"I'm glad." Miss Hattie plucked at the skirt of her green floral dress. "You'll have him realizing he still loves you long before then."

"Good grief, Miss Hattie." Bess laughed only so she wouldn't cry. "Jonathan doesn't love me."

She stilled. "He doesn't?"

"No, of course not." Her face warmed. "He's in lust."

"Ah, I see. Do you love him?"

Bess opened her mouth to answer, then closed it without uttering a word. Did she? "No. No," she said more emphatically. "It'd be foolish to love the man again."

"Then why, if you don't mind my asking, dear, did you agree to his proposal?"

"To keep him from suing me for custody of Silk." That was true, wasn't it?

"I see."

Bess feared the dear woman did see — far too much. More than Bess herself wanted to see. "I know it sounds crazy, but truly, you only have to understand John. I think he's jealous of Miguel, you see, and because Miguel gave me Silk and I won't take John's money, he wants to punish me. He doesn't understand that we're only friends."

"You and Silk, or you and Miguel?"

"Both."

"And so what you're telling me is that for your friend — a dog — you've given yourself to your husband for a week."

"Not exactly." Bess again sipped from her mug. The warm milk felt good going down her throat. She propped her elbow on the desk, then dropped her chin into it. "I'm keeping him from filing the lawsuit and making fools out of both of us."

"So you're using Jonathan to spare him humiliation?"

"I'm not using him." Bess bristled at the crass sound of that. "He's being an arrogant pig on the settlement and I'm trying to encourage him to be decent about it." *Encourage* worked for Tony, right? When a wheel works, there's no need to reinvent it.

"I'm sure you know best, dear." Miss Hattie tilted her head. "I have to wonder though why you'd agree to sell yourself to a man you don't love. It doesn't seem at all like you."

It wasn't like her. Or like the woman she had been when she'd arrived here. For a long moment, she stared at the antique washstand in the far right corner of the room, at its pretty cream-colored bowl and pitcher. "I'll tell you the truth, Miss Hattie. I don't know who or what I am anymore. When I came up here, I was seeking peace and refuge. Nothing has gone as planned, though, and now I don't know what to think."

"Maybe you need to give yourself some time before making any life-altering decisions."

"Life-altering?" Bess stilled. Again getting the sensation that something important had been revealed to her.

"Dear, you seriously don't think you can spend a week —"

"Seven days. We settled on seven days because of him going to Portland."

"Seven days, then. You can't expect to live with John again as his wife for seven days and for things not to change between you."

"I know it's risky, Miss Hattie." Bess rubbed at her neck muscles. They were again as tight as a drum. "And if I didn't say I was scared, I'd be lying. I'm finding out things about both of us that are changing the way I'm seeing things." She glanced over to the terracotta berry box John had said he hated. "Frankly, I fully expect a good heartbreak out of this deal. But what else can I do? He won't bend on the settlement agreement."

"Why should he?"

"Because I can't touch that money. I won't."

"Why not? You did help earn it, dear."

"You don't understand."

"Explain it to me, then."

Bess dropped her hands into her lap. She couldn't meet Miss Hattie's gentle emerald gaze. She wanted to, tried to, but failed. "If I take a single cent of that money, then it'll prove John's parents had been right about me."

"But Bess, dear —"

"No, it's true, Miss Hattie."

"What do John's parents have to do with this?"

Bess grimaced. "They're rich."

"They are?"

"I'm not."

"Yes?" A puzzled frown creased Miss Hattie's delicate brow.

She didn't understand. But, bless her, Miss Hattie had such a heart of gold that she wouldn't understand. "I wasn't good enough for their son."

"Oh, dear. Are you certain about this? You're a lovely woman, and I'd think that so long as you loved their son, they'd be proud to have you in their family."

"They weren't."

"Did they tell you so?"

"No, ma'am. They couldn't."

"Couldn't?" Her perplexed brow-crease now had the company of a frown, and she fidgeted with the single strand of pearls at her throat. "Why ever not?"

"Because I've never met them."

"Bess, you've been married to Jonathan for seven years and you've *never* met his parents?"

"No." She sighed. "Not once."

"Then how do you know they disapprove of you?"

"Why else wouldn't I have met them?"

Miss Hattie stood up and threaded her way through the files to the door. "Did Jonathan tell you this, dear?"

"Of course not. He refuses to speak of his parents." Bess rubbed at her cheek. "I'm not sure he even speaks *to* them. The subject is taboo."

"Ah, I see now." Miss Hattie visibly relaxed. "So you've just figured this out on your own."

"I've had to. Jonathan won't discuss them at all, Miss Hattie. I don't even know his mother's name. Isn't that just the most awful, insulting thing to have to confess? A wife should at least know her husband's mother's name."

"Hmmm, yes, I would say she should."

Relieved at Miss Hattie's affirmation, Bess again sipped from her mug, swallowed, then returned it to the corner of the desk. "I know it's confusing, and I probably seem very foolish, but the truth is that they were wrong about me. And, well, I guess part of me agreed to his proposal because I need this time with him, too."

Miss Hattie smiled softly. "Because you still love him."

"No, I don't. I'd be a fool to love a man I know is ashamed of me."

"*Ashamed* of you?" Miss Hattie forced her voice lower. "Bess, I can't believe you'd honestly think Jonathan is *ashamed* of you."

"He hasn't introduced me to his parents."

"Despite our short acquaintance, I know you well, and I don't believe for a second that you've given yourself body and soul to a man you don't love. Not for a moment, much less for a week."

"Seven days," Bess automatically corrected, then again sipped from her burgundy marble mug. "Actually, I agreed for more reasons than I told you. Aside from the custody suit for Silk, and to spare us public humiliation — honest, Miss Hattie, John has no idea how cruel the public can be — I agreed because . . ." Bess stopped cold. If she disclosed the truth, Miss Hattie would think Bess a terrible person. That would hurt. What Miss Hattie thought of her mattered; Bess respected the woman.

"Because?"

Bess couldn't lie. She stiffened, bracing to see the concern in Miss Hattie's eyes turn to disappointment, then to revulsion. "Because once we're divorced, I want him to remember what he's missing in losing me." Bess lowered her gaze to a strip of bare floor. "Not very noble, but true."

"It isn't my place to judge you, dear. But I daresay in your position, I'd want the man to know he'd lost a good woman, too."

Bess looked up. "Really?"

"Of course." Miss Hattie grunted, fluffing up the first of three brown-and-green-print throw pillows on the bed. "What woman wouldn't feel that way? Why, none who's honest, I'd wager."

"I . . . well, I agreed for me, too, Miss Hattie. Because, like I said, I need this time with him." Getting used to losing him would take all of their seven days together and, she feared, more. Much, much more. A lifetime. Eternity. Infinity.

Cuddling the last of the pillows to her chest, Miss Hattie's eyes twinkled. "Ah, the magic."

Bess sighed, no longer surprised that Miss Hattie, like Tony, knew her deepest secrets. "I've called it lust with a kick, but you're right. The magic."

Miss Hattie smoothed the skirt of her dress. "Be careful, hmmm?" Worry deepened a soft wrinkle at the side of her mouth. "I've grown fond of you and John, and I'd hate to see either of you hurt. Lust is powerful, and that kick makes it more so. Unless it's tempered with love, lust can be painful."

Didn't she know it? "Pain is exactly what I'm trying to avoid."

Looking as if there were more she'd like to say but wouldn't allow herself to, Miss Hattie nodded. "I'm sure you'll do what's best, dear." She put the pillow back onto the forest green comforter, then left the room.

Bess again sipped from her mug. What else had been on Miss Hattie's mind? What had she wanted to say but held herself back from saying? Whatever it —

You made promises, Doc. No more lies.
What happened to no more lies?

Tony. A furious Tony. Bess shivered.
"What's wrong with you? I didn't lie to Miss
Hattie. I don't think if anyone wanted to
lie, they could lie to her. I didn't want to.
And I didn't lie. So what are you so riled
about?"

A stack of files near the foot of the bed
lifted from the floor and flew throughout
the room, their contents scattering, fluttering to the floor, to the bed, onto the rug.
Look at them, Doc. Look at them!

He wouldn't hurt her. He wouldn't. Two-
handed, she set her mug down and stood
up. Her knees felt as weak as water and at
any moment she expected her heart to burst
right out of her chest. "Would you just calm
down? You're scaring me."

I hope I am. I hope I frighten you right into
facing the truth.

"What truth?"

Crimney. Look at the papers, Doc!

He wasn't going to hurt her. Furious, yes,
but not harmful. She inched over to the
bed, praying her legs would hold her upright, then looked down at the first paper.
"It's a report on a false lead."

For goodness sake, woman, not the report.

Look at the important stuff.

"What important stuff?"

The doodles, Bess. Look at the darn doodles.

She'd ignored doodles all afternoon. Now he wanted her to look at them, calling them and not the reports important? "John scribbles on everything. It'd take a month to read all his doodles."

You're trying my patience here. Look at the blasted doodles.

"All right, all right!" Geez, the man was a pain in the tush. She lowered her gaze to the paper. "Bess the Beautiful?"

Look at the date.

"Two years ago. Right after I filed for the legal separation." Her heart started a low, hard beat. "He thought me beautiful then?"

Evidently. Check out the one over there, on the pillow. No, no, no. The other pillow.

She moved around to the other side of the bed then looked down at the page. "Miguel the Intruder?" She lifted the page and frowned. "Is that how John feels about Miguel? That he's intruding on John's turf?"

Well, I don't know, Doc. What do you think?

"I don't know."

While you're deciding that maybe you should know, take a gander at that note on the nightstand, the one by the clock.

Bess grabbed it and zoomed in on the doodles. "Bess the Betrayer." Her heartstrings felt a vicious tug and her eyes burned. This he'd written recently — right after Elise's death. The day of the funeral. That Bess hadn't gone *had* upset him.

"What do these mean, Tony? I don't want to read too much into them." She didn't dare to read too much into them. One thing she couldn't forget. John didn't love her anymore.

Think about it.

From cryptic, to fury, to sarcasm, and now back to cryptic. The cryptic that sent cold chills racing up and down her spine. "Do you interpret these to mean John felt betrayed because I left him? Because they can't mean that. He was hurt because I didn't show up at Elise's funeral. That's all."

Is it?

She didn't know. "Maybe. He is jealous of Miguel." She flipped her hair back from her face. "I should have told him we were just friends, but I didn't."

You wanted him jealous.

"I wanted him to think I'd built a fine life without him."

And have you?

"I don't have to answer that. You know the truth."

383

Jonathan is jealous of Miguel. And you perpetuated that. You don't have to explain why to me, but you certainly should understand yourself.

Bess plopped down on the bed and snapped her eyes shut. "He didn't want me, Tony. He didn't love me. Do you know how humiliating it is to have your husband forget you exist for three days and to put another woman first indefinitely? Regardless of the reasons, regardless of how well intended or founded they are, it hurts, darn it. It . . . hurts."

Maybe if you'd been honest about your feelings rather than burying them, he'd have understood. You say he didn't love you, but I have to wonder, Doc, if you loved him. You didn't trust him, or share with him, or have faith in his love. Sounds to me as if you got a good dose of what you dished out.

"That's not true!" Bess opened her eyes and jerked upright. "You don't —"

A luminescent man, very handsome, very concerned eyes, wearing an old-fashioned Army uniform stood not two feet from the edge of the bed. No, not a man. Not . . . solid.

A ghost.

And in his left lapel was a yellow carnation.

She gasped. Her knees gave out. Staring gape jawed at him, she collapsed back onto the bed. "Good . . . grief."

CHAPTER 10

It's me — Tony. Crimney, Doc, don't faint! I never did know what to do with women who cry or faint.

"Faint?" The shock had passed. Well, sort of. And now she was the one who was furious. "Oh, no, Tony. I'm not going to faint. I'm going to phone." She scooted off the bed, demanded her knees knock off the gelatin act, then moved to the desk and the brown, streamline phone. The smell of Tony's *Old Spice* cologne made her nostrils tingle.

Phone? Who are you going to call?

Bess lifted the receiver. "Maggie Mac-Gregor. She's got a queen-size backside-chewing coming and, by gum, prego or no, she's going to get it." Bess started dialing. "She knew about you all along and didn't tell me. And I thought she was my friend."

She was, er, is. He folded his arms over his chest. *Now just how would you have re-*

acted if she'd told you the truth about me? And, if memory serves me correctly, she did hint. He tapped at his lapel, jiggling the yellow carnation there.

"She didn't *tell* me. She should've told me."

You wouldn't have believed her, Doc.

She probably wouldn't have. She probably would have thought Maggie had overdosed on prenatal vitamins or something. Still . . .

The phone's out, anyway. You'll have to wait to call her.

The receiver at her ear, Bess stared at him. The phone *was* out of order, its static-free line as silent as a tomb. He'd done it. "I'll have to wait until I calm down?"

He smiled. *Works for me.*

She cradled the receiver and sat down at the desk. "You're intruding again."

Just doing my job, Doc.

"Scaring the socks off me keeps you gainfully employed? Why aren't you just rattling a few chains or something?"

His golden eyes twinkled. *That's one of my hobbies. This is more interesting.*

"I see."

No, you don't. Not yet. But you will.

"That sounds almost like a threat, Tony." Was she really sitting here holding a conversation with a ghost? *Really?* Maybe she'd just lost her mind. Yes, insanity. That had to be it. She'd been under a lot of stress — who could deny it? It'd gotten the best of her and she'd slipped right on over, beyond twilight. Yes, insanity. Had to be insanity because she felt no fear. Only being insane could explain the absence of fear.

You're not insane, woman, just stubborn.

"There's not a stubborn bone in my body," she insisted, shoving aside a stack of folders. She folded her elbow, then propped her chin on her palm. "Since you're here, and bent on intruding, can you tell me what all these doodles mean?"

What do you think they mean? Wait, let me rephrase that. What would you like for them to mean?

Nothing seemed easy anymore. No black and white, only a million shades of gray. "Straight out, my head doesn't want them to mean anything. But my heart, well, it wants the doodles to mean that John might —"

Might? Knock it off, Doc. Hearts don't deal in mights. They desire, yearn, crave, but they don't mess around with mights.

Her face went hot. "All right, then. The truth is, my heart wishes they mean he still cares for me."

You're doing it again. Cares for. What heart

would worry itself with a nit-picking thing like caring when it loves unconditionally and prays — not wishes, prays — it'll be loved back?

Bess went stiff. "I will *not* love Jonathan again, Tony. I will *not.*"

I'm convinced. He looked down at her as if he were wearing glasses and peeking at her up over the rims. *Are you?*

Her chin quivered. "He'll break my heart."

We've been through this before. You're not thinking. Why aren't you thinking?

A knot of tears clogged her throat. Bess gulped them down. "I've been thinking, but I've been spending a lot more time on feelings. I've about decided neither is smart."

On the contrary. Your discussion with your father was a very healthy one. Even if he didn't hear it.

"You were eavesdropping?" Bess gasped.

Tony laughed. *Not exactly. I can't not hear anything that goes on around here — even when I'd like to. Beaulah Favish comes to mind. I'd really like to not hear her.*

"I expect the sheriff does, too." Bess smiled. Not being able to turn off sounds must be as deafening as silence. When she and John had first separated, she'd finally had to move out. Two days of silence in their home and it had become purgatory to her. Yes, silence could be deafening. Sound, too, for Tony. Could he get away from it as easily as she had? For some reason, though purely speculation, she doubted it. She'd have to ask him about that some time. When she got used to the idea of conversing with a gho— with him.

Along with thinking about my message to you, the tide one — you haven't forgotten it, have you?

If she didn't know better, she'd think he was deliberately trying to be cute. But she did, and he wasn't. He was serious. "Not at all." It plagued her night and day.

Ah, good. Along with it, I suggest you think about the doodles, Doc. They're very telling.

For the first time, Bess tried looking at their situation from John's perspective. "He felt betrayed," she told Tony. "The way he sees it, I walked out on him and got involved with another man. I betrayed him. Is that how he felt?"

Feels, Bess, not felt. And, yes, I'd say that's about right.

"But that would mean that he'd tied his feelings of worth as a husband to the success of Mystic Investigations. Surely John wouldn't have done that. Surely he knew —"

Bess, Bess, Bess. Man's feelings have become inbred over thousands of years. You

390

can't negate the power of innate feelings in the blink of an eye. These things take time. To him, your independence and reserve translated to you not wanting or needing his protection. More accurately, to you not needing him. Your refusal to accept half of your combined assets only reinforces those feelings.

"But that doesn't have anything to do with it."

Doesn't matter. That's how he sees and feels about it. You have to understand. Man has long been the protector and provider of women.

"Thousands of years. So you've mentioned."

Right. And your actions, intentional or unintentional, scorn John following his natural instincts, trying to do both. In a real way, you've neutered him.

"For goodness sake, this is the twenty-first century, Tony. Men don't want helpless, dependent women anymore. They expect us to be capable of handling things. Who'd want a victim for a wife, anyway? And who'd want a man who wanted his wife to be a victim? No. No, you're in the wrong century, Tony."

You misunderstand me, Doc. We've talked about this before, but it's obvious now you

391

missed my meaning. *All John wants is to feel needed. That desire — feeling needed — is universal to any man in any century. Or to any woman, for that matter. Being needed is what all this boils down to. And that's what you've denied John.*

Bess just stared at him, taking all this in, unsure what, if any, of it held value.

Tony slid a hip onto the edge of the desk. *You're still looking baffled. Let me clear a little of the mud. If you love someone and they don't need you, what do you consider yourself worth to that person?*

The truth hit Bess like a hammer blow. "I get it. It's not just being needed. It's a question of self-worth. Because I didn't share my trials and challenges with him, because I didn't share my feelings with him, John felt unworthy. He felt I had weighed his value as a husband, a provider — as a man — and he didn't have any value." Her stomach curling, she licked at her lips, then returned her gaze to Tony, sitting perched on the desk's edge, his hands laced in his lap. "John didn't neglect me. Oh, Lord, *I* neglected *him.*"

Well, as John himself would say, truth is truth, and I think you both did a fair share of neglecting, Doc. But you've nailed the upshot of the situation from his point of view.

"But that's *not* how it was!"

Doesn't matter. We're not talking reality here, Doc. We're talking perception. And, right or wrong, this is how John perceived your relationship and what he perceived to be the truth.

Tony stilled, tipped his chin toward the door as if listening. *Oh-oh. Jonathan's back. Don't mention that you've seen me, Bess. The man isn't ready yet and . . .* Tony's voice trailed. He cocked his head, then grimaced.

"And? That's a heck of place to drop the conversation, Tony."

He's ticked to the gills.

"At who?"

Tony shrugged. *Beats me, but I'm outta here. He's got a wicked temper, and I've got chains to rattle.*

"Chicken."

Now isn't that fine? Tony grinned. *Bess Cameron Mystic, who shook like a leaf at the sound of my voice yesterday, now teases me in my natural state. Crimney, but I'm pleased, Doc.*

He was pleased. And she wondered if he ever got lonely. Though she'd wanted to ask Miss Hattie about him, she feared upsetting her, and so Bess had kept her questions to herself. But she hated the thought of Tony or Miss Hattie feeling lonely. "If you're so pleased, then hang around and help me get John unticked."

I'm pleased, not stupid. You handle him.

"Tony, are you the only ghost around here?"

Tony smiled enigmatically. *Leap, Doc. Leap!* Then in a blink, he disappeared.

"I would leap — maybe," she shouted out. "If I knew what the heck you meant!"

Jonathan took the steps two at a time up to the second-floor landing, then stormed across the hallway's white Berber rug. The little *Occupied* sign hung on the nail on the bathroom door, but the light was off, and the bathroom empty. Bess had forgotten to take it down. He looked back down the hall to her room, double-checking. The door was closed, but no streak of light seeped under it onto the planked floor outside it. Her room had been dark from the drive, and it was still dark.

A surge of panic swelled in his stomach. He slammed the bathroom door shut, then went on toward his room. What if Jimmy had fixed her car? What if she'd left? What if he'd blown this second chance? *Darn it!* Hadn't he learned *anything* from the first time she'd left him?

He opened his bedroom door — and there

stood Bess, wearing her pink silk robe and, if the white splotch over the front of it was an accurate indicator, half a cup of milk. Papers were strewn and stacked all over the room. And her face glowed bright pink.

"You're back."

He stood statue still and just stared at her.

"Jonathan?" She stepped out from behind the desk and over to him.

Not *John* but *Jonathan.* Gosh, but she was beautiful. His heart swelled and his anger at himself doubled. He knew she felt she'd ranked second to Elise and the case. He knew he had only seven days to solve the case and to make Bess realize how much he loved her. He knew, and yet he . . . "You didn't leave."

She blinked, clearly wary. "No."

"Your car isn't fixed." There had to be a reason — one that had nothing to do with him — that explained her still being here. Maybe the jail threat. The fine issue still loomed and, if she returned to New Orleans, Judge Branson would incarcerate her. "I thought Jimmy would have it repaired by now and when I didn't see it in the parking area . . .

"You thought I'd gone."

He nodded.

"Oh."

How could one little word hold so many feelings? Disappointment, hurt, sorrow . . .

He was crazy for asking, but he'd go crazy wondering if he didn't. "Is that the only reason you're still here?"

"We have an agree—" She paused mid-sentence and some recognition flickered in her eyes. "No. No, that isn't the only reason I'm still here." She held open her arms and smiled. "Welcome home, Jonathan."

In his mind, he again saw her standing on the front entry landing of their New Orleans home, smiling, arms open and welcoming, and the past and present merged in a poignant blend that had his emotions raw, his heart racing right up his throat, his soul singing a joyful refrain. "You're not angry."

"Should I be?" She lowered her arms to her sides.

"Yes!" He lowered his voice, and chastised himself for shouting. How could she *not* be angry? Before, he hadn't realized, but now, now he knew how she'd feel and yet he had taken off like a rocket, chasing a lead, and had left her behind again anyway. Why hadn't it even occurred to him to ask if she'd like to go along? "I'm sorry, Bess."

"Okay.' She sounded wary, and her lip twitched double-time.

She didn't understand his apology. He was

396

mucking it up. He clasped her hands in his. They were cool. From the damp spill, he'd figured they'd be warm. Evidently, she'd been here in his room with that mug of milk for quite some time. Looking at the mess she'd made, she had to have been here since he'd left.

And why her making a mess of his case files pleased him when he should be mad as heck, he hadn't a clue. Maybe because she was still here. Maybe because the mess proved she'd not even thought of leaving him. Maybe because he felt so grateful that he'd not blown their second chance, and he had the opportunity to make this latest infraction up to her.

"Did I do something wrong?"

"No." He met her gaze. "No, I did. I'm sorry, Bess. Here we had agreed to seven days of marriage — no mention of the divorce, no mention of anything negative, only seven days to be together — and with one phone call on the case, I take off." He dropped her hands and stepped away. "I shouldn't have gone."

"You had to go."

"I should've asked you to come with me."

"You needed to do this on your own. I know that. This case, well, it's special to you, and you had to handle this facet of it as you've handled the whole thing — with total focus."

"Would you quit defending me?" He turned his back to her. With the clenching of his fists, his gray-suited shoulders bunched. "I put it first, Bess. Knowing how you felt last time, fool that I am, I did it again."

She walked over and hugged him from behind. "You're not a fool, darling. You're dedicated and concerned." Her cheek vibrated against his back. "You couldn't not follow up on this lead any more than you could postpone following the one over Christmas. You still don't know what happened to Dixie, what might be happening to her. And now that Elise is gone, you feel even more pressure to solve this case and see to it that her daughter is okay."

"You forgive me." He didn't deserve it. But he wanted it. Gosh, how he wanted it. He covered her hands at his waist with his.

She kissed his broad back. "There's nothing to forgive."

He spun around then pulled her into his arms, clutching her to him, telling himself not to hug her too tightly or he'd crush her. But warm and giving, she hugged him just as fiercely.

A long minute passed . . . then another . . .

then yet another, and still they stood there in the middle of his chaotic room, just holding each other.

"Jonathan," she patted his back, "sit down. I have a surprise for you."

Because it was closer than the desk chair and he was reeling, he chose the bed.

"Close your eyes." Bess's eyes shone bright.

Tears? Or mischief? He'd take either. She wasn't angry. She'd understood. And that's all that mattered. He unbuttoned his suit jacket, loosened his tie and top shirt button, then dutifully closed his eyes. Bess had gotten him a present. If only he'd solved the case, he'd tell her that the only present he wanted was the only present he'd ever wanted: her.

But he hadn't solved the case, and until he did, he wasn't worthy of her.

"Ready?"

"Yes." *Ritz* and Bess. Man, what a heady mix. Tomorrow, when he called Bryce, he'd also call his broker and buy stock in the company producing it.

"Okay." Her voice went husky-deep, sexy. "Open your eyes, Jonathan."

He lifted his lids and took the small, glossy white bag she held out to him. In the folds of crackling tissue paper, he felt something hard . . . something oval . . . then pulled it out of the bag.

A terracotta box with blueberries and vines atop it, just like the one she'd bought for Miss Hattie. His words came back to haunt him. *I hate that box. You chose it.* So what did this mean? He glanced from it up to Bess.

Her eyes glistened with tears. "It's a symbol of good faith and our agreement. I've chosen you again, Jonathan."

His heart felt so full it nearly burst. And his eyes stung like fire. She'd chosen him again. Yes, only for seven days. But each day was an unexpected blessing — one he'd never dared to dream of. "Thank you, Doc."

She gave him a watery smile and drew in a breath that heaved her shoulders. "So, what happened in Portland? Good news?"

He put the box on the desk, then reached for Bess. "We'll talk about it later. Right now I've got something more important to do."

She went into his arms willingly. "Priorities, right?"

"Definitely." He nodded, his gaze locked with hers. "When a man's wife gives him a gift, he should show his immediate appreciation. Don't you agree?"

She smiled up at him and looped her arms

around his neck. "Wholeheartedly — provided he is appreciative."

"He is."

"And how is he going to show his wife his appreciation?"

Her heart was thumping as hard as his. "This particular wife is fond of having her feet rubbed," he said. "So he'll start there."

She snuggled closer. "Start there?" Rearing, she met his gaze. "And where will this particular husband's appreciation end?"

"That depends on my wife." What if she refused? She'd agreed to seven days, but without feelings for him that went beyond the magic, could Bess follow through on their settlement proposal? Would she? Did she want even affection from him? And what about Santos? Before John had left for Portland, when they'd been so close to making love, she'd said only she and John had been there. Santos's ghost hadn't been between them then. But had that been only the heat of the moment? Had she had second thoughts? Was the man between them now?

Bess rubbed the tip of his chin with her nose. "Why don't you start and we'll see where it ends?"

"There's something I have to do first." He nuzzled the shell of her ear, then guiding her chin with a fingertip, he lifted her mouth to his. "I missed you, Bess. I missed you so much."

A little groan escaped from low in her throat. "I missed you, too."

Their lips touched and, in a mingle of sighed breaths, touched again. Bess curled her arms around him, working her fingers along the ridge of muscle at his side. He started to tremble and then to shake, wanting her, having spent the last hours fearing he'd lost her, and now holding her in his arms. More than anything else, he needed to make love with her, to show her all she made him feel, to confirm that this wasn't a dream but a miracle. She was in his arms. *His* arms. Loving him. Loving *only him.*

He needed her. And the words she'd given him echoed through his mind. *I needed you then, and I need you now. Only you, darling. Only you . . .*

Bess wanted only him. He shuddered, groaned deeply from the back of his throat, and she savored the feel of him, the signs that sparked, ignited, and set to flame her own passion, and then mercilessly strengthened it. Memories of how wonderful they'd been together whirled in her mind, snatches of images of him loving her, whispering endearments, murmuring loving sighs. She broke their kiss. Cupped his face in her hands, then rubbed tiny circles on his jaw with the pads of her thumbs. "Jonathan, I loved you . . . then. With all my heart. And I want you more right now than I've ever wanted anything in my life."

His eyes stretched wide. He held her, not moving, not breathing, just staring deeply into her eyes. "I loved you, too, Doc . . . then."

Then. They'd both been honest, yet protective, self-survival ranking imperative because of the divorce. Now understanding their needs in ways she'd never understood them before, she accepted their instinctive reactions without searching for deeper meanings. Seven days. And then divorce. Seven days, and then never again would she be free to tell him anything, or to ask anything of him. "Tell me you . . . want me, Jonathan. I need to hear you say you want me."

"I want you, woman. Never doubt it."

A long while later, his breathing returned to normal and he tugged the covers, sending papers flying. Holding her to him, he rolled onto the sheets, then jerked the bed clear of debris and covered them. Bess smiled against his hair-roughened chest. Even physically satisfied, he didn't want to let her go.

For seven days.

A tear sprang to her eye, then trickled down her cheek. Seven days.

On his back, he sandwiched her legs between his thighs. "Bess?" he whispered against her forehead.

"Hmmm?" A second tear followed the first.

"For the record, we didn't just have sex. At least, I didn't."

He'd given and wanted reassurance. The tears in her throat melted. "Me, either." She tilted her face up to his and looked into his eyes. "We made love, Jonathan."

His eyes went solemn and he lifted a finger to her face, touched it to the skin just under her eye. "Is that why you're crying? Because you regret it?"

Her chin quivered. "No." She wanted to say more, but couldn't. Too many emotions churned close to the surface.

"I need to know why, Doc."

Need. Not *want,* but *need. We all need to be needed.* She swallowed hard. "Because it was so beautiful. You touched my heart."

His eyes went soft and his lip curled into a wondrous smile. "You touched my heart, too."

Another tear slipped to her cheek and she smiled back. "I'll be awake for hours."

He stretched over to turn off the lamp. "You'll be asleep in under a minute. You always said making love revved you up, but —" John looked down at the angel cradled to his side. Her lashes lay golden against her cheeks. She was asleep.

A poignant tear stealing from his eye, he clicked off the lamp, then settled in, his wife in his arms. A contentment he'd never before known blanketed him. Tomorrow those shadows would be gone from her eyes. Tonight, together, they'd rest.

He burrowed his nose against her neck and inhaled her sweet *Ritz*. Life just didn't get any better than this. Bess in his arms, the scents of their loving filling him . . . He'd touched her heart. John smiled. No, life didn't get any better than this.

And Tony's message to Bess again came to John's mind. *Leap upon a mystic tide and have faith the sand will shift and an island will appear.*

John snapped open his eyes and stared at the high, sloped ceiling awash in midnight shadows. *Shifting sand.* His relationship with Bess was shifting. John's mind slipped into overdrive — and the truth pumped through his veins.

Tony's message wasn't merely a message. It was a map!

CHAPTER 11

John intended to kiss Bess awake. And he would do it — just as soon as he got his fill of looking at her. In unguarded sleep, she looked angelic. Feeling tender, he fought the urge to touch her face. Last night, she'd loved him. She'd not held back physically, but she hadn't totally let herself go emotionally. That *was* asking for the impossible. They only had seven days and, for complete inhibition, a woman like Bess needed a lifetime assured of a man's love.

He'd give it to her. He'd love to give it to her . . . if only he had the right.

Because he didn't, he stared at her. At the smooth, clean line of her jaw, the gentle curve at the cove of her neck, the sweep of her lashes resting softly against her cheek. Her lips were parted, and between them he glimpsed her teeth, the tip of her tongue. On her side, she had her knees curled to her chest, one hand slung over her head, the other tucked under her pillow, and her hair was a wreck. The tender hitch in his chest tugged tighter, and he smiled. The woman was beautiful to him in every way.

He probably was as crazy as Selena accused him of being. Pretending for seven days that the divorce didn't exist. Pretending he and Bess were happily married. Pretending she loved him now as she'd said she'd loved him then. The back of his nose stung and his eyes burned. It might be crazy, but it was also the only way he stood a chance of making it through the rest of his life without her.

As if feeling his gaze, her lashes fluttered. Before she could open her eyes and maybe refuse him, he dipped his chin and kissed her. He tasted her surprise, then her recognition of him and, when she purred and lazily curled her arms around his neck, a warm ray of joy as pure and as good as sunshine spread through his heart. Cherishing it, cherishing her and this moment, he lingered, kissing her lips until she stretched awake and opened her eyes.

"Good morning."

"Hmmm, it's looking promising." She arched a brow and her eyes sparkled through the haze of sleep.

He pecked a kiss to her forehead, then

rubbed it with his chin. "I called Bill Butler at Fisherman's Co-op. In an hour, his son Aaron will meet us down at the dock with a bushel of clams and a burlap bag full of seaweed."

"What for?" She grunted, shaking off the last of the netherworld fog of sleep.

"I promised my wife we'd bake clams, and Bill says Little Island is the place to do it." Picturesque. Private. And no Beaulah Favish with her binoculars, spying on them.

"But, Jonathan," Bess pressed a hand to his thigh, "only villagers can go to Little Island. Miss Millie donated it to the villagers because the coast was getting too *touristical* and —"

"Touristical?"

"Too many tourists," Bess explained. "Anyway, only the villagers can go there. We're from away. We won't be welcome there."

"We are. Bill invited us." John forked his fingers through her hair, pushing it away from her face. "And if you're interested, we also can get a complete tour of the lighthouse — if we can bribe Miss Hattie into baking Hatch some blueberry muffins. Hatch offered the tour, even though he's *summercating*."

"Summercating?" Bess wrinkled her nose.

"I'm not sure — these Mainers have a language all their own — but I think it's when you spend an afternoon under a shade tree with a good book, or on the porch swing watching the grass grow."

"Summercating. I like it." She smiled. "So we're going to spend some of our seven days summercating, then."

"I thought we would — if the idea appeals to you." He'd go anywhere to be with her, even Death Valley, his least favorite spot on earth.

Bess smiled. "It appeals."

John let his hand slide along her curves. She appealed. Enormously. "Good."

She stretched into his stroke, and her voice went needy-soft. "Jonathan, how much time do we have?"

"Why?"

She dropped her gaze to his chest. "When a husband gives his wife a gift, she should show her immediate appreciation. Don't you agree?"

"A gift?" What gift had he given her? Another of her subtle messages? Maybe. And the same words he'd given her. He'd tease her a little. That's something they'd done far too little before. Bess wasn't the only one who didn't want to repeat past mistakes. "But I haven't —"

Staring at him, Bess interrupted. "Keeping a promise is the right thing to do, but it's also a gift, Jonathan. Now ditch the clothes and come here so I can show you how grateful I — hmmm, wait. I'm feeling pretty grateful. How much time do we have before meeting Aaron?"

She wanted him. John's heart skipped a rugged beat. Not once in all their time together had Bess ever been the aggressor in their lovemaking. Not once. That she was now, that she was openly telling him she wanted to make love with him, inflamed him. Eager to give her what she wanted, all thumbs at her hunger and the emotions in him it stirred, he yanked at the buttons of his shirt. "Enough."

John glanced down at his watch. Bess would be ready to leave for Little Island in fifteen minutes. They'd be a good forty-five minutes late, but it'd been worth it. An aggressive Bess was worth anything. Everything. He'd called to warn Bill Butler, and he'd tip Aaron extra for the time. Heck, for another hour like the last, John would buy Aaron a new boat. Grinning at the little terracotta boxes, side by side atop the chest, John again felt that tender hitch in his chest. She'd chosen it. And she'd chosen him.

411

Riled, Bess was magnificent. But open and loving, she went beyond magnificent. And she'd taken him with her — straight to heaven.

Six more days. Even if they held only half the promise of this one, they'd be enough. He could handle living with only the memories. He'd miss her. He'd never stop missing her, but he could do it. He could survive.

Sitting at the desk, he tapped the end of his pen to the file open before him. He'd rather have her. To do that, he had to solve the case. And Tony's mystic tide message. That message was a map; John was convinced of it. But to what? To where? For what? And for whom?

The phone rang.

Still deep in thought, John answered it. "Mystic."

"John, it's me — Bryce."

"Hey, buddy." John leaned back and put his thoughts on hold.

"How are things coming on the divorce settlement with Bess? You two reach a compromise?"

Oh, boy. "Several, but not yet on the money."

"Progress is progress. Dare I ask on what?"

"Not just yet." John looked down to the

mop curled into a ball, resting her head on the toe of his shoe. "For now, let's leave it at there probably won't be a custody suit on Silk."

"Wonderful." Bryce let out a sigh, obviously relieved. "Hang tight on the money end. Millicent Fairgate has been spewing insults all over town about Bess's keeping the divorce under wraps and making the station look bad. She's furious."

"Expected she would be." John grimaced and folded an arm over his chest. "Any of these insults slanderous or libelous?"

"Just short of it."

"Watch her. If she steps over the line, sue her. Bess has enough to contend with without that vulture circling her."

"Will do, but I think the problem of Millicent Fairgate is about to dissipate." Bryce paused and static filled the phone wires. "I would've waited until you got back to New Orleans to go over this, but considering the circumstances, I figured I'd best call."

"Okay."

"I just got today's mail, John. There's something in it from Elise. It was addressed to me, so I opened it."

John swallowed hard. "And?"

"It's a codicil to her will, duly executed and notarized — by Judge Branson, no less."

Judge Branson? Now why would Elise have him notarize a codicil rather than her attorney? John frowned. Sooner or later Bryce would get around to explaining.

"She's directed her executor — you — to buy WLUV 1-0-7.3 from Millicent Fairgate for fair market value."

"What for?" Odd twist, and totally unexpected.

"She doesn't say. Only instructs you to buy it."

John dragged a hand through his hair. "Man, Bryce. How am I supposed to do that? Millicent isn't going to sell the station. It's her legacy."

"She won't have any choice," Bryce said, deadpan serious. "In fact, the only way she can save face is to pretend to sell it."

Pretend to sell it? "What are you talking about?"

"There are documents along with the codicil, John. Elise already owns the station. She bought it from Millicent's husband — right after Bess filed for the legal separation."

"Now why would Elise do that?" And why would Millicent pretend she still owned it? She *was* still running the station. This didn't make a lick of sense.

"I don't know. But in the letter, Elise says

to publicly buy the station from Millicent. To disclose the fact Elise already owns it only if Millicent won't play ball."

Odd. No, weird. John cocked his head. Another puzzle he couldn't figure out. "Well, I guess you'd best buy it then. Offer her fair market value today."

"If you insist." Bryce huffed his displeasure. "John, you knew Elise better than anyone else alive. Why would she go through the motions of buying a station she already owns? She's even stipulated which account the money is to be drawn from to pay Millicent."

Turning in his chair, John stared out the window, down over the copse of trees to the sleepy Sea Haven Village. Fog rolled in off the ocean and only hints of the rooftops were visible. It wouldn't ruin their outing to Little Island. In five minutes, the sun would be shining again. Maine weather was nothing if not changeable. "I don't know why she would, but I suspect she's giving someone — possibly Millicent's husband — a day of grace."

"A chance to save face, you mean."

John shrugged. "Same thing, isn't it?"

"I guess so. But don't you want to find out before we proceed? This isn't small change we're talking about."

"No, I don't. If Elise wanted to disclose her reasons, she'd have done so. Since she didn't give them, she didn't want us to know them. We have to respect that."

"But Elise could get burned. Well, her estate could. You know what I mean."

"She was a smart woman with a good heart. She's not doing anything she didn't want done. Don't dig, Bryce, just get the ball rolling and close the deal."

"Will do, buddy. But it strikes me odd and I'm really curious."

"Forget it, okay?" A light tap sounded at his door. "Got to go. Bess and I are going to bake some clams."

"Bake clams? John, this isn't a vacation with your loving wife. You're supposed to be working on a property settlement for your divorce. Judge Branson —"

"Can get his own clams, and his own woman."

"I'll pass that tidbit along when he tosses both you and Bess into the slammer."

"Get us one cell, mmm?"

"Do I smell a reconciliation in the air here?"

John's heart wrenched. "Only for six more days."

"What?"

"Never mind. Is Suzie sleeping better?"

"Not really. But we're working on it. Her therapist says it just takes time."

"Give her a hug from me."

"I'll do that. She'll be all right — the doctor assures me of that. Getting used to the idea of losing her mother really has body-slammed her. I'd be lying if I didn't say I was worried, John. It's going on too long."

"Time's a funny thing, you know? For her, it's going a lot slower without a mother there to soften the day-to-day blows. Give her some time, like the doc says, and let her know how much you love her. Lots of hugs." Hugs John hadn't gotten, and had needed so desperately. "And let her know how much you need her, and how special she is to you." Elise had given him that. She'd called him *dear heart.* Suzie needed to know she was dear to someone. Desperately needed to know she mattered. "And get her a mother," John added before thinking better of it.

"Yeah, I'll just phone Macy's and order a mom." Bryce sucked in a breath. "In the meantime, you forget baking clams and get that property settlement resolved."

"Working on it." John hung up the phone then opened the door, eager to see Bess. The woman didn't know it, but if Elise owned the station, then Bess's job was no longer in jeopardy. But he thought he'd wait a while to tell her. Bringing up their lives away from Seascape might bring reality crashing down around their ears and, right now, he was happy for the first time in six years. He didn't want reality. He wanted his wife. And, at Seascape, he had her.

For six more days.

Little Island was one of the most gorgeous places on earth. No electricity. No phones. No bridges. The only way to it was by boat and, once there, the lush foliage and graceful trees wove a magical spell around those fortunate enough to visit it.

Aaron dropped Bess and John off at the end of a rickety wooden pier near a little sign that read: *Leave only footprints. Take only photographs.* And nearer to the rocky shore, nailed to the pier's last post, was another sign. It was older, faded, and the sun glared brightly on it. Bess couldn't make out the words.

They walked on and, under the shade of a craggy old oak, she and John spread out a patchwork quilt. The day had started out cool but had warmed to a very pleasant upper seventy degrees — a welcome respite from the sweltering nineties pegging the mercury at home. And now sitting knee to knee with John, Bess inhaled the fresh, salt-tinged air deeply and gazed out beyond the orange tiger lilies some thoughtful soul had planted, onto the ocean. "I'll bet this place is breathtaking at sunset."

John slid his gaze down the face of the rocky slope to the narrow strip of a pebbled beach, and nodded. "I'll bet it is. We'll have to come back one day and see."

Bess smiled, feeling a little melancholy. If they did come back, it'd have to be within six days. After then . . . no. No, she wasn't going to think of them now. She was going to take all she could get from these six days. Live each of them to the fullest.

"So," John stretched out, grabbed a rock, and anchored the edge of the quilt against the steady breeze, "what did Miss Hattie send?"

Bess peered inside the basket, then grinned. "Miss Millie's infamous chocolate chip cookies!"

"Really? T. J. raves about those." John reached for the green-covered container.

Bess pulled it back. "Not so fast, Jonathan. Those are for dessert."

He came up on his knees, the devil dancing in his eyes, captured her in his arms, then leaned forward, forcing her down on the quilt, onto her back. "I had different plans for dessert," he breathed against her mouth, then captured her lips in a spellbinding kiss that left them both breathless. "But if my wife wants cookies, then she'll have them."

Bess darted her slumberous gaze from him to the container, then back to him. She dropped the container onto the quilt and smiled. "Your wife wants cookies. Later."

He grunted, let his hand drift down her side, ribs to hip. "What does she want now?"

Her smile faded. She eased her hand between them, cupped him, then gently squeezed. The twinkling in her eyes darkened her irises to the blue of the ocean. "You," she whispered, urging him back to her. "She wants you."

"I do love a woman who knows what she wants." John grunted, rolled away, then stood up. Bess laughed out loud, watched his shenanigans with youthful delight, then joined him with her own rendition of bawdy and brass. She was lousy at it, but he didn't seem to notice. A seductive temptress was out of her realm, yet the way his eyes heated to that heart-stopping cobalt blue, Jonathan didn't know that either, and she sure had no intention of telling him. They'd never laughed like this, teased, and taunted, and acted totally ridiculous when making love.

And only now did she notice, or wonder why.

It was enticing, exciting — fun.

As bare as he, she stood on the quilt in the stark sunlight. They faced each other openly, all flaws exposed. The hunger burning in his eyes matched that in her soul, and catching a glimpse of white pickets behind him, feeling ultra-mischievous, she darted around him to the little fence.

He ran after her, then stopped. "Two graves? Out here?"

There were no names on the headstones, only slate crosses marking the burial sites and red impatiens blooming at their bases. Bess reached for Jonathan's hand, laced their fingers and squeezed tightly. When he looked at her, she blinked hard and gazed up at him. "I hope they were as happy here as I've been here today with you."

Jonathan swallowed a knot in his throat. "I'm sure they were. I'm sure they stood on the shore and watched the sun set, and held each other, and were content."

"Sometimes I love the way you think, Jonathan." She smiled up at him. "I want to come back here and watch the sun set with you."

"I'd like that."

Her eyes went solemn. "Promise me."

He'd kept his promise to come back. To come here and bake clams. She wanted him to keep this one, too. "I promise." He hugged her, again wondering if life would ever again be this good. "I never knew you were a nudist, Bess."

"I never have been." She nipped at his shoulder. "I've decided I like it."

"Me, too." He growled deep in his throat.

She laughed and swatted his backside. "You're bad, Jonathan Mystic."

"To the bone, darling. Bad and mad," he looked into her eyes, "about you."

"Oh, Jonathan. Why didn't you get slouchy on me?"

"What?"

"Never mind."

"Wanna go for a swim?"

She cocked a brow at him. "First?"

He gave her a ghost of a smile. "Or last."

"First. And then we'll bake clams, gorge ourselves on Miss Millie's cookies, and drink Moxie —"

"Moxie?"

"It's a local soft drink. Lucy Baker loves it."

"Can't wait."

"You're going to have to." She pulled out of his arms then darted down to the water.

Jonathan followed. And hours later, when

they had played like children in the surf, had made slow, sweet love on the quilt under the shade of the old craggy oak, had skipped stones across the water's surface, and had stuffed themselves on the absolute best clams cooked in rocks and seaweed John ever in his life had eaten, they dressed and then made their way back toward the old pier.

On the way, they stopped at the little graveyard. Their hands clasped, their heads bowed, Bess wished those who had passed on peace, and John thanked them for sharing their island with him and his wife. Then John and Bess walked on, hand in hand and content, back to the rickety pier.

Gripping the basket handle more firmly, John stepped onto the wooden planks. Today had been the best day of their marriage. Before, they'd both been too busy wanting to make their career marks to enjoy the things most important in life. Now, it might be too late for them, but at least they'd had today. And John regretted all the days they'd lost, because now he knew what he'd been missing.

Bess stopped at the first pier post and shoved aside some kind of berry vine that half-blocked an old, faded sign. He hadn't noticed it when they'd arrived.

The empty burlap bag in her hand puddled on the planks. "Darling, what does this say? Can you make it out?"

He set down the picnic basket and the bushel basket of cooked clams, then stepped around her and squinted, focusing on the faded gray letters. "Beware . . . of . . . shifting . . . sand."

"Shifting sand?" Bess straightened up and stared at him, her eyes wide. "Tony's message had shifting sand in it."

It had. A road map. John stared at the little sign. Definitely a road map.

And an island will appear.

This island? Was that it? The message was a road map to this island? But why?

The sounds of a boat motor grew louder and louder.

"Darling, Aaron's here."

Something flashed yellow on the planks. John bent down and pushed back the vine for a better look.

And there against the weathered wood lay a single flower petal from a yellow carnation.

Tony. Definitely a message. Definitely a road map to this island. But whatever for?

John pulled out his wallet, put the yellow petal inside the clear photo-holder next to the one holding Elise's petal, then returned his wallet to his pocket.

Unfortunately, that was a question John couldn't answer . . . yet.

CHAPTER 12

"They're positively the best, aren't they, Miss Hattie?"

Miss Hattie slowly chewed a clam, clearly savoring it, then delicately removed a clump of seaweed from her mouth with her lacy-edge hankie. "Wonderful. My, but I haven't had clams cooked on the rocks in years. What a delightful surprise."

Bess smiled. "There are plenty enough for dinner. Jonathan bought an entire bushel."

At the sink and rinsing her hands, Miss Hattie elbowed the dishcloth to wipe at a water spill on the countertop. She grunted. "He must have been hungry."

"I'll bet Vic would enjoy some."

"He'd love them. I'll take some over tomorrow for lunch. He's still down, bless his heart, and fighting it tooth and nail. The man has always been hard on his feet. Now, he's added his back to the list." She rubbed her hands dry with the dishcloth. "I try to tell him we're not fifty anymore, but will he listen?"

"No." Bess grinned. "He's a man, Miss Hattie. Men don't listen."

Miss Hattie giggled.

The lights went off.

"Oh, my." Miss Hattie sighed. "I suppose they do listen, on occasion."

The lights flickered, then came back on.

"What's that all about?" Bess looked at the overhead fixture. "Do you think there's an electrical short in the wiring?"

"There's a short, all right," Miss Hattie emphatically nodded, "but not in the wiring."

Bess sent the woman a puzzled look.

She frowned at the clams for tempting her, ate another one with a resigned sigh, then returned to the sink to again rinse her hands. "It's nothing, dear."

The phone rang. Miss Hattie looked down at the water dripping from her hands. "Goodness."

"I'll get it." Bess sprang up from her chair, her heart lighter than it'd been since her wedding day. This had been positively, absolutely, unequivocally the best day of her life. Perfect, from the moment she'd opened her eyes and seen John looking at her with love. Oh, she wasn't under any illusions. It was temporary lust — well, lust with a megakick. Might as well call a spade a spade — but it was better than the sad-eyed despair she'd been seeing in them. If only in a small way, she was helping him to focus on living, rather than on his grief at losing Elise.

Hoping the next six days would be as fulfilling as this one, Bess reached for the phone. That was asking a lot, but if you're going to dream, why dream brass and not gold? She lifted the receiver, and placed it to her ear. "Hello, Seascape Inn."

"Bess?"

Sal Ragusa. And he sounded surprised.

Bess laughed. "It's me. Miss Hattie's devouring clams so I answered the phone for her." *Sal! Oh-oh.* Her stomach quivered. *This had to be bad news.* "How are things at the station?"

"Not so good, Bess." An undertaker couldn't sound more sober.

This was *the* dreaded call. And Millicent Fairgate hadn't had the courage to make it herself. Bess forced a smile into her voice. "It's okay, Sal. I know what's coming."

"I'm sorry, Bess. I did what I could —"

"I know you did." What was she going to do? No job. Little money. Big fine.

"She made the firing effective as of noon today."

"High noon. Typical Millicent." Bess dragged a hand through her hair. "I appreciate you calling. When I get back, I'll clean out my office."

"It's already done," he mumbled. "I did it for you and took the stuff to Maggie MacGregor. I figured it'd be kind of hard for you and . . . well, heck, Bess, I didn't think I could stand seeing you do it."

Her smile turned genuine. "Thank you. It would have been hard and I really appreciate your . . ." the word 'help' stuck in her throat, "thoughtfulness." She'd tried. She still couldn't say it, but at least she'd tried. Honest effort was a kind of positive growth. Not the best, but better than burrowing into the sand and ignoring a challenge.

"Yeah, well. You're special. It really ticks me off that Millicent did this."

"I know. But it's okay." How she prayed that proved true. "If it weren't for you, I'd head straight to the competition." Bess laughed. "Now wouldn't that frost Millicent's cookies?"

Sal laughed. "She'd have a fit."

"Yeah."

Static filled the line. Neither of them knew what to say. The dreaded news had come and been imparted, and all that was left was goodbye. "Sal, I want to thank you for all you taught me. I've learned a great deal working with you."

"You're welcome. I've learned from you, too. And I'll miss you."

The old Bess would never admit it. The new Bess might not yet be able to say that awful "H" word, but she could tell the truth. "I'll miss you, too. Bye, Sal."

Bess hung up the phone, fighting the urge to fly up the stairs to John and cry her eyes out. But she wouldn't. This wasn't the end of the world. Only the end of a job. Six days from now. That's when she'd need him to hold her while she mourned.

Only then, he wouldn't be there. And she'd be mourning him leaving her.

Miss Hattie looked at her through worried eyes. "Bad news, dear?"

"None that wasn't expected." She gave Miss Hattie a watery smile. "So how do you like those clams?"

It was nearly dark. Twilight. That moment of time during each day when nothing is exactly as it appears. When the haze of deception makes magic seem ordinary, desire as natural and attainable as drawing breath. That miraculous instant when dreams don't seem nebulous, but real and reachable and concrete.

And John's dreams were of the future, one for him with Bess.

Standing out on the headland cliffs, he watched the sun drop down past the horizon. Twilight had come and gone. Had his chance for dreams come and gone with it?

Within minutes, a wall of fog rolled in with the roaring surf, crashing onto the shore. The fog rolled up the cliffs then over his skin, its cold mist chilling him to the bone. He stuffed his hands into his windbreaker pockets and swore that as long as he lived he'd never forget this day. The sights and sounds of Bess laughing, her bare and splashing in the surf, and the tenderness. Oh, the tenderness . . . When they'd stood side by side before those two unmarked graves and she'd bowed her head and prayed for two people she'd never met, wishing them peace, he'd felt more tenderness in that moment than in his entire life.

She was perfect. Today had been perfect. And, though he'd had no right — no right — to do it, God help him, he'd fallen in love with her all over again.

When they'd returned from the island, she'd gone off to shower. Miss Hattie had told him then about Bryce's call. "The deal

431

is closed," she'd said, passing along Bryce's message.

The station was bought. Elise's estate now owned it. Well, it had owned the station for years, but now the estate publicly owned the station. Using John's power of attorney, Bryce had signed the documents. Bess's job was safe.

The fog swept in, cloaking him with misty tendrils and swirls. John closed his eyes and whispered a prayer. *Thank you. For letting me see how good love can be. For finding a way to ease my mind on Bess being taken care of after this divorce. Thank you for letting me dream and pretend for a little while that she loves me again. I know she doesn't, and I can't blame her. If only things had been then as they were today. But they weren't. And done is done. I hurt her. I didn't know how much until we came here. I know I should tell her about my parents . . . but I can't. I . . . can't.*

How do you tell a woman you want to respect and admire you — a woman you've hurt and are trying so hard to make things right with — that you're such an awful person even your own parents couldn't love you?

Selena could learn the truth. He couldn't risk that. Couldn't put her through what he'd been through because of the secret about the cult. The shame. The feelings of worthlessness. The guilt and not knowing what he'd done wrong, why his parents had rather live in it than with their own children. No. No, he couldn't put her through that. No one deserved that kind of pain. No one — especially not Selena. He couldn't tell Bess to put her mind at ease about his parents and why he refused to discuss them. She'd act differently. Selena would pick up on it. She'd wheedle it out of him and then she'd be devastated. No, the costs of truth were just too high.

It was a cozy kitchen.

Bess and John and Miss Hattie had dinner there, rather than in the more formal pink and navy blue decorated dining room. Bess loved the feel of the kitchen, the warmth it radiated. With white, lacy curtains at the windows, the basket of yellow porcelain bisque daffodils in the center of the light oak table, the old antique radio softly playing big band era music from its nook beside the fireplace, and the pretty ceramic canisters lined up like soldiers-at-the-ready on the white-tile countertop, the kitchen welcomed people into it, invited them to linger, and to chat. And when the low hum of the fridge clicked off, the gallery's grandfather clock's sure and steady ticks sounded like a heart beating. The heartbeat of the house. Yes. A gentle smile tugged at Bess's lips, and she made a mental note that the first item on her Things-To-Do list was to buy a grandfather clock, just as soon as she and John got home and —

Bess and John wouldn't be going home.

Reality crashed down around her ears, and Bess stiffened in her chair. Their home stood empty now. They lived in different homes, led different lives separate from each other. And they would be separate forevermore.

Blinking hard, she looked across the table at him. Smiling at Miss Hattie, he looked so gorgeous. His thick black hair gleaming in the light from the lamp above the table. And Bess's heart ached. Six more days of pretending, and then she'd have only her memories of him. Six more days, and they'd be divorced.

She didn't want to do it.

She wanted more days like today. Years of more days like today.

She wanted him.

"More cobbler, Bess?" Miss Hattie stood at her side, cobbler and serving spoon in hand, a splash of a blueberry stain soiling her white apron.

"No, thank you." Her voice didn't want to work. She coerced herself into snapping to, into forgetting about mourning until she was forced to remember it.

"I'd love some more," John said.

Smiling, Miss Hattie obliged him, spooning another serving of the cobbler into his white petal bowl. "I do love men who aren't afraid to eat. It's very disheartening to cook and to not have an appreciative man around to — Bess? Are you all right, dear?"

John looked at her and worry filled his eyes. "Bess, what's wrong?"

"I'm fine." Heat surged up her neck. "I think I ate too much. Miss Hattie, you're a wonderful cook."

"Thank you, dear." She smiled, but the concern didn't leave her eyes.

John finished his cobbler, but he too clearly still worried. Bess smiled more than she wanted as a way of reassuring them she was okay. "John and I will do the dishes, Miss Hattie. We insist."

"Well, if you insist, then let's do them together," Miss Hattie said, then filled her tone with a conspiratorial edge of mischief. "More free time for all of us."

John washed. His hands buried in hot, soapy water at the sink, he cocked his head.

"I thought you had a cook to help you."

Miss Hattie carried her bowl and cup over to him. "I do. But I only bother Cora to help when the inn is busy. I prefer to do things myself as much as I can." She nodded toward the coffeemaker. "Bess, dear, why not put on another pot of coffee? It's chilly tonight."

John dried his hands on a dishcloth. "Would you like for me to build a fire?"

"I'm afraid it's too warm for that, dear. It's in between right now. Too warm for a fire, and too cool without one."

"Like twilight."

"Excuse me?"

"Nothing, Miss Hattie."

What had he meant by that? Bess studied him, but couldn't imagine.

They finished the dishes. He folded the cloth, draped it over the little pull-out rack in the cabinet under the sink, then sat down at the table. After Bess had the coffee brewing, she joined him.

Miss Hattie eased down into her rocker, reached to the fireplace's stone ledge for her reading glasses, decided against wearing them, then picked up her sewing bag and returned to embroidering her new napkins.

"Are you ready to tell me yet?" Bess asked John.

436

"Tell you what, sweetheart?"

Her heart beat a little faster. *Sweetheart.* Not the sarcasm-laced *darling.* True, they'd made an agreement, and he'd called her darling many times since without the sarcasm, but that first time he'd said it still made the word sting. "How things went in Portland." She laced her fingers atop the table. "I've been wondering all day but every time I ask, you say 'later.' Is it later yet?"

John grinned. "It went well, as a matter of fact. I met Gregor Samuels at Dockside, and he said he personally had seen Dixie aboard *Southern Pride* three days after the kidnaping."

"I knew it!" Bess rapped the table with the heel of her hand. "I knew it. I knew it. I knew it!"

"What did you know, dear?" Miss Hattie asked, looking lost in a mental fog.

"*Southern Pride* is Thomas Boudreaux's yacht, Miss Hattie," John said. "He's missing, too — same time as Dixie. They were engaged, according to some sources, and he's a prime suspect in Dixie's kidnaping."

"Or her elopement, whichever the case may be," Bess chimed in.

"There's still doubt?" Miss Hattie paused

sewing, her needle midair, and looked at John.

"The FBI talked with a few of her friends who insisted Dixie was eloping with Boudreaux, but her mother, Elise, believed she'd been kidnaped." John paused to hike a kink from his shoulder. "Dixie had told Elise that Boudreaux had been too possessive. He was pushing Dixie to marry him, and she'd agreed because she was afraid of him. As soon as she figured out how to gracefully get away from him, she intended to do it."

"Hmmm, she must have been very young, to try that type maneuver." Miss Hattie slid out of her rocker then over to the cabinet where she poured two cups and a mug of steaming hot coffee. "Why did Dixie fear him?"

"I read his case report," Bess said, watching Miss Hattie bring a cup to her and then set the mug onto the table before John. She'd already claimed a man with hands the size of John's needed something more substantial than a fragile china cup to sip from, and he did seem more comfortable holding the burgundy marble mug. "Boudreaux had a long history of episodic violent behavior. Not a nice man."

Miss Hattie retrieved her cup, then settled down into her squeaky rocker. "He sounds dangerous."

"He was." Bess frowned. "Nothing has been found on him, either, has it? Not since back then?"

"No, it hasn't." John blew into his mug. Steam lifted from it and swirled in the light shining down from the overhead fixture.

"Dixie might have been wise, being wary of him." Bess dragged a fingertip around the rim of the salt shaker, near the floral centerpiece. "Those type of personalities have a lot of triggers, and rejecting him could have set him off on a tangent."

"She was young, too," John said. "Far too young to be dealing with violent men or to be contemplating marriage. Boudreaux was violent, but he was also charming and slick — a lot like Miguel."

"Jonathan," Bess warned. "There's no comparison between those two men. Miguel is not violent, nor is he slick."

"Sorry." John's eyes twinkled. "Old habit." He wasn't sorry at all. "Uh-huh." But he was jealous of Miguel, all right. To the bone jealous. Bess shouldn't, but there was a nasty part of her that totally enjoyed it. It proved Jonathan wasn't indifferent toward her. His love cost too much. His hatred rankled. But both sat easier on her shoulders and in her heart than his indifference.

Miss Hattie sipped from her cup, then set it near her glasses on the fireplace ledge and looked at John. "This doubt about whether she was kidnaped or eloped must have created a lot of difficulties for you in trying to solve the case."

"It has," Jonathan said. "A lot of them." He tapped the curve of the mug handle with his thumb. "I believe she was kidnaped. Bess agrees with the FBI, that Dixie eloped."

"Oh my. Sounds a lot like Lucy and Fred Baker's angel discussion." Miss Hattie sighed. "Spirited, at times."

"I'm sorry, darling." Bess gave John's hand atop the table a gentle squeeze. "I know we disagree on this, but I swear my position has absolutely nothing to do with questioning your judgment."

He frowned. "We said no games, Bess. That was the agreement." He slid his gaze pointedly to Silk, curled in a ball at Miss Hattie's feet.

"I'm not playing games. To me, it's a logical deduction. Well, a likely deduction. If Dixie was kidnaped, Boudreaux kidnaped her for breaking their engagement. Anyone else would have demanded a ransom. And if Boudreaux kidnaped her, wouldn't he come back for the money now that Elise is dead?"

"Unless Dixie refuses to claim it. Or can't claim it," John agreed.

Even thinking that she might not be able to claim it hurt him; Bess could see it in the shadows in his eyes. Hadn't she thought the same thing? That Dixie could be dead? Why should she think John so shallow that the idea wouldn't have occurred to him? Lord, but Bess had been arrogant. "If Dixie were alive, I'd think she'd have come home to claim her inheritance. I mean it's ludicrous to believe a money-grubber like Boudreaux would walk away from all Elise's money, unless . . ." her voice trailed.

"Unless?"

Bess met John's gaze. "Unless *he* were dead."

"Or Dixie was." John gazed off into the black hole of the fireplace, looking as if he wished he'd built a fire there anyway. "Logical, and possible — provided Boudreaux and/or Dixie knows Elise is dead." John sat back and stretched out his legs. "I know all the evidence points to an elopement, Bess, but Elise knew in her heart Dixie was kidnaped. A mother knows these things about her child. And we know Dixie was alive four months after the kidnaping. Samuels made a positive ID on her at Dockside three days afterward and again four months later. He said Dixie and a man fitting Boudreaux's description had left on *Southern Pride* heading for Nova Scotia."

"Positive ID?" Bess frowned. "Was he absolutely sure? No margin for error?"

"He described her amulet, honey. We both know there are only two like it in the world."

"Amulet?" Miss Hattie put her sewing down.

Bess nodded. "When Dixie was born, her father had matching ruby amulets made for her and her mother. They always wore them." Bess turned to Jonathan. "Darling, you did bury Elise with hers, didn't you?"

He nodded.

"Of course you did." Bess looked back at Miss Hattie. "If this Gregor Samuels described the amulet, then it must have been Dixie. Or a woman matching her description wearing it. Most likely Dixie. I can't imagine her willingly taking off that amulet."

"She wouldn't," John agreed. "Neither would Elise."

Miss Hattie stilled for a long moment, lifted her gaze ceilingward, and didn't so much as breathe. Then she refocused, letting her gaze drift between Bess and John. "I don't want to interfere, my dears, but —"

"Please, Miss Hattie," John said, sounding

desperate. "If there's anything you can suggest that will help, I'd love to hear it. I want . . ." He slid his gaze to Bess. "Solving this case is *extremely* important to me."

"Something happened here a long time ago which might or might not be useful."

"Miss Hattie, you're sounding awfully mysterious." Bess leaned closer to John and rested her hand on his thigh. He cupped her fingertips with his palm and just being close to him eased her apprehension.

"I'm sorry," Miss Hattie said. "If they were en route to Nova Scotia, then they had to come by here. May I strongly suggest that you two talk with Hatch about this? He knows more about the sea and the goings on in it than any other man alive."

John shrugged. "I'd planned on checking with the Coast Guard to see if they have any records of a *Southern Pride* —"

"Bah," Miss Hattie grunted. "Hatch was born and raised in that lighthouse, Jonathan. The Coast Guard comes to *him* for information, dear."

Seeing that this ranked important to Miss Hattie, Bess squeezed John's thigh. "We'll talk to him first thing in the morning, Miss Hattie."

"Can we bribe you into making some blueberry muffins to take to him?" John gave her a winning smile. "He's promised us a tour of the lighthouse, but only if we bring him some of your muffins."

"No bribery is needed. I'd be delighted to make the muffins." She tilted her head. "Vic probably would enjoy some, too."

"Is he any better?" Bess asked, rubbing John's thumb with her forefinger.

"A few more days of bed rest and he should be fine. If he misses the Scottish festival and gets cheated out of doing the Highland Fling with the MacInnes twins, he's going to be challenging to live with for the next year."

Miss Hattie stood up, then rinsed her coffee cup at the sink. "It's time to turn in. I'll see you children in the morning."

"Good night, Miss Hattie."

" 'Nite," Bess said.

The phone rang, and Miss Hattie waved. "It's for you, Bess."

Bess hiked her brows at John.

"Don't ask me. She just knows." He shrugged, then stood up. "And don't forget our agreement. We sleep —"

"I won't," Bess interrupted him, then lifted the phone. "Seascape Inn."

"Bess, my angel."

"Hello, Miguel." Bess's gaze locked with John's.

444

"I'll see you upstairs," he said stiffly.

Bess nodded, and he left the kitchen, looking so angry a black cloud might as well have been riding shotgun over his head. Silk, the little traitor, dogged his heels.

"You sound upset, Angel. What's wrong?"

"I got fired a while ago." She twisted the phone cord around her index finger. John had looked pretty upset. For a day that had been beautiful until twilight, it'd sure gone to the dogs since.

"I'm afraid it's just as well," Miguel said. "That's why I'm calling."

Bess frowned. What had she missed? "Why?"

"To tell you that the station has been sold."

"*Sold!* Dang it, Miguel, I asked you not to do it. I even said please. Why did you — ? Oh, never mind. I don't even want to know." She slammed the phone onto the hook, then snapped off the lights.

By the time she got to the stairs, her muttering had turned to mumbling and the frustrated tears burning her eyes had started to fall. How could he do this to her? After she'd asked him not to? After she'd explained how humiliated she'd feel if he did? Some friend.

Like a homing pigeon, she headed straight

for John's room and shoved open the door without so much as a cursory knock. It was dark, and he evidently was already asleep. In the old days, she'd have miserably slunk off to her room and cried her heart out alone. But these weren't the old days. For six more days, she had a husband with strong arms and big shoulders, and he was going to wake up and let her use them.

"Jonathan? Wake up."

"I'm not sleeping, Bess. I'm fuming."

"Great. Terrific." She stubbed her toe on a box, cursed it, then, at the side of the bed, crawled over John. Snuggling down beside him, she sniffled.

"You're crying?" He reached for the lamp. She grabbed his arm. "Don't. Please."

"Bess, honey, what's wrong?"

"What isn't?" she wailed. "Oh, I thought I wanted to talk about this, Jonathan, but I don't. I just want you to hold me while I have a good cry."

"What did that jerk do to you?"

"I might kill him," she muttered. "No, I'm going to kill him. I just have to decide how. Slowly. Definitely slowly."

"You don't go around killing men, darling." John wrapped his arms around his wife. Whatever Santos had done had knocked her to her knees. John might just

446

kill the jerk for that himself. "If you did, I'd have been dead a long time ago."

"Well, I should." She curled her fingers against his chest, letting their tips drift through his hair. "He humiliated me, Jonathan. After I begged him not to —" She let out a deep sob, then shuddered.

She'd *begged?* Bess? Impossible. Asked, maybe. But not begged. No way. "What did he do?"

No answer. Just another sob.

And another.

And still another.

John gritted his teeth. The man was definitely going to die. Never in all their years had John seen Bess so upset. He turned on the lamp. "I asked you, what did he do?"

"Don't you yell at me, Jonathan Mystic."

"Then answer me and I'll shut up. How did Santos humiliate you?" She had to love the man. Had to. Otherwise she'd never be this hurt.

"He bought the station!"

Oh, crud. John clicked off the light. What did he do? What did he say? She thought Santos bought the station. Should he tell — no. No. He couldn't. Not yet.

John swallowed hard, praying he was handling this right. "I'm sorry, honey." He tugged her into his arms and held her tightly. All this because she believed Santos bought the station? Santos. The man did know what buttons to push when it came to Bess, John had to give him that. Even if this button wasn't actually his.

John held her while she cried, murmuring gentle reassurances, feeling guilty as sin, and worrying the entire time. When her sobs lessened to sniffles, then to an occasional sigh, he still worried, and his guilt heap had doubled in size. "How did him buying the station humiliate you?"

"Because it's absurd. Ridiculous."

"It's a lucrative business, Bess."

"It's a billboard to the entire city of New Orleans, is what it is, Jonathan. He might as well take out an ad in *The Times-Picayune* telling everyone at once that I can't keep my job without him running interference for me. I'll be a laughingstock. But that's not the worst part of it."

He should tell her the truth. Santos *hadn't* bought the station. Obviously, before the man could tell her that, she'd gotten fired-up and hung up on him. "You won't be a laughingstock."

"I will."

"What's the worst of it?"

"He was supposed to be my friend. He was supposed to believe in me. He was supposed to show the others that he knew I could do my job alone because I'm good at it. Instead, he shows them the exact opposite."

Oh no. That's exactly how she'd feel on learning John had bought the station for Elise. It wouldn't matter to Bess that he'd done it under explicit codicil instructions. From Bess's vantage point, the bottom line would be that once again he'd put Elise and her desires first.

And the kicker of it was, to a point, Bess would be right. What a colossal mess. Even though Bess had told him that she'd envied Elise, he'd never, not once, considered how Bess might feel about working for Elise's estate. He'd been caught up in thinking that with Sal running the station, Bess's job would be safe. She'd have some financial security. John hadn't thought beyond that. Still, even now, after loving, and losing, and falling in love with the woman again, he hadn't learned a darn thing from before.

John grimaced and rubbed at his jaw. And how was he supposed to tell her that Santos hadn't done the dirty deed? Seeing her reaction to believing Santos had bought the station, knowing she didn't love the man or she'd never have made love with John and yet she'd still come unglued, how could

John tell her that her loving husband had been the jerk who'd humiliated her?

Heaven help him, she'd kill him dead.

No. No, worse. She'd slip back behind that cool cashmere, eel-skin facade.

She dried her face on the edge of the quilt, then snuggled back to him. Her *Ritz* filling his senses, he closed his arms around her. A boulder of fear of losing her again stuck squarely in his throat. How could he handle this honestly without alienating her?

He had to tell her the truth, of course. If he had an ounce of decency, he'd tell her now. But if he did, then their agreement would be shot. She'd be furious with him, stomp back to her room, and not speak to him. He'd not see her laughing in the surf. She'd take his ring off and sling it in his face. Get her car from Jimmy's Quick Service Garage and leave Seascape Inn. They'd never go back to Little Island and share that sunset.

He'd promised.

Yes, he'd promised. And she'd promised him six more days. Six days in which he could build enough memories with her to last him a lifetime. Could he face a life without them *and* her?

He had to tell her. It was the right thing to do. No secrets, they'd said. No games or lies. He *had* to tell her. And he would.

In six more days.

It wasn't right or fair or honest. But after those six days, then he'd already have lost all he had to lose.

Chapter 13

Bess stumbled past the grandfather clock. It chimed eleven times. She'd awakened in John's arms feeling as if a cactus had taken root and sprouted in her throat.

Walking on into the kitchen, she saw Miss Hattie, hanging up the telephone.

"Are you all right, dear?" Miss Hattie looked adorable in a white cotton bathrobe with lace edging the collar and cuffs. "Shall I warm you some milk?"

"No, thanks." Bess opened the fridge and pulled out a bottle of Moxie. "I need something a little more thirst-quenching." She popped off the top of the brown bottle and took a long drink. It felt ice-cold going down her throat.

"I didn't realize you were still awake." Miss Hattie poured herself a glass of milk and sat down at the table. "Your attorney phoned a moment ago."

Bess sat down across the table from Miss

Hattie. "I'm sorry. She must have forgotten about the time change. Francine's a terrific attorney, but she's kind of unconscious about everything else."

"She said it was urgent, Bess, but she didn't want me to awaken you."

"With Francine it's always urgent." Bess sipped from the bottle. The Moxie was quite different from a cola, but very good. She licked at her lips.

"No, Bess. You need to call her right away." Miss Hattie lowered her gaze to her glass. "I don't want to intrude, dear, but may I say something?"

The tilt of her head, the tone of her voice, set Bess's nerves on edge. Battle-worn and grateful for the temporary reprieve of momentarily postponing the return call to Francine, Bess nodded.

"I'm delighted to see you and Jonathan truly together, dear."

"It's still only temporary, Miss Hattie. We made a deal and essentially, unfortunately, nothing's changed."

"Oh my, this doesn't sound at all encouraging. But don't give up hope, dear. It's early in your week and there's plenty of time for him to see the light."

Embarrassed, wishing she'd kept her business to herself, Bess sighed. But the damage was done. She only hoped Miss Hattie didn't think her a bigger fool than she already did. "This whole Happy Marriage Agreement isn't reasonable, or logical, or anything else that's wise."

"Ah, the magic's working hard, I see." Miss Hattie propped an elbow on the table then sipped from her glass, a wistful look in her eye.

Her lack of condemnation had Bess relaxing, mimicking the angelic innkeeper's pose, then propping her chin on her hand. "It's getting worse, Miss Hattie. It *was* lust with a kick. Now it's lust with a megakick, and growing stronger every time I see the man. Absurd, isn't it?"

"Oh, I don't know. There's a lot to be said for the magic." Miss Hattie gazed off into space. "It's really a matter of pride, isn't it? Yours and his."

That was part of it. Bess shrugged. "I suppose."

"I wouldn't presume to speak for either of you, dear, but I'll tell you this. Were it my pride, I'd toss it to the wind forever for a second more of magic."

"You would?" Miss Hattie, the practical, the thoughtful, the loveable, would opt against pride? Or was she just saying so? Hard to imagine Miss Hattie ever speaking

454

an untruth, but she was a gentle, if an iron-willed, soul. Not sure which she'd done, Bess frowned.

"In a village minute." Miss Hattie nodded to add weight to her claim.

She *really* would! "I'm surprised."

"Why on earth would that surprise you?"

"Because you're a Mainer." Bess flushed at that undiplomatic remark. "What I mean is, Mainers are frank people, and very proud."

"Of course." Miss Hattie lifted a hand, palm up. "But we're also very intelligent, dear."

"I'm afraid I'm lost."

"We have a lot of cold nights up here. And pride can't hold you and keep you warm, dear. A special man, one who makes you feel the magic, well . . ." Miss Hattie's cheeks tinged pink and she scrunched her delicate hankie in her hand. "Pride comes in a poor second to the magic, and that's that. Don't you agree?"

By the time Bess figured out the question had been a rhetorical one, Miss Hattie had risen, rinsed her glass at the sink, and was walking out of the kitchen. "Do call Francine right away. She sounded . . . nervous."

Francine? Nervous? The shark who made excellent attorneys shake in their shoes at coming up against her in court? The attorney who'd sent more than one judge to hitting the books to keep up with her in court? Francine didn't *do* nervous, she inspired it.

Bess took a double swig of Moxie for fortification, then walked straight to the phone. She dialed, praying another bomb wasn't about to blow up on her head.

Francine answered on the first ring, and immediately started spouting. "I spent a solid hour on the phone with Miguel — he's extremely upset at your hanging up on him, Bess — then I called Millicent Fairgate to chew on her rear and inform her of just how many laws she'd broken in firing you, but she wimped out and refused to talk with me. Her husband, that lily-livered, sorry excuse for a man, said she was 'indisposed' with a migraine." Francine grunted. "She's going to have a lot more of them before I'm through with her on this, I promise you that. Do you want me to file suit tomorrow, or wait until you come back?"

Bess's head whirled. When she talked with Francine, it always did. "Yes. No. I don't know." She let out a heartfelt sigh and forked her fingers through her hair. "Let me think about it."

"What's there to think about? Madam

'Indisposed' Fairgate blew it. You've performed well for over six years — all of which time you've been separated from John. Your work record is clean — excellent, in fact — and that's straight from Sal Ragusa's mouth. Millicent is firing you because you're divorcing, straight-out, open and shut case, and *that,* darling, is discrimination." Francine harrumphed. "I'll have her backside for breakfast."

"I don't know that I want you to." Bess shifted her weight, foot to foot. So she'd sue and win. And be locked into a job with resentful bosses. Well, a resentful owner. Sal would be fine about it — until he got sick of Millicent being on his back. He'd be miserable. Bess would be miserable. In cases such as these, could there really be a winner? Bess worried her lip with her teeth, then again spoke to Francine. "Let me talk it over with John."

"What?"

Bess jerked. "Good grief, Francine. My ears will ring for a week."

"This is a joke, right?"

"No." Bess bristled and tapped the phone with a nail.

"No, of course it isn't. You don't joke about John or your job."

Bess frowned at the receiver, then put it

457

back to her ear. Not a very pretty picture of herself, and she would be miffed, but she couldn't honestly pull it off. She *didn't* joke about John or her job. Both mattered to her.

"Bess, sit down a minute and just listen to me. You know I think you're the greatest, but that thin air up there must have your blood too thin and your brain suffering serious oxygen deprivation. You're divorcing John, right? When a woman is divorcing a man, she doesn't ask him for advice. Alimony? Yes. Advice? Never. It's simply not done."

Bess grimaced. "It is done if she's me and she's asked for his advice before and it's proven sound. Excellent, in fact. And John's has."

Francine's sigh rattled static through the phone. "I've been asking this for years, and I'm going to ask it again. By all that's holy, woman, why are you divorcing this man? You're crazy about him."

Maybe she was just plain crazy. "He doesn't love me." She'd be even crazier to not divorce a man who didn't love her. Staying married to him under those conditions would be absurd. Ridiculous.

"Look, I'm your lawyer but I'm your friend, too. The friend in me says you're out of your mind for staying at Seascape while

he's up there. You're vulnerable and confused. He'll steal your heart and cut it to
ribbons. Don't give him the chance. Get
out of Dodge — before it's too late."

"I tried that." How Bess feared Francine
was right. "My car's broken and I can't
leave until it's repaired."

"Leave it."

Running would be so easy. So easy. But,
like Tony's message, her feelings for John
ran deep in her heart. She couldn't run.
And if she did, her heart would stay with
him.

She couldn't. She stared at the bowl of
fruit on the counter's edge, at the slope of a
banana. Should she tell Francine about the
Happy Marriage Agreement? Bess probably
should, but Francine already thought Bess
had lost her mind. She didn't want to prove
it, and disclosing that surely would. "You've
told me your opinion as a friend. What does
my lawyer advise?"

Francine didn't hesitate so much as a
second. "Forget the divorce — at least for
now — and reexamine how you feel about
this man. I've seen a lot of divorcing couples
and you, darling, just don't fit the mold."

"But *he* does." And he'd not once asked
her to come back — aside from for the
seven days, which tied to his ego, not to

their marriage. He didn't seem to mind her being gone so much as he minded her walking out on him. Why was that? "We've been separated six years."

"Physically. But what about in your heart?"

Bess opened her mouth to answer, then realized she couldn't. "I don't know. Sometimes I think he's always been in my heart. Sometimes I swear he hasn't, and won't ever be again." Bess rubbed at her forehead. "I'm so confused, Francine."

"Exactly. And until you're not confused anymore, I don't think we should proceed any further on the divorce."

The only thing left to do on the divorce was the property settlement. She couldn't tell Francine yet that there wouldn't be a custody suit over Silk, because then she'd have to disclose the terms of the agreement or to lie and she'd rather not do either. Francine was a friend, but also an officer of the court. Sleeping with Jonathan legally zapped the separation. In the eyes of the law, by making love, they'd reunited. The entire process would have to be repeated. And, while Bess didn't give two figs about that, Jonathan might.

She sighed. Never had she heard of him being interested in another woman. But

Jonathan was a private investigator, a darn good one from all accounts, and weren't they notoriously discreet? She couldn't stand the thought of him with another woman. The suggestion alone had the green-eyed monster in her rearing its nasty head. But she'd have to accept it. Like Fred Baker had said, some woman would snatch John up in a heartbeat. Her stomach sank. And wasn't it absurd that she would have to do her best to accept this too with grace?

Starting next January, she vowed to herself, there would be *no* annual mottoes.

"Bess?"

"I'm sorry. I drifted, Francine. It's been a long day and I'm just too weary to think. Don't do anything for now. I'll weigh it all out and then let you know what I want to do."

"On the divorce or on suing the snobbery out of Millicent Fairgate?"

"Both." Weary, Bess leaned a shoulder against the wall.

"I have to admit, I'd get a lot more satisfaction out of suing Madam Millicent."

So would Bess. She yawned and finished her Moxie. Maybe she'd sue Miguel, too. For being a lousy friend. No, she wouldn't. She'd just blister his ears and make him miserable. He'd had good intentions. Then

461

she'd find herself another job, because even if she did sue, and she won, she'd still lose. "It really doesn't matter what I decide on the divorce, Francine."

"Of course it matters."

"No, it really doesn't. Jonathan won't lift a finger to stop it." And Bess couldn't blame him. Maybe if when she'd left him, she'd told him explicitly why she'd left him, things wouldn't have gotten so out-of-hand. Big mistake on her part. Not her first, and surely not her last, but one with painful, long-term repercussions. "I'll call you tomorrow or maybe the day after. I need to sleep, and then to think."

"All right, Bess. 'Nite."

" 'Nite." Bess cradled the receiver and headed toward the stairs, feeling so low she'd have to look up to see down. "Tony, if you can hear me, I sure could use a friend."

You have one, Doc. He's waiting for you right up those stairs.

"I let him down. I should have trusted his judgment on the kidnaping/elopement thing with Dixie. It really didn't occur to me that he'd take my stand as a lack of faith in him personally."

We all make mistakes, Bess. But I'm not sure your opposing view on that issue was one.

"It was." The third stair creaked. Holding onto the banister, she looked up at Cecelia's portrait. "She never would have sided against Collin."

She did. Often.

"Then she did it differently. Collin didn't doubt her belief in him. Not if the legend is true."

It's true. And he didn't doubt her; that's true, too.

Bess turned the corner at the landing then continued on up the stairs. "We're back to worth, aren't we?"

Looks that way to me.

"That's the difference, then. Cecelia opposed Collin, but she didn't threaten his sense of worth."

That's right.

"I'm not sure how I threatened Jonathan's worth."

You'll figure it out. I have every faith in you, Doc.

Could she? "Tony?"

Yes?

"I'm scared."

I know, Bess.

"I don't want to get hurt anymore. I don't want to hurt John anymore either. I'm so tired of trying so hard and still losing what's important to me. Miss Hattie says it's pride, but it's a lot more than that."

There's an old saying about everything coming out in the wash. When your wash is done, is there really more than fear and pride left soiling the washtub? You have a man lying awake waiting for you, Bess. A man who loved you enough to marry you. A man whose ring you still wear. He's seen you without your mask now and he didn't run. He didn't condemn you, or seem mortified, or give you the silent treatment as your parents did. He asked you to again be his wife.

"For seven days."

Seven days, yes. But isn't it interesting how much can be accomplished in seven days, Bess? How long did it take to create an entire universe? Hmmm, I wonder how long it would have taken if pride and fear had stood sentry? And I wonder, if you felt seven days was seven more than you deserved, would you have dared to ask for a lifetime? Think about it, Doc. Think about it . . . and leap.

Bess crawled over John and snuggled up against him. "Are you asleep?"

"No." On his back, he shifted his weight and curled an arm around her bare shoulder. He'd lain here spitting nails of green envy because she'd talked with Santos, because he'd had the ability to touch her emotions so deeply when John did not. He'd lain here feeling like a slug for not telling her Santos hadn't bought the station, and wondered how he was going to tell her that he had without her walking out on him again. And he'd wondered what was going on in her mind. Though she'd drifted off to sleep, awakened, gone downstairs, and then had come back to his bed, he still didn't have the foggiest notion about that — or about how to untangle and resolve this mired mess.

She cuddled close, stroked his chest with her hand. His insides quivered. He wanted to make love with her. On that level, he could communicate with her. But he couldn't do it. Not now. Not with deceit between them. He wanted to; gosh, but he wanted to. He wanted to mark her as his in every way a man can mark a woman. But his pride and reverence wouldn't let him. He'd never touched Bess to mark her as his possession, or in jealousy, or in fear that a deceit would be discovered and she'd leave him. He wouldn't start now. He might have no right to love her, but he did, and his heart wouldn't let him touch her with anything in his heart but love.

He loved her. But he didn't know her, not anymore. Bess wasn't Bess. He didn't know who exactly this new Bess was, but he liked her. He liked her telling him her feelings, her laughing and splashing in the surf, and her asking him for his promise to return to Little Island with her to watch the sunset. And he liked that she clearly wasn't in love with Santos. Surely if she had pursued the divorce so she could marry the man, she'd never have agreed to John's proposal — and she'd surely never have made love with him or come directly to his bed for comfort after talking with her sorry Spaniard. What kind of relationship they had, John didn't know, but on Bess's part, it wasn't love. At least, John didn't think it was. With this new Bess, who knew? Maybe she did love the man. Could she? No. No, of course not. Well, maybe.

"Hold me, John. I'm chilled."

His heart in his throat, he wrapped his arms around her. She snuggled closer to his side, bent her knee, then rested it on his thigh. He lay staring at the shadows on the sloped ceiling, knowing they were both holding their thoughts to themselves, both upset, both hurting. Why didn't he talk to her about this? He'd started to earlier, but then she'd gone downstairs. The stair had creaked then, and again on her return. He'd heard her footfalls hesitate at the landing, too. She'd debated between returning to her own room and to his. That she'd come back to him had that tender hitch in his chest swelling, and his heart feeling full. And all of him determined not to again make the mistake he'd made before she'd gone downstairs.

He eased his hand over her ribs, splayed his fingers on her skin. "Bess?"

"Hmmm?"

"Can we talk?"

She let out a little sigh that reeked of relief. "I'd really like that."

He dragged a gentle thumb down the side of her face, then curled his fingers at her nape to thank her. "I want you to know that today has been really special to me."

"To me, too."

His heart tripped a beat. "This is hard to put into words, but . . ." He was lousy at this talking-about-his-feelings business.

"Just say it." Her voice was soft, coaxing, encouraging.

"I've been thinking about what you said — about me putting Elise first. I know I did it, and I think that had a lot to do with why you left me. I didn't mean for anything to drive us apart, Bess. I want you to understand that. I was just so hungry to prove myself. And I guess I took you for granted."

Never, never in his life, would he be so foolish as to do that again. "Anyway, I just wanted to say that I know a lot of the blame for the divorce is mine."

"Jonathan." She swallowed hard. "Thank you."

"I'm sorry I was so slow to catch on to why you left me. I just . . . wasn't thinking about things from all sides."

"We all make mistakes, including me."

He pressed a kiss to her forehead to apologize further. "You're a hard act to follow, you know?"

"Me?"

"Yeah." He let his hand drift down her hair. Soft. Silky. Sexy. "You're always in control, always calm."

She grunted. "Jonathan, I just spent an hour soaking your shoulder. That's hardly controlled or calm."

He smiled against her cheek. "I liked it."

"You hated it."

"I hated you crying. I liked you choosing my shoulder to cry on."

"You did?"

"Yeah." He rubbed at her cheek with his nose. "Before, you always knew what to do. I loved you, Bess, but I never felt like you needed me. Tonight you did. I liked it."

"Me, too. You do good shoulder, Jonathan."

He smiled. He didn't want to, but he couldn't help it. His soul was too hungry and this morsel fed to it tasted too delicious not to be savored. "I've been a loner all of my life, Bess. When we got married, I thought things would be different. But they weren't. I was still a loner, only married. From the sidelines, I watched you conquer one mountain after another . . . without me."

"Jonathan, no. It wasn't like that."

"It was. You were always so sure of everything."

"I wasn't. I'm not." She reared up to look at him, moonlight from the window flooding her face. "I'm not sure of *anything,* Jonathan."

"Bess —"

"No, really." She lifted the hand rubbing his side to his shoulder. "I wanted to share things with you. I just didn't know how." She pressed a kiss to his chest. "We can't go back, Jonathan. But we can do things differently now." She dragged in a deep breath. "I got fired today. Millicent didn't have the guts to do it herself. Sal called. And then Millicent sold the station to Miguel. And do you know what I feel about all that, Jonathan?"

"I imagine you're hurt and angry."

"I am. But the sad truth is, more than anything, I feel relieved."

"Why?" His surprise riddled his voice.

Bess stared down at him, praying she could get through the telling. Praying he didn't hate her when she was done, or worse, that he'd lose every ounce of respect he'd ever had for her. She could take a lot of things, but losing Jonathan's respect wasn't one of them. "I've wanted to leave my job for a long time. But I had no place to go and I needed the money to live."

"I don't get it." He clasped her shoulder, his fingers firm yet gentle. "You love your job."

"Because I've felt like such an arrogant fraud!" She let her head dip to his chest, then let out a self-deprecating laugh and looked at him. "Who am I to give advice to the lovelorn? I've made a shambles of my own love life. Physician, heal thyself!"

"You're not a fraud."

"I am!" Tears she'd fought since her talk on the stairs with Tony crawled up her throat. "I loved you so much, and I still couldn't hold onto you. I tried, Jonathan. I really, really tried. But I just . . . couldn't."

"Bess, honey, don't." He pulled her down until she half-draped his chest, then rolled her onto her back, following her over until he rose above her. "Don't cry. *Please.* I hate your tears."

"I'm . . . sorry. It's just that for the first time since we separated, we were happy. Today was just perfect. It was just so beautiful and perfect, and then I got fired, and Miguel, the traitor, bought the station — after I asked him not to do it — and then Francine called and — everything is just so screwed up now, and I'm so confused and angry. They . . . ruined . . . our . . . perfect . . . day."

"Shh." He pressed tender kisses to her eyelids, her salty cheeks, her nose. "They didn't. We won't let them. They can't ruin our day, if we won't let them. Things will look better in a few days, darling, I promise."

"They won't. In a few days, I'll still be fired. Everyone in New Orleans will be laughing at silly Bess Cameron, the doctor to the lovelorn who can't keep her husband *or* her job — not even with her friend buying it for her. And in a few days, then you'll be gone, too. How can things be better if you're gone, too?"

A hand at her shoulder, the other at her

ribs, John went still. "Will you miss me, Bess?"

Bess swallowed a sob. Would she miss him? Absurd question. His heart jackhammered against her ribs and his eyes looked so solemn. So very solemn. Pride should keep her from telling him the truth, but pride paled to the magic, just as Miss Hattie had said. "I will, Jonathan. I'll miss you so badly I'm not sure I can stand it."

He looked stricken. Stunned. Then stricken again. He cupped her face in his hands, his voice a gravelly whisper that poured his sincerity straight to her heart. "Right now, I can't give you the words, Bess. Or forever. The fault for that is mine. You have no reason to believe me, but if I could give them to you, I would. I'd go back and undo the hurt. I failed you, but I swear to you, woman, I loved you."

"*Then.* You loved me, *then.*"

He hesitated, and sorrow filled his eyes. "Yes, I loved you then."

She clasped his head, urged him down, then kissed the soft skin beneath his eyes, hoping to take away the sorrow. "I believe you, Jonathan. And I'm sorry I failed you, too."

A soft keening erupted from his throat and he clasped her hand, laced his fingers with

472

hers, pressed their palms, then placed light kisses to each of her fingertips. "I want to show you, Bess."

Tender, touched, needing to know that he felt the healing between them, too, she rubbed her nose against his neck.

Spreading his fingers on her jaw, he tilted her face and looked deeply into her eyes. "I want to show you all the things you make me feel. There are things you should know first, but I need to show you, Bess. I . . . need."

Her breath caught, her chin quivering, she reached for him. "Hurry."

But Jonathan didn't hurry, he lingered, lavishly loving her. Lusty, yes, a man like Jonathan couldn't deny his lust any more than he could deny drawing breath. But this wasn't a lustful coupling, it was more gentle and tender and caring. Less physically demanding, but more emotionally powerful. Giving, not taking. Sharing, fearless of vulnerability. Pleasing, without concern or thought for being pleased. It was loving. A loving communion of bodies, of souls, and of hearts.

The power of his selfless ministrations set off a series of shudders that rippled through her body. Bess gasped her enchantment, and gave over to the love flowing between them.

So poignant the moment, the recognition and acceptance of the precious gift they'd shared, a new tenderness flowed between them, and tears blurred Bess's eyes. She smiled at her husband and wept openly. For the first time in her life, she'd overcome her fear of censure and held no part of herself back. She'd given freely and completely, all she'd had to give, determined that in this Jonathan would not feel like an outsider, not feel married yet alone. And now, she reaped her reward.

Her giant of a husband, so strong and formidable and insistent on closing topics that dared to touch him emotionally, looked down at her, a single tear trickling from the corner of his eye.

And never in her life had she felt so blessed.

CHAPTER 14

John awakened alone. Slowly coming out of the dregs of sleep, he heard a knock. But it wasn't at the door. It was inside his mind.

He opened his eyes. "Tony?"

It's me.

"Why the knock?"

I considered rapping your skull, but I thought I might scramble what's left of your brains.

John sat up. "Obviously you're ticked. Any particular reason, or is this a general all-purpose kind of ticked?"

No, it's specific. You leaped and fell flat.

"Ah, the station." Finally Jonathan understood.

Yes, the station. You're lying to her, Jonathan. After what you shared last night —

"Are you playing voyeur, Tony? Watching Bess and I —"

Don't be ridiculous or insulting. Bess and I had a chat on the stairs. Only an idiot wouldn't know — I resent that voyeur bit, John. More even than you calling me weird.

"Well, excuse me for the offense. I've never had a ghost looking over my shoulder before, so I didn't know just how much looking a ghost did."

Good grief.

"You sound like Bess."

So did you. Tony laughed. *Sorry for the fit of temper. Guess that's a lot like her, too.*

"Not really." John ruffled his hair and rubbed a kink out of his neck. "But maybe one day. She's definitely moving in new directions."

I meant inside. She's very moody inside.

"Why?"

Ask her. I'm here to do some serious encouraging.

"Here it comes."

Well, crimney, Jonathan. You're lying to her. You've got to tell her the truth about the station.

"I know it's wrong, Tony. But — well, before last night, it didn't seem half as wrong as it does right now."

You don't want to lose her.

The truth sounded so selfish. So selfish. "No, I don't want to lose her."

I want you to think about this. You and Bess share something beautiful and magical together. It's a special gift. But lying to her, well,

that kind of makes what you have a mirage.
Isn't all you feel for each other too special
and too beautiful to be denigrated to a mirage?
Don't spoil it, Jonathan. Tell Bess the truth.

"Darn it, Tony, don't you see? If I tell her,
I will lose her!"

But if you don't tell her, Jonathan, then have
you ever really had her?

"Don't drop those muffins, Jonathan. Hatch
won't give us the guided tour."

Walking down the gravel drive between
Seascape and Beaulah Favish's green clapboard house, John gripped the bag of blueberry muffins tighter. "I won't drop them."

"Hmmm." Bess laced their hands. "Penny
for your thoughts."

He forced himself to lighten up. He'd
weighed the pros and cons of telling her the
truth, and the cons won. For now, he
couldn't tell her. They veered left at Main
Street, then walked past the freshly painted
Fisherman's Co-op. Two black men sat at a
wire-reel table on the slab-slate porch playing checkers. Bill Butler and his uncle,
Mike. They were laughing, and the sound
made John realize just how serious he and
Bess had become. Only yesterday, they'd
laughed and splashed in the surf. And he
wished he could go back to that time, and

477

feel that happy again. "I was thinking that you smell good. And that I love your dress."

"Liar." She laughed. "But I'll take both your compliments."

"You do smell good, and I've always loved you in red." After passing the pier, they left the street and took to the sloping path that led to Land's End, the wooded headland jutting out into the ocean where the lighthouse rose like a stone sentry. "It makes your hair look like spun gold."

Her cheeks tinted pink. "I meant that those weren't your thoughts." She stiffened and stopped suddenly. "Jonathan. There's someone —"

"Shh, it's all right. It's Batty Beaulah pulling her binocular patrol."

"Ghost-hunting."

He nodded. "Everyone in the village thinks she's got a loose screw, except you and me."

"Hmmm, and Miss Hattie." Bess continued on up the sand-swept path. "She told me once when we were having lunch at the Blue Moon Cafe, that Beaulah had suffered some challenges that trouble her. I didn't understand then, but now I think that challenge was coming face to face with Tony."

Near a giant clump of bunch berry vines, Beaulah stepped out from the evergreens in front of them. "Have you seen him yet?"

"Who?" John asked.

"Don't you be playing games with me, boy. I was teaching kids nearly your age before you were a gleam in your daddy's eye. And I saw what he did to that paint on your car, little lady. Took the shine right out of it." Beaulah moved the binoculars from her eyes and let them swing from the black band around her thin neck. "It's over at Jimmy's, and it sure is shining now."

John had noticed that, too. He'd passed Jimmy's on the way to the store for Miss Hattie yesterday, and the car *had* been as glossy as if it had been freshly painted. "No," he answered her original question, finding it easier to answer. "I haven't seen him yet."

"He's real." She said, taking off down the path, back toward the village. She stomped through a clump of chickweed and swiped at a lacy-edge fern encroaching onto the path. "If they tell you he ain't, don't you believe 'em. He's as real as you and me. I saw him myself the day his mama died. Twice. Once, I saw his face in that attic room window. And then I saw him on the widow's walk, not a half-hour later."

Bess's hand went clammy cold in John's. "I believe you, Miss Favish."

"Of course you do. You ain't a fool, and I ain't lying. Why wouldn't you believe me?"

Terns squawking overhead, Jonathan looked at Bess. Something in her tone triggered a suspicion. Had she seen Tony?

A twig snapped. Miss Hattie came up near Beaulah from a fork in the path. "Ah, there you are, Beaulah. I was getting worried that you'd be late to church for quilting. We've got twelve more to make before Christmas."

"I'll get there, Hattie. But first you tell these two the truth. He's real, I say. As real as you and me."

"Of course he is, and I've never said otherwise." Miss Hattie gave John and Bess an indulging smile. "Bess, I talked with Jimmy a few minutes ago. Your car is repaired and he's bringing it home."

"Thanks, Miss Hattie."

John nearly panicked at that news, until he looked at Bess and saw no signs in her expression or manner that warned him she meant to get into that car and leave.

Looping their arms, Miss Hattie urged Beaulah back toward the village. "Pastor Brown has some slides of his trip to California to share with us today."

"Humph!" Beaulah snorted, then stomped down the path, holding her hat on her head against a stiff breeze. "A Pastor ought not be going to California to surf, Hattie. He ought to be doing holy things — like going to Jerusalem, or something."

"Even spiritual men need a rest every now and then to rejuvenate, don't you think?" She waved John and Bess on down the path. "You children enjoy your tour."

Amen to that. Crimney, of course spiritual men need breaks, too. Even progressive ones like Pastor Brown.

Tony! Good grief. Would you please give me some warning that you're going to jump into my mind?

Sorry, Bess.

Me, too. Jonathan sighed. *She smashed the muffins. Hatch is going to be ticked to the gills.*

Oh, Lord, you hear him, too?

Jonathan nodded.

Hatch won't be ticked. I've known him more years than I care to recall. He won't mind their condition so long as they're Hattie's blueberry muffins. Shape won't change the taste. I think she uses orange in them. Hmm, or maybe it's lemon.

The upward slope of the path leveled. Bess stopped under the shade of a lone oak. The underbrush had been cleared away, and someone had mixed peat moss and dirt into the rocky soil and planted a small bed of orange tiger lilies.

I don't mean to be nasty-tempered here, Tony, but whenever you come around, bombs start falling — usually on my head — and if that's the case, could you —

Tell her, Tony. She's shaking like a leaf again.

I am not.

You are, darling.

Okay, I am. But, good grief, who wouldn't be?

Point taken. Actually, Bess, I came to talk with Jonathan, so I'll go solo with him and you can relax.

Shoot. He gets the bomb, and I miss it.

Thanks, darling. I adore you, too.

She grinned. *Welcome.*

Can she still hear us?

No, Jonathan.

I know what this is about, and I've already decided you were right. I have to tell her the truth. But on the way back — after we talk with Hatch. She's looking forward to the tour, and I don't want to spoil it for her.

Enough said. Leap, Jonathan. Follow the map then leap.

John stared at Bess and frowned. Tony's message. It really *was* a map. But to what specifically? And what could Little Island have to do with him and Bess?

"Jonathan," Bess said, sidestepping a

sharp stone on the pebbly path. "Francine called me last night."

Oh gosh. "I should have told you sooner, Bess. I didn't want to wreck the tour." He didn't want her to walk out on him, is what he didn't want. "I made a bad decision to wait and I'm sorry."

Bess stopped, squinted against the sun, up at him. "Should have told me what?"

John swallowed hard. "What did Francine say?" Why hadn't he asked that first? Stupid question. Guilty conscience.

Bess folded her arms over her chest. "You should have told me what?" she asked again.

There was no way around it. Done was done. "That Miguel didn't buy the station."

Her pupils widened, then narrowed to points. "He didn't?"

"No."

"Then who did?"

John stared at her tense face for a long moment. Reached for her hand, but she kept her arms folded tightly against her chest. Whether to keep from reaching back to him, or to hold in the hurt, he didn't know. But he felt guilty as heck for rousing either. "Me."

Her eyes went hard, accusing, and her trembling chin hardened to granite. "Why?"

At least she'd asked. She hadn't just

walked out, like before. Unfortunately, his explanation wouldn't help him. It'd only hurt her more. "Elise directed me to, Bess, in a codicil."

"I see."

"Do you?" Hope laced his voice even as he warned it away.

"Yes, I do." She turned and started walking toward the lighthouse, her shoes slipping on the pebbly path. "Ego. Money. Yours. Just like I said the day you came here. You wanted even my dog, and now you've got my job — not that I want it, but it sure irks me to have you take it."

As he feared, she thought he'd ranked her second. All this other was just bluster to hide behind. "No, Bess. It's not like that. I swear —"

She stopped and spun around. "Don't you swear squat to me, Jonathan Mystic. Not squat. I'm trying very hard to hang onto a sliver of patience and grace here, and you've already made it nearly impossible. I don't want to talk about this anymore. Not now. We're going to go see Hatch, like we promised Miss Hattie, and, after we have, then we'll settle this."

"But, honey, if you'll let me explain —"

"Not now!" She held up a hand and lowered her voice. That she'd raised it clearly surprised both of them; her face was as red as her dress. "I'm angry and humiliated, Jonathan. And I'm hurt that you'd be the one to do this to me. I can't be logical or rational yet."

She was hurt. "But not as hurt as when you thought Miguel had done it."

She laughed, but there was no humor in it. "What? You expect me to cry again? To run to you for comfort when you're the one who did this to me? Jonathan, please. This is the real world, darling. We're divorcing. You can't —"

His jaw went tight. "We agreed not to mention that for six more days, Bess."

"We *agreed* to be honest. You weren't. That negates —"

"I'm holding you to our agreement, woman. Don't doubt it. I mean to have my time with you."

"Why?" She guffawed. "Haven't you humiliated me enough? You won't break me, Jonathan. I won't let you. But you can hurt me, and I won't lie about that. So why don't you just tell me how much hurt you have to inflict to feel vindicated, and then we can call this charade done. And while you're at it, maybe you can tell me why hurting me is so important to you."

Before he could answer, she turned and

strode up the path lined with spiky ever-greens so dense that their sun-shadowed trunks looked black.

Near a clump of intruding hawkweed, the evergreens thinned. He caught up with her, then clasped her arms, the bag of muffins dangling from his left hand. "I don't *want* to hurt you. I've *never* wanted to hurt you. After last night, how can you even *think* I'd want to hurt you?"

He squeezed his eyes shut, dipped his chin, and fought for control of his emotions. When he thought he had a grip on them, he again met her eyes. "We made love. For the first time ever, we made love. I never really understood the difference before, but now I do, and I can't believe that you don't. I won't believe it unless you look me in the eye and swear it, Bess. Can you do that? Can you look me in the eye and swear it?"

She groaned. "I can't." Dropping her forehead against his chest, she groaned again, deeper. "Why do you do this to me, Jonathan? I should be furious with you — I am furious with you. But all I want to do is to kiss and make up. I hate me for that. And I don't much like you for it either. It's absurd. Ridiculous. And if you tell me it's the magic, I think I might just sock you in the nose."

486

"It's not." She wasn't going to leave him. She would calm down and give him his chance to explain — later. But she wasn't going to leave him. His heart twisting, he hugged her to him. This much he had to tell her now, before her anger could fester, before she let too much old baggage interfere, and he talked but she couldn't hear. "Elise bought the station when you filed for the legal separation, honey. I don't know why, and I just learned of it yesterday. The sale taking place now is just a formality — that's confidential. I think she's giving Millicent a way to save face. I don't know. I don't need, or even want, to know." He buried his face in the cove of Bess's neck. "I just know I don't want to lose you again over this. I —"

Bess looked up at him, her eyes wide. "You don't want to lose me?"

He shook his head, let her see the truth in his eyes.

"But you knew this last night. And you didn't tell me. You made love with me, and you didn't tell me." She paused to steady her voice. "You don't trust me, Jonathan. How can either of us lose what we don't have?"

"Bess, please." Emotionally, she was sliding away, distancing herself, he could feel it.

487

"Please, let's just go sit out on the cliffs and talk this out. Please."

"I'm not ready yet. I need time to think. And Hatch is expecting us. We'll see him, and then we'll talk."

"All right." Jonathan would have agreed to anything. And he would agree to anything — just so long as she didn't run out on him again. That, he couldn't take. People who mattered had run out on him his entire life, and he couldn't take losing anymore. Especially not Bess. Please, not Bess.

They walked on to Land's End in silence.

The path split.

One fork dead-ended at the base of the lighthouse tower, the other led to the side door of the attached house. A gray fence enclosed a small area at the tower base and, just outside it, Hatch sat on a bench made of two concrete blocks and a plank of wood, whittling. Tiny shavings clung to his beige, long-sleeved T-shirt and blue slacks.

Hearing them approach, the bent old man lifted his head and smiled, softening his weathered face.

Bess smiled back, though her heart wasn't in it. Looking into his wizen eyes, an odd sensation crept over her and seeped inside. *Tony, I'm scared.* The memory of what she'd told him that night on the stairs flooded back. She had no reason to be afraid, but she was, and she couldn't shake the feeling, or identify its source. For some reason, anticipation and anxiety filled her. Something life-altering was about to happen; that standing-on-a-precipice feeling already had her suffering an adrenaline surge, already had aroused her fight-or-flight instincts.

"What are you whittling?" Jonathan asked Hatch.

Wood shavings sprinkled down onto his scuffed black boots. He blew at them, then held up the wood. "A gull."

"It's pretty," Bess said. "We brought you some muffins from Miss Hattie."

He cocked a brow. "Blueberry? I like her apple, but her blueberry's my favorite." He set the gull down then lay his whittling knife beside it, careful not to nick the bench and dull the blade. "Ready for the tour?"

Bess couldn't do it. She wanted to leave. Now. Jonathan had made love to her, lied to her and made love to her, and she wanted to get this done and be by herself for a while so that she could get their relationship and everything that had happened settled in her mind. "Another time, Mr. Hatch."

"Hatch. No mister. Just Hatch." Brushing at the shavings clinging to his thigh, he

489

sniffed. "Don't smell like apple. Hattie's got a heavy hand with cinnamon in her apple."

"They're blueberry," Jonathan said, then passed the bag.

Hatch set it down on the bench beside him. "Didn't figure today was a good day for the tour, so I didn't figure on getting any muffins. Nice surprise."

Feeling about as up for a tour as for the coming confrontation with John, Bess frowned. "Why did you think we wouldn't want to tour —"

"Hattie called and told me about the *Southern Pride* and the girl you're looking for."

Bess's heart picked up its beat. "Do you know anything about her?"

"It's a distinct possibility." He looked from Bess to John. "Done some checking, though I really didn't need to. Memory like a steel trap." He tapped a gnarled fingertip to his temple. "About four months after your little lady went missing, which I hear from Hattie would be about the time *Southern Pride* was headed up to Nova Scotia, me and Vic was out fishing. Seen signs of wreckage, though none that identified a specific craft, in our estimations."

John had stiffened, squared his shoulders, and hung onto Hatch's every word. "Could it have been *Southern Pride?*"

Hatch shrugged. "You'll need to weigh the matter, but I'm thinking it could've been. We found a young lady's body near Little Island. Coroner said she'd drowned," he paused to make the sign of the cross, "and Sheriff Cobb didn't have a sandmite's shade of luck identifying her. She was eighteen, according to the coroner."

"Dixie's age," John said in a voice that sent a tremor quaking through Bess. "Was she ever positively identified?"

Hatch rubbed at his jaw, rustling his stubbly gray whiskers. "Nope, but we tried long and hard. Not knowing who the little lady was, Miss Hattie worried something fierce. Closest I ever seen Hattie Stillman to being sick, aside from when her soldier died, of course. Said there had to be kin worried about the little lady, and until they knew what had happened to her, they'd never know a minute's peace." He leaned back and shook his head. "Yep, we tried long and hard, but had not a sandmite's worth of luck. Buried her out on Little Island."

A shiver raced up Bess's backbone. The graves she and Jonathan had stood before just yesterday. Could one of them actually have been Dixie's?

John's dark brows knitted and he fisted

his hand alongside the thigh of his jeans. "Why was she buried out there rather than in the cemetery behind the church?"

Bess had wondered that, too. The church had a pretty little cemetery behind it. Why the isolation of the island?

"Miss Millie insisted," Hatch said. "The little lady had on an amulet with a ruby the size of your thumb in it. When the sunlight caught it, Miss Millie said it reminded her of the ocean view from Little Island at twilight. So," he shrugged, "we figured the little lady would rest easy there."

Bess gasped. "A ruby amulet?"

"Yep. Stone as big as the end of my thumb." Hatch reached into the pocket of his worn blue pants and pulled out something shiny.

"We'll have to have the body exhumed to be positive but, Hatch, I'm nearly certain the young lady was Dixie Dupree."

John's face was pasty white. In a show of support, Bess reached for his hand and laced their fingers, certain his inner turmoil matched or doubled her own. The wind tugged at his pale yellow shirt, whipped through his glossy black hair, carrying his scent and that of the sea . . . and that of rain.

Looking out onto the horizon, Bess's heart

sank. Above the angry white-capped waves, the sky was a sleety, dark blue, almost navy. She stiffened, emotionally battening down for yet another storm.

"Ain't no need to go disturbing the dead, boy." Hatch passed John the shiny disc, his voice low and steady.

"A doubloon?"

Hatch nodded, his wise eyes solemn.

Jonathan frowned. "What am I supposed to do with it?"

"You're needing proof, boy, and this old man knows it. But disturbing the dead resting peaceful would upset Miss Hattie, and we try to avoid that. She's had enough upset in her life. We do our best to protect her against suffering anymore."

"I don't understand."

"Don't need to." He picked up his knife and gull and put the blade to the wood. "Just take that doubloon and go out to Little Island. Aaron Butler will run you out there."

"Why?" Bess's frightened feeling intensified, and she had to remind herself to breathe. Tony must have something to do with this. He wouldn't want Miss Hattie upset. But how could going out to Little Island with a doubloon give Jonathan any proof that the woman who'd drowned had been Dixie?

"Because Little Island is where the little lady's grave is, Mrs. Mystic."

Besieged with eerie feelings, Bess didn't bother telling him her preference for Cameron. Neither did John. He stared into the old man's eyes, long and hard and deep.

"There are two graves there, side by side," Jonathan finally said. "Did you find the body of a man out there, too?"

Thomas Boudreaux. Bess tightened her grip on Jonathan's hand. Could his be the second grave?

"No. Only the little lady."

"Who's in the other grave?"

"Don't matter, in my estimation," Hatch said in a tone warning the subject wouldn't be discussed further. "If you're standing facing the graves, the little lady's is the one on the left."

John squeezed Bess's hand. "Thank you, Hatch."

The old man cocked his head, stared at Jonathan a long moment, then nodded. "You go to the island, John Mystic," he said, his voice gentle with an understanding and a grasp of the situation that went beyond Bess's, "and you do what you've got to do there, then you bring that doubloon right back to me." His voice turned hard. "Don't take it to Seascape Inn, boy, and don't ever mention it to Miss Hattie."

"Why?"

"Because I said." His expression shifted to enigmatic, his tone uncompromising. "Either give me your word or leave here without that coin and don't ever come back. Those are my terms."

Bess silently urged Jonathan to give the man back the doubloon. To turn and leave and not come back — to forget all this. Now. Before whatever was about to happen, happened. Her honed instincts were pounding out a distress signal, a warning more dire than any she'd ever felt before. But in her heart, she knew he wouldn't do it. Her instincts screamed that, too, just as they screamed that Hatch's little lady was indeed Dixie Dupree. And Bess held no illusions as to what this new development meant.

With this trip to the island, Jonathan would end his six-year search. He would fulfill his promise to Elise by solving the case. He'd no longer feel like a failure, which meant he'd no longer feel the need to prove his worth by controlling Bess. And that meant he'd no longer need her.

Their relationship would be over.

He'd leave here.

He'd leave her.

This time, forever.

The magic was strong, but not strong enough to hold him. And in keeping the news of the station sale to himself, he'd proven to them both that the magic was what they had together. The magic, but nothing else. Nothing . . . more.

Jonathan stood rigid, his jaw as hard as the cliffs. "I accept your terms, Hatch."

Inside, Bess crumbled and cried and begged him not to do this. Prayed for a miracle that would keep him from taking Hatch's doubloon. But miracles didn't happen for people like her. She knew it. She'd learned that lesson six years ago. Just as she'd learned that, regardless of how painful, acceptance is positive growth. And so outwardly, she slid behind her protective mask, appearing passive and accepting.

Like before, she'd mourn losing him, alone.

CHAPTER 15

John stood on the pier facing Bess, his back to the angry ocean, to the wall of fog seeping inland and enshrouding them to Aaron Butler who busily readied the boat.

She looked devastated, her eyes filled with so much pain it wrenched John's heart. "I should be elated. I've worked a long time for this. Instead, I —"

"You're grieving," she said in a deadpan tone, distant and pulling farther away. "I'm grieving, too."

He nodded, longing to reach out and touch her, to beg her to not hide from him behind that cool cashmere facade. The moment he'd taken the doubloon from Hatch, she'd summoned it back into place — and John had begun grieving. He didn't know how to stop this. How *not* to lose her again.

If the woman buried on Little Island proved to be Dixie, irony would have come full circle. For years, he had been obsessed with solving this case. For Elise, yes. But also for him and Bess. She'd walked out on a failure. A failure who couldn't crawl to her and ask her to come back. But a success could ask her to come home. If he solved this case, then he'd have earned the right to ask her again to be his wife. To hold his head up and walk back to her as a man she could be proud to call her husband.

Or so he'd thought.

Now, looking at her pain-filled eyes, at the resignation in her bowed head, in the aura of loss surrounding her, he grieved, just as she'd said, because he knew their situation was hopeless. He'd lost her again. She didn't trust him, and he couldn't blame her; he'd lied to her. Yes, out of fear of losing her, but still he'd lied. He hadn't trusted her either. She'd been right about that. And without trust, what did they really have?

The magic.

Beautiful. Special. But not enough.

Santos calling her no doubt had brought him sharply to her mind, reminded her vividly of their relationship. She didn't love him, but she cared for him. Him, she trusted. From him, she accepted gifts. Things were different for her with John. She likely regretted their agreement and them making love. Likely had decided, just as he had decided, that the magic wasn't enough. Heaven knew, she deserved more. She'd loved him *then*. Not now. *Then.*

She couldn't love Santos. Or could she? She had changed. When she'd believed Santos had bought the station, she'd turned to John for comfort. He loved her, and yet he'd betrayed her, hurt her. And, from the look in her eyes now, he didn't stand a prayer of being forgiven. Ever.

His eyes burned. "You're not coming with me, are you, Bess?"

"No, John, I'm not."

John not *Jonathan.* His heart sank.

Bess's heart shattered. She fisted her hands behind her back, praying she wouldn't humiliate herself further by crying in front of him now. "You going out there, well, it closes this chapter of our lives." A repulsive shudder trying to deny the truth rippled through her. She stiffened against it. Acceptance was positive growth. She *must* accept. "All that's left is for us to go ahead with the divorce —"

"But we made love, Bess."

"No, John." Lord, how that truth hurt. "I thought we had, but it wasn't honest. It wasn't making love."

He stared out at the water, his eyes as turbulent as the violent waves crashing against the shore. "It was for me."

"We have to be realistic." The wind tugged at her hair. She pulled it back from her face and held it with her hand. "We tried and we failed. We have to accept that and to go on our separate ways."

His jaw went rock hard. "We can work this out."

"No, we can't. There'll always be a case, John." She'd always rank second. He'd always omit telling her whatever might bring them discord. There was no trust. There was magic, but no trust.

"We can," he insisted.

"All right, maybe we can." She looked him straight in the eye. Arguing with him wouldn't work, but proving her point would. "When do I meet your parents?"

The color drained from his face. "You don't."

She'd expected it, and yet the flat-out denial stung. It stung, then burrowed in and hurt deeply, filling her with a pain so fierce and forceful that she feared she'd stagger and fall to her knees. *Ashamed.* "That's why we can't work it out."

"Mr. Mystic?"

John turned. "Yes, Aaron?"

"Boat's ready. We better hurry if we're gonna beat the storm."

John looked from Aaron to the thunderheads swirling ever closer, then back to Bess, his expression torn. "Tell me you'll be here when I get back. Tell me —"

Her heart breaking, she raised her hand.

He pressed his to it, palm to palm. *"Please, Bess."*

The temptation burned so strong, so strong she almost gave in to it. But that would only delay the inevitable. Only prolong the intense pain that would demand its due before the healing and acceptance could again begin. He knew it, just as she did, and one of them had to be strong enough to do what was best for both of them. One of them. Her. But once more, once more, she had to have the words. "I loved you."

He swallowed hard, his Adam's apple rippling his throat. "I loved you, too."

She drew the words in, deep into her heart, where she could always cherish them. Then, burying her emotions more deeply than ever before, she shored up her courage, stepped back, and lowered her hand, fisting her fingers into her palm to hold his warmth to her a moment longer. Her chest went tight, her muscles stiff. Her heart numb. "Good-bye, John."

Resignation burned in his eyes, settled over him, dark and oppressive, and he lowered his hand. "I'll miss you, Bess," he said softly, his eyes bright.

She'd miss him, too. Oh, but would she miss him, too.

He paused to look at her, then blinking hard and fast, he turned and stepped into the boat. "Let's go, Aaron."

Bess stood on the dock, demanding her feet to stay planted to the planks and not run after him. She laced her arms tightly over her chest, as if trussed they could hold inside the pain exploding in her. The fog thickened, and with it came the first sprinkle of rain. Blinking against the pelting drops, she held her gaze on John, praying he'd turn around and come back. Praying that just this once he'd put her first.

He didn't look back.

The tears in her heart welled, sheening in her eyes.

If you want him, then you've got to fight for him, Bess.

Tony. How like him to sense her in trouble and to come. She blinked and thought back. He always had. Since his first phone call to the station, whenever she'd needed him, Tony had been there. "I can't fight for him, Tony."

Why not?

The rain came harder and faster, and still

she stood there on the pier, looking out at the fog. The storm outside paled to the one raging within. The boat was now only a vague outline on the horizon, and its image was dimming. "Because if I do," a sob tore from her throat, "I lose him . . . and me."

I don't understand.

"He doesn't love me, Tony. He desires me, but he doesn't love me. He can't because he doesn't love himself."

He wants you to be proud of him, Bess. Is that so wrong? For a man to want to be respected and admired by a woman who means so much to him?

"He lied."

He feared losing you.

"No, Tony." The sadness in her soul seeped into her voice. "He feared me learning the truth."

The truth?

A gust of wind tugged at her clothes. She lifted her face to it, welcoming the stinging rain because it she only could feel outside, not within. "He's ashamed of me."

No.

"If he weren't, he wouldn't separate me from his family," she insisted, straining to catch one more glimpse at John. The fog swallowed the boat, and it disappeared.

Bess, listen to me. No, just listen. Is sex or

control or shame powerful enough to touch a man so deeply at loving a woman that he sheds a tear?

"Don't, Tony, please. *Please.* I don't dare believe. I don't dare."

You don't dare not to believe. The sand has shifted, Doc. Leap. Leap and have faith that an island will appear.

Uncertainty stabbed at her. Was there a chance for them? No. No, there couldn't be. Even after all they'd been through, still John had refused to let her into his family's life. But Tony seemed so sure. Once, she'd been sure, but she'd been wrong. And yet, John *had* cried. He had explained that he'd not put Bess's needs but her desires second because he trusted her capabilities.

Trusted her capabilities.

A spark of hope ignited in her heart. He *trusted* her capabilities. A man who trusted a woman capable of caring for her needs wasn't a man ashamed. He was a man who had faith. And yet . . . he acted ashamed. Why?

The spark grew to a flame. She tried to tamp it. She'd only get hurt. Only be wounded more deeply. "I don't understand."

Don't you? Maybe you don't want to understand. Maybe it's emotionally safer not to un-

derstand.

Thunder rumbled overhead. No, a boat. Her stomach in knots she watched it break through the fog, slicing through the waves. Aaron. Alone. Her hope died.

Remember what Hattie said about pride, Bess?

Oh, no. "It can't hold you."

Neither can fear.

His words cut through her like a sharp knife. Fear? Was that it? She loved John Mystic. Had she succumbed to letting the fear of being hurt again steal the joy of them reuniting? Had she used his lying about the station as an excuse? One to protect herself from pain?

She could leap. Could give them another chance. She could go to him and tell him that she loved him, and then ask again about his family. If he was sure of her love, and he loved her back, then he'd share his reasons for the separation with her. And maybe he'd let her into all those closed parts of his life he'd forbidden anyone to enter.

Aaron pulled up alongside the pier, grabbed the rope, and started tying the boat to the dock.

Decision time, Doc. Do you take one more chance on love? Or do you forfeit it in fear, and mourn?

"Aaron!" She hurried down to the end of the pier. "I need to go to Little Island."

"But I just got back —"

"I'll pay you double." Double should appeal to a boy not yet in his teens. Good grief, she'd stooped to bribing a minor? Awful. Scrap grace, but desperate circumstances call for desperate measures.

"I dunno. It's storming, Mrs. Mystic." He shrugged, lifting his slender shoulders.

Mrs. Mystic. It felt right. Comfortable on her shoulders. "Please, Aaron. It's very important."

He scratched his head and checked the sky. Bess prayed it wouldn't be too dangerous to make the crossing. Now that she'd made her decision, she wanted to carry it out immediately. She couldn't wait. John had looked so devastated. So hopeless.

"All right, Mrs. Mystic. Fish prices at auction being down, I'll do it. But it's gonna cost you triple."

Bess smiled at the boy. Who was taking advantage of whom here? "It won't put you in any danger, right?"

"Spit, no." He dropped the rope and pointed to a life vest. "But you put that on. My dad says folks from away have to wear jackets when it's a little rough."

Bess pulled on the life jacket. Her clothes

were already soaked. Chilled to the bone, she felt sure she looked as miserable as she felt. The rain had to have washed her makeup into streaks down her face and her hair lay plastered to her head. Aaron, bless his heart, had been wise enough to grab a yellow slicker and hat, though he had the brim folded back, which meant his sweet, cocoa-colored face was as soaked as hers. But at least his clothes were dry. He wouldn't catch cold.

The fifteen-minute ride was rough, the boat rocking and lurching into massive waves. By the time Aaron pulled up to the dilapidated little pier, Bess's stomach was lodged somewhere between her ribs and throat.

"You all right, Mrs. Mystic? You look a little green around the gills."

She felt green around the gills, too. "I'm fine." She stepped onto the dock. "Do you think you should wait before crossing again?"

"Yes, ma'am. I'll be riding out the storm right here. I should'na come this time. Dad'll blister my ears, but," he shrugged, "you said it was important."

"Thank you, Aaron." Bess clasped his wet hand in hers. "You wait right here, okay?"

"Yes, ma'am."

Bess hurried down the pier. As she passed the last post, she tapped the little sign warning of shifting sand, then rushed on.

When she first glimpsed the little fenced grave site, her instincts shouted danger. Within seconds, the temperature plummeted.

A veil of icy mist gathered on her skin.

And a pressure at the soft hollow in her right clavicle had her stopping dead in her tracks. She was losing her breath, her focus. Her head swam. She pressed her fingertips to her temples and staggered. Her feet seemed to turn to lead. She couldn't lift them. Couldn't move anything at all. Staring at John's broad back, she opened her mouth to scream.

Cold bands of frigid air pressed against her lips. She couldn't make a sound. *Tony! Tony! Help me!*

Shh, it's all right. I'm here, Doc.

Thank goodness. I thought I was dying.

I had to stop you. You've no idea what you were about to do.

Why didn't you just tell me?

I'm sorry, Bess. I panicked. You can't interfere.

Tony, please let me go to him. I won't interfere. I promise. I won't.

The pressure eased slightly and Bess

gulped in air. The rain whipped through the trees and pelted against the rocky sand, muffling her sounds. Holding the doubloon, John stood head bowed at the grave on the left. He clearly had no idea she was here.

Don't move, Bess. Not an inch. And don't make a sound. You can't go to him just now, and I'm trusting you to stay put. You can't hear anything. Do you understand? You can't hear a word that's said or it could ruin everything.

I understand. I won't move. I swear. I won't hear, either. She lifted her hands and cupped them over her ears.

The pressure ceased and, shaky inside, Bess did her best to stand shadow still. She glimpsed a flash of gray, then one of dark green, just inside the grave site fence.

Tony.

He looked exactly as he had when last she'd seen him in the Cove Room. Exactly as Maggie MacGregor had described him at Lakeview Gallery. Aged yet ageless, like Miss Hattie. Golden eyes, a gentle expression, wearing an old-fashioned Army uniform and a yellow carnation in his lapel. Unlike before, when he'd seemed more luminescent, more an essence than a human being, now he looked as solid as Jonathan. His brown hair streaked golden, he was tall and handsome, and, having gotten to know him, Bess easily understood how he had captured and held Miss Hattie's heart.

Jonathan! He'd never before seen Tony! Could he see him now?

It didn't appear that he could.

Rest easy, Doc. In a minute, you'll understand.

John held the doubloon and stared down at it. What exactly did he expect to happen?

No idea. If not for his experience with Tony, he'd have thought Hatch had slipped over the edge and joined Beaulah Favish. What *could* happen here that would make exhuming the woman's body unnecessary?

The possibilities sent cold chills through him that had nothing to do with wet clothes and rain.

Jonathan?

Tony? Is that you? You sound funny.

I'm emotional.

Why?

Because I'm going to materialize. I don't do it often. It frightens people.

I know you're a ghost, Tony. And I'm not afraid of you. I understand your message.

You do?

Yes. Though I suspect its meaning is very different for Bess, for me, it was a road map.

*Here, to the island. You helped me through
Elise's death, and then you led me here to
find Dixie.*

The doubloon suddenly felt very cool.
John closed his eyes, and when he reopened
them, a man wearing an old Army uniform
and a yellow carnation stood before him,
holding the other edge of the coin. "Tony."
John smiled.

Looking more than a little relieved, Tony
smiled back. *Hi, Jonathan.*

"I can't believe I'm seeing you."

*I can't believe you're seeing me and smil-
ing. I was worried I'd still give you the creeps.*

"You don't."

Tony chuckled. *I'm glad. That really bothers me — the initial reaction I get. But enough
of that and onto why I'm here — or rather,
why you're here. I know trust doesn't come
easily to you — and I know why, Jonathan.
I'm glad you've chosen to trust me, though if I
had to choose, I'd have chosen for you to trust
Bess.*

"Telling her about my parents."

Yes.

"She thinks little enough of me as it is."

*And their actions, in your eyes, make you
less loveable to her.*

"Don't they?"

Only Bess can answer that. Her parents

511

weren't kind to her, Jonathan. You look at Bess and see a cashmere, eel-skin facade. You recognize it as a mask, yet you don't see the pain that drove her to hide behind it. Haven't you wondered about that? About why she hides behind that facade?

"Why does she?"

You asked me that once before. I told you then to ask her.

"I intended to, but I got sidetracked."

Well, maybe one day you'll get around to asking her and she'll tell you. I could, but some things are best discovered firsthand. Bess thinks I'm a meddler, and she's probably right. But meddling by telling you about her past isn't my purpose here today.

"What is your purpose?"

Tony reached into his pocket. To give you this.

John's muscles all clenched at once. "Dixie's amulet!"

Actually, it isn't.

"Tony," John insisted. "I've seen her mother's every day for years. It's Dixie's amulet." He stared past Tony's shoulder to the grave, relieved and happy and sad, so very sad — all at once. He'd found Dixie. Dead. Not from murder, but from drowning.

It isn't Dixie's, dear heart.

Dear heart? John's breath caught in his throat. He couldn't be hearing what he thought he was. He couldn't! Only one woman in his entire life had called him *dear heart*. Only . . . He lifted his gaze from the dirt. *"Elise!"*

She stood not three feet behind Tony, dressed in dove gray, as she had been when last John had seen her — at her funeral. But she didn't look like the frail and wan woman she'd been at her death. She looked radiant. Vibrant and healthy. Like the woman she'd been before her illness. Tears surged to his eyes and ran down his cheeks, his chest squeezed into a vise. Thirsty, he drank in the sight of her. "Oh, oh, Elise."

I knew you wouldn't give up.

John tried to move, to go to her, but Tony raised a hand and stopped him. *Don't cross the fence, Jonathan.*

Feeling certain if he did, he'd never return, John nodded. "Tony, you were there in the hospital to help me, but to help Elise, too. That's why she held the yellow carnation petal."

He's clever, Tony. Elise grunted and slid Tony an I-told-you-so-smile. She looked back at John and her expression softened. *Tony came to guide me here. To my baby, John.*

John's chest throbbed with a pain so intense he couldn't tell where it began or ended. For six years, he'd dreaded having to say these words to her. And now, heaven help him, the time had come. "Dixie's dead, Elise."

Yes. A wistful smile touched the curve of her generous mouth. *But so am I, dear heart, and thanks to Tony, we're together again. Me, and Clayton, and Dixie.*

The rain slowed to a drizzle. "I'm glad you found them."

I had to come. In the hospital, Tony promised he had a wonderful surprise for me. When I arrived here, Dixie and Clayton were waiting. Her smile faded. *I couldn't bear to be so happy, knowing you weren't yet at peace.*

"I love you, Elise," the words tumbled out of John's mouth. "I never told you that, and I've regretted it more than I can say."

Oh, John. I know you do. I've always known. You didn't give me the words, but you showed me in many, many ways.

"Bess said you did."

She was right. I'm delighted you and she are reuniting. I can truly be at peace now, knowing you won't be alone.

He shouldn't rob her of peace, but he couldn't be dishonest with her. Not again. Not ever again. "I can't lie to you. I'm sorry

I did when you were . . . passing. I tried with Bess, but I failed."

Oh, but you didn't try because of my death-bed promise. Though, knowing you as I do, you've surely spent considerable time trying to convince yourself of that fact. I thought I was pretty clever, giving you that crutch — making you promise — to soothe your conscience.

"My conscience?"

Well, she shrugged, *your ego.*

He smiled. She had been clever. Very clever, in making him swear it on his mother's grave. "No, I didn't follow through for you, though I did tell myself that for a long time. I tried because I love her."

Of course you do, dear heart. You always have. Which is why you must try again. The third time is a charm, they say.

Bess would never again give him the chance. He knew it and, deep in her heart, Elise had to know it, too. Rather than be put in the position of leaving something unsettled, he changed the topic. "Why did you buy the station?"

Millicent was in dire financial straits — though she didn't know it. Her husband liked the ponies. They faced disaster, and I couldn't see me standing by and doing nothing. What kind of person would that have made me?

"How could Millicent not know it?"

She's too socially oriented to be bothered with piddling financial matters. Still, like everyone else, she has her redeeming qualities. But she doesn't know how to struggle, John, and being poor would have destroyed her. I couldn't have that on my conscience.

A flash of insight had it all making sense. "You owned the ponies."

A substantial share in the track, actually, which I sold when I saw how it nearly destroyed Millicent.

"I see."

Yes, and I hope you'll keep your insight private. I don't want Millicent to be embarrassed by this, John — not unless she insists on being uncooperative. I've taken great pains to protect her, and I'd like for you to continue doing so.

"I will."

But I won't have her treating Bess shabbily either. I feared she would, which is why I insisted on the station rather than other Fairgate assets. I thought that if all else failed, with Bess working for you, you two would at least be forced together short-term. I hoped short-term would be long enough for you to realize you still loved each other and to get pride out of the way. Of course, I didn't know about Tony then, or about Seascape, or I could have saved myself considerable worry and money.

The money. Elise's fortune. "What should I do with it, now that Dixie is . . . ?" He couldn't say it again.

The word is dead, dear heart. Truly, it's not so bad. We're together and happy. And I don't hurt anymore. That relief from pain is such a treasure, John. Don't waste a breath mourning us, or fearing joining us — though don't be in a hurry — I'm hoping to watch over you until you and your children grow old.

She stared off into space for a moment, as if listening, then looked back at John.

As for the money, your sister Selena's business is a worthy one, dear heart. The money is yours to do with as you wish, with the exception of a million dollars per year. That I wish you to donate to Selena so that she and her partners can carry on with their work. She glanced at Tony. *Do you approve?*

Most definitely. Children and seniors are most vulnerable.

Clayton agrees — Dixie, too. Wonderful! Elise giggled. *It's unanimous, then.*

It'd been a long time since John had heard Elise laugh. The sound warmed his heart. "One more question," John said. "Who is in the other grave?"

Another lost soul, dear heart.

"I thought it might be Thomas Bou-dreaux."

No, he's still alive.

"But the wreckage —"

Was faked. Elise pursed her lips into a tight little line. *He did kidnap Dixie, John. They were caught in a storm here, and she sighted the island. She thought she could swim to it and dove overboard. Dear child didn't count on the undertow. Thomas Boudreaux was a terrible swimmer, and a coward too fearful to assist her. And too fearful of being jailed, as well, I expect. The wreckage actually was no more than a few things he tossed overboard to make it appear as though she'd been in a ship that had gone down.*

"I'll hunt him down," John vowed. "He'll pay for this, Elise. I give you my word."

Don't bother, dear heart. Thomas Boudreaux has paid. He's gone quite mad — literally. He'll be institutionalized for the rest of his life. Some people react rather strangely to seeing spirits. The greater the burden on the conscience, the greater the fear. Naturally, Thomas Boudreaux was terrified. When riled, Clayton always has been rather formidable.

A part of John felt cheated that Thomas Boudreaux had caused so much pain and hurt and that he'd eased into insanity and escaped retribution. But insanity forfeited life; John really shouldn't feel that way. And once he got over the shock, and accepted the truth by talking through all this with Bess, he knew he wouldn't.

Clayton and Dixie are waiting, Elise. I'm sorry, Jonathan, I wish there were more time.

John nodded. "You were a wonderful mother to me, Elise." He'd told her he loved her. And just once, he wanted the words.

And you were a wonderful son to me.

"I'll miss you," he said, his chest tight. "All the rest of my life, I'll miss you."

A part of me will always be there with you, just as a part of you will always be here with me. Remember what Miss Hattie said?

"You know Miss Hattie?"

Indirectly. Elise smiled. *Miss Hattie said a part of Tony lives on in her every breath. When you love someone, that's how it is, dear heart. I never gave you the words, but I felt them with every fiber of my being. You couldn't have been more precious to me if I had given birth to you, John. I loved you. And never forget this: I will always love you.*

A warm flow of contentment seeped through his chest. His eyes blurred, his throat went husky, and a single tear spilled to his cheek. "I love you, too."

Isn't it wonderful that the love lives on, John?

"Wonderful."

Good-bye, dear heart. Think of me.

"I will. You know I will." John tried but he couldn't say good-bye. His throat locked tight and kept the words inside.

Tony stepped between them, and again touched his hand to the other side of the doubloon. *Be at peace, Jonathan.*

The drizzle of rain stopped and the giant of a man nodded, then closed his eyes. "Thank you, Tony."

Someone else is waiting for you.

"Who?"

Your wife.

Bess, here? She'd come? His heart raced and his stomach lurched. John opened his eyes. Elise and Tony were gone.

Footfalls sounded behind him. He spun around and saw Bess, rushing toward him. She had come!

Two feet from him, she stopped cold and stared at him, her eyes turbulent, clouded with worry. "Are you all right?"

"I'm fine." Did he dare to tell her what he'd just experienced?

"Was it Dixie?"

A test to see if he'd be honest; he sensed it. "Yes."

"And Boudreaux?" Bess asked, looking no less worried. "Is he in the other grave?"

"No. It's, um, another lost soul. I wasn't

520

told who."

A breeze gusted through the trees. Rain-drops that had collected on the leaves fell to the ground and shimmered on the sandy rocks. "I saw Elise, Bess."

Bess squeezed his upper arm, knowing how hard that had been for him to admit to her. "I know, darling. I saw her, too. And Tony. I couldn't hear anything, but I saw them both." Just as she saw that the haunted grief no longer plagued John's eyes. He was again content. Without her.

Her heart plummeted. She couldn't tell him what she'd come here to tell him, after all. It'd be awkward. He'd never lied to her about still loving her. Never once had he said he wanted more with her than two weeks — which she'd foolishly, foolishly, downgraded to one in their agreement negotiations. No, she couldn't tell him. Couldn't risk making him feel forced into admitting the things he didn't feel. Couldn't risk being rejected by him. In this relation-ship, she'd been humiliated enough. And they'd both been hurt enough. One of them had to be gracious, grounded. Her.

"You saw them, too?"

That clearly had surprised him. "Yes."

"Bess, why are you here?" A flash of yel-low on the ground caught John's eye. A petal from Tony's yellow carnation. John picked it up then put it inside his wallet in the third photo holder, near Elise's.

"I came to tell you something. And to ask you something."

He turned away from the graves, stepped closer to Bess, then looked down at her upturned face. "What is it?"

"The case is solved?"

"Yes."

"That was my question," she said, looking as guilty as sin. Her face had gone red and she didn't meet his eyes. Lying.

Disappointment shafted through him. She never could lie to him. They both knew it. So why was she trying to lie to him now? "And what did you want to tell me?"

"That I'm glad it's over for you, and you can get on with your life."

"Anything else?" She hadn't risked coming to him during a storm for this. Not Bess. Not the way she feared storms.

Her eyes widened, then clouded. "No."

"After what we just experienced here, after all we've meant to each other, I can't believe you're looking me in the eye and lying to me, Bess." Oh, it hurt. And it had been so hard to say that and stay civil.

"I'm not lying. I swear it."

He studied her. No dilation of her pupils,

no wringing of her hands, no leaning away from him, no looking anywhere but right into his eyes. Okay, so she hadn't lied. But she hadn't told him the whole truth. And that proved beyond all else that she still didn't trust him. Proved that the case had been solved, but, as he'd always feared it would be, it had been solved too late.

How in the world was he supposed to go on without her? He wanted to keep his promise, to come back here with her to watch the sun set. He wanted a life of days and nights with her. But now the truth had evidenced itself. He'd never have the chance. She wanted him. But she didn't want him forever. She didn't love him.

He'd thought the pain of that could get no worse. He'd been wrong. He swallowed hard, then cleared his throat. "We'd better get back to the pier. Aaron's family will be worried about him being out in the boat in this kind of weather."

With a soulful nod, Bess agreed. Maybe she should have risked telling Jonathan the truth. Maybe she should have risked more humiliation. More . . . pain.

No. No, she'd done the right thing. She'd put him through far too much already. Nearly as much as Meriam had inflicted on Bryce. Bess couldn't risk harming John more. She had to be strong. She'd done the right thing here. So why didn't it *feel* right?

They walked back to the dock in silence. At the end of the dilapidated pier, Bess noted something amiss. "Jonathan, the second sign. The one about the shifting sand. It's . . . gone."

"Maybe it was never there."

Maybe it *had* been an illusion, as her secret hopes of them reuniting had been an illusion. "When we get back to Fisherman's Co-op, I'll walk with you to bring the doubloon back to Hatch."

"Okay." He boarded the boat, then reached back, offering her a steadying hand. "Afterward, we need to talk, Bess. Really talk."

But even as he said the words, the truth hit her like a center-targeted arrow. They could talk forever and it wouldn't change a thing.

Alone, the magic wasn't enough.

CHAPTER 16

After returning the doubloon to Hatch, Bess and Jonathan headed back to the inn. Walking up the front drive, John glanced up toward the roof and grunted. "Have you ever noticed that attic room?"

Bess looked up at it. A raccoon that obviously had its days and nights mixed up ran along the widow's walk railing. But after the experience on Little Island, nothing that happened here could surprise her. "What about it?"

"I don't know. I get the eeriest feeling looking at it."

Bess walked on, glancing at the pretty planter of pink zinnias on the porch, then opened the door. "It was Tony's room, John."

"I see." He followed her past the registration desk and on into the kitchen.

Silk greeted them. A sheet of Seascape stationery lay on the kitchen counter. John lifted the dog; Bess, the note.

She read it, then put it back down on the counter. "Miss Hattie's gone to see about Vic."

"Good. Are you ready to talk?"

Her gaze slipped from his eyes to his chest. "I'd rather not. I've decided to go home." Did he have any idea how hard this was for her? Any idea at all? "We could talk about everything, but it won't change anything."

"We made an agreement."

"I know." She leaned against the cabinet for support. "I'll share Silk with you. You don't have to file suit." Looking at the dog in his arms, Bess shrugged. "She adores you."

"We have five more days."

"No, we don't." She walked to the windows and looked out back, to the lean-to where guests parked, and saw her car. "I'm going to go pack." She looked back at John and said the word that had brought nightmares with it for as long as she could remember. "Will you help me bring down my bags?"

"Of course." John's eyes burned bright. "But Bess, we haven't agreed on a settlement."

He hadn't looked at her as if she were

helpless, or as if her asking for help repulsed him. He only hurt because she'd chosen to leave. Or had she misread him? She must have. Wishful thinking. "I know. I don't know what to say about that. I can't touch the money, though, I can tell you that. It isn't a matter of not wanting or needing it. It's principle. I . . . just can't."

"What principle?"

Ashamed. "It doesn't matter. Not really. It's me, and what I'd think of me, if I touched so much as a dime."

"But you earned some of that money."

"Yes, I did." She turned and started toward the door. "But that doesn't matter either."

He followed her through the gallery, up the stairs, and then to her room. At the closed door, he paused. "It matters to me, Bess. I won't let you leave this marriage with nothing. It isn't right."

Her hand on the knob, she pressed her head against the cool wood. It smelled of lemon oil and, reminded of Miss Hattie and her nurturing, Bess inhaled deeply. "Choose a sum you feel is fair and donate it to Selena's company. I hear she's doing wonderful things for seniors and kids."

"But that won't pay your rent, Bess."

"No, but it will feed my soul, Jonathan."

She gave him a watery smile. "That's far more important."

Two hours later, John stuffed the last of her bags into her car. He didn't want her to go. He didn't want to lose her again, and yet there seemed no way to stop her. Bess had decided for both of them. Again. He'd had a second chance, and he'd blown it. Why had he lied to her? *Why?*

He slammed the trunk shut, then stuffed his fists into his pockets. "I wish you wouldn't leave."

"I can't stay." The wind pulled at her hair. She didn't reach up to smooth it. Instead she fished through her purse, rifling for her keys. "It'd only prolong the inevitable, and I think we've already hurt each other far too much."

They had. He stepped closer to her. "I'll miss you, Bess."

She didn't smile. "I'll miss you, too."

"May I kiss you goodbye?" His heart oozed pain that thrummed through his veins and left a burning ache in its wake.

"I don't think that's a good idea." She took in a shuddered breath then got into the car.

John stood there, watching her buckle Silk into the passenger's seat, her hands trembling. Something shiny caught his eye.

She still wore his ring.

Tony. Tony, do something! I know you can. I need time to figure out how to make it up to her. Please, Tony. Help me!

Bess keyed the car. It roared to life.

And a part of John died. No help would be coming. And Bess would be leaving.

The car didn't move. John blinked and waited, then waited some more. But still Bess didn't drive away.

She cut the engine, then opened the door and got out. "The gearshift won't move. Can you get Silk while I go call Jimmy?"

A smile spread across John's face. She'd done it again. Asked him for help. Did she realize she'd done that only twice in their entire married life — and both times had been within the last five minutes? "Sure."

She nodded, then walked toward the house. John pulled out the pup and scratched her ears. He should have offered to look at the gearshift, but maybe Jimmy would keep her car tied up a couple more days, and John needed the time. *Thanks, Tony.*

No answer. Odd, that. Silk licked at the back of John's hand, claiming his attention. "Elise says the third time's a charm, squirt. Let's hope she's right."

■ ■ ■ ■

John sat at the kitchen table with two of Miss Hattie's mouth-watering blueberry muffins and a cup of hot coffee. Silk lay on the rug before the fireplace snoozing. He hadn't seen Bess since returning to the house, and figured she was hiding out to avoid him.

Miss Hattie came in, her face flushed from the wind and her tidy bun springing loose tendrils around her sweet face. "Jonathan, where is Bess, dear?"

He smiled up at the angel who sounded panicked. "I think she's up in the Great White Room. Why?"

Miss Hattie's eyes went wide. "Oh, my. Bess *was* leaving again, wasn't she?"

He nodded. Now how had Miss Hattie known that? Likely the same way she'd known that the phone had been for him when Selena had called, and for Bess when Miguel Santos had called her.

Miss Hattie plopped down into her rocker. The dangling seat cushion string swept the floor on her forward rocks. She cocked her head, slid her gaze ceilingward, and her emotions flitted over her face: concern, confusion, and finally understanding. With that, came a heart-warming smile.

"Jonathan?"

He finished his muffins and downed the last of his coffee. "Ma'am?"

She stopped rocking. "I asked about Bess because I thought I'd seen her car on Main Street."

"You likely did. Jimmy towed it to the shop."

"No, dear." Miss Hattie shook her head, her reading glasses sliding low on the bridge of her nose. She looked at him over the top rims. "I mean I saw her car being *driven* down Main Street."

"Driven?" Rinsing his dishes at the sink, John stilled. He grabbed up a dishcloth and dried his hands. "But the gearshift was stuck. The car wasn't driveable. Unless . . ."

Miss Hattie hiked her brows. "Unless?"

"Unless Bess didn't want to leave." Of course. She'd asked for his help. She'd given him her trust and he'd missed picking up on it. That's why Tony hadn't answered. He *hadn't* interceded!

"There's nothing wrong with that car, Miss Hattie." A bubble of excitement burst in John's stomach. "Bess didn't *want* to leave!"

Miss Hattie nodded. "Far be it from me to say I know your wife better than you do,

Jonathan, but if I were a wagering woman, which I'm not, my wager would be that our Bess has taken the leap."

Tony's message. The leap upon a mystic tide message. Bess *had* leaped. And now, if they had a snowball's chance of a reunion, so must he. He headed toward the gallery, his gaze already focusing on the steps.

Miss Hattie smiled at the spring in Jonathan's rushed steps. "Ah, Tony. I think our dear Jonathan has just realized that his wife has stopped running. How clever of her, to use the car. I didn't think our Bess would do anything so mischievous, but then she has, bless her heart, suffered more than her fair share of humiliation, hasn't she?

"Now, we've only to wait and see about Jonathan. He hasn't realized it, of course, but he's run farther and harder and faster than she . . ."

CHAPTER 17

Bess stared out the turret room window, watching the afternoon sun sparkle like diamonds on the ocean. The tears blurring her eyes slipped down her face, and she folded her arms over her chest, warning herself to bury the pain, to bury it deep inside. It didn't stop. Disgusted with herself, she ached to the marrow of her bones.

Why had she done it? Pretended the gearshift had jammed? Why had she deceived John? Why hadn't he seen the action for the symbol it'd been?

It'd been a snap decision, and those always brought about regret. She'd known better, and yet the idea of leaving him again had made her feel frozen inside. She couldn't touch that gearshift. Knowing it was wise, that by not touching it, she was dooming them both to more pain, she still could not do it.

And so she'd lied. She'd done the very

thing to John that she'd so strongly objected to him doing. And, might as well call a spade a spade, she'd done it for one reason: she loved him. She still loved him.

She looked down at her wedding band and again remembered the promise she'd made him on their wedding day. She'd vowed never to take off his ring. That promise, she could keep. She never would take it off. Even after the divorce, she never would.

Permitting herself one last sniff, she dried her eyes and opened the window. The sounds of the sea would soothe her, and looking out on the horizon, seeing infinity, would help her gain perspective. It had so often since she'd come here. Today she'd lacked the courage to do what was best for both her and John. Maybe the constancy of the ocean's tide, the rhythm of it, would help her find her own rhythm. Maybe its steady waves would carry on them acceptance. And maybe then she would have the strength to do what she had to do.

John lightly tapped on the Great White Room's heavy door.

Bess didn't answer, but the door opened, its hinges not making the slightest creak. He walked into the room and saw her standing on the little braided rug in the adjoining turret room, her arms folded over her chest, staring out the open window at the sea, the sheer white curtains billowing in the breeze. She didn't know he was there, he realized, and stopped to just look at her. Wisps of her hair blew free in the wind, and her face was red, her eyes slightly swollen and too bright.

She cried.

For them.

A tender hitch formed in his heart then spread warmth through his chest. Man, she was beautiful. So beautiful. And so fragile. How many times he must have hurt her . . .

He closed his eyes and whispered a prayer. *Please, please, give me one more chance with her. I'm going to tell her everything. Everything. Please, don't let me lose her, too.*

When he opened his eyes, Bess was looking at him. He didn't know what to say. How to start baring his soul. He'd been concealing all his life, and he was good at it. But he didn't know how to be open, and to tell her the truth.

"I know nothing is wrong with the car, Jonathan."

Jonathan. Not *John* but *Jonathan.* He nodded, afraid to say anything for fear she'd stop talking. "The gearshift wasn't stuck." She lowered her gaze to his chest. "I lied."

His heart rate doubled. "Why?"

She looked down at her hands. "Because I didn't want to leave."

She wears your ring.

Memory. Not Tony. Memory. John looked at Bess's left hand. It was there. His ring was still there. "Why didn't you want to leave?"

She shrugged. "I'm a glutton for punishment, is all I can figure."

He nearly smiled. "Is that why you didn't go to Little Island with me? Because you're a glutton for punishment?"

She sighed then sat down on the window seat, her spine stiff, her hands folded in her lap. "No."

He walked over, stopped on the braided rug, then looked down on her bent head. "Can you tell me why?"

"I'd rather not."

"Please."

She looked up at him, her face still tear-streaked, though she'd stopped crying. "I didn't want either of us to go out there."

That he hadn't expected. "Why?"

"Because my instincts told me the woman buried out there was Dixie. And I knew that once you solved the case, you wouldn't need me anymore."

"Why would you think that?" Amazing

536

conclusion. But where had it come from?

"Because you wouldn't feel like a failure anymore, and you wouldn't need to prove anything with me."

More than amazing. Baffling. "I thought you refused because you didn't trust my judgment."

"I trusted your judgment. Our instincts agreed."

He could stop there, but if this was to be a baring of souls, he wanted it done right the first time. Once was hard enough. "And I thought you'd compared me and your sorry Spaniard, and he'd won."

She shook her head and flushed guiltily. "He's just a friend, Jonathan. I should've told you that before. But . . ."

"You liked seeing me jealous."

She opened her mouth to deny it, but paused, then told him the truth. "Wicked of me, but, yes, I did."

"Why?"

Again she dropped her gaze, this time to his waist. "Because it showed me that you weren't indifferent."

He smiled, though she didn't see it. "No, I'm not indifferent. Not about anything when it comes to you."

Her fingers were laced, and she started wringing her hands. "I wanted to come first with you. Never in my whole life have I come first with anyone, or felt loved unconditionally. My parents loved me, but they never liked me. I was too exuberant, too demonstrative, too emotional. I embarrassed them."

"So you buried the parts of you that they objected to, hoping that then they would love you unconditionally."

"You would have, too, if your parents looked straight through you as if you weren't there, and didn't speak so much as a single word to you for a month at a time."

He didn't know what to say. He'd had no idea that they'd ever done anything like that to her. They'd spent time with her parents, and he'd never seen any signs of friction or tension, or . . . he thought back. Or signs of any affection. None.

How could he not have seen that?

Bess's gaze dropped lower, to his knees, then to his shoes. "That's why getting to know your parents meant so much to me, Jonathan. I wanted to see if maybe I —" She hushed and shook her head. "It was a silly notion."

"I had no idea, honey." Tony had told him to ask her about the facade. And he'd meant to, but he'd gotten sidetracked. There was a lesson there. One he now considered learned.

She blinked hard and fast, and raised her gaze to his. "Your parents disowned you because you married me and I wasn't wealthy, didn't they?"

"What?" He hadn't meant to shout but, she'd surprised him. Where could she have gotten that idea?

"You were ashamed of me."

"No! Never!" He dropped to his knees in front of her and clasped her arms. "Gosh, Bess, I wasn't. I'm not."

"Don't lie to me," she whispered, looking ready to break.

"I'm not. Honey, I was ashamed, but not of you. Never of you."

She stared at him, waiting for an explanation. And the time definitely had come for one. Good grief, all this time she'd thought he'd been ashamed of her? Because she wasn't wealthy —

A truth hit him with the force of a thunderbolt. "That's why you wouldn't touch our money. You thought my parents saw you as some type of fortune-hunter and in taking the money, you'd prove them right. So you refused to touch it to prove them wrong."

"They were wrong. I never cared about the money, Jonathan. I loved you."

"Then," he said softly, the puzzle pieces sliding into place. "You loved me, then."

"Yes." She drew in a breath that heaved her narrow shoulders. "Then."

He cupped a hand to her cheek. "You're so wrong about all this. I was heartless not to explain. I'm sorry, Bess. I can't take the hurt I've caused you away, but I'm going to tell you the truth so you don't hurt over this anymore."

He paused to collect his thoughts, to look into her eyes once more before they filled with disgust. "Selena doesn't know what I'm about to tell you. I don't want her ever to know it. I'm trusting you, Bess. I've never in my life trusted anyone, but I'm trusting you."

"I won't tell her, or anyone else, Jonathan. I swear it."

He steeled himself for her response, knowing it'd hurt bad no matter what he did. "Grace and Mitchell Mystic are dead."

"Who?"

"My parents." He swallowed hard. "Selena thinks they died when she was three, but they didn't. They decided they were tired of being parents and just walked out."

"But you were so little!"

He had been. But he'd been determined. "For three days, I wouldn't accept it, that

540

they weren't coming back. Then I called Uncle Max. I don't know what would have happened to us if he hadn't taken us in."

Too wired to crouch, Jonathan stood up and paced. "We never saw them again."

"How do you know they're dead?"

"After they died, a lawyer called Uncle Max. He told me. Selena was so little she didn't remember them ever being alive. We decided it was best left that way. I knew they were dead, but I didn't know how they'd died. Uncle Max had said a tragic accident, but he couldn't lie any better than you."

"You found out."

Jonathan nodded. "Yes, I did. But I wished I hadn't."

"Whatever it is, Jonathan, it doesn't matter."

"It matters." He paced from the bed back to the braided rug, then stopped. "They were in a cult situation, Bess. They committed suicide. They must have seen it coming and had an attack of conscience, because shortly before their deaths is when they went to the lawyer and willed their worldly goods to Selena and me."

And he would have traded their fortunes for a simple smile. For a single *dear heart*.

"I'm sorry, darling." Bess looked up at him, tears in her eyes.

Bess's tears. Man, nothing could get to him like Bess's tears. He stiffened against them, against the pity he saw in her eyes. "So you see, you were wrong, Bess. I *was* ashamed. But not of you. I was ashamed of me."

"Why?" She jumped to her feet.

A bolt of pain rammed through him, so intense he mentally staggered. "My own parents couldn't love me. Didn't you hear me? My own parents . . ."

She clasped his arms and squeezed, digging her fingertips into his flesh. "No. This isn't about you, Jonathan. It wasn't about you. They got caught up in this cult thing. It was them, not you."

He clenched his jaw. "They walked out on me."

"And then I did, too." Her chin quivered. She worried her lip, trying to hide it, but tears sheened her eyes. "I'm so sorry, Jonathan. If it helps, know that I walked out because I loved you. Maybe they did, too. Maybe they had misgivings about taking you with them into that kind of life. Maybe they knew you'd be better off with Max than with them. Just as you knew learning the truth would hurt Selena. You couldn't risk telling me about them for fear she'd find out and she'd feel . . . unloveable. Isn't that right?"

"Yes." He stared hard into her eyes.

She dropped her gaze, paused. "Maybe, in their own way, your parents leaving you proved just how much they loved you."

"Bess, are you trying to tell me that you left me because you loved me?" He didn't dare to believe it. Didn't dare!

She nodded.

He touched a gentle fingertip to her chin. "You said we'd closed a chapter of our lives. You were right about that."

"Yes." She sounded sad, so very sad.

"I want to open another chapter, Bess."

She looked up at him, her eyes searching.

"You said once I solved the case, I wouldn't need you anymore. But that's not true. I'll always need you."

"Elise —"

He pressed a fingertip over her lips. "Was the mother I never had. I loved her for that, and for loving me. I'll always love her. This wedge between you and me wasn't her fault. It was mine. I muddled what mattered most — you. I don't want to lose you again, Doc. I don't ever want to lose you again."

Devotion. Bess saw it in his eyes, heard it in the low, throaty timbre of his voice. She'd been so . . .

Sometimes you have to leap upon a mystic

tide and have faith the sand will shift and an island will appear.

Her heart started a low, hard beat. Yes. Yes . . . she understood.

Mystic tide. Speak your heart, confident your beloved will understand.

That's right, Bess. Go on. You can do it.

Her blood pounded through her veins.

Shifting sand. Flexibility. Assumptions voiced, truths revealed.

Come on, Bess. Yes! You're almost there. Come on!

Oh, no. Her heart thumped hard, threatening to beat through the wall of her chest.

An island will appear . . .

Bess gasped, "Jonathan, the island! It's love!"

Ah, Bess. Bess. Finally.

"What?"

"Tony's message. The island is love. That's what he meant for us to know."

Jonathan shook his head. "For me, it was a road map, honey, to solve the case."

"Yes, it was. But it was also a road map for me *and* you and our relationship."

"I don't get it."

Oh, thank you, Tony.

Anytime.

"For the right fee, I'll explain it to you, Jonathan." Bess shrugged. "I'm unemployed, if you'll recall."

"How can you joke?"

"Because I've figured out the message."
She smiled.

"Will you pay my price? I know how you
love agreements."

"I'll pay." His eyes twinkled. "Wait. What's
your price?"

"I'll tell you . . . later."

"I don't know if I like going into a deal
with you without knowing the terms, but I
do love that sparkle in your eye, so I'll bite
the bullet and go for it."

"Thank you, darling." She squeezed his
arm. Trust. Sweet trust.

"Okay, so tell me."

"I can see patience is going to be perpetual
for you, too."

"What?"

"Annual mottoes, darling. Never mind.
We'll discuss that later, too."

"Bess."

She wrinkled her nose at his warning tone.
"People change during a marriage and,
when they do, they've got to trust love to
sustain them through those changes so they
grow closer and not apart."

Jonathan looked thoughtful, then he
smiled. "The island is love."

"Yes." She smiled back at him.

Wonderful! Finally! Leap, Bess! Leap!

I am, Tony. Good grief, give me a minute. I'm new at this stuff.

He chuckled.

Men.

"What's your price?" Jonathan asked.

Oh, Tony, my heart feels like it's coming out of my chest. What if he laughs at me? Lord, I'm nervous. Never mind. Trust love, right? Right. See, I did get it.

Quit stalling.

All right, all right, but if I end up crying, I'm going straight to Miss Hattie on you.

Duly noted.

Bess licked at her lips and looked Jonathan straight in the eye. "My price is the divorce. I don't want it."

He blinked, then blinked again. "Because of media reaction in your job?"

"No." *Oh, Tony. What if he hates me now? What if he doesn't give a flying fig that I'm crazy about him? I'm so . . . scared.* "Because I loved you . . . then."

Chicken.

Thanks so much for your support. This is hard, you know. Oh, why don't you go rattle a chain?

No way. I've worked hard for this moment and, by gum, I'm going to see it.

"I know you did, sweetheart." Jonathan

dragged the pad of his thumb along her chin.

If he gives me heck, Tony, I'm going to be so angry. Hurt, too. Hurt? Did I say hurt? I'll be devastated, is what I'll be. Oh, I must be nuts to try this leaping. It's a wonder anyone survives it.

You're doing fine. Hold tight. Faith, Bess. Faith.

Faith. Oh, I do love him so, Tony. I really, really do. "And because I love you now."

The look in Jonathan's eyes softened and he stared at her, then groaned from deep in his throat and pulled her into his arms. He buried his face in the cay at her neck, and hugged her tightly, rocking back and forth on his feet. *I love you, too, Bess.*

Good grief! You heard every word. Tony, how could you!

Um, I think I hear some chains calling me.

Wait! Thank you, Tony.

That goes for me, too.

Anytime. Hold tight to the magic.

Jonathan reared back and looked at her, his eyes shimmering. "I heard, Bess. And I meant what I said. I love you. I don't want the divorce, I never did. I want you. I've always wanted you."

He kissed her deeply, longingly, lovingly. And by the time he lifted his lips from hers,

Bess believed him. He wanted her. He loved her.

He was not ashamed.

He smiled, his eyes tender and bright.

She smiled back, from the heart out.

"Let's go," he said, rubbing their noses.

"Where?"

"I made a promise to you. It's almost sunset."

She hugged him tightly, her heart so full it was overflowing. "First we're calling Francine and Bryce and stopping this divorce nonsense."

"Great idea." He laughed. "Judge Branson will love it. I'm going to send him a new set of golf clubs for levying that fine on you."

"What?"

"It got me up here." He lifted the phone receiver at the desk.

"Add a new putter, too," her arms around his waist, she squeezed, needing to hold him tight, "from me."

He frowned and hung up the phone. "It's out of order again."

"Fine. We'll use the one downstairs."

Laughing and holding hands, they hurried down the stairs together. At the bend, beneath the portraits of Collin and Cecelia, Bess paused, pulling them to a stop. She looked up at the portrait of Cecelia, the healer, and smiled. *Legend says miracles happen here. And they do. I think you must have loved so much that it lingers. That's the magic here, isn't it? Love. And, Cecelia, bless you for saving one of those miracles for John and me.*

"Honey, why are you crying?"

A flood of peace and contentment filled her. One such as she'd never known. One she'd forever fail to fully explain, but never fail to appreciate. "I'm happy." Bess smiled at her husband.

He pecked a kiss to her lips. "Me, too."

She curled her arms around his neck. "I love you, Jonathan. With all my heart."

"I love you, too, Doc." He kissed her long and deep. "I love you, too."

Miss Hattie heard John and Bess's exchange on the stairs and sighed her content. Healed. At peace. "Lovely. Isn't it lovely, Tony? Just lovely."

The phone rang. She answered it, and was still on the line with Bryce Richards when Bess and John came into the kitchen. They were smiling, their faces flushed and exuberant. Their joy seeping into her heart, she held up a finger for them to wait, then spoke into the phone. "I'll have your word, dear, that you'll come and bring the children. You need a little rest, and they need pampering."

After listening for a moment, she smiled. "Well, I think the odds of getting them a mother from Macy's are rather slim, dear." She laughed softly. "All right, Bryce. We'll see you then."

"Bryce?" Jonathan asked.

"Just a moment, dear. Jonathan has a question, I — think."

"I'm sorry, Miss Hattie. Is that Bryce Richards?"

"Yes, it is." She held her earring in her hand. "Did you need to speak with him? We've finished our chat."

"Please."

Miss Hattie passed John the phone, then turned to Bess, who hugged her and whispered close to her ear. "We're not getting the divorce, Miss Hattie."

"Of course not, dear." She smiled, gave Bess's back a solid pat, and then sat down in her rocker.

"Yes," John said. "And tell Francine, will you? We're in a bit of hurry." Jonathan slid Bess a smile. "We're going to watch the sun set."

Bess smiled back at him and the love flowing between them had Miss Hattie pulling her lacy hankie from her pocket and dabbing at her eyes.

Jonathan hung up the phone and folded an arm around Bess's waist. "We're not getting a divorce," he told Miss Hattie.

"Of course not, dear." The angelic woman smiled then looked at Bess. "Promises are made to be kept."

A light in Bess's eye said she was remembering the words Miss Hattie had said to her at the Blue Moon Cafe, when they'd first discussed why Bess still wore John's ring. Bess nodded, confirming it. "True love *is* always like that, Miss Hattie. You were right about that, too."

"Speaking of promises," Jonathan backed away, then clasped hands with Bess, "we're going out to Little Island to keep one. We'll be back after dark."

"Fine." Miss Hattie sniffled. "I'm going to Millie's to play cards, but dinner will be warming in the oven."

"Do you have a bridge group, Miss Hattie?"

"Oh my, no, dear. We play poker. Penny-ante. But please, don't mention it to Pastor Brown."

Bess grinned, then explained to Jonathan. "If provoked, the Pastor gets long-winded, and then the mayor nods off during the sermon and snores, and that mortifies his snooty wife, Lydia."

"I won't breathe a word," Jonathan swore.

Laughing, Bess kissed Miss Hattie's cheek, then Jonathan pecked one to her forehead. "Thank you, Miss Hattie. For everything."

"Of course, dear." She shared with them a secret smile. "I keep my promises, too."

Hattie watched them leave, arms curled around each other's waists, heads bent together, laughing. Healed. At peace, content, and healed. Lovely . . .

To the grandfather clock's steady ticks, she climbed the stairs to the attic. The white drop cloths that were supposed to be covering the furniture were again heaped on the floor, and the temperature was decidedly cool. *Tony.*

She lifted the photograph of him and Hatch, again pulled the hankie from her apron pocket, then touched it to her eye. "Well, my darling, it appears Jimmy again won the bet at the Blue Moon Cafe. And I couldn't be more delighted."

Feeling tender, she sniffed, and noticed something floating midair. Her heart lurched, a knot of tears swelled in her throat. She lifted her palm and watched a tiny object flutter lightly into her hand.

The petal from a yellow carnation.

"Oh, I love you, too, Tony," she whispered, reassured he was near and content. "With all my heart, I love you too."

Together, they'd again helped those in love find the magic at Seascape.

ABOUT VICKI HINZE

Vicki Hinze is the award-winning author of 24 novels, 4 nonfiction books and hundreds of articles, published in as many as sixty-three countries. She is recognized by Who's Who in the World as an author and as an educator. For more information, please visit her website.

You can visit Vicki here:

Facebook at:

http://www.facebook.com/vicki.hinze.author

Twitter at:

http://www.twitter.com/vickihinze

http://www.vickihinze.com